No Harp for My Angel

— — — —

Booty for a Babe

— — — —

Eve, It's Extortion

— — — —

Three Novels by
Carter Brown

Introduction by Rick Ollerman

Stark House Press • Eureka California

NO HARP FOR MY ANGEL / BOOTY FOR A BABE /
EVE, IT'S EXTORTION

Published by Stark House Press
1315 H Street
Eureka, CA 95501, USA
griffinskye3@sbcglobal.net
www.starkhousepress.com

NO HARP FOR MY ANGEL
Originally published and copyright © 1956 by Horwitz Publications,
Sydney, Australia.

BOOTY FOR A BABE
Originally published and copyright © 1956 as by Horwitz Publications,
Sydney, Australia.

EVE, IT'S EXTORTION
Originally published and copyright © 1956 as by Horwitz Publications,
Sydney, Australia. Revised as *Walk Softly Witch!*, Horwitz Publications,
1959, and further revised for the U.S. as *The Victim*, Signet Books,
New York, 1959)

Reprinted by permission of the Estate of Alan G. Yates, and licensed via
publishing representatives, Xou Pty Ltd, Australia. All rights reserved under
International and Pan-American Copyright Conventions.

"Alan Yates, Meet 'Carter Brown'…" copyright © 2018 by Rick Ollerman.

ISBN-13: 978-1-944520-44-1

Book design by Mark Shepard, SHEPGRAPHICS.COM
Proofreading by Bill Kelly

First Stark House Press Edition: May 2018

FIRST EDITION

NO HARP FOR MY ANGEL

While in Florida on vacation, Lt. Al Wheeler tangles with—

- a redhead with green eyes who is "Nobody's girl but my own!"
- her club-owning gangster boyfriend, who is involved in some very shady business…
- and his gorilla henchman, who is seven feet of muscle and bone, just waiting for the chance to crush him to a pulp when Al becomes the decoy sent in to bring their racket down.

BOOTY FOR A BABE

When Lt Al Wheeler tries to solve a murder at a science fiction convention—

- he discovers a professor who wants to stop time by tricking the elusive Delfs…
- meets an intellectual gangster who wants to get his hands on the professor's *latest* invention…
- is frustrated by the generously proportioned convention organizer, who somehow manages to keep one step ahead of Al's wolfish designs.

EVE, IT'S EXTORTION

Which finds Lt. Al Wheeler trying to solve a hit-and-run murder involving—

- the victim's wife, who is all too glad to have lost her lush of a husband…
- the beautiful skip-tracer who tracked down the victim right before he met his untimely end…
- and her dubious boyfriend who may not be as innocent as he professes, but is certainly up to no good.

Contents

Alan Yates, meet "Carter Brown".....

by Rick Ollerman

Richard S. Prather is one of them, with Shell Scott, his main creation, as the star of 42 novels and short story collections. Edward S. Aarons is another—in addition to a number of other novels, he wrote 42 "Assignment" books featuring CIA operative Sam Durell. James Atlee Phillips (as "Philip Atlee") wrote 22, or 23 or 24 (depending on how you count) "Joe Gall" books. Between Perry Mason, Doug Selby, Lam & Cool and a few others, Erle Stanley Gardner tops all of them, and even John D. MacDonald, a name better known to writers than today's readers, belongs on this ill-fated list.

Who exactly are these guys? They're just a sampling of the writers who sold at least tens of millions of books, sometimes many more, but who are barely remembered, if at all, by the book readers of today. Prather sold over forty million books and both he and his main character—the 6'2" silver-haired, wisecracking, alcohol-fueled PI—likely wouldn't raise an eyebrow outside the perfect corner of the right mystery writers' conference. The same goes for all the above, really, including one of the bestselling writers of *all time*, Gardner. And like MacDonald, it's the name of his most famous character, Perry Mason, or in MacDonald's case, Travis McGee, who would most likely garner the actual spark of recognition. Ask around, like I have. It's true.

And what of the writers who once shared dominance on the spinner racks of the fifties through the eighties? Names like Harry Whittington, Gil Brewer, Day Keene? Unfortunately for them, for their own reasons they chose *not* to write series. Without a strong character readers could identify with book after book, their chances of surviving their own futures turned out to be fairly dim. It appears that oftentimes it is the series that brings new readers to a writer, even long after they no longer write. Those of us who are hard-core Whittington/Brewer/Keene fans often feel relegated to feeling like we're in some sort of cult when we're talking to people *who should know better* about how Whittington did this in *Web of Murder* or how Brewer did that in *13 French Street*.

The group of writers listed above are far from the only ones who fall into this lamentable classification. Frank Kane had Johnny Liddell; Leslie Charteris wrote about Simon Templar, The Saint; the duo of Manny Lee and Fred Dannay had the multimedia superstar of Ellery Queen (as written by "Ellery Queen"); Stephen Marlowe wrote about Chet Drum, collaborating with Prather on *Double in Trouble* (Fawcett Gold Medal, 1959), which featured both their PIs, Drum and Shell Scott.

There was another one, a monster bestseller from Australia by way of England who was born with the name Alan Geoffrey Yates. After a brief dalliance with the house name "Peter Carter Brown" the first name was dropped but the rest kept when the name's owner, publisher Stanley Horwitz, struck a deal to have the books published in the United States. This was the country where the stories took place though Yates himself had never been there until well established in his literary career (similar to British author James Hadley Chase).

How do you explain the massive commercial success of a writer like Yates, who it's claimed sold as many as 70,000,000 to 80,000,000 books in his three decades of writing, and still be "forgotten"—whatever that really means—today?

Yates wrote about several characters: Detective Al Wheeler, his first; private investigator types Mavis Seidlitz and Rick Holman; and even an amateur sleuth, Larry Baker. Each of these series has their own flavor, their own sense of place, but Yates's first character, Wheeler, always remained his most popular, both with his publishers and his public.

When Yates was discharged from the Royal Navy following WWII, he and his new Australian wife spent some time living in a suburb just outside of London. After a year and a half of an unremarkable career as a sound cameraman, the job he'd held before the war, the Yateses emigrated to Sydney with the help of both their parents. His next job in the movie industry fell through and Yates was left in his adopted country with very few prospects.

He became a salesman of sorts and worked for a number of different companies. At one point he'd applied for so many jobs that when better offers came in he jumped occupations four times, sometimes in a matter of weeks, eventually ending up in the publicity department of Qantas Airlines. There he was responsible for the airline's official magazine as well as the employees' internal publication, but there were problems for Yates from the start. The salary wasn't much. And while Yates seemed to enjoy the work and the people he worked with, he could do the math and knew that only time, and a lot of it—decades—would allow him to work his way up the salary scale. The work itself would only change if he were granted promotions and of course, there were never guarantees in that department.

In 1939, Australia had placed a tariff on printed matter that included reading material from the United States. The tariff lasted until 1959 and in those two decades homegrown talent had a chance to blossom. Yates had been reading stories of the American West until he eventually decided the writers didn't appear to know any more about the place than he did. In his time away from his day job, he began writing his own stories.

First there was a failed entry to a short story contest, but that led to an opportunity to write dialogue for scripts for radio shows. Unfortunately, that didn't work out either. Yates kept writing though, and eventually he sold a story for twenty pounds, or one pound per thousand words. He'd turned pro.

Another effect of the tariff had been to transform Australian publishers who specialized in one form of work, to another. This included Horwitz Publications, which was founded in 1921 as a printer of trade and sporting magazines but, post-tariff, turned to the robust fiction market looking for locally sourced writers.

Stanley Horwitz, son of the original founders, had the idea of creating a number of house names that he could use, hiring enough writers to produce sufficient content to keep a rapid-fire stream of content of Horwitz books on the racks. They needed to move and move quickly in order to make room for the next month's offerings. The strategy worked, and Stanley had turned the company into an Australian powerhouse.

As for Yates, he had been selling not only more westerns but also a few romances, a horror series, and some of what he called "scientific thrillers." Eventually he sold stories to imprints belonging to Horwitz Publications and at the age of twenty-eight, with the prospect of a slowly mandated progress up the corporate ladder at Qantas, he signed an eye-raising contract with Horwitz.

Yates wrote well and Yates wrote fast. Horwitz wanted more of a commitment from him but he balked; he simply couldn't do it and still keep his day job. So they offered him a deal for thirty pounds a week against advances. No more corporate ladders, no more set-in-stone salary structures. Not only would he be a professional writer, he would be a full-time professional writer.

And all he was asked to do was produce two novelettes and one novel each month—that's all!—under the house name of "Carter Brown." The term of the contract?

Thirty years.

At the time, Dexedrine was legal and Yates had gotten used to it in the war. He said that his usual process was to write a first draft with the drug's help in forty-eight hours, let the book sit for a few days, then do a rewrite. He later said the hangover effects were barely worth it and eventually he stopped doing it altogether. He couldn't understand people taking speed recreationally.

In the meantime, while the Australian tariff prevented American books from coming in, nothing prevented local-grown books from going out. Stanley Horwitz cut a deal with the paperback arm of New American Library (NAL), Signet Books, to supply a new "Carter Brown" book every month. Signet could also accept a reprint, or a book already published in Australia, but for some reason they were reluctant to do that, even later when it could have given Yates a much needed break.

The books themselves started out with police detective Al Wheeler as the "unorthodox" main character. Favored by his boss because of his results, it was Wheeler's attitude on life as a single, jazz-loving bachelor that gave him his charismatic appeal. Later, the tone of the books would change to an even lighter atmosphere, with his screwball sergeant on hand giving Wheeler the opportunity to play the straight man. This was something you'd expect to see more in the movies of the time than in a hard-boiled novel, but the books are very much of their era. From the fifties to the eighties, Yates went through the same trials of life as anyone else pounding out a living on a typewriter; he not only had to keep himself challenged but he also had to match the public's varying tastes in fiction—if he wanted to stay in the game.

Something that rarely fluctuated was the cover art and its depiction of sexy, impossibly long-legged and partially clad women. With many of the covers painted by the artist who is no doubt the most identifiable and popular crime fiction cover artist of all time, Robert McGinnis, these Carter Brown books are collectible for that reason alone. The portrayal of women in the Brown books is very much of their time. When a book features a main character who is cast in the mode of an alpha male, what does it mean when the covers feature these gorgeous works of art that highlight, not the series star, *but a scantily clad or sometimes naked woman, instead?*

Possibly part of the reason that many of these writers have faded to the background may be that in their original editions—certainly in many of their original mass market paperback editions—the cover art is sexy, designed to appeal to a male audience, and doesn't reflect much of anything that happens in the book. Look at the U.K.'s Corgi Books, a mass market paperback house started in 1953 whose usual practice was to use a black cover with the photograph of a lingerie-clad or other suggestively dressed woman. You don't see "literature" or even "crime fiction," you see sex, you see books to be bought quickly and then hidden away. They're designed to move quickly. Unless the consumer is familiar with the author, a more "serious" reader may very easily stay away.

We like to teach "you can't judge a book by its cover" but when it comes to selling sex, a different set of rules seems to apply. As does censorship, which appears to be making a comeback of sorts in the new millennium. There were things one could write about, and things one simply didn't mention in the Victorian era. Like out-of-wedlock pregnancies and divorces, over time these things became socially non-stigmatic. Yet now we seem to be creeping deeper into an age where sexual attraction or overt mating rituals of any sort are viewed as sinister and must be abolished. If these attitudes persist—and extrapolating the news, they look like they will be around for a while—will they begin to affect literature as well as all forms of culture before a new hippie movement returns to enlighten? Who knows?

Needless to say, Yates accepted the contract from Horwitz and with the help of the amphetamine Dexedrine, he started cranking out the stories, despite the effects of the drug. He had to have some sort of secret for keeping up that manic pace for the next ten years, or at least keeping close.

After Yates accepted the contract, with his natural talent, ambition, and the speed, he mostly kept up with its terms for the first ten years, though in the end he was struggling more and more. For all his hard work he just couldn't quite make it work. The contract with Signet called for ten brand new books every year, and it was a strain for Yates from the start. There was a dispute between Yates and Horwitz, the details of which remain undocumented, and legal action was threatened, but in the end Yates hired an agent and a new deal was struck. All talk of legal action was dropped, and Yates's commitment dropped from ten new books a year to six.

Not only did this help Yates's state of mind, but the quality of the books went back up. He'd been so pushed for time his normal practice of first draft, set the book aside, then rewrite, had sometimes been reduced to barely completing the first draft. At one point, concerned with the quality of the stories they were getting, Signet brought in author Frank Kane (mentioned earlier) to help edit the manuscripts. Earlier in the contract, Yates had professed his approval for Signet's editors. At this point it seems there was doubt on both sides.

Signet appeared to only be interested in the Al Wheeler character but Yates was anxious to branch out and write about new ones, and the editors at Signet finally agreed, though with a set ratio of Wheeler to the new cast that tilted heavily toward their old favorite. This was also part of the renegotiated contract, so in addition to awarding Yates more writing space and breathing room, he'd been allowed some additional creative freedom as well. This is important because even the deepest wells run dry and some of the books during this time come awfully close to repeating each other in spots.

Toward the end of Yates's career, which ended with his death in 1985, Tower/Belmont Books took over as the publisher of "Carter Brown."

Throughout his entire novel-writing career, Alan Yates wrote something in the neighborhood of three hundred novels and was translated into nearly three dozen languages, clearly becoming a global literary phenomenon. Not many writers have achieved worldwide success on this kind of level and have been translated into so many languages. And all of it had been done under a name that wasn't his, under copyrights he didn't control, another remarkable set of circumstances one would be hard-pressed to find duplicated today. It should be noted that one of Horwitz's editors, C.J. McKenzie, was hired to write six "Carter Brown" books while Yates was in New York on a kind of working vacation. Other than these titles, whichever they are, Yates wrote all the rest.

Aside from two French films, Detective Al Wheeler, as well as Yates's other creations, have been ignored by filmmakers. Erle Stanley Gardner has had Hollywood incarnations of his Perry Mason, followed by the nine-year television run starring Raymond Burr, another season of the "new" Perry Mason with Monte Markham, and dozens of made-for-TV movies. It seems Hollywood won't let us forget the esteemed lawyer, but what of the author, what of Gardner himself?

When an author can be as successful as Gardner or Yates/"Carter Brown," Richard S. Prather, or any number of others, how is it that their names can disappear so quickly as the public mood or literary fashion changes? The books themselves are physical objects, they're out there, they do not disappear.

At least with Gardner, and to a lesser degree with John D. MacDonald's Travis McGee, their characters seem to have lives greater than their creators. In the case of Yates and Detective Al Wheeler, both author and character seem to have been somewhat blown over by the sands of the new century.

Perhaps nowhere is there a more stark example than the cousins who wrote as "Ellery Queen." Not only was their most famous character the eponymous Queen himself, but one cousin lived on the east coast, plotted each book and founded and edited the magazine that still bears their name to this day. The other cousin, Manfred B. Lee, lived on the west coast, wrote the actual novels from the detailed outlines that Frederic Dannay provided, but he wrote the scripts for the popular radio show of the time that starred their fictional sleuth. These were classic mysteries, where all the clues were presented during the show and before "Ellery Queen," the character, solved the mystery, the play was paused and the audience given the chance to work out the puzzle on their own.

Queen was featured in Hollywood movies, had a popular television show starring Jim Hutton and David Wayne, and then… nothing. The name may be known, but the books, the stories.…

In the end, the "Carter Brown" story is difficult to quantify. As an author, Alan Yates certainly gives us fast moving, entertaining and well-told stories in the optimistic vein of post-WWII America. They're fun, escapist reading; they're "entertainments," to borrow Graham Greene's term.

It is important to recognize that books from certain publishers, though borrowing the "sex sells" tactic from the publishers of other sorts of stories, are in fact very different. Certainly some readers must have reacted poorly to the provocative photos and paintings of the cover beauties and assume the contents were as cheap and tawdry as they appeared. Still, these covers were only a marketing gimmick. One can look at the difference between Chase's or Gardner's hardcover books and compare them to their paperback releases to see the difference immediately.

Whether or not this worked for these authors' sales, the storytelling talent was always there, in black and white, right there on the page. Yes, they're pure pulp, written fast and with all the energy and verve that implies, and written by someone with the talent of true prodigy and not prolixity. Pulps were written for breakneck entertainment with an eye to giving their audience what they wanted. You could generally tell the best writers by the ones who did it longest.

The paperback publishers who took this to heart after the pulp market collapsed in the fifties followed the same model. Some trusted the power of their content, some didn't, instead using the kinds of sexy photos that adorned hundreds of Gardner's, Chase's and Yates's/"Brown's" books. Others like Signet would commission a Robert McGinnis painting—no less sexy but every bit as suggestive. Whatever the outer package, the contents were nearly always a satisfying blend of action, adventure, mystery and women to the reader willing and waiting for that month's offering.

There's no analog today, nothing that has supplanted this original thrill, this type of reading entertainment. The closest thing we actually have are reprints and the rediscovery of what we've lost, seeking what the last generation already had. The most important thing for all of the writers mentioned here was that they *kept you reading*, and when you compare their output with today's mostly book-a-year writers who sell but a fraction of some the oldsters, you can't help but wonder how much we've given up versus how much we've lost, how much today's marketing techniques have taken from us as readers. Publishers of old weren't worried about saturating the market so much as meeting its demand.

None of the writers mentioned in this piece are still with us today. As of this moment, Robert E. McGinnis is 92 years old. And still painting. I wonder if he's our generation's version of Edward Hopper, his work nearly instantly recognizable, from his James Bond movie posters to his hundreds of book covers and everything in-between.

In-between.

I wonder, too, if that word best describes that lost world of pulp, of the Erle Stanley Gardners, the Leslie Charterises, and yes, the Alan Yateses of the writing world. It's still there, *between* the old and the new, still holding up, still entertaining, still doing exactly what it was supposed to do.

In Yates's case, he kept the world reading for thirty years in as many languages. Now, more than two decades after his death, he's still doing it. Is there a better tribute?

—Littleton, NH
February, 2018

No Harp for My Angel

Carter Brown

CHAPTER 1
Tonight We Live

I picked up a handful of sand and let it dribble slowly through my fingers onto her tanned midriff. She moved slightly.

"That tickles," she said.

"How about we swim again?" I suggested.

"You swim, Al," she said. "I'll just lie here and soak some more sun."

I looked down at her. Her blonde hair was being bleached even more blonde by the sun. She was wearing a black two-piece swimsuit which was nearly the ultimate in minimum.

I remembered my vacation had only one more week to run. "The hell with swimming," I said. "I'll stay here. What does swimming get you?"

"I'll buy it," she said. "What?"

"Wet—that's all!"

She opened her eyes, crinkling them against the glare, and looked up at me. "I guess I'm flattered," she said. "You'd rather stay here with me than swim!"

"There's lots of things I'd rather do with you than swim, honey," I said. "You can feel flattered some more."

"Your trouble," she said lazily, "is that you're just a hick. A hick on vacation is twice the hick he is at home!"

"What are you trying to do? Flatter me, now?"

"There's something about Florida," she said. "It must be the fresh air and the ocean and the beach or something. Every little jerk who gets down here thinks he's a Casanova or something!"

"I am not little," I said.

There was a piece of genuine saltwater-saturated seaweed close by. I picked it up, then carefully dropped it where I'd previously dropped the sand.

She sat up with a shrill scream.

"A jerk likes to see a jerk," I said happily. "What makes you think I'm a hick?"

"Nobody but a hick would do something like that!" she glared at me.

Then she got onto her feet and looked down at me. "Get lost!" she snapped. "And stay lost!"

I stood up so I could look down at her: "You don't like me?"

"I wouldn't like you if I had a hole in my head!"

"You mean," I said plaintively, "that soda I bought you, it was fifty cents—wasted?"

She picked up her towel and purse from the sand, and then flounced off along the beach. The rear view of that flounce was really something. I stood and admired it until she disappeared out of sight.

Then I sat down and lit a cigarette. Three hours before, Ocean Beach had started to look exciting—that was when I first saw her. Now it was looking the way it had looked the last two weeks—one hell of a lot of ocean and one hell of a lot of beach.

Maybe it was my fault for taking a vacation without being properly organised. I remembered at least they sold liquor in Ocean Beach and there was nothing to stop me having a drink.

By seven that evening I had acquired a nice, unhealthy glow and was intent on turning that glow into a neon sign. I took half an hour out to go back to the hotel and shower and change. I dressed up into a tuxedo, black tie and the trimmings. I gave the tie a final flick and check-over in the mirror.

"Tonight," I said gravely to the image in the mirror, "we live!"

Then I headed back towards the last bar I'd been drinking in. It was called *Toby's Tavern*. When I got back I noticed a difference as soon as I walked in.

There had been people there when I left, there were still people there. But the redhead in the white sharkskin dress hadn't been there when I left, otherwise I would never have left.

She was sitting on a stool at the bar, with an old-fashioned in front of her. It looked to be the only old-fashioned thing about her. She didn't seem to have an escort. I eased myself down on the stool next to hers and ordered a Scotch on the rocks.

She looked at me slantwise for a moment, then looked straight ahead of her again. Her eyes seemed to be green. A redhead with green eyes and a figure Jane Russell could have accused her of plagiarising.

"The thing I like about Ocean Beach," I said gently, "is the informality of the place, don't you?"

She turned her head towards me: "I beg your pardon?"

"Most other places," I explained, "you have to wait to be introduced to people. Here in Ocean Beach you just say hello."

"Hello," she said, and sipped her drink.

"That," I said, "is as good as a formal introduction. I can now ask you to have dinner with me. Will you have dinner with me?"

I got the slantwise look again.

"You do eat?" I asked.

"It's never been a problem," she said.

"Then we'll have dinner?"

"I'm waiting for somebody," she said. "A man."

"He may have been hit by a truck," I said hopefully.

She sipped her drink: "He's about your height, maybe twenty pounds heavier and very short-tempered. He wouldn't like me even talking to you."

"He doesn't sound the sort of guy you should know," I said.

"His name is Johnny Lynch," she said.

The name didn't mean anything to me. The way she said it, apparently it should.

"I wouldn't be worried if it was Rocky Marciano," I told her. "Well, not very much."

"You should be worried," she said. "You're a stranger in town?"

"Vacation."

"If you lived here, you would know the name," she said. "You have yourself a good time and find another girl."

"That's what they all say," I said.

Her eyes widened a fraction as she looked over my shoulder.

"Friend of yours, Julie?" a voice grated from behind me.

I looked around and saw him standing there. Her description had been accurate as to weight and height. He was dark and good-looking, and he was burning.

"Not exactly," I said. "I was trying to persuade the lady to dine with me, but she was just giving me the gypsy's warning about a character named Lynch. You know him?"

"That's me," he said. "And for two cents, I'll ..."

"You can't be Lynch," "The way she described him, Lynch looks human. He doesn't have ears that stick out from his head like bat wings and ..."

He gave a strangled sort of grunt and swung at me. It wasn't scientific. I ducked and his fist whistled over my head. I hit him under the jaw with the heel of my hand and his head jerked back painfully. Out of the corner of my eye, I saw the look of alarm in the redhead's eyes as she looked behind me.

I came quickly off the stool, grabbed Lynch by the lapels of his jacket and swung him around onto the stool just in time for him to collect the baseball-bat the bartender swung, on his cranium.

Lynch gave up all interest abruptly. I let go of his lapels and watched him slide gently onto the floor.

"Wise guy!" the bartender said. He had a worried look on his face.

I grabbed the end of the bat nearest me, tearing it out of his hands, then lunged forward with it. The other end hit the bartender squarely in the solar plexus so he was more concerned with breathing than talking.

There was a faint smile on the redhead's face. "I think we'd better get out of here," she said.

We got out onto the sidewalk. A cab ambled past and I hailed it. "*The*

Gourmet," I told the driver.

I settled back into the seat and offered the redhead a cigarette. She took it and I lit it for her and one for myself.

"Johnny will kill you when he catches up with you," she said.

"That Johnny," I grinned. "He wants to watch out the wind doesn't get behind his ears—he'll take off!"

"Johnny plays in a big league," she said, "and this is his home town. If you were smart, you'd be making a reservation on the next plane out."

"I have a whole week of my vacation untouched," I said. "And now I've met you, I just couldn't leave Ocean Beach ahead of schedule. In fact, I may never leave Ocean Beach."

She smiled again: "If you want to be big and brave, I guess I can't stop you."

"Julie," I said. "It's a nice name. Sort of suits you."

"Thank you," she said.

"Call me Al," I said generously. "It's short for something, but for what I'd rather not tell you. Al is just fine."

"Do you always bulldoze your women like this?"

"Only the green-eyed redheads," I said. "They do something to me."

"How many green-eyed redheads have you known?"

"You're the first," I admitted.

We arrived at *The Gourmet.* I paid off the cab and the head-waiter found us a table close to the dance floor. We ordered drinks and dinner. We lit cigarettes, the drinks arrived; we were organised.

She sat opposite me, looking somehow remote.

"Thinking about something?" I asked.

"I was thinking about Zero."

"Thinking about nothing?"

"This Zero isn't nothing. This Zero is something. He's Johnny's playmate. He's about seven feet tall and looks like an overgrown gorilla. He acts like one, too."

"Now you're trying to frighten me," I said. "Just because you know I'm scared!"

Julie shrugged her shapely shoulders: "I'm just warning you. Johnny will have half a dozen men looking all over town for us."

"Are you frightened?" I asked her.

She shook her head slowly: "Not for me, only for you."

"I can look after myself."

"I doubt it."

The waiter put oysters in front of us.

"What does this Johnny Lynch do that he's so tough?" I asked.

"Johnny's got lots of interests," she told me. "He owns the *Paradise* for one.”

“That’s where you can play the tables and dice if you’re that way in-clined?”

She nodded: “You’ve been there?”

“Only once,” I said. “I lost fifty bucks, so I got out while I had my clothes left.”

“You know something?” she said. “You don’t talk like a tourist. You don’t even look like one.”

“What do I talk and look like?”

“I don’t know,” she said. “You’ve got me wondering, Al. I’ll tell you something—I’m not Johnny Lynch’s girl, although he thinks I’m going to be.”

“Glad to hear it,” I said.

“I thought you might be disappointed,” she said softly.

I looked at her. I was getting that slantwise look again.

“Why would I be disappointed?”

“I thought that just maybe you thought I was his girl.”

“And I made a play for you so I could take a poke at Johnny?”

“So you could annoy him, anyway.”

“It was the red hair and the green eyes,” I said. “Truly.”

“It flatters a girl to think it was, anyway,” she said.

We ate. We danced. We drank a little, maybe a little more than a little. We left around midnight and I called a cab.

“The night is young,” I said originally, as we got into the cab. “Let’s go drink somewhere.”

“You can take me home,” she said, and leaned forward to give the driver the address.

She settled back then: “I’m sorry, Al. I’m a working-girl—I have to be up early in the morning.”

“We could fix that,” I said. “If you don’t go to bed first, you can’t over-sleep.”

She shook her head: “But I have to stay awake tomorrow!”

Twenty minutes later the cab stopped. It was one of Ocean Beach’s more expensive pieces of real estate. A dozen cabins grouped strategically around a big swimming pool. Each cabin was completely self-contained with its own carport. We walked down to one of the cabins in the centre.

She fumbled in her purse for the key, found it and turned it in the lock. She pushed open the door and switched on the light.

“You can come in,” she said, “for one drink.”

Suddenly we had company.

“Let’s all have a drink,” Lynch said pleasantly, and gave me a push which sent me stumbling forward, off-balance. The next moment a steam-hammer hit me between the shoulder-blades and I finished up flat on the floor.

I heard the door slam and the next moment the sound of a slap. I looked up. One side of Julie's face was bright crimson.

"I don't like girls who walk out on me, baby," Lynch said pleasantly.

I hauled myself onto my feet and took a step towards him, then I stopped abruptly. I bumped into somebody's chest. That is, my head did.

I took a pace backwards and looked up.

Julie hadn't exaggerated at all. He must have been so close to seven feet tall that it didn't matter. And he did look just like a gorilla with a broad, flattened nose and a receding forehead. His eyes were slits set in concrete.

"You going someplace, buster?" he asked. His voice was gravel being tossed in a cement-mixer.

"Me?" I said. "Whatever made you think that?"

He reached out with a scoop of a fist, scooped my lapels together and lifted me up so that my feet dangled six inches above the floor.

"Put me down" I said and tried to break his grip on my coat.

I got the frustrated feeling a fly gets when it tries to swat a man.

Then he ran his free hand over me expertly. "He's not heeled, Johnny," he said.

"Put me down!" I repeated.

"Sure!" He let go of me suddenly and my heels hit the floor with a thud that jarred right through me.

Lynch lit himself a cigarette. "Get us a drink, baby," he said. "We're thirsty."

Julie walked across to the drink cupboard, her face expressionless. Lynch looked at me with a sneer on his face.

"Who is this jerk?" he asked.

That hurt—it was the second time that day.

"I don't know," Julie said, her back to him as she poured the drinks. "He started talking to me at *Toby's Tavern*. I told him about you and you came in as I was telling him."

"But you went with him!"

She shrugged her shoulders: "What else could I do?"

"I'm not so sure about that," he said. He looked at me again. "Where do you come from?"

"Little Rock, Arkansas," I told him.

"Brother! I'd believe it! How long are you staying in Ocean Beach?"

"A week."

"They should have told you about Johnny Lynch, punk!"

"They did," I said. "But I didn't believe it until I saw you. Not the ears, anyway."

"You're too smart, pal," he said. "I think we ought to make sure you have a quiet week for the rest of your vacation. Zero!"

"Yeah, Johnny?" The giant looked at him enquiringly.

"The tourist wants to sleep," Lynch said softly.

I got one last glimpse of the redhead, half-turned from the drink cupboard, giving me that slantwise look. Then Zero's bulk blocked out everything else. I threw a punch at him and bruised my knuckles. Then his hands came around my throat and started to squeeze.

CHAPTER 2
Of My Own Free Will

There was a jumble of blurred impressions ....

Sitting in an auto. What the hell was I doing there? The reek of whisky everywhere. Voices. Angry voices ... "He might have killed somebody!" ... "Drunk! Hopelessly drunk!"

Then official voices ... "He's loaded!" ... "Hey! Toss this lush into the wagon and get him down to the precinct!"

Then I was sitting in a chair and my head was clearing slowly. I squinted against the brightness of the light and saw a cop looking down at me.

"Coming out of it, huh?" he said.

"I guess so," I said. The words sounded thick and blurred.

"You'll have a long time to stay sober, pal!" he said.

I shook my head and suddenly my eyes clicked back into focus. There were three or four cops looking down at me and a couple of guys in plainclothes as well. It looked like a party.

"What happened?" I asked.

The cop snorted: "What happened, he says! You get drunk and steal a car, then run it up on a sidewalk into a plate-glass window and what happened, you say!"

I felt around cautiously in my pockets and found a pack of cigarettes. I lit one and somebody else came into the room. A white-haired character with a face that looked as if it had been stamped on. He looked at me incuriously, then did a double-take.

"Al Wheeler!" he said. "What the hell are you doing here?"

"I'm trying to work that one out," I said. "How are you, Ben?"

"I'm around the same," he said. He looked at the cop who had been talking to me: "What's this guy here for?"

"Stole a car, drunken driving, then finished up in a plate-glass window, Lieutenant."

Ben Jordan raised his eyebrows: "Maybe I should have a talk to him."

"Routine case, Lieutenant," the cop grunted. "The guy's a lush, anybody can tell that just by looking!"

Jordan fought down the grin that started to spread across his face: "I think I should still have a talk to him. You booked him yet?"

"Not yet, Lieutenant. We only just got him here."

"Better come into my office," Jordan said, looking at me.

I heaved myself to my feet and followed him along a corridor and then into his office. I dropped into a chair and Jordan closed the door.

"Better have some coffee, Al," he said.

"I could use it," I said. He rang through and told somebody to produce some coffee, then relaxed in his chair behind his desk.

"Well, well, well," he grinned. "Lieutenant—or is it Captain Wheeler? Chief of a Homicide Bureau and getting rolled for a lush!"

"Very funny," I said sourly. "And it's still Lieutenant. That Commissioner of ours moves like a guy with no legs when it concerns promotions!"

"What are you doing in Florida?"

"Vacation."

"Why didn't you look me up?"

"Like I said—vacation. I wanted to get away from cops."

"It figures," he said. "The unorthodox cop takes the unorthodox vacation!"

A cop came in with the coffee, then went out again. I broke the lid off the carton and drank. It tasted good, raising some of the fur off my tongue.

"I might as well tell you the story," I said sourly. "If it sounds stupid, okay, I'm stupid!"

So told him the story, from the time I met the redhead until the time I woke up in the precinct. When I finished, I waited for Jordan to finish laughing, but he wasn't laughing. His eyes were bright with interest.

"Why didn't you tell Lynch you were a cop?" he asked.

"Because for one I figured he wouldn't believe me and for two it would have scared off the redhead. Dames always scare when they suddenly find out you're a cop. Their consciences get the better of them and they start remembering—and get nervous. Trying to make love to a nervous woman is like trying to race a mountain goat up a mountain!"

Ben nodded. "This Lynch is quite a character," he said. "He's still almost new around here. Bought the *Paradise* around three months back."

"How about his gorilla?"

"Zero? He came along with Lynch."

"You want me to make a statement?"

He thought for a moment, then shook his head: "No, Al."

"You want me to take the rap?" I grinned at him.

"That's it," he agreed.

The grin was sponged off my face: "What!"

"Take it easy," Ben said. "I'm thinking."

"I thought you had the gripes!"

"How'd you like to do us a favour, Al?"

"My instincts tell me no," I said. "When a cop asks a cop for a favour ..."

"Seriously," he said. "You might be able to help us quite a lot."

"I'll listen, anyway," I told him.

He lit himself a cigarette: "A lot of funny things are happening in this neck of the woods—most of them seem to have happened since Johnny Lynch settled in. There's nothing directly connected with him, of course. But we've got a sort of feeling about him."

"I know what you mean," I said.

"Florida is one hell of a place for missing persons," he went on. "But lately we've had three or four listed who just shouldn't be missing. They had a lot of things in common. They were all young, all dames, all came from reasonably wealthy families and all, apparently, had no reason to disappear."

"Sounds interesting," I said. "Don't tell me the Road to Rio runs straight through this precinct?"

"We don't know what the hell it is, Al, and that's the trouble. None of them were in any trouble, so far as we can make out. Two of them were engaged to be married to nice guys who are still running around in tight circles trying to find them."

I lit myself another cigarette: "Any link between them and Lynch?"

"Only in a vague sort of way, Al. They all visited the *Paradise* a few times. So do maybe a couple of hundred people every night."

"Then why are you so interested in Lynch?"

"Because he's got the boys scared. All the hoods around the town are frightened stiff of the name Lynch. But we can't find out why."

"So what do you want me to do?"

Ben looked at me hard for a moment: "This bum rap that was pushed onto you tonight: if you make a statement, we can't prove anything. They'll deny it, of course. There'll be three of them to deny it. They'll furnish themselves with alibis. You can't swear they put you into that car, because you were unconscious then. I've got a better idea."

"Such as?"

He leaned forward across his desk: "We'll let you walk out from under the rap. We'll let it out that you're Al Wheeler, from Chicago. A big-noise racketeer who's down here on vacation. We will tell it that you pulled a mouthpiece out of your hat and even got political pressure to bear. We'll make you sound like a big-shot. A real big-shot!"

"And where will that get me?"

"I don't know, Al," Ben said thoughtfully. "But we could also let it filter around that you're most annoyed with Johnny Lynch and you've said something about making it your personal business to take care of him before you finish your vacation."

"So he gets all jumpy and nervous and maybe does something stupid?" I said. "I push him around until I push him into a panic?"

"You got it, Al!" Ben said happily.

"Nuts!" I said.

He didn't look so happy: "What?"

"I said, nuts! And I meant just that. Maybe Johnny doesn't get panicky at all. Maybe he just tells that seven feet of concrete to take care of me. And maybe Zero does just that!"

"Al!" Ben said in a hurt voice. "You aren't scared?"

"Of course I'm scared," I said. "Even the thought of that Zero frightens me. And I'm still on vacation, remember!"

"You won't do it?"

"In a word—no!"

"Not even for an old pal?"

"Not even for five old pals or their widows!"

He shook his head slowly: "I thought better of you, Al, I really did!"

"You're breaking my heart!" I told him. I got onto my feet.

"Where are you going?" he asked vaguely.

"Back to my hotel," I said. "I have had a trying evening."

"Al," he said gently. "You can't go there—we haven't booked you yet."

"What!"

"You heard what I said, Al."

I glared down at him: "Are you kidding?"

"Of course not," he said easily. "You've got at least six counts to be booked on. We can check with Commissioner Lavers that you are Lieutenant Al Wheeler in charge of his Homicide Bureau and then I guess we'll drop the charges."

"My pal!" I said bitterly.

"Your old pal," he corrected me.

I looked at the nasty grin on Jordan's face. I could imagine the Commissioner's reaction when he heard Lieutenant Wheeler had been arrested and booked on six different counts in Florida. I could imagine the reaction of the boys in Homicide. I could imagine …

"Okay," I said. "Take your hands off my throat. I'll do it."

"I'm glad to hear you say that, Al." he grinned. "I knew you wouldn't let me down!"

I went back to the chair and sat down again. "One thing I'll need is an equalizer."

"Are you referring to a gun, Lieutenant?"

"Just that! I left my working clothes at home."

"I guess we can fix that, Lieutenant," he said. "What else, Al?"

"Any more information you've got," I said. "What about the dames who've disappeared?"

"I can send you down to the Bureau in the morning," he said. "Hennessey down there can give you what dope we've got on them."

"It seems awful thin to me," I said. "To try and tie it onto Lynch, I mean."

Ben shrugged his shoulders: "There it is, Al. That's what we figure. Or if we don't figure it, we're curious about the coincidences that have happened since Lynch came to town."

"What about the *Paradise?*" I asked him. "What sort of joint is that?"

"The tables are straight," he said. "So are the dice. You know how it is with that sort of joint. The house takes a percentage all the time and they can't lose. It wouldn't pay them to be crooked."

"You know anything about my redhead?"

"Your redhead? I thought she belonged to Lynch!"

"That was before tonight, maybe," I said.

"No, Al, we don't know anything about her. I'd never heard of her until you mentioned she existed."

"Okay," I got onto my feet again. "I guess I can go home now, huh?"

"Sure, Al—we'll forget all about the lush and the car. The car wasn't badly damaged at all. We'll even get it fixed and returned to its owner."

"You know who owns it?"

"Sure—it was reported stolen an hour ago. A dame by the name of Julie Adams. Lives at Palm Court."

"Now there's a coincidence," I said.

I walked towards the door and stopped when I reached it. I looked back. Ben Jordan was sitting there with a look I didn't like in his eyes.

"You're pulling a fast one," I said.

"Why, Al!" He looked at me reproachfully. "Whatever makes you think that?"

"I've just got a feeling," I said. "But I'll find out—I guess."

"I don't know why you can't trust a pal," he said.

"Never trust a copper," I said. "You should know that."

I opened the door, then I remembered something else: "How about that gun?"

"I'll have it for you in the morning."

"Okay," I said. "I'll need it when I meet Zero again. In fact, I'll probably need three guns and a couple of hand grenades when that happens."

"If you shoot him, we'll probably give you a medal," he said.

"Don't kid me!" I snarled. "If I shoot Zero, the only thing I'll get out of you will be a first-degree murder rap!"

CHAPTER 3
Compensation

Came early evening and I dressed in the tuxedo and trimmings again. They had been to the dry-cleaners and back and they looked reasonably respectable. I packed the .32 with the filed off serial number in a shoulder-holster under my left armpit. I hadn't asked Ben where he'd got it and he hadn't told me.

My watch said it was six-thirty. I looked up the phone directory and found a Miss Adams was listed at the Palm Court address. I lifted the receiver and dialled the number. It rang half a dozen times and then a husky voice answered.

"Miss Julie Adams?" I asked.

"That's right," she agreed.

"This is Al Wheeler," I said. "Hello."

I thought I could hear her breathing gently into the phone and that was all.

"Are you doing anything tonight, Julie?"

"Yes," she said, "I am."

"Nothing important, I hope," I said. "Nothing that couldn't be postponed while you had dinner with me?"

"After last night," she said, "I didn't think you'd want to see me again in a million years!"

"I'm the guy who can't take a hint," I said. "Not even the gentle sort of hint I got last night."

"I'm supposed to see Johnny at ten," she said. "At the *Paradise*."

I looked at my watch. "It's only seven now," I said. "I can pick you up in twenty minutes. That gives us plenty of time for dinner and then I can deliver you at the *Paradise* right on time."

There was just her gentle breathing again.

"A date?" I asked her.

"All right," she said. "You pick me up in twenty minutes."

I put the receiver back on the cradle.

I got there in fifteen minutes and paid off the cab. Palm Court looked much the same as it had the night before. I walked down to her cabin and knocked on the door.

She opened it almost straight away.

"Come in," she said. I followed her into the living-room, closing the door behind me. She turned to face me: "Would you like a drink before we go?"

"It sounds like a good idea," I said.

She was wearing a strapless sheath of black barathea. A silver snake was clasped around the wrist of her right hand. She walked over to the drink cupboard and got out a bottle and a couple of glasses.

"I don't understand you," she said.

"That's because you don't know me well enough," I said. "That can be taken care of."

"After last night," she said. "After what they did to you, you come back for more?"

"I came back to see you," I told her.

She turned around with the drinks in her hands: "Why?"

"There's just something about green-eyed redheads," I said.

She came over and handed me my drink. Her eyebrows lifted.

"You have to have an angle," she said slowly. "Everyone in this business has an angle, don't they?"

"Or curves," I looked at her pointedly.

She shrugged her shoulders and for a moment I felt anxious for the black barathea: "I'm just wondering what your angle is?"

"It started off being a vacation," I said. "Then you came along."

"All right, Al," she said. "It's your secret."

We ate in one of those intimate places that has candles instead of electric light, so they can serve you lousy food and add up the bill their way. The conversation was sparse and didn't mean anything. We left around nine-thirty and I got a cab and told the driver to take us to the *Paradise*.

We arrived at five to ten. I helped her out of the cab.

"Thank you," she said. "It's been very nice."

"I'm not going yet," I said. "This place has a horrible fascination for me."

Her eyebrows lifted for the second time that night: "You mean you're coming inside?"

"Sure," I said.

I paid off the cab and turned back to her.

"But Johnny will be in there," she said. "And Zero is sure to be there as well."

"You don't have to introduce us," I said as I took her arm. "We have already met."

"I suppose you know what you're doing," she said.

We went inside.

The *Paradise* is divided into roughly two halves. In the first half you can sit and eat and drink and dance and watch the floorshow. In the second half you can gamble. You can play roulette, chemin-de-fer, baccarat, dice—almost anything you want.

We walked through the first half into the second half. Julie kept on going past the tables. We came to a door marked *Private* and she pushed it open. It led into a corridor and I kept with her. She closed the door behind us, then stopped and looked at me.

"I'm going into Johnny's private office," she said. "You're still sure you want to come?"

"Still sure," I agreed.

We walked down the corridor and then she stopped at a door, knocked twice, opened it and walked in. I followed behind her, closing the door and leaning against it.

Johnny Lynch was sitting behind a desk and Zero blocked off half the wall behind him.

"He insisted he wanted to come along," Julie said. She walked away from me over to an armchair and sat down gracefully, then proceeded to light herself a cigarette.

Lynch had hardly noticed her—he was watching me carefully.

"Al Wheeler," he said softly. "Again."

"How are you, Johnny?" I asked. "And that Missing Link of yours?" I nodded towards Zero.

"I been hearing things about you, Al," he said gently. "They tell me you got influence. You swung that rap last night without any trouble at all."

"A little organisation," I said. "That was all that was needed."

"I hear you're a big-shot in Chi," he said.

"They've been exaggerating," I said, "but not very much."

"I guess I was hasty last night," he said. "I made a mistake."

I lit myself a cigarette. "You made a mistake," I agreed.

"I'm sorry, Al."

"That's fine," I said. "How about the damages?"

"The story I also hear," he went on, "is that you're looking for Johnny Lynch?"

He was tensed, waiting for me to start something.

I grinned at him: "Maybe the story has gone a little haywire, Johnny. I'm down here on vacation. So you messed up my evening—so I need compensation." I shrugged my shoulders: "I don't bear a guy a grudge, Johnny. I'm down here in Ocean Beach for pleasure, not for business. If you take some of my pleasure away, then maybe you can compensate me for it."

"How much is an evening worth to you, Al?"

"Two thousand dollars," I said.

"Your entertainment comes high!"

"Ain't that the truth!" I agreed.

He looked at me for a few seconds longer, then he pulled out a drawer of his desk and took out a bundle of notes. He counted out two thousand

and pushed them across the desk towards me.

"There's your two thousand, Al," he said. "Compensation."

"That's what I'd call a reasonable attitude, Johnny," I said.

I walked across to the desk and picked up the money and put it into the inside pocket of the tuxedo.

"No hard feelings, Al?" he asked.

"Johnny!" I grinned at him. "Of course not!"

My hand was still inside my coat. I grabbed the butt of the .32 and pulled it out in one movement. I continued the movement through the air so the barrel of the gun hit him across the side of the head with a nasty dull sound. He slumped sideways in the chair.

Zero growled, pushed himself off the wall and started towards me.

I pointed the .32 at him. "Can you spit bullets, too?" I asked gently.

He stopped where he was. I took a quick look at Julie. She was still sitting in her chair, smoking her cigarette. There was a blank expression on her face.

"Turn around!" I told Zero. He hesitated for a moment, then turned around. "Get back to the wall!" I told him.

He moved forward until he couldn't move any further without walking through the wall—not that I doubted he couldn't do that if he tried.

I moved around the desk softly and came up behind him. I reversed the gun in my hand and let him have the butt across the nape of his neck with all I'd got. He grunted and sagged at the knees. I hit him again the same way and this time he rolled onto the floor and lay still.

I turned away from him.

"Is it my turn now?" Julie asked.

"I think we should go and have a drink," I said. "I don't think Johnny will be good company the rest of the evening."

"If you say so," she said.

We went out of the office, back down the corridor. A minute later and we were outside on the sidewalk again. The commissionaire picked up a cab for us and we drove back in silence to Palm Court.

She didn't say a word until we got inside the cabin again.

"I understand you even less," she said.

"Let's have that drink, honey," I said. "I'm all tuckered out with the exercise."

She was pouring the drinks when the phone went. She looked at me questioningly and I shrugged my shoulders. She walked to the phone and lifted the receiver.

"Hello—yes, Johnny? Are you all right? No, I'm gone. He made me leave with him. He insisted we have a drink in a bar and then he put me into a cab and told the driver to bring me here. No, I don't know where he went.

All right, Johnny, tomorrow afternoon. 'Bye."

She hung up and went back to the drinks.

"Why didn't you tell him I was here?" I asked.

"You might have shot me," she said casually.

I sat down on the couch and she brought the drinks over and sat down beside me.

"Johnny was worried when we went in," she said. "You almost had him scared. He was going to give you that money without any trouble at all. It wasn't necessary to hit him. Why did you hit him?"

"I owed it to him," I said. "He and his tame gorilla."

"But you got the money."

"Sure, but that isn't enough with a guy like Lynch. You have to impress him that he's a punk."

"Johnny's no punk!"

"He acted awfully like a punk tonight."

She lifted her glass and drank sparingly: "You come from Chicago?"

"That's right."

"Are you in business there?"

"Sure—the same line of business as Johnny, but in a bigger way. A much bigger way."

"You mean you're a hoodlum?"

I looked at her. "Don't say that, honey," I said. "A hoodlum's small-time. Me—I'm big-time! I'm called a racketeer."

"After your act tonight," she said, "I believe you."

I emptied my glass: "Mind if I refill this?"

"Go ahead."

I walked over to the drink cupboard and busied myself with the bottle.

"Al," she said.

"Yeah?"

"You don't like Johnny, do you?"

"Not much."

"He'll hate you after tonight. He'll kill you—or try to. His ego won't be satisfied until he does."

"So what?"

"Are you going back to Chicago?"

"Not till my vacation is finished."

"That means you're going to have to fight Johnny—you realise that?"

"I guess so."

I turned around with the refilled glass and headed back towards her.

"Maybe I'm stupid," she said. "But I think you have a chance of winning."

"That's nice to hear," I sat down beside her again.

"Would you listen if I made you a proposition, Al?"

"I always listen to a proposition, honey."

"The dice are loaded against you, Al. This is Johnny's town—he knows it and you don't. He also has a lot of men here he can use whenever he wants to."

"Sure."

"You need help, Al."

"Maybe."

"I could give you a lot of help. Inside information."

"I thought you were Johnny's girl?"

"I'm nobody's girl but my own!"

I looked at her. I was getting that slantwise look again.

"If you won," she said, "you could take over Johnny's set-up." She snapped her fingers: "Just like that!"

"It's a thought."

"If I help you, you've got three times the chance. And if you're successful, you can do something for me."

"What?"

"I'll tell you that when the time comes."

"Maybe I won't do it then?"

"I think you will," she said confidently.

I finished the second drink. "I don't understand you," I said. "Or weren't we talking about understanding people? I don't dig you at all!"

She turned her face towards me.

"Sometimes I don't even understand myself," she said softly. "So you don't have a chance, do you, Al?"

Her lips were soft and moist. She moved closer to me and her fingernails dug sharply into my shoulders.

"What do you want, Al?" she whispered. "An illuminated address?"

CHAPTER 4
Decoy

Hennessey looked at me as I tossed the files back onto his desk: "Find anything interesting, Lieutenant?"

"Not very much," I said. "It's just the way Ben Jordan told it to me. Four dames, all young, all pretty, all disappear. They all come from well-to-do families and they have no apparent troubles. No corpses turn up, no ransom notes."

"That's it," Hennessey nodded, "and it stinks!"

"You think they're all connected in some way?"

"Sure! They all happened within the last couple of months."

Hennessey grinned suddenly: "Tell you something else. Over the last three months we had reports that three or four big-shot hoodlums were on their way to Florida. But we ain't seen any of them. I got a theory they met up with these girls, married 'em and went to Cuba for their honeymoons."

I grinned obligingly: "Why does the Department think the disappearance of these girls is connected with Johnny Lynch?"

"It doesn't," he said flatly. "Ben Jordan's got a sort of hunch about it, that's all. All the local hoods are frightened of Lynch. They clam up when his name's mentioned. So we figure there must be more to Lynch than just the *Paradise*—which is pretty well legal, anyway. And those four girls would have visited the *Paradise* sometime or another."

"You're sure of that?"

"Sure!"

"But they wouldn't have gone there alone?"

"I guess not," he agreed.

I lit myself a cigarette: "Thanks for a look at the files, anyway."

"Anytime, Lieutenant," he said.

I went down to the precinct and found Ben Jordan in his office.

"Still alive, I see," he said brightly.

"And still buying insurance," I told him.

"Sit down, Al. Something on your mind?"

I sat down and looked at him: "I've been down with Hennessey having a look at the files on those missing girls."

"Got any bright thoughts?"

"No."

"Seen any more of Lynch?"

I told him what had happened the previous night. I didn't tell him about my deal with Julie Adams. I thought something had to be sacred and, anyway, why should he know everything?

He sat there grinning at me after I had finished: "So you got Lynch good and mad? That's good!"

"Sure," I said. "And I want the works when you bury me—an address from the Mayor, too."

"You're out of luck, Al," he said. "The Mayor don't speak a word of English. They made him Mayor because he can't understand what they're saying when they tell him about the g   raft in City Hall—that way he never asks for a share for himself."

"You're wasted as a cop," I said.

"I know it," he agreed modestly.

"You should be pushing a broom around the streets!"

He leaned back and lit a cigarette: "What are you going to do today?"

"Try and stay alive firstly," I said. "And secondly, spend some of Johnny's dough. I want to spend it fast in case he catches up with me and takes it back."

"You could always give it to me," he said hopefully.

"These dames who are missing," I said. "I had a thought about them."

"Yeah?"

"Did you handle any of the investigations?"

"The last one," he said. "Girl called Lucille Randle. Why?"

"Did she have any girl-friends?"

"I guess so."

"Anyone in particular you remember?"

Ben thought for a moment: "Yeah—she did. Girl called Dawn Blair."

"What sort of girl was she?"

"Blonde and attractive. Her old man owns a hotel. Plenty of dough."

"I was wondering," I said. "Maybe there's an easy way to find out if Lynch's got anything to do with the girls' disappearance."

"Tell me."

"If you think this girl Dawn Blair is worth the approach. She might play decoy."

"Just how would she do that?"

"She might suddenly get a yen to gamble. Start playing the tables regularly at the *Paradise*. She wouldn't have to risk a lot of money—just be there."

Ben bit his lip dubiously: "We'd be taking a hell of a chance, wouldn't we?"

"I could keep an eye on her," I said.

"That would be taking even more of a chance!"

"Thanks, pal!"

He thought about it some more: "She seemed to be a smart sort of girl. Maybe you've got an idea there."

"If I kept an eye on her, you wouldn't need to have one of your men tailing her the whole time. And that stops the risk of Lynch or one of his men spotting the tail and getting wise."

"I guess so," he nodded. "Okay—I'll try and talk to her today."

"If she's agreeable, you could tell her about me," I said. "Then I could meet her."

"I think you're just trying to get yourself a girl!" he grinned. "Okay, Al, I'll try it. You just might have something there."

"I'll ring you this afternoon," I said. "Around four?"

"Sure," he said.

I left the precinct and got out into the sun again. I had Lynch's two thousand bucks in my wallet and I felt rich. Rich enough to think I should have some transport of my own and stop worrying about hacks.

I walked three blocks and found a second-hand auto yard. For nine hundred bucks I bought a little Austin-Healey with twelve thousand miles on the clock. It made a satisfactory burbling sound when I drove it out of the yard and the pick-up down the street brought a smug grin to my lips.

It was only eleven-thirty and the sunlit day stretched ahead of me. Who was it said something about improving the shining hour? I drove over to Palm Court and put the Healey under the carport, but not under Julie's carport.

She opened the door on my second knock. She was wearing a black silk shirt and tailored shorts.

"Back so soon?" she said. "What did you want—breakfast?"

"I'll settle for coffee," I said.

I followed her into the living-room. She went into the kitchen to make the coffee and I lit a cigarette. She came back into the living-room into my arms. I kissed her the way I didn't think was possible in the mornings.

"Nice," she said.

She lit herself a cigarette. "Nice seeing you, Al," she said. "But I don't think it's smart."

"Why not?"

"I never know when Johnny may turn up," she shrugged her shoulders. "If he keeps on finding you here, he's liable to wonder, isn't he?"

"I guess so," I said.

"Besides, he might have somebody following you, checking up on what you're doing."

I shook my head: "I'm not being tailed—I've been looking for that. I moved out of my hotel this morning so they won't pick me up easily."

"Where are you staying now?"

"Palm Court."

"What!" Julie stared at me.

I grinned: "Four cabins away."

"Is that wise?"

"I figure it is. One thing I'm close to you and another thing I don't think Lynch will look for me this close."

Julie went back into the kitchen and reappeared a couple of minutes later with the coffee.

"'What number is your cabin, Al?"

"Eight."

"I might call," she smiled. "You'd better not cheat on me, living so close."

I took the coffee and sat down. "When are you seeing Johnny again?" I asked. "This afternoon?"

She nodded: "He said he'd pick me up."

"How long have you known him?"

"A couple of months."

"What's his racket?"

"You've seen it, Al."

I shook my head: "Johnny's racket is more than the *Paradise*—it has to be. Otherwise he wouldn't play it so tough."

"All I've seen is the gambling," she said. "What else do you think he's doing?"

"I don't know," I said. "But I'm interested—if there's money in it."

"What do you do back in Chicago, Al?"

"A little here, a little there," I said.

"You give things away like a pawnbroker," she said.

I finished the coffee: "You could be right about it not being smart for me to be around here. I'll ring you this evening, honey. Okay?"

"Sure," she said. "If I tell you it's a wrong number, you'll know I've got company."

"Okay," I said. "And don't forget my new address."

I drove the Healey into town and bought myself a couple of drinks and then some lunch. I went for a drive after that, getting the car up to ninety-five on the highway. I came back to Palm Court around four.

I rang Ben Jordan.

"I went and talked to her, Al," he said. "It looks like she might help us. I told her about you and suggested the two of you should get together and have a talk. She suggests you go up to their place for dinner tonight. Okay?"

"Sure," I said. "What the address?"

He gave me the address and I made a note of it.

"She said to be there around seven," he said. "Her folks will be out so the two of you can talk freely."

"Fine," I said.

"And I did say talk!"

"Why, Lieutenant! What a nasty mind you have!"

I was ready to leave at six-thirty. I rang Julie's number and nobody answered. I hung up and went out to the car. Half an hour later I reached Dawn Blair's house.

It was quite a place. It was down the coast, out of town, with its own private beach. A concrete drive ran off the road and I parked the Healey outside the house. It was a ranch-type which seemed to go on and on forever.

I pressed the buzzer and waited.

About twenty seconds later the door opened and a blonde stood there. I looked at her and felt my mouth drop open. She was wearing a blue shirt and dark slacks. One glance told you how vital her statistics were.

"You're Mr. Wheeler?" she smiled at me.

"That's right," I croaked.

"I'm Dawn Blair. Won't you come in?"

I followed her through the house onto the sundeck, which ran the whole length at the back. It was about fifteen feet above the beach and the moonlit ocean made a perfect backdrop to the scene.

"My mother and father are out," she said, "and it's the servants' night off, or one of them. I thought it was better that we should be alone after Lieutenant Jordan telling me how secret this was."

"Sure," I said.

A shaded lamp lit a table in the corner which was set for two. An intimate set-up. But then Dawn Blair looked an intimate sort of blonde. She talked in a sort of husky whisper and I got the impression that if she was exposed to daylight, she'd vanish.

"Would you like a drink, Mr. Wheeler?" she asked.

She was talking my language. She poured the drinks from a trolley alongside the table. We sat down facing one another. Her hair was long enough to fall forward around her face when she inclined her head, leaving her face in shadow.

"I think this is terribly exciting, Mr. Wheeler," she said. "I'm breathless!"

"Let's skip that Mr. Wheeler routine," I suggested. "My name is Al."

"How wonderfully quaint!"

I thought about that for a moment, then decided to let it ride.

"Lieutenant Jordan said I could help to find Lucille Randle."

"We're hoping so," I said. "Did he tell you how?"

She shook her head: "No, he was terribly mysterious about the whole thing. He said you'd explain it all to me—Al."

A nice guy, that Jordan.

"Should we eat first?" she suggested.

"Sounds like a wonderful idea," I said. "Do you mind if I help myself to another drink?"

"Of course not. I drink hardly anything myself. You just pour yourself a drink whenever you want one."

That was something. We ate. Oysters, lobster mayonnaise and strawberries and cream. I passed up the strawberries and got myself another drink instead.

Dawn cleared away the dishes, put the coffee on the table, and I lit her a cigarette and one for myself.

"Now," she said eagerly. "Tell me all about it!"

So I told her all about it, or some of it. I pointed out the vague suspicion we had that Lucille Randle's disappearance and that of the other girls was somehow linked with the *Paradise* and Johnny Lynch.

She listened, absorbed.

"I'm working on it from one angle," I said. "A sort of undercover angle. If you help us, you can work on it from another angle."

"Of course I'll help!" she said.

"There may be some danger attached to it," I told her.

"I'm not frightened!"

"Okay, what we want you to do is this. Go to the *Paradise*; start tonight, maybe. Go every night. Play a little on the tables, not very much. Go unescorted or with an escort; that doesn't matter very much, either. But go there. I'll keep an eye on you while you're there. You won't see me, but I'll be around. When you get home, I'll ring you a little later. Tell me everything that's happened while you were there, however unimportant it might seem.

"If Lynch makes any suggestions to you—that you might like to do this or that—stall him until you've spoken to me. And that's all there is to it."

"Of course I'll do it," she said. "It sounds fascinating, really fascinating!"

I managed not to wince. "That's fine," I said. "We appreciate it a lot. And don't tell anyone what you're doing—not even your mother and father."

"Not a soul!" she promised.

I finished my drink and refilled the glass.

"Do you carry a gun, Al?"

"Sure."

"Could I see it?"

I took the .32 out of the shoulder-holster and handed it to her, making sure the safety was on. She held it reverently for a moment, then handed it back to me.

"Gosh!" she said.

CHAPTER 5
That Julie, With The Double Face?

Dawn Blair went to the *Paradise*, driving a Packard convertible. I followed in the Austin-Healey. I smoked half a pack of cigarettes, then she came out and got back into her car.

I was the only guy who followed her home. When I saw her car turn off the road onto the concrete drive, I turned the Healey around and headed in the opposite direction.

Ten minutes later I stopped at a drugstore and used the phone booth. She answered on the first ring.

"Al Wheeler," I said. "Anything interesting happen?"

"Nothing!" Dawn's voice was remorseful. "Absolutely nothing, Al!"

"Well, never mind," I said. "That's a start. Same time tomorrow night?"

"Of course!"

"Okay. Goodnight."

"Goodnight, Al," she said huskily.

I drove back to Palm Court. I thought it was going to be fun standing around in the rain while a blonde, who was made for almost anything but detecting, was inside the *Paradise*. It was one hell of a way to spend a vacation.

I got inside the cabin, poured myself a drink and looked at my watch. It was just before midnight—the night was still young by Ocean Beach standards. I picked up the phone and dialled Julie's number.

The phone rang for a while before she answered it.

"Al, honey," I said.

"I'm sorry," her voice was polite and remote. "You must have the wrong number."

I hung up. So Julie had company. Johnny Lynch, I wondered? Maybe if I took a walk, I could find out. The night was hot, she might even have a window open. Julie was my partner ... she thought. Or was it she was my partner ... I thought? The old question of who was kidding who, which has kept man and woman interested in each other for the last few thousand years.

I finished the drink before I went. I left the lights on in the cabin, remembering that the windows at one side could be seen from Julie's place. If she happened to look out, she'd see the lights still on and figure I was inside—maybe.

I took my time about walking the short distance between the two cabins. There were no lights showing in any of the others. I wondered if they only rented them to honeymoon couples.

I approached her cabin with more care than a lover would take when he isn't quite sure if the husband is home or not. I eased myself around a corner and saw the light shining through the big living-room window, making a patch of brightness on the ground outside. I got as close to the window as I could, keeping myself flat against the wall. The window was open, I noticed.

I got down on all fours and crept along until I was directly underneath the window, and I listened. I heard a man talking, but it wasn't Lynch's voice.

"Johnny said you'd entertain me this evening," he said. His voice was smooth and confident. "You take a long time to warm up, don't you, doll?"

"If you wanted that sort of entertainment," Julie said flatly, "you should have made yourself clear to Johnny. He's got plenty of girls around the club who'd be only too pleased."

"I like my dames to have class," he said. "You've got class, baby."

"One of the reasons I keep it," she said, "is because I'm a one-man woman. And that man happens to be Johnny."

He laughed softly: "Sure. Okay, baby. I'm not a violent type. I always prefer a girl to like me for my money alone. Pretty soon I'll have a choice of classy dames, according to what Johnny says."

"If he says so, he would be right."

"He'd better be right," there was an edge to the smooth voice. "For what I'm paying, I could take over a floor of one of Hilton's places and have the food served on golden platters!"

"But Hilton couldn't offer you all the advantages that Johnny can."

"Maybe not."

An elephant-sized mosquito hummed happily onto my nose like a homing pigeon. I went to slap it, then remembered they would hear it inside the room. I shook my head violently. The mosquito hummed away six inches with a sort of enquiring hum, then came back again.

"Kind of late," the guy inside said. "I guess I should be making tracks. You weren't going to ask me to stop the night, were you?"

"No."

He laughed again: "I thought not. How long do I have to stick around Ocean Beach, anyway?"

"I don't know," Julie said. "Didn't Johnny say?"

"He said it wouldn't take long."

"That probably means only a few days," she said. "Don't you like it here?"

"Me? I'm a Coney Island character. I get sort of lost with all this ocean!"

"I wonder you bothered to come all the way down to Florida?"

"You know why—it was a little too hot in New York. The smart thing to do was let things cool off."

"Police?" Julie asked. "Or is that none of my business?"

"It's not particularly any of your business," he said. "But it's not cop trouble—or Feds, either. It's—how will I put it? A shift of emphasis."

Julie made an impatient sound: "That's double-talk!"

"The Syndicate wanted a shift of emphasis," he said easily. "I was the guy who shifted it. Some people wouldn't like it—not till they got used to it. So I'm taking a vacation till they get used to it."

"Then you don't have to worry about how long you stay here if the police or the F.B.I. aren't after you?"

"They aren't the only people who can trail a guy," he said.

"Were you ever in Chicago?" she asked suddenly.

There was a slight pause. "A few weeks," he said. "That was a year ago.

Why?"

"Ever run across a guy by the name of Wheeler? Al Wheeler? He's mixed up in the rackets somewhere."

"Big-shot?"

"I think so."

"I don't remember him," he said. "If he's really big-time, he'd be tied in with the Syndicate or dead by now."

"I just wondered," Julie said indifferently.

"Johnny asked me the same question," the guy said. "What's with this Wheeler?"

"He's been around," Julie said. "Getting into Johnny's hair a little, that's all."

"Surely Johnny can take care of that?"

"Johnny's cautious," she said. "He could take care of him like that!" I heard Julie snap her fingers. "But he wants to place him first. You know— if he did something hasty, it might be bad for business."

"Sure," the guy didn't sound very interested. "Well, I guess I'll be on my way. Thanks for the evening—good clean fun that it was. See you around, Julie."

"Wouldn't you like another drink before you go?"

"No, thanks."

I heard their footsteps receding. I crawled back until I was past the window, then stood upright. I edged my way down towards the corner of the cabin until I could see the path that led from the front door to the carport, and the Cadillac underneath the port.

A square of light hit the path as the front door opened.

"Goodnight," the guy said. Then he walked across to the car. The front door shut again. For about four seconds I got a good look at him.

He was around medium height with broad shoulders. His hair was iron-grey and curly. He was wearing a tropic-weight blue suit that must have set him back a couple of hundred bucks. He walked confidently. I watched him until he got into the car. I waited until he'd backed out onto the roadway and driven off.

Then I went back to my own cabin.

The phone was ringing as I opened the front door. I raced across the floor and answered it.

"Where were you?" she asked.

"In the shower," I said. "Been ringing long?"

"It seemed a long time," she said. "I thought you might have gone to bed."

"We Wheelers never sleep," I told her. "Your company gone home?"

"Johnny has to keep an eye on his club," she said lightly. "He gets worried the staff might cheat on him."

"Now he's gone," I suggested, "how about asking me over for a drink?"

"I think you should ask me over," she said.

"You're asked."

"I'll be a couple of minutes," she said. "Just give me time to resurrect my face."

"Sure," I said.

I hung up, dived into the bathroom and turned on the shower, reefed off my clothes, dived in and out of the shower and towelled myself half-dry. I put on a shirt and a pair of slacks and was rubbing my hair dry when I heard her tap on the front door.

I answered it, still towelling my hair. She smiled as she walked past me into the living-room. I finished towelling my hair, ran a comb through it, then joined her.

She was pouring drinks.

"What sort of day did you have, lover?" she asked.

"Just a day," I said. "How about you?"

"Just a day," she said.

She turned around and handed me a drink. She was wearing a scoop-necked blouse and a multi-coloured flared skirt. Her green eyes held the alert languor of a leopard.

"Johnny's trying to check up on you," she said.

"What about me?"

"Who you are. Just how big you rate in Chicago."

"Why is he going to all that trouble?"

"Johnny's just naturally cautious."

"He wasn't very cautious the other night, when he tried to swing that drunken driving rap onto me."

"But he was mad then," she said. "Mad jealous! Because of me, naturally!"

I reached out and ran the fingers of one hand into the back of her hair, pulling her towards me. I kissed her, still holding her head so that her lips were pressed hard against mine. It seemed to last a long time.

"H'm ..." she said when I let go of her. "You nearly made me spill my drink."

"That's what I like about you," I told her. "Hot-blooded!"

She shrugged her shoulders. It did dangerous things to her scoop-neckline. "Tell me about Chicago, Al," she said.

"Like what? Like it's a big place?"

"Like what you do there!"

I drank some of my drink: "Honey-doll, who's making these enquiries for Johnny Lynch?"

"I'm making enquiries for Julie Adams," she said. "We're in partnership, remember?"

"Sure," I said. "We trust each other."

"Okay," she said.

She sat down on the couch and looked at me: "I'm taking an awful risk with you, Al!"

"Sure," I grinned. "Any dame who looks the way you look, takes an awful risk being in the same town with me!"

"Let's forget this man-woman stuff for a minute!"

"Are you crazy?"

"No, just serious. I can fix it so you take over Johnny's set-up, Al. I'm risking my neck to do it. If Johnny had the slightest suspicion about it, I'd be pulled out of a ditch inside a couple of hours!"

I sat down beside her and lit myself a cigarette.

"Look, honey-doll," I said. "Maybe what you say is true and I appreciate it—almost as much as I appreciate you. But you'll pardon me if I don't get hysterical at the thought of taking over Johnny's set-up. Sure, I guess the *Paradise* makes good money. But I've got a set-up in Chi that makes good money too, maybe better than Johnny makes. And I know the set-up in Chi. It works smoothly, it has no problems. If I took over Johnny's set-up here, I'd have a lot of problems. That's why I'm not crazy about the idea. I'm just crazy about you."

She didn't say anything for a moment and I thought maybe she wasn't impressed.

"The *Paradise* is Johnny's front," she said finally. "It isn't his real racket."

"You mean he peddles bubblegum on the side?"

She moved her shoulders impatiently: "I mean his racket—his real racket—is worth ten or twenty times what the *Paradise* is worth."

"Okay—what is his real racket?" I tried to say it as casually as I could.

Julie didn't answer. I didn't press the point. I took her glass along with mine and refilled them both.

"I can't tell you," she said finally.

"That's what I like about our partnership," I said. "We trust each other so much!"

"I have to be sure of you first, Al," she said. "I'm being honest. I'm not sure of you right now."

"Fine," I said. "What happens meanwhile?"

"I'll know in a few days," she said.

"You waiting for the crystal ball to clear?"

"I don't need a crystal ball. Johnny's check in Chicago will be thorough."

I brought the drinks back to the couch and put her glass into her hand.

"I don't know that I can wait that long," I said. "Maybe my vacation's beginning to bore me."

She smiled at me: "Don't worry about the waiting time, Al. I can keep that interesting for you."

"You mean this man-woman stuff?"

"Since when did you get tired of that?"

I sipped my drink. "That Johnny," I said. "He must be really worried."

"Why?"

"What else would turn a guy's hair grey overnight?"

Her lips tightened a little: "What are you doing, Al? Spying on me?"

"Just curious, honey," I said. "I guess I'm built the same way as Johnny. I get mad jealous, naturally! So when I ring you and you give me the wrong number routine, I know there's someone with you. So I take a walk onto the front porch where I can see your front porch, and after a while this grey-haired character leaves."

"That shower routine was just a gag then?"

I shook my head: "No, I went into the shower straight after. I wanted to feel cleaned up a little."

"You don't have to worry about the grey-haired man," she said.

"That's fine," I told her. "I was just wondering how many partners you had."

She put her hand on my knee: "Al! Don't be stupid! He was a business contact of Johnny's."

"Why lie about him then? You let me think it was Johnny—or you tried to."

"Because," she shook her head impatiently. "Because I thought it was too involved ..."

"I've seen him before," I said casually. "In Chicago—maybe twelve months ago now. Comes from New York, doesn't he?"

Her face was expressionless: "Yes, he does."

"I don't remember his name," I went on. "But he's a Syndicate man."

"Salvador Tinetti," she said.

"It doesn't ring any bells," I said. "But he being a Syndicate man, I wouldn't know him well."

"You're a freelance, Al?"

"Sure."

"The way I hear it, there isn't much room in Chicago for freelances."

"You don't want to believe all you hear. Look at me—where would I be if I believed all I heard?"

She smiled: "All right, Al. I asked for it! Johnny wanted me to entertain Salvador this evening, so I did. And you can take that look off your face— I didn't entertain him like that at all!"

"I'll believe it," I told her. "Otherwise Johnny wouldn't have suggested it."

Julie snuggled close to me, her thigh pressing tightly against mine: "Now—are you satisfied?"

"I guess so," I said. "Except if I'm going to do something about Johnny, I'd like to do it fast!"

"It will only be a few days."

"You said that before and I don't like it. While I'm not doing anything about Johnny, I'm a sucker for Johnny to do something about me. I don't like giving the other guy first try!"

"I'll try and hurry it up a little," she said. "Promise!"

"I'll give it two days," I said. "I mean this, Julie. If you haven't come up with something concrete by then, I'm skipping the whole idea and going back to Chi."

"All right," she said. "I'll try."

"That's fine," I said. "Another drink?"

Her lips came close to mine. "No, Al," the whispered. "Not another drink. Let's try some of that man-woman stuff we've been talking about."

CHAPTER 6
Salvador And Salvage

I was out of bed, wearing a robe over my pajamas and smoking a cigarette to go with the coffee, when the door buzzer went. It was eleven o'-clock on a bright sunny morning at Ocean Beach, making truth out of the posters on the billboards. I put the .32 into the pocket of the robe, then answered the door.

Julie stood there dressed in a bright smile, halter bra and shorts. Behind her stood the grey-headed guy, wearing a blue shirt with yellow palm trees dotted all over it and a pair of light tan slacks. He was also wearing dark glasses. Maybe he didn't like the sunlight.

"I'm glad you're up anyway, Al," Julie said.

"Come on in," I said. "There's still some coffee."

They followed me into the living-room.

"Al," Julie said. "I would like you to meet Salvador Tinetti. Salvador, this is Al Wheeler."

"Hi," I said. We shook hands. His grip was firm. I couldn't tell the expression in his eyes behind the cheaters.

"I'll go and get us some coffee," Julie said brightly. "While you boys can make it old home week!"

It was as subtle as a punch in the nose.

I grinned at Tinetti: "I was telling Julie I thought I'd seen you in Chi about a year back."

"That could be right," he said.

"Lynch isn't sure of me," I said, still grinning. "And Julie's his girl. So she'd think it would be a golden opportunity to introduce us so we could swap stories of Old Chicago and you could maybe place me, huh?"

He grinned slowly, showing white, strong teeth: "Could be."

"We can talk about the stockyards and the Loop, if you like. Or Grant Park and Madison Avenue. The only thing I'm not prepared to talk about is the rackets."

I lit another cigarette from the stub of the first: "I'm not a Syndicate man, Salvador. I'm what you might call a freelance. And to give you a picture of me, just maybe I'm giving the Syndicate an all-too-clear picture of my racket—and they might get interested."

Tinetti shrugged his shoulders gently: "It wasn't my idea, Al. I came along for the walk."

"And there's one final point," I said. "I don't really care if Johnny Lynch places me or not. Lynch is a punk and I make a point of never worrying about punks!"

Julie came back with a tray, balancing cups, saucers and coffee on it.

"You boys getting dewy-eyed for Chicago?" she said brightly.

"We're both getting dewy-eyed over the way you're hamming it, honey," I said. "It's as obvious as the Statue of Liberty!"

She put the tray down on the table, then straightened up and looked at me. Her green eyes were greener.

"Sure," I said. "I know you're trying to do right by Johnny. But like I was just saying to Salvador, Johnny's a punk!"

"I guess I made it a little obvious," she said.

"I guess you did," I agreed.

We sat there drinking coffee without anybody saying anything. A couple of minutes later Julie got onto her feet.

"Well, thanks for the coffee anyway, Al. I think we should be going."

"Nice of you to call," I said.

I walked with them to the front door. I thought if I was going to be the clay pigeon, I might as well get up there into the air so they could really get me in their sights.

"See you around, Al," Salvador said, holding out his hand.

"Sure, Salvador," I said. "You look a nice guy and a guy who can take care of himself. I'd like to tip you off to something."

"I'd appreciate it," he said smoothly.

I could feel Julie's eyes practically boring holes in my face.

"It's like this, Salvador," I said. "Lynch is a punk. And while he's checking on me, I've been doing some checking on him. I guess you're down here on vacation the same as me. My tip is not to let Johnny organise your vacation for you. I really wouldn't advise it."

"Why not?"

I looked at him carefully: "I've been picking up information in this town. A little here, a little there. They tell me dames have a habit of disappearing when Johnny's around. Nice-looking dames who come from nice homes and have nice parents and nice young men who want to marry them. It's a sucker play, that's what it is. Too many questions get asked when dames like that disappear. Too many people, with too much influence for the cops to ignore, start asking too many questions."

"It sounds interesting," he said in a flat voice.

"The way I hear it," I went on, "the heat is on. Johnny's almost ready for the big bounce."

"Well, thanks, Al," he said slowly. "I appreciate it."

I watched them get into the Cadillac and drive away. Then I went back inside the cabin. I had a shower and a shave. I got dressed in a grey tropic-weight and wished Palm Court provided a hi-fi set-up like the one I had at home. I needed something to soothe my nerves.

Music. Yeah, music. Julie did a lot to my nerves, but the one thing she didn't do was soothe them.

I rang Dawn Blair. A servant answered and I waited until the phone was switched through.

"Hello?"

"Al Wheeler. Can you speak freely?"

"Yes—I'm in my room. Matter of fact, Al, I'm still in bed. Awful, isn't it?"

"I think it's very sensible," I said. "I wish I was there."

She giggled: "You say the most awful things!"

That's me—a character. Are you going to the *Paradise* again tonight?"

"Of course, if you want me to."

"I'd like you to. Get there around nine. I'll be waiting outside."

"Are you going to escort me?"

"No, ma'am. Lynch won't come within a hundred feet of you if he sees me alongside."

"Pity," she said. "You're the first man I've ever gone out with and spent a whole night without even seeing him!"

"It's an original twist," I said.

"When I leave," she said, "I'll stop about a mile down the road."

"What for?"

"For you to join me, silly!"

"It might not be smart."

"I'll pretend I'm worried I've got a flat or something. If you don't come, I'll know it's dangerous and I'll drive on home."

"Okay," I said.

"Sound more enthusiastic, Al!" she complained. "You're the first man I've ever thrown myself at."

"You sure it's me, or that .32?"

I hung up and thought Jordan had picked me a screwball okay for a partner. But then it isn't every screwball that has long blonde hair and an eager look in their eyes.

The phone rang almost as soon as I'd replaced the receiver. I picked it up again and said hello.

"Wheeler?"

"Sure."

"Tinetti here."

"Yes, Salvador?"

"You know a bar called *Harbour Rest?*"

"I've seen it."

"I'd like you to meet me there in half an hour."

"What's the pitch?"

"Leave that till you get there."

"Okay," I said.

I strapped on the shoulder-holster and put the .32 into it before I left. I had the hood down on the Healey and the convertible cover in place. I was wearing dark glasses and, idling down the main boulevard, I felt almost young.

The sidewalks were loaded with dames. Black-haired dames, yellow-haired dames, red-haired dames ... Dames in shorts and shirts, dames in swimsuits, dames in bikinis. Dames that walked, dames that strode, dames that waddled and dames that bounced.

I calculated I got a twenty-five per cent head-turn as I went past.

Which all goes to show what an Austin-Healey can do for you, particularly with a convertible cover.

That's the trouble with getting old—it makes you cynical.

I angle-parked opposite the *Harbour Rest.* I noticed the cream Cadillac that had been under Julie's carport the night before, parked three cars away.

I crossed the street and went into the bar. There were booths alongside one wall. Salvador was sitting in the third one along, a drink in front of him. I sat down opposite him.

A waiter appeared. "I'll have a Scotch on the rocks and a beer chaser," I told him.

The waiter served the drinks. Salvador paid for them before I could and the waiter disappeared. Salvador looked at me through his dark glasses and

I looked back at him through mine.

"What was the idea?" he said. "Shooting off your mouth to me about Johnny, in front of his dame?"

"Johnny's a punk," I said. "If she doesn't know it by now, it's time she did."

"And what happens to you if she runs straight back to Johnny and tells him what you said?"

"Nothing," I said casually. "Anything that Johnny throws my way, I can take care of."

"You're damned sure of yourself, Wheeler!"

I sipped the Scotch and let the beer fulfil its chasing function.

"Why not?" I said.

"Where did you get this story on Johnny?"

"Around."

"Don't be cagey, Wheeler. I'm asking you to put it on the line."

"Salvador," I said. "You look like a nice guy and that's why I gave you the tip-off. But there's no reason for me to put it on the line for you or anybody else."

"You know who you're talking to?"

"Sure," I said. "Salvador Tinetti. You may be a big-shot in New York, but right here in Ocean Beach, pal, you're just a breeze!"

His face darkened for a moment, then he relaxed: "Maybe you're right, Wheeler. You being independent of the Syndicate, you wouldn't know much about me."

"Enough," I said casually. "You made a few changes for the Syndicate in New York and that's why you're down here—until the heat cools off."

"I don't have any cop trouble," he said.

"Who said anything about cops? Or Feds even? I'm talking about the part of the opposition you didn't eliminate."

"How the hell do you know this?"

"I told you—I get around. I pick up the information I need to know."

He finished his own drink and beckoned to the waiter to refill it.

"I'll tell you something else, Salvador," I said. "The cops know you're in town. They're watching—watching close. They figure if they tag along right behind you, they might be there when Johnny gives you the choice of classy dames."

He jumped like I'd stuck a knife into him. He lit a cigarette very deliberately, giving himself time to calm down a little.

"What's your angle on this, Wheeler?" he asked hoarsely.

"Do I have to have an angle? I'm down here on vacation. I took an interest in Julie, before I knew she was Lynch's girl-friend. Johnny didn't like it. He organised me into a fake drunken driving rap and it took me a little trouble to organise myself out. I didn't like that, so I started taking an interest in Johnny."

He took off his sunglasses and looked at me. His dark eyes were very cold.

"If Johnny's really on the skids," he said, "maybe the Syndicate should know about it."

"He's not member, is he?"

"No—he's an independent who's giving good service—or he was."

"I was thinking to myself," I said slowly, "that maybe Johnny's set-up could really work—with an efficient guy running it. And me—I'm so efficient I even surprise myself!"

Salvador put on his dark glasses again.

"It might be a thought," he said. "I shall have to think about it myself. Lynch definitely doesn't seem to be so—so reliable as I understood him to be. I can contact you at Palm Court?"

"Anytime," I said. "Anytime at all."

He got up from the table and walked out of the bar. I watched him go, then lit a cigarette and called for another drink.

I was still wondering who was kidding who?

CHAPTER 7
The Long Vacation

It was around eleven when Dawn Blair came out of the *Paradise* and got into her Packard. It went off down the street and I waited a couple of minutes. Nobody else followed her, so I rolled the Healey.

A mile or so further on, the Packard pulled off onto the grass and Dawn got out, making a great play of looking at her tires. I parked the Healey behind the Packard and came up to her.

"There's nobody else around," I said.

"That's wonderful!" she said. "Where are we going?"

"Who said we were going any place?"

"But that's the whole point of meeting you, silly!"

"Okay," I shrugged my shoulders. "You suggest a place."

"Don't you have a place?"

I stared at her.

"I mean," she said nervously. "It wouldn't be good for us to risk being seen together, would it?"

"I guess not. Yeah, I've got a place."

"That's fine, Al," she said. "Somewhere we can be private by ourselves!"

I took another look at her. There wasn't a lot of light—all I could see was the long blonde hair, the rest of her face was in shadow.

I should argue with a blonde.

"We have one other problem," I said. "That of transport."

"That's no problem—I have my car."

"And I have mine. Okay—you follow me. But when I turn off the road, leave your car parked outside. I'll wait for you in the Healey."

"Anything you say, Al."

I went back to the Healey and got in. After a hundred yards I checked in the rear-vision mirror. The headlights of the Packard were right on my tail.

Twenty minutes later I turned off the road at the entrance to Palm Court and waited. A minute later she opened the door and dropped into the seat beside me. I drove along the concrete and ran the car up underneath the port.

We got out and I fumbled for the key.

"You live here, Al?"

"For the time."

"Maybe we could have a swim in the pool?"

"I don't think so," I said. I had visions of Julie watching us from her windows. "The water isn't any good at night."

"Why not?"

"It's all black."

"Oh," she nodded her head.

I pushed the door open and switched on the lights. I let her go inside first.

"This is nice, Al," she said. "I bet it's expensive!"

She took another half a dozen steps forward that brought her into the centre of the room. I shut the door and started to follow her.

It was the first look I'd had at her in decent light. It was worth taking my time over that look. She was wearing a silver lame sheath that fitted her like duco and moved when she moved, breathed when she breathed. Her tanned shoulders were bare and her blonde hair brushed them as she turned her head.

"Is something the matter?" she asked.

"It's me," I said. "I'm having trouble breathing, that's all. But don't let it worry you—after a while I'll get used to looking at you."

She smiled at me and took a deep breath, a deadly combination. She looked as demure as a cobalt bomb.

"You say the nicest things!" she said.

What the hell? I couldn't expect an original line of dialogue along with everything else.

I poured us a drink. Dawn sat down on the couch. I wouldn't have thought there was enough room in the silver lame for sitting down, but then the world is full of surprises. I sat down beside her.

"Johnny Lynch spoke to me tonight!" she said breathlessly.

"What did he say?"

"Hello!"

"Hello, huh?"

"Then he said he owned the place and was I having any luck at the tables and I said no I'd just lost a couple of hundred and he said too bad let's try another table and he took another hundred dollars from me and said he'd play it for me. And ..."

"You won."

She looked disappointed: "How did you know?"

"I sort of guessed. How much?"

"Five hundred."

"And you said thank you."

"Yes, and ..."

"He said you should buy him a drink to celebrate."

Dawn pouted: "If you know it all there isn't much point in me telling it, is there?"

"I'm sorry," I said. "Go on."

"Well, we had a drink and he asked me my name and I told him and then he asked me what I did and I told him I didn't do anything if he meant what sort of job did I have and he said it must be nice to have a rich father and I said yes it was. Then he asked me if I liked to gamble and I said why else would I be there and he said he guessed that was right."

She took a deep breath: "And then—and then he said had I ever seen the really big games and I said weren't they really big games that were being played at the *Paradise* and he laughed and said no they were only piker games by comparison."

I finished my drink and got myself a refill. She hadn't touched her original drink.

"Then he said if I liked he would let me in on one of the big games, just to watch. He wouldn't let me play because he said the people who played in the big games would be too tough for a beautiful girl like me. So I played along with it, Al, and said I thought I might like to see a game like that. And he said there was one scheduled for the night after tomorrow—Thursday. If I wanted to see it I could give him a ring on Wednesday evening and he'd let me know the arrangements."

I lit us cigarettes: "And that was that?"

"Yes—oh, he talked a lot more but it wasn't about very much. About gambling and all the different games. He was sort of trying to make himself out as a nice guy. You know, Al—sort of trustworthy."

"With you playing Little Red Riding Hood," I said. "Sure!"

"So what do I do, Al?"

"You ring him tomorrow night and say you'd still like to go along," I said. "And we take it from there."

"It's so—so pulsating!" she said.

Her lips were full and soft, slightly parted, showing the even, white teeth underneath. She was looking at me with her china-blue eyes dancing with excitement.

"You keep on looking at me that way," I said, "and I'll have to kiss you."

"Good," she said. "I was hoping you'd say that!"

Ten minutes later she shrugged away from me: "Al, darling, take that gun away—it's hurting me!"

"Sure," I said. I took the gun out of the holster and put it down beside me on the couch.

"That's better," she said, and came back into my arms.

With Dawn, things were simple. She liked to be kissed, liked to be held. She enjoyed it without any repressions or psychological quirks. I remembered how Julie used her sex consciously, aware of every movement that she made, every word she said. With Julie, her sex-appeal was a usable asset. With Dawn, it was something she didn't even think about. So anyway, I was the lucky guy to be in the position to draw a comparison.

And you can say that again.

Pick a phrase ... Time flew by on gilded wings. We didn't know what time it was—then I just happened to catch sight of my watch and saw it was three a.m.

"Does your mother know you're out, honey?"

"Why—is it late?"

"Three o'clock."

"I suppose I should go home. They know I went out alone and I've got my car. If I don't turn up soon, they'll be phoning the police and the hospitals."

"Sure," I said.

She stood up: "I must look a fright! Is there somewhere I can put my face back?"

"Use the bedroom," I said. "There's a dressing-table with a good-sized mirror in there."

"Thanks," she said.

She walked into the bedroom and closed the door behind her. I thought I'd get myself a drink, but I didn't. I heard a soft moan from inside the bedroom, then a thump as something hit the floor.

I dived across the room and opened the door. Dawn lay in a heap on the floor, out cold. I knelt down beside her and patted her hand. After a few seconds her eyelids fluttered and then she opened her eyes.

"What happened, honey?" I asked her. "Why did you faint?"

Her eyes opened still wider: "Is he still there?"

"Who?"

"That man—on the bed! I ..." She went limp again.

I wondered what had started her seeing things. I got onto my feet, looked at the bed—and nearly shared the floor that Dawn wasn't using.

There was a guy on the bed, sitting there with his back propped up against the bedhead, his legs neatly stretched out in front of him. His eyes were wide open, staring at me. If it hadn't been for the bullet-hole in the centre of his forehead, I'd have expected him to say something. He wasn't wearing his dark glasses.

Salvador had taken the long vacation.

I was still looking at him when the door buzzer went.

I wished I was someplace else.

Dawn's eyelids fluttered again. I knelt down beside her.

"Someone's at the door," I whispered. The buzzer went again just to prove my point. "Stay right here and don't make a sound until I come back."

"But I can't!" She sat bolt upright. "With that—that ..."

"Just till I find out who it is!" I said. "It won't take long."

"But I ..."

"You have to!" I said savagely.

Somebody began to beat out a jump tune on the buzzer. I went back into the living-room, closing the bedroom door behind me. I picked up the .32 from the couch, thumbed back the safety and then went to the front door. The buzzer stopped abruptly as I opened it.

She walked in right past me. "In the shower again?" she said in an acid voice.

I followed her into the living-room. She was wearing a negligee of black nylon and lace. Her eyebrows lifted as she saw the two glasses, the lipstick-stained butts in the ashtray.

"What's with you?" I asked her. "Insomnia?"

She turned around to face me: "I see you don't believe in being lonely, Al?"

"Why should I?" I said. "After you double-crossed me!"

"Me! I double-crossed you!"

"Sure! Bringing Tinetti here this morning to see what he could find out about me and Chicago!"

"And what about you? What about that story you gave him about Johnny?"

"Hell!" I said. "Why not? How dumb do you think I can get! You string me along with the story of taking over from Lynch and all the time you're still working with him!"

Julie looked at me, stupefied. Her mouth opened and closed a couple of times: "You don't think that!"

"What else should I think?" I asked wearily.

"I wasn't trying to check on you for Johnny's sake," she said. "It was for me. I gave Salvador a story. I told him not to tell Johnny we had seen you because I was scared Johnny would kill you, and it wouldn't be good for business. Salvador is down here on vacation—he doesn't want to see any trouble start. I knew he would keep his mouth shut."

I walked over and poured myself a drink—a long one with no water.

"Don't I get a drink?" she asked.

"Were you figuring on staying?"

"Don't give me that, Al Wheeler!" she said. "I've been burning all day and half the night at the thought of you. I got so I couldn't stand it any longer—that's why I came over here now."

She moved closer to me. Her arms came up and wound around my neck.

"'You dope," she said softly. "You big dope! Don't you know I'm crazy for you?"

I reached up and pulled her arms from around my neck. "No," I said, "I don't know it. I'm not sure of it. I need time to think about it, Julie. Maybe by tomorrow ..."

"I was forgetting, Al," she said in a hard voice. "You've been consoling yourself, haven't you? I was wondering why you were so anxious to get rid of me. Maybe she's still here, huh? Some cheap little broad with fluffy blonde hair and ..."

She started to walk towards the bedroom: "Well, we'll get rid of her first and then ..."

I didn't really have much of a choice. If she opened the door she was going to see Salvador's body, which would be awkward. But she was also going to see Dawn Blair and that could be fatal for Dawn. If Julie told Johnny she'd seen Dawn Blair with me ...

I took three quick paces and came up behind her as her hand twisted the doorknob. I sliced the side of my hand down onto the nape of her neck and she crumpled onto the floor at my feet.

I picked her up and carried her out of the cabin and across to her own. I put her into bed and tucked the covers around her. She seemed to be sleeping peacefully.

Then I ran back to the cabin and into the bedroom. Dawn gave me a wan sort of smile and her eyes started to glaze. I slapped her face hard and she jerked to attention.

"We have to move fast!" I said. "Get out of here, get into your car and drive home."

"All right," she said, with her teeth starting to chatter. "But what are you going to do about—about ..." She gestured feebly towards the bed.

"I'll take care of him," I said. "The vital thing for you is to get out of here. I'll ring you in the morning—or later this morning."

"All right, Al," she said limply. "I—I ... Gosh!"

Then she went.

I closed the door behind her and locked it. I lit a cigarette and poured another drink.

One thing about being a cop—having a corpse in your bed doesn't give you goose-pimples the way it gives the ordinary citizen goose-pimples. At least it wouldn't if I'd been a straightforward cop. But I was an undercover cop—or something.

I tried to think rationally. There wasn't any doubt that Johnny Lynch had either done the job himself or ordered it done for him. The body had been dumped in my cabin for a variety of reasons. The first one was as a warning, maybe. Salvador must have made the fatal mistake of either confiding in Johnny or trying to strong arm him. The second reason was it showed me that Johnny knew where I was. And the third reason was it made a simple means of getting rid of the body for him and left me with the problem.

I thought there was one obvious move—to get him off my bed. You can get used to a cadaver, but not that used to it you can sleep with it.

I finished the drink, then went into the bedroom. I dragged him off the bed and out into the living-room, then out of the cabin and under the carport. I sat him in the Healey and got in beside him and started the motor. I drove out onto the road and headed towards town.

I still didn't have any definite ideas, but I thought I might get some on the way.

My watch said it was four-thirty as I came into town. In an hour or so it would be getting light. I drove past the *Paradise* and saw it was closed, dead, with no lights showing. I kept on going. I idled down the boulevard past the *Harbour Rest* and then I saw it.

The cream Cadillac was still parked where it had been that morning. I swung in beside it and cut the motor. I transferred Salvador back into his own car, propping him behind the wheel. As an afterthought I lifted his wallet.

I drove back to Palm Court. As I passed Julie's cabin, I saw it was in darkness. I wondered if she was waiting for me in my cabin with a sawn-off shotgun in her hands. The thought didn't make me nervous—much. I gumshoed in the back door with the .32 in my hand. But she wasn't waiting.

I had another drink—it was practically breakfast—and took Salvador's wallet out of my pocket. There were the usual things. There was a couple of hundred in folding money, two credit cards, driving licence with a New York number. And there was a letter.

It was dated New York, two days before. It was from a guy named Jackson Slade. The letter said that Slade hoped Salvador had made his contact in Ocean Beach okay and hoped he'd enjoy his vacation. It said there was no reason for him to hurry back to New York, he could take a couple of months if he wanted. It also said he'd be glad to know that the business alterations that had been made before he left were working very satisfactorily and that by the time he returned, there should be no resentment to the new methods by anyone.

I folded the letter and put it back in the wallet, then tossed the wallet into a drawer. I locked both front and back doors and went to bed.

I thought it would have made life a hell of a lot easier if I'd let Commissioner Lavers' hair stand on end at the thought of one of his Lieutenants facing a drunken driving rap.

A hell of a lot easier!

CHAPTER 8
Maybe

I got up around ten. I made the routine from shower-taking to tie-tying. I rang Dawn's number and asked for her. Her voice sounded sleepy when she answered.

"Al," I said. "Everything under control?"

"Everything's all right with me," she said. "How's everything with you?"

"Under control."

"You got rid of ..."

"My visitor?" I said quickly. "Sure! That's okay. How were your folks?"

"Worried but not desperate," she said. "I told them I got a flat."

"Did they believe it?"

"No—but they thought it was probably better to believe that than keep on asking questions, I guess. I think they got scared at the thought of what might turn up as answers."

"Yeah—you'll ring Lynch tonight?"

"If you say so, Al."

"Fine. Ring me around ten tonight. 'Bye."

"I'm going back to sleep," she said. "Wish you were here, Al. 'Bye."

I depressed the cradle-bar and let it lift again. I asked for long distance, then told the operator I wanted a person-to-person call to Mr. Jackson Slade and gave the New York address that was on top of the letter. She said she'd ring back.

I went out into the kitchen and made some coffee. I brought a cup back with me and lit a cigarette that tasted like the ashes of yesteryear.

The phone jangled. It was the New York call.

"Slade here," a flat voice said. "Who's that? You, Salvador?"

"You wouldn't know me," I said. "I've got some information I think you should have."

"Who is this calling?"

"Names don't matter," I said. "Get this and get it fast. Salvador is a memory!"

"What!"

"That's right. He's taking a permanent vacation. And if you want to know who sold him the ticket, I'd ask Johnny Lynch if I were you. Lynch is coming apart at the seams and Salvador got wise. He thought you should know but bad luck for him, Johnny got to hear of it first."

"Who is this calling?"

"Groucho Marx," I said. "You'll excuse me now, I have to go paint on my moustache."

I hung up.

There was a knock on the door. I felt automatically for my gun and held it down at my side as I opened the door. It was Julie again.

She didn't look any the worse for the late night she'd had. She was wearing another scoop-necked blouse and a tight gabardine skirt.

She half-smiled at me: "Can I come in?"

"Sure," I said.

"Promise you won't slug me again?"

"Cross my heart!"

She came in. I closed the door and followed her into the living room.

"Coffee!" she said. "Smells good!"

"I'll get you a cup."

"Are you alone, Al? Or am I intruding again?"

"I'm alone."

I got the coffee and brought it back into the living-room. She sat on the couch, that half-smile on her lips.

"My neck's a little sore this morning," she said. "Otherwise I'm all in one piece."

"I'm sorry about that," I said.

"I had it coming, I guess," she said. "Who was she?"

"Like you said," I grinned. "A fluffy little blonde I met in a bar."

"Why didn't you want me to see her?"

"It would have given you a superiority complex," I said, "and me an inferiority one."

"I can't blame you," she said. "I've been thinking about what you said last night. I can see the way it must have looked to you."

I shrugged my shoulders: "Skip it. I've cooled down, too. What you said about Tinetti makes sense. Let's forget the whole thing."

"Of course, Al," she said warmly.

"The fluffy blonde was the direct result of me being mad at you," I said. "You can take that as a compliment."

"Thank you!"

"How's Johnny?"

She lit a cigarette carefully: "I was with him last night, for a while."

"How is he?"

"He has me worried."

"Why?"

"It wasn't a very exciting evening. We sat around in his office most of the time. He didn't do anything, but just sat there with a big grin all over his face."

"The grin worried you?"

"He looked awfully pleased with himself. When Johnny looks pleased with himself, someone's probably dead. He wouldn't say anything to me about it, he just kept on saying he felt good."

I thought I could tell her why Johnny had been so happy, but maybe she already knew.

"So Johnny was looking pleased with himself," I said. "Okay. When do we start to do something about Johnny?"

"When Salvador starts his real vacation," she said. "I think that is the time, don't you?"

"You're telling me," I said. "I'm just listening."

"You know what I'm talking about," she said. "You tipped off Salvador. Is it true about the cops watching Johnny that closely?"

I shrugged my shoulders: "I wouldn't know. I just thought it might be a good idea to worry Salvador—shake his confidence."

"Sometimes I get to thinking you're smart," she said. "And then sometimes I don't."

"What's with that crack?"

"You undermine Salvador's confidence too far and the next thing you know, we'll have the Syndicate around our necks!"

"Why not?"

"Are you crazy?"

"Like a fox! By the time the Syndicate gets organised to take Johnny over, we've already done that. We save them the trouble. We're reliable—

Johnny wasn't."

She chewed her lower lip: "You could have something there, and maybe you couldn't."

I was standing facing her as she sat on the couch. I reached out with one hand and grabbed the scoop neckline of her blouse and pulled. She came onto her feet. She either did that or lost the blouse.

"I'm getting tired, honey," I said gently. "Getting tired of your maybes! Maybe I'm smart and maybe not—maybe I could and maybe I couldn't!"

I put the flat of my hand against her face and pushed so she sat down again abruptly.

"Make up your mind," I said. "I've been stalling long enough on this deal. We either move in on it together or I move in on it alone!"

"How far do you think you'd get alone?"

"Far enough to take care of Johnny," I said gently. "And you!"

She licked her lips: "The way you say it, I could believe it."

"Get smart," I told her. "Believe it!"

"I think I shall," she said. She got onto her feet: "I'm almost sure Salvador starts his real vacation tomorrow night. I'll let you know, Al. I should know by tomorrow morning at the latest."

"Okay," I said. "Do that."

She walked to the door, then looked back at me: "I'd still like to know why Johnny's laughing!"

"Maybe he caught sight of himself in the mirror while he was shaving," I said. "Who cares?"

She went out, closing the door gently behind her. I thought it was late enough in the morning to start drinking. I poured myself a drink and wondered how Al Wheeler's celebrated impersonation of a hood had gone down with Julie Adams. I hoped it had.

I thought maybe it was time I had another talk with a certain Lieutenant Jordan. I rang the Bureau and was put through to him.

"Al Wheeler," I said.

"How's the vacation going?"

"You funny little man!"

"Not good?"

"I think we should have a talk about it."

"Come on in."

"No," I said. "I have an idea I might be hot. I'll meet you sort of accidentally."

"Okay—where?"

"There's a bar called the *Harbour Rest*. I'll be in there in half an hour— okay?"

"Okay, G-man. See you!"

I hung up and thought I loved Ben Jordan's sense of humour.

I was there half an hour later, tucked away in a booth at the back of the place. I ordered a double Scotch and drank it, then ordered a replacement before Jordan arrived.

He sauntered down past the booths like he was a guy with no place to go, then sat down opposite me. My new drink came and I ordered for him. I waited until his drink had arrived and the waiter was out of earshot.

"How are things?" Jordan asked.

"I don't know," I told him.

"You bring me down here to tell me that?"

"Let's remember this was your idea in the first place," I said. "And all I've got out of it so far is two thousand dollars!"

"What!" Ben's eyes popped.

I grinned at him: "And a load of grief!"

"How did you get the two thousand?"

"Johnny Lynch gave it to me."

"What for?"

"Compensation for the phony drunken driving rap."

"You're not serious?"

"Didn't you see that glittering new Austin-Healey outside? It's mine—paid for!"

Ben grinned: "I'm a sucker—I'll believe anything once. What else?"

"How are things with you?"

"So-so, Al. We picked up a corpse across the road from here this morning."

"Littering the street?"

"Neatly seated in a Cadillac with a hole through its head. Guy by the name of Salvador Tinetti. A Syndicate man from New York."

"Any connection with Johnny Lynch?"

"We're still trying to find out. It was in the morning papers."

"You know I can't read," I said.

He drank some of his Scotch: "What else is cooking with you, Al? What's fermenting in that unorthodox brain of yours?"

"You remember," I said, "you mentioned something about some big-time hoods were reported heading your way, but they never arrived?"

"Sure."

"Did you know Salvador Tinetti was here?"

He moved his shoulders irritably: "Nobody tipped us off he was coming. We get a few million people coming here through the summer—we should keep tabs on all of them."

"I wonder if any of the other big-time hoods got here without you knowing?"

"Okay—if they did?"

"I don't think they stayed here," I told him. "I think they went someplace else."

"It's a reasonable deduction!" he said sarcastically.

I lit a cigarette moodily.

"Why don't you stop the double-talk?" Ben asked.

"Because I can't make sense out of it myself," I said.

"I don't wonder that Commissioner of yours gets grey hairs with you around all the time! How are you getting on with Dawn Blair?"

"Most times I can't believe she's real," I said. "Until I look at her."

"I was talking to her on the phone this morning," Jordan said. "Something's cooking with Lynch."

"Yeah—she's ringing him tonight."

"If Lynch snatched those other dames," he said wonderingly, "what the hell did he do with them?"

"You're not subscribing to the White Slave theory? The Road to Rio— the awful warning to all young girls to stay home?"

Ben shook his head: "Not with the type of girls these were. You know as well as I do, Al, that White Slavery is almost dead; in the States, anyway. You know, if it was that, the way they operate. They pick their girls. They like the orphans, the floozies, the kids who've run away from home and ended up in another state a thousand miles away. They like the girls that nobody's going to miss when they've gone. But these girls were the opposite of that. I've said all this before—good families, wealthy families, lots of friends, and fiancées even! If it's White Slavery, then it's screwball!"

"Yeah," I said.

Jordan grinned wryly: "This gets us one hell of a long way, doesn't it?"

"I guess so. Maybe we'll be a bit closer to the answer after tonight when Lynch has talked to the girl."

"I hope so, Al."

I finished the Scotch and looked around for the waiter.

"You haven't told me very much, Al," Ben said. "About what you've been doing. Maybe I should put a tail on you?"

"I'd lose him," I said. "I'm being unorthodox about this, Ben. The thing that worries me is that maybe Johnny Lynch is being unorthodox, too!"

CHAPTER 9
Boys From New York

I ate some lunch after I left Ben Jordan. I drove back to Palm Court and spent the rest of the afternoon sleeping. I went out and bought myself dinner at the *Cabano*. I could afford to live high on the balance of Johnny's two thousand bucks. It was times like these I could almost feel grateful towards him.

I got back to the cabin around nine, with four bottles to replenish the liquor supply. I opened one, had a couple of drinks, listened to a soap opera on the radio and thought if anything kills radio, it won't be television—it'll be radio.

That brought the time to around ten. I thought Dawn should have made her call by now—why the hell didn't she ring me? I had that thought again at eleven, only more so.

Then the door buzzer sounded. I opened the door cautiously. I'd got into the groove of opening that door with a gun in one hand and sort of standing sideways, trying to pretend I was invisible in case anybody took a shot at me.

A bright, smiling blonde bounced past me into the living-room. I slammed the door shut and followed her.

She was wearing a tight, crisp green print dress. As I followed her, I noticed that she and Marilyn Monroe had something in common when they walked away from you.

"So now they've got TV with the telephone system!" I said. "It's wonderful—I can see you quite clearly and the phone didn't even ring!"

Dawn turned around and looked at me, wide-eyed: "I thought I'd come over and tell you myself, instead of ringing. Aren't you glad to see me, Al?"

"I guess so," I weakened. "Where'd you leave your car?"

"I took a cab," she said simply. "That way, my mother and father won't worry so much if I'm home late."

"What makes you think you'll be home late?"

"I'm in the mood for it," she said. "You're a difficult sort of person, Al!"

I lit myself a cigarette: "You don't mind if I pour myself a drink?"

"Not if you pour me one."

"You won't drink it."

"I will tonight—I'm in the mood!"

So I poured the two drinks and when I turned around with them, Dawn was sitting down. Her dress had ridden well up over her knees. Her knees had dimples, I noticed. She patted the couch beside her, encouragingly. I sat there and gave her the drink.

"Here's to the hours of darkness!" she said. She shut her eyes and drained the glass in one gulp.

I took the empty glass out of her hand and replaced it with my full one. Her eyes were still tight-shut and her face was a mottled red colour. I got up again—got another drink. By the time I was back, she could speak again.

"I'm in the mood!" she said defiantly.

"You said that."

"I just thought I'd let you know. I feel reckless and hell-bent!"

"What sort of bent?"

"You know what I mean, Al. Tonight I feel a woman!"

"What do you generally feel like—a monogrammed ear-ring?"

"Very funny!" she said coldly.

I sipped some of my own drink before she got down on it.

"You did ring Lynch?" I asked.

"Of course!"

"And what did he say?"

"There's a big game on tomorrow night and would I like to come along and see it. I said I'd be thrilled. He said the game wasn't being held in the *Paradise* and he couldn't tell me where over the phone. But he'd pick me up."

"At your house?"

She shook her head: "He suggested I get a cab into town and then he'd drive me from the *Paradise* to where the game is being held. And he'd drive me home. But he said on no account was I to tell anyone about it."

I stubbed out my cigarette: "What time are you to meet him?"

"Ten-thirty."

"Have you spoken to Lieutenant Jordan about it?"

"Yes."

"What did he say?"

"He said he'd talk to you about it in the morning."

The phone rang. I got up and walked over to it, then lifted the receiver: "Yeah?"

"Al?"

"Check."

"Julie."

"Yeah?"

"Don't sound so excited! Did you see the papers?"

"Tinetti? Sure."

"I don't like it, Al!"

"Why? It's him that's dead, not you!"

"You can be big and brave if you want. That explains Johnny's big grin last night."

"Could be."

"I guess it takes care of Salvador's vacation—permanently!"

"Sure."

"So now I don't know what Johnny's going to do."

"You had any word about anybody coming down from New York?"

"I haven't heard anything—why?"

"Won't they be curious about Salvador?"

"You mean the Syndicate boys there?"

"Who else?"

"I hadn't thought about it. I suppose they will. I'll stop by later and see you, if you're still up."

"Where are you ringing from?"

"The *Paradise*. I think I'd better hang up now, Al, otherwise Johnny's likely to wonder how long it takes me to powder my nose!"

"Sure," I said.

I put the phone down and went back and sat down beside her.

"Look, honey," I said. "This deal with Lynch tomorrow night could be dangerous. If you want to pull out, you pull out. There's nothing to stop you."

"Why should I want to pull out?"

"I just told you why!"

"Don't be so rude!"

"Don't be so dumb!"

The door buzzer went.

"My!" she said coldly. "You're kept busy, aren't you? Another woman can't stay away from you?"

"I attract them like flies," I said modestly. "Maybe I smell like honey!"

"Maybe you just smell!" she said sweetly.

I went to the front door and yanked it open. I had forgotten my routine. One second later it was too late to worry about the routine.

A gun rammed into my solar plexus. I took a step backwards. A guy followed the gun into the cabin and another guy followed him.

The guy holding the gun was tall and thin, not wearing a hat. His hair had thinned on top and was grey around the sides. The other guy was short and powerfully-built, with a mashed-in nose and the sort of face that needed a plastic surgeon.

"Say something!" the tall guy said.

"Like, *Help!*" I suggested.

"You're Wheeler—Al Wheeler?"

"That's right," I agreed.

He stared at me for a moment: "It sounds like the voice on the phone. My name's Slade—Jackson Slade. That mean anything to you?"

"No," I said. "Should it?"

"Maybe, maybe not," he said. "Ask us in for a drink!"

We went into the living-room. Dawn's eyes bulged as she saw the two of them.

"Not bad!" the chunky guy said, looking at her admiringly. "That's the sort of dame you need for a winter in the Adirondacks!"

Dawn got to her feet. He walked over and pushed her shoulder so she sat down again abruptly.

"Take it easy, sister," he said. "Don't wear yourself out for nothing—it would be a waste!"

He came back and patted me down, relieving me of the .32, which he stuck into his hip pocket. Then he moved over to the liquor cupboard and started pouring a couple of drinks.

Slade was still staring at me: "The name of Salvador Tinetti mean anything to you?"

"Sure," I said. "He was the guy who was shot this morning. I read about it in the newspapers."

"Johnny Lynch figures you're the guy who killed him!"

"Why would I kill Salvador?"

"I don't know, pal," he said. "I'm asking you!"

"You mind if I light a cigarette?"

"Go ahead—there's no hurry about this."

I lit myself a cigarette, then went over and sat down beside Dawn. Slade sat down in an armchair and put the gun on the arm. The chunky guy gave him a drink.

"Thanks, Toni," he said.

"I'm the guy who called you this morning," I said. "You're right about that."

"Go on."

"Lynch is on the skids—losing his grip. I told Salvador that. I also told him I could take over Lynch's organisation and run it efficiently. It would save the Syndicate moving in and taking it over themselves. Salvador was listening to me. I think he made a mistake. I think he went back and told Johnny more or less what I'd said and that he was believing it. So Johnny had to do something fast. He bumped off Salvador and had his story ready for you when you arrived—that I had done it."

Slade didn't look impressed: "Where do you come from?"

"Chicago."

"You aren't tied in with the Octopus there."

"No—I'm an independent."

"Doing what?"

"Minding my own business, mostly."

I saw the glitter in his eyes and the movement as the chunky guy started towards me.

"Mostly," I added, "doing a heist here and a stick-up there. I wouldn't have tangled with Lynch—I came down here strictly on a vacation—but I made a pass at Johnny's girl and he tried to put a frame around my neck. I didn't go for a punk like him doing that. I took him for a couple of thousand to make up for the frame and he wasn't hard to take. Then I started hearing rumours around the town. Better than rumours: there's a certain lieutenant of detectives here who used to be in Chicago. I did him a favour once ..."

"Like squealing on a pal?" Toni asked.

"Like stopping a shiv getting stuck into his back! He tells me that Lynch is falling apart. Then I meet Salvador and I figure he should know what goes on."

Slade studied the fingernails of his right hand carefully: "The way Johnny tells it, Salvador told him the story of you trying to muscle in. Johnny wanted to take care of you last night, but Salvador says he'll do him a favour—he'll take care of it himself. And that's the last time Johnny sees Salvador alive!"

"He's lying," I said.

Slade gestured noncommittally with his hand: "Salvador could do a thing like that. He was just a little bit trigger-happy. He'd sooner shoot anybody that had to be shot, than not. It could make sense."

"That's ridiculous!" Dawn said suddenly. "I was here last night and nobody came in here."

"It was late—Johnny says," Slade looked at her.

"I was here late," she said defiantly. "Till morning!"

"I said she was an Adirondacks' babe!" Toni said admiringly, "Anytime you got a spare winter, kid, you give me a ring!"

Slade jerked a thumb in Dawn's direction: "She come from Chi, too?"

"Local talent," I said.

"I'll have to spend my vacations in Ocean Beach," Slade said. "What's your name, kid?"

"Ruby," I said quickly, "Ruby Ryan."

"She can tell me, can't she?"

"She happens to be my dame," I said.

"Maybe she was!" he said.

He finished the drink and held up the empty glass. Toni took it and refilled it, then brought it back to him.

"Heists," Slade said. "Stick-ups. Free-lancing. You don't sound the sort of guy to take over Lynch's set-up."

"I'm not a slob like Lynch," I said.

"I wouldn't say that," Toni said amiably.

"Get off your knees when you speak to me!" I told him.

His face darkened and he started to pad across the floor towards me.

"Relax!" Slade told him.

"Only want to teach him to talk polite," Toni pleaded. "Only one hit!"

Slade didn't say any more—he sat there, watching.

Toni came up in front of me. "You want to watch it, pal," he said. "Watch it all the time!"

He had his gun in one hand. He raised the other and brought it down in what would have been a vicious backhander if I'd left my face where it was.

I didn't. I ducked and brought my knee up into the pit of his stomach. He doubled and that brought his face down on a level with mine where I still sat on the couch. I hit him twice with the heel of my hand across the bridge of his nose.

He rocked back on his haunches and sat on the floor, shaking his head slowly, the tears streaming out of his eyes.

"Just take it easy, Wheeler," Slade said. He'd picked up the gun from the arm of the chair and it was pointing steadily at me.

"Sure," I said. "I could take that punk if I was tied in a sack!"

"There's no guarantee you won't be yet," he said gently.

Toni heaved himself off the floor and started to walk towards me again with murder in his eyes.

"Toni! Get me another drink!" Slade said in an incisive voice. The chunky guy hesitated for a moment, then turned around and did as he was told.

"Have you made any plans for taking over Lynch's set-up?" Slade asked me.

"Of course," I said.

"May I enquire what they are?"

"You can," I said, "but it won't get you anything."

"You really think you can do it?"

"I know I can do it."

"That would mean getting rid of Lynch first."

"I had thought of that," I told him.

Slade put the gun back onto the arm of the chair again.

"It's Salvador I'm chiefly interested in," he said. "Who killed him? It's obvious it was either you or Lynch. If it was Lynch, we shall save you the trouble of disposing of him. If it was you, then you'll very soon lose interest in everything."

I didn't say anything—it was too obvious to need a reply.

Slade finished his drink, then got onto his feet. "We'll be seeing you around, Wheeler," he said. "Toni—give Mr. Wheeler his gun back."

Toni took my gun out of his hip pocket and tossed it to me reluctantly. I caught it and put it back into my pocket.

"So long, honey," Slade said to Dawn. "Don't do anything I wouldn't do."

Toni stared at me, his eyes hot. Then he picked up the half-full bottle of Scotch by the neck and broke it on the edge of the table. Good Scotch dripped over the carpet. Still looking at me, Toni tossed the broken half of the bottle he still held in his hand, onto the floor.

"I'll make a point of seeing you around, punk!" he grated.

"Bring your step-ladder," I told him. "Then we can meet face to face!"

They walked out slowly. Half a minute later I heard a car start.

Dawn's eyes were round and staring. "Those men," she said. "Who were they?"

"Hell!" I said. "Hasn't anyone ever tried to sell you a vacuum cleaner before?"

"Al! They were gangsters!"

"You just could be right, honey."

"But you weren't frightened of them—were you, Al?"

"Not very much," I said. "I think!"

"You hit the little one, anyway!"

I winced: "He tried to hit me first!"

"I know," she said. "I was proud of you. The way he kept on looking at me! As if I was dressed in cellophane!"

I looked at her: "That's an interesting thought!"

"Stop it, Al!" she said. "You've got the same look in your eyes now!"

I needed a distraction. I got up and opened a new bottle of Scotch and poured us a drink. I picked up the pieces of broken bottle and took them out to the ashcan in the kitchen. The carpet would have to look after itself.

I came back and gave Dawn her drink and sat down beside her, my own drink in my hand.

"The boys from New York," I said. "Looks like things are going to develop."

"And another thing!" she said suddenly. "Ruby Ryan! What was the idea of giving me an awful name like that?"

"Maybe they go back to the *Paradise*," I explained patiently. "Maybe they say to Johnny Lynch that they've been calling on Al Wheeler and he had a blonde with him. And they say this blonde's name was Dawn Blair. And Johnny smiles all over his face and says isn't that a coincidence, he has a date with a Dawn Blair the very next night."

"Oh!"

"Yeah—oh! Likewise—ah!"

She looked crestfallen: "I'm sorry, Al. I didn't think of that."

"Whereas now if they mention you, they say there was a gorgeous blonde there by the name of Ruby Ryan. Ocean Beach is full of gorgeous blondes, so it isn't going to mean very much to Johnny."

She finished her drink. I finished mine. We had two more and then two more again.

"You're a dirty, lousy stinker, Al Wheeler!" she said suddenly.

"Who—me?"

"Yes—you!"

"When did you work that out?"

"Saying things like that. You ought to be shot. I'm sorry that little man didn't shoot you. It would have done you a lot of good!"

"What did I do?"

She closed her eyes for a moment, then opened them again.

"Stay still, can't you!" she said.

"I am."

"You're not, Al—you're weaving about all over the place! And making nasty, dirty remarks about me!"

"What the hell are you talking about?"

"Ocean Beach is full of gorgeous blondes! I suppose you think that blondes like me are a dime a dozen?"

"I think blondes like you are unique!"

"There you go—insulting me again!"

She looked at the empty glass in her hand, thought about it for a moment, then threw it suddenly. It hit the opposite wall and splintered into fragments.

"If you want a chair to tear the legs off," I said coldly, "I'll get you one!"

"You are the most frustrating man I ever threw myself at!"

Then she threw herself at me—literally. One moment we were sitting side by side and the next moment she was on my lap, her arms around my neck, her lips pressed against mine.

I reacted the way any other guy would have reacted. I'd been full of good intentions so far as Dawn was concerned. Suddenly I was just full of intentions.

She stopped kissing me for a moment and looked at me hard.

"That unique," she said. "Was that a compliment?"

"Sure," I said. "You're not only unique, you're impossible!"

"Darling!" she said. "You say the sweetest things!"

And then she went back to her frontal attack.

CHAPTER 10
Everybody Loves Me

I handed her the drink. She sat on the sofa, her legs tucked up underneath her, making little purring noises.

"What's the time?" she asked.

I looked at my watch: "One a.m. Shouldn't you be going home now?"

"You are rude to me, Al darling. I told you I was going to stay out late. I don't have the car with me, remember?"

The door buzzer sounded. I suddenly remembered Julie had said she'd call in.

"Do you think it's those men back?" Dawn asked.

"Could be," I muttered. "Maybe you'd better get out of the window or something."

"I'm not leaving you, Al," she said firmly. "I'm staying by you, bullets or no bullets!"

"Well, how about ducking into the bedroom and waiting there until I get rid of whoever it is?"

"No," she said. "A woman's place is by the side of her man. I am not going to desert the sinking ship!"

"I look like a sinking ship?"

She giggled suddenly: "You are listing just a little to one side!"

The buzzer sounded again, impatiently.

"Please!" I said. "Dawn, honey. Please just wait a while in the bedroom."

"If you're frightened," she said generously, "I'll go answer the door for you."

She got onto her feet unsteadily and headed towards the front door. I didn't have any choice. I felt bad about it. I hit her a slicing chop across the nape of the neck and caught her as she fell.

I took her into the bedroom and put her on the bed under the covers, then raced out again, slamming the door shut behind me. I went to the front door frantically wiping the lipstick off my mouth.

I opened it and Julie came in.

"You took your time about answering!" she said.

"I had visitors earlier on," I said. "I just wanted to make sure who it was this time."

"What visitors?"

"A couple of guys from New York."

She turned to stare at me: "From New York? Those two men who were with Johnny earlier on? A tall man and a short, fat one?"

"That's right. The tall guy's name is Slade and the short one is Toni."

"What did they want?"

"To find out whether I killed Salvador or not."

"You told them you didn't?"

"Naturally! I don't know whether they believe me. They think it's either me or Johnny."

She looked at the liquor-stain on the carpet, the broken glass on the floor: "Did you have a fight?"

"Only with the short guy," I said.

"They made a mess."

"You should see what I did to Toni!"

She took off her wrap. Underneath she was wearing a sheath of gunmetal grey. When she turned to face me, I could see more of Julie than you can of the girls who do the TV commercials.

"Al," she said, "I'm getting frightened!"

She moved closer—right into my arms. She pressed up against me. "For the first time in my life," she said huskily, "I'm really scared!"

"Why?"

"Those men Slade and the little one. I've never seen anyone like them before. They make Johnny and Zero look like Santa Claus and his reindeer!"

"We don't have to worry about them," I said. "So long as we can convince them that Johnny killed Salvador, we won't even have to worry about Johnny, either. They'll give us his set-up on a plate!"

"I wish I could feel as confident as you sound," she shivered. "I need comforting, Al. I still feel frightened." She looked up at me: "Kiss me!"

I kissed her. She kissed me. It took quite a time. In the middle of it, I thought I heard a faint movement inside the bedroom and my pulse doubled. But Julie didn't hear it. Finally she broke away from me.

"I don't like it here, Al," she said. "That broken glass and the liquor on the carpet—it keeps on reminding me of Slade and his man. I want to forget them—for tonight, anyway. Let's go to my place."

"Okay," I said. I couldn't think of anything else to say.

She took a handkerchief out of her purse and gently dabbed my mouth.

"Lipstick doesn't become you, honey," she said. She wrinkled her nose: "I must look a fright, too. Just wait for me—I won't be a minute."

And before I could stop her, she turned around and walked into the bedroom, closing the door behind her.

I stood there with my eyes closed, waiting for the explosion. Nothing happened. I wondered if I had enough money left to buy an air-ticket to Peru—quickly.

The silence was hellish loud. I took the chance to pour myself a drink. I thought if ever I needed one, it was right now.

I heard the bedroom door open and I didn't dare look around. An exploring finger poked me in the spine.

"Are you taking me home?" a sweet voice asked.

My glass shattered on the floor and I spun around, ignoring the fact that more good liquor was staining the carpet.

Dawn stood there, a sweet smile on her face.

"It's getting late," she said. "You are going to drive me home, aren't you?"

"S'sure," I stammered. "But ..."

"Thanks, Al," she said.

She had what looked like a rag in her hand. She tossed it carelessly onto the couch: "I'll leave that with you—it might come in handy for cleaning up the place afterwards."

"Thanks," I said. I noticed the rag was gunmetal grey in colour.

I thought maybe it was better not to make any enquiries. I took her arm gingerly and escorted her out of the cabin, and into the Healey.

Half an hour later I stopped outside her house.

"I'll ring you in the morning," I told her. "After I've talked to Lieutenant Jordan."

"Fine," she said. "Goodnight, Al."

"Night," I said.

She got out of the car, then remembered something. She turned around and leaned towards me.

"I forgot to express my appreciation for a beautiful evening," she said softly.

Then she hauled off and let me have it right between the eyes. None of this effeminate, slapping stuff. She hit me with a clenched fist and the night sky was suddenly bright with stars.

By the time the stars had disappeared, Dawn had, also. I let in the clutch and drove back to Palm Court.

I let myself into the cabin and heard thumping noises coming from the bedroom. I crossed my fingers and then opened the door and stepped inside.

The light was still on. There was a muffled figure, swathed from head to foot in a sheet, writhing on top of the bed. I went over and had a look.

Dawn had made a job of it. A girdle had been pulled over Julie's head and down across her shoulders, effectively pinioning her arms to her sides. Another sheet had been tied around her legs, binding them together.

I untied the sheet that bound her legs, and pulled the girdle back over her head. Then I unwrapped the sheet that completely enveloped her from head to foot.

Her hair was something straight out of Salvador Dali. Her face was a bright red. She sat up with a murderous look in her eyes. Dawn had made a concession to modesty—she'd left Julie in a bra and pants.

"Get me my clothes!" Julie said slowly.

"Yes, ma'am!" I said hastily.

I picked up the girdle between my thumb and forefinger and offered it to her. She snatched it out of my hand. I scouted around and found her slip on the floor. Then I went into the living-room and got the gun-metal grey sheath. By the time I got back into the bedroom with it, Julie had the slip on and her stockings were straight again.

She snatched the gown out of my hand and pulled it on over her head, then wriggled into it. She pulled it down, then froze suddenly.

I stared at her. Before, when she'd been wearing it, the cleavage had been noticeable. Now it extended down almost to her knees. The gown had been neatly ripped almost in two.

Julie sat down on the bed, put her head in her hands and began to cry. I began to wonder why that character, Casanova, had ever bothered.

"Would you like a drink?" I suggested.

She picked up a shoe and threw it at me. I thought maybe she'd like to be left alone. I went out into the living-room and poured myself a drink. Alcoholism was safer, I figured.

Some five minutes later she came out of the bedroom. She was clutching the gown in front of her. She looked like a survivor from a shipwreck—a survivor who'd spent fifty days in an open boat.

"I shall probably shoot you," she said in a muffled voice. "But that might be too quick. I could cut you into little pieces with a knife. I could boil you in oil. I could bury you alive. I could ..."

"Julie," I said, "I'm sorry. Honestly, I am."

"You're sorry!" she said. "That's just fine! That makes everything all right, doesn't it? You're sorry!"

She headed for the door. I watched her go. The door slammed shut behind her and the cabin rocked gently. I had one more drink and then I went to bed.

I was up around ten in the morning. I had a call from Jordan, who suggested I meet him at the *Harbour Rest* again in an hour's time. I showered, shaved, got dressed.

This time Jordan was already there when I arrived. I sat down opposite him and ordered a drink.

"You heard from Dawn Blair?" he asked.

I rubbed my hand gently between my eyes: "Brother! Did I!"

"How do you figure it?"

"You mean what's going to happen?"

He shook his head: "I'm not asking you to get out your crystal ball! I mean how do we handle it?"

"If you have a lot of flat-footed cops around the place," I said, "you'll frighten Lynch off. And this is the one time we don't want him frightened off."

"I agree," he said. "You have any suggestions?"

I lit myself a cigarette: "Yeah. Wherever Lynch's taking her, it won't be a gambling game. If she's going to disappear the way the others did, I'd think he can't take her too far. He'll either leave her somewhere or hand her over to somebody else. He'll have to get back to the *Paradise* as fast as he can."

"Okay. What then?"

"If I tail them when they leave the *Paradise*," I said, "as soon as they make a stop, I can find a phone and ring you. You can get a wagon-load of cops out there as fast as you like. That way, I should be able to tail him without making it obvious to him that he is being tailed. And we can handle the job as a routine with no heroics from anybody."

"Wheeler!" he said. "For a moment there, I thought I heard you talking common sense!"

"It gets into me at times," I admitted. "When I'm not looking."

"All right," he said. "I'll have a couple of prowl-cars ready at the Bureau, to move as soon as you ring."

"Fine," I said. "I'll be glad when you've got Lynch in a cell and I go home and back to the quiet life of being a cop again. This secret agent stuff is beginning to give me the screaming heebie-jeebies!"

"You got paid, didn't you?" he asked. "Two thousand bucks!"

"It's still not enough!"

"After it's all over," he grinned, "we'll make you an honorary member of the Bureau down here—how's that?"

I told him.

I had lunch in town, then went back to the cabin. I cleared up the debris and except for the stains on the carpet, the place looked reasonable.

I rang Dawn.

"Yes?" Her voice was cold.

"I've been talking to Jordan," I said. "About tonight."

"Yes?"

"We've arranged it this way. I'll be watching the *Paradise* when you arrive. When you leave, I'll tail you. When you get to where you're going, I'll ring Jordan and he'll arrive with a couple of carloads of cops."

"I see."

"Okay?"

"Yes." There was a click as she hung up.

I had a vision of Dale Carnegie shaking his head sorrowfully and saying: "Son, you're not trying!"

It was a hot, sunny afternoon. For once in my life I felt healthy. The pool outside looked inviting. I got into a pair of trunks and took a towel and a pack of cigarettes with me.

I lit a cigarette, then stood on the edge of the pool and tentatively dipped my big toe into it. It felt cold. My healthy feeling was vanishing fast. I thought it was just as healthy to sunbake as it was to actually swim. After all you get water—hot water—out of the shower anytime you wanted. It was exactly the same sort of stuff—wet.

I was still thinking about it when something hit me violently in the back.

I hit the water face-first with the cigarette still between my lips. It wasn't cold—it was freezing. I came up to the surface, opened my mouth to breathe and two feet landed painfully onto my face, driving me to the bottom again. I wasn't sure whether I'd only lost the cigarette or swallowed it. One thing was for sure, I'd swallowed half the pool.

I came up to the surface, opened my mouth again and a hand clamped around my face and pushed me under. It was getting monotonous. Not only that, I was drowning. I thought maybe I could fool whoever it was by coming up feet-first the next time, until I remembered you can't breathe through your feet.

I swam half a dozen yards underwater, let my feet touch the bottom, crouched, then pushed myself off the bottom with all the push I could get. If whoever it was was waiting for me on the surface, I was going to torpedo them.

I broke surface like a porpoise and kept on coming. I came out of the water as far as my waist. I took a great, gulping lungful of air and made four furious strokes, which took me to the side of the pool. One convulsive heave got me out of the pool.

I got my breath back and looked around for the gorilla who'd tried to drown me. There was only one person in sight. A sultry-looking redhead in what could be laughably called a two-piece swimsuit. There was a wicked smile on her face and her green eyes were greener than the grass.

"Having fun?" she asked.

"Did you do all that?" I asked her in an awed voice.

She nodded happily. "I was going to drown you," she told me. "But then I thought they'd have to drain the pool to get you out and I wouldn't be able to swim when I wanted."

"I'm glad you remembered that," I told her.

She put her hands behind her head and lay back. The two-piece seemed to shrink even more as she did so.

"How's the fluffy blonde today?" she asked.

"I wouldn't know," I said. "Last night when I took her home, she hauled off and socked me. I don't think we're speaking—or if we are it will be only through a third party. And that third party will be a referee!"

"Light me a cigarette," she said.

I did as I was told. I lit two cigarettes and gave her one.

"What a great big hero you are," she said thoughtfully. "The way you stood there just now—at the edge of the pool—bravely plunging your big toe into the water ..."

"That girdle around your head," I said conversationally. "Did it hurt very much?"

We smoked in silence for a while.

"I didn't ask her to come around last night," I said. "She just arrived. I tried to get rid of her before you came but she wouldn't go."

"Why didn't you knock her unconscious the way you did me?" she asked in an acid voice.

"Well," I cleared my throat. "As a matter of fact, I did. But she must have come round before you went into the bedroom."

"She hit me like a tornado!"

"I can imagine," I said.

"You still attract me, Al," she said. "In a repulsive sort of way! You sure that fluffy blonde has gone out of your life?"

"Cross my heart!"

"Then I suppose we're on talking terms again," she said.

I looked down at her: "Is that all?" I brought my head down so that I could kiss her. I kissed her. It was much better than swimming—warmer.

After a while she moved her head away: "What will the neighbours think?"

"We have neighbours? I never see anybody. I always thought they were honeymooners."

"Even if they are, they're still neighbours."

"You ever hear of honeymooners looking out of a window?"

"They might want to know whether it's day-time or nighttime?" she suggested.

I shook my head slowly: "You don't have the right outlook on a honeymoon, I can see that."

"I'm open to suggestion," she said.

"Let's get Johnny fixed first," I said. "And then I shall be very forward with my suggestions."

"Talking of Johnny," she said, "I saw him this morning. I think he's worried about Slade and the other man. He hasn't sold them the idea that you murdered Salvador. He wasn't very happy this morning."

"You know if he's planning on doing anything about it?"

"He's doing something tonight," she said. "He told me that he couldn't see me tonight and he'll be away for a couple of days."

"A couple of days!"

"He goes away periodically. You look worried, Al?"

"It's just a reaction to all that water I swallowed out of the pool!"

"The only consolation," she said lightly, "is that while Johnny's away, I don't have to worry about him calling me or coming out here."

"Yeah," I said.

"I am, as it were, a free woman. Would you like to take a free woman to dinner tonight?"

"I'm sorry, honey," I said. "I can't."

"The fluffy blonde came back into your life very smartly!"

"This is business, honey."

"What business?"

"My business."

"You're a trusting partner, aren't you?"

I grinned at her: "It is business, honey. But I don't expect to be out very late. Can I call when I get back?"

"If you bring some liquor with you," she said. "And I haven't found another man first."

"You'll never find another man like me, honey," I told her.

"I know, Al," she said earnestly. "That's what makes me so eager to go out looking for another man!"

I stubbed out the cigarette and looked at her again. For a redhead, she was building quite a tan.

"You wouldn't like to come over to my cabin?" I asked her hopefully. "I'll make some coffee—or something."

"No, thank you," she said lazily. "I can see by that look in your eye you've got or something in mind. I'll stay in the sun—it'll be safer!"

CHAPTER 11
Sucker

At ten-fifteen, I had the Healey parked fifty yards down the road from the *Paradise*. I'd put in a full tank of gas and I only hoped Lynch wasn't going to spend those two days driving. Ten minutes later I saw a cab stop in front of the club and Dawn got out. She was wearing the silver lame again. She looked terrific.

I thought it was a pity we were only speaking through a third party.

I lit a cigarette and waited. Twenty minutes went by without anything happening. Then a Cadillac went past me and drew up outside the entrance. I saw the commissionaire go forward to it, salute, then drop back again. It looked like Johnny was maybe in the Caddy.

Then the commissionaire hurried forward and opened the door.

There was a flash of blonde hair and silver lame as Dawn hurried across the sidewalk, and then she was in the car. A few seconds later it moved away from the curb.

I started the motor, let in the clutch and pulled the Healey out into the street. I kept up fairly close through the city traffic. The Cadillac headed north, getting out onto the coast highway and opening up a little.

I had the top down in the Healey and the fresh air felt good against my face as the speed built up to seventy-five.

About fifteen miles further on, the Cadillac turned off the highway, making a sharp left-hand turn. I dropped back a little, then made the turn. I could see the tail-lights up ahead of me. Then the Caddy pulled into the side of the road and stopped suddenly.

Maybe Johnny knew he was being tailed or maybe he was just checking up. There was only one thing I could do and that was keep going—overtake him. Then when I got round the next bend I could pull off the road and stop, hoping he'd go on again.

I slowed so that I went past them at about thirty-five. Or that was what I intended to do, anyway. But as I came up on the car, the rear door bounced open suddenly and the silver lame seemed to spill out onto the road.

"Al!" I heard her high-pitched scream. "Al! Help me!"

I slammed on the brakes and the Healey stopped almost dead alongside the Caddy. I jumped out, grabbing the .32 out of my shoulder-holster and raced up to the Cadillac.

"Dawn!" I said. "What happened? What ..."

A gun jammed into my ribs.

"Drop it!" she said in a hard voice. "Drop it or I'll let you have it—I mean it!"

She did, too. It was there in her voice. I dropped the .32 and someone else got out of the Caddy and picked it up. When he straightened up, he seemed to blot out half the sky.

"Hi," he said. "I been waiting a long time for you to show up!"

"It's my night for a Zero!" I said.

"Get in the back!" he ordered. "You drive, doll."

With my own gun poking me in the ribs, I didn't have much choice. I got in the back with Zero beside me.

She got into the front seat, behind the wheel and switched on the interior lights. She put her hand to her head and took off her hair casually. She dropped the blonde wig on the seat beside her, then turned around to look at me.

The interior lights made her own hair burnished copper. Her green eyes were almost black as she looked at me.

"Hello, sucker!" she said.

The car moved away and I slumped back in the seat.

Sucker was the objective word, all right. I had been fooled by a blonde wig and a silver lame gown. I had only seen her for a fraction of a second as she hurried from the *Paradise* to the waiting car—and that from fifty yards distance.

The more I thought about it, the less I liked it. It meant first of all that they had known about Dawn. Julie wearing the silver lame gown was proof enough of that. And secondly, they had gone to a lot of trouble to pick me up. Maybe to make sure I was on my own.

I remembered with a nasty jolt that Ben Jordan was waiting with his posse of police for me to ring. It looked like he was going to wait a long time.

The Cadillac swung back onto the highway, but headed north in the opposite direction to Ocean Beach.

"We going to see the sights?" I asked.

Zero's gun was still hard against my ribs. "You got no idea, pal!" he chuckled. "You got no idea!"

And that, I supposed, was a cryptic remark.

"You mind if I light a cigarette?" I asked him.

"Go ahead," he said. "You got time to smoke it!"

That was another cryptic remark.

I lit the cigarette: "What's the pitch?"

"You'll find out, pal," Zero grunted. "I been saving myself for you!"

"You needn't have bothered," I said. "Who wants garbage?"

"Funny thing, Al," Julie said softly from the front seat. "I got to thinking about you and came up with the same conclusion."

"It was the wrong one," I said. "You haven't been smart."

"I think I have," she said. "And I got tired of the competition. You know something, Al? That blonde isn't fluffy at all!"

"Her gown fits you," I said.

"A little tight in places," she said complacently. "The right places!"

The Caddy swung off the highway again. I looked out of the window. After a mile or so, there weren't any more lights. Julie slowed the car and the going got rougher.

"A shot in the back and dumped in the wilderness?" I asked. "You want to see it, lover—or are you going to pull the trigger?"

"Worry about it, Al," she said. "It makes me feel good to hear you worry. Maybe we won't even waste a bullet—Zero can break your neck without any trouble at all."

"With one hand!" Zero grunted.

The road had become a track. We bumped along it for maybe a mile, then turned again and stopped at a gate. Julie got out and opened the gate, then drove the car through.

Five minutes later we stopped beside another car. Somebody walked over. Julie cut the motor and switched on the interior lights again. The somebody stuck his head into the car and it was Johnny Lynch.

I can't say I was surprised.

"You collected him okay," he said.

"No trouble," Julie said. "No trouble at all. Chivalrous—that's what he is."

"That some sort of sickness?" Zero grunted. "I been close to him—I don't want to catch nothing."

"Don't worry," I told him. "You won't."

"Everything's okay," Johnny said. "We're all ready to go."

"I get him out of here?" Zero asked.

"Sure," Johnny nodded.

Zero looked at me. "We can do this two ways, pal," he said. "You do like you're told or I slug you and carry you. You please yourself."

"I'll do as I'm told," I said.

"Okay—get out of the car!"

I got out of the car, with Zero coming close behind me.

Then I saw it. I didn't believe it. I closed my eyes tight and opened them again but it was still there, so I had to believe it. It wasn't so new—just unexpected. Go to an airport and you expect to see airplanes. Go out into the middle of nowhere and you don't expect to see one—but it was there all right.

"I own three acres here," Lynch said. "The only thing you can say about it is that it's flat. You can't grow anything on it and people around here thought I was crazy when I bought it. But you can land a plane on it."

"What do you want to land a plane on it for?"

"That's what I figured," he said. "You don't know, do you? You've been guessing."

"All right," I said, "so I've been guessing. Now you can tell me the answer."

"I'll do more than that for you, Wheeler," he said. "I'll even let you see for yourself. Get into the plane!"

I got inside the plane, with Zero following me close and then Julie and Lynch coming up behind him. There were three other people in the plane. The pilot, sat at his controls and not taking any notice of anything, Jackson Slade—and Dawn Blair.

"Sit down beside your girl-friend, Wheeler," Lynch said.

I did as I was told. Zero sat next to Jackson Slade in the seat behind us.

Opposite us, Julie and Lynch sat together.

"Okay, Vince," Lynch said to the pilot. "Take it away!"

The engines roared into life a moment later. I looked at Dawn. She was wearing a man's topcoat much too big for her, but on her it looked kind of cute. Her eyes were frightened.

"You all right?" I asked her.

She nodded: "This isn't exactly according to plan, is it, Al?"

"Not exactly," I agreed.

"Where are they taking us?"

"I know as much as you do about that," I said.

The engines reached a deafening crescendo. The plane started to bump forward. Dawn reached out and held my hand tight.

"I'm frightened!" she said.

"That's okay," I said. "So am I!"

A few moments later the plane was airborne. Nobody asked me to fasten my seat-belt. After a few minutes when the engines had settled down to a steady drone, I saw Slade and Lynch light cigarettes, so I thought it was okay for me to do the same.

Dawn still had that frightened look on her face.

"What happened to you?" I asked her.

"I walked into the club," she said. "When I got to the tables, a man came over to me and said Mr. Lynch was waiting for me in his private office and he'd take me there. So I followed him. When I got into the office there was only that—that redhead! She had a gun in her hand. She made me take off my gown and give it to her. Then Lynch came in and she went out. He gave me a topcoat and told me to keep quiet otherwise something unpleasant would happen to me."

"Gosh!" I said.

She gave me a nasty look I could treasure: "So I kept quiet—of course, I'm not a hero like Al Wheeler! After a while he took me out the back way to a car. I sat in the back with him—there were two men in front. We drove out to the plane and waited there. Ten minutes later you arrived with the others."

I told her what had happened to me.

"I don't see how you could possibly mistake that woman for me!" Dawn said coldly when I'd finished explaining. "Even if she was wearing a blonde wig!"

"I was fifty yards away," I said.

"Even if you were five hundred yards away. We have nothing in common!"

"I wouldn't say that, honey."

I got another nasty look.

"Anyway," she said, "what's happening now?"

"I don't know."

"Where are we going?"

"I don't know."

"What are you going to do about it?"

"I don't know."

She looked at me as if she was disenchanted. I couldn't blame her.

"Are you sure you're a policeman?"

"Right now I'm not very sure of anything," I said. "Except I wish I was someplace else!"

Dawn pulled the collar of the topcoat higher around her face and slumped back into the seat. I lit another cigarette and hoped nobody bumped into the Austin-Healey while I was away.

Outside the plane the night was bright with moonlight. I looked out of the window and saw a pattern of lights on the ground beneath us. I thought a lot of the people down there would be worrying about things that weren't worth worrying about.

Things like how they were going to pay their rent, whether their girlfriend would ask them inside to say goodnight or whether she wouldn't. I wished I was down there so I could worry about things like that.

Half an hour and two cigarettes later, I looked out again and this time there was no pattern of lights. There was only ocean. I slumped back in my seat and saw Johnny Lynch watching me with a grin on his face.

"Coast to coast," he said, "Florida isn't very wide down here."

"And where now?" I asked. "Australia?"

"Not quite so far," he said. "Cedar Keys."

"What happens there?"

"You'll find out," he grinned. "Zero's looking forward to it!"

He turned away. I felt Dawn's elbow nudge my ribs.

"Cedar Keys," she said. "Where's that?"

"Just off the West Coast," I said. "Half a dozen islands—little bits of something in the ocean."

"Why are we going there? Why is Lynch taking us there?"

I shrugged my shoulders: "Maybe it's the gypsy in him!"

I felt the pressure in my eardrums rise slightly and swallowed to get rid of it. I had another look out of the window. The ocean was much closer now. And then as I looked I saw a dark smudge in the middle of the ocean. The plane dropped lower still and the smudge became clearer.

Five minutes later and I could see some twinkling lights.

"Looks like we're there," I said.

"I don't like it, Al," Dawn grabbed my hand. "I'm scared!"

"Stay close to me, honey," I told her. "You couldn't be as scared as I am!"

I took another look out of the window and saw a tree flash past. I wondered where the hell it was going in all that much of a hurry. Then the wheels bumped down, the plane lifted off again for a moment until the wheels bumped down again and the plane rolled along on solid ground.

We had arrived.

CHAPTER 12
Tourist's Paradise

We walked maybe a quarter of a mile from the plane before the lights of the buildings were close. There was one quite large cabin in the centre of a clearing, surrounded by a dozen or more smaller ones.

I looked at Lynch: "What is this—Injun country?"

"You could call it that, pal," he agreed. "Only out here there aren't any Texas Rangers!"

We went into the big cabin. Inside, it was a surprise. It was expensively furnished. Music was muted from a phonograph in one corner and beside the phonograph stood a big-screen TV set.

There were a couple of couches and a dozen or more armchairs set around the room. Along half the length of one wall ran an ornate bar, with a white-coated barman in attendance.

There were three other people in the room. Two men and a girl. The two men were tough-looking characters, both wearing gaudy shirts and slacks. The girl was brunette, good-looking and no signs of toughness about her at all. She looked out of place.

She was wearing a white print dress and was dancing with one of the men.

It was the look in her eyes that worried you. A lack-lustre look that didn't belong. Her eyes were twenty years older than the rest of her. Moving around the floor in time to the solid beat of the music, she looked young and alive, but her eyes were dead and they looked as if they'd been dead for a long time.

Dawn stopped suddenly. She was walking just ahead of me and I nearly bumped into her. She was staring at the girl.

"Lucille!" she said. "Lucille Randle!"

The girl stopped dancing as her head jerked around. "Dawn," she said tonelessly. "Dawn Blair. So they got you, too?"

"C'mon, baby!" the guy said irritably. "We dancing or ain't we?"

Obediently she started dancing again.

Dawn still stood there, staring at her. "Lucille!" she said. "I ..."

Lynch took her arm, jerking her forward again.

"You got plenty of time to talk to your pals later," he growled. "Right now we got things to do!"

"You mean we're going to have a drink?" I said, looking at the bar hopefully.

"Not here," he said.

He opened a door and stood to one side. The rest of us went into the room. It was a room much smaller than the one we had just left. It was furnished as an almost exact replica of Johnny's office at the *Paradise*.

Zero was the last one in and he shut the door. The pilot of the plane hadn't come with us. That meant there was Johnny, Zero, Slade, Julie, Dawn and myself.

Johnny went over to a miniature bar in the corner and started making sweet noises with bottles. He handed the drinks around and even gave me one. I drank it quickly before he changed his mind and felt a little better. Not very much.

"All right, Lynch," Slade said abruptly. "Let's get down to business!"

"There's plenty of time," Johnny said. "Plenty of time!" His eyes flickered towards Dawn appreciatively.

"I want to get this thing straightened out first," Slade said. "Then we've got plenty of time."

"If that's the way you feel," Johnny shrugged his shoulders indifferently.

I lit myself a cigarette.

"Wheeler," Johnny said easily, "I'll tell you what we want to know. Who are you?"

"I'm Wheeler," I said, "from Chicago."

"You're Wheeler, maybe," he said. "But not from Chicago. I checked. I checked very carefully. Nobody has ever heard of Al Wheeler in the rackets in Chi. So maybe you'd better think again, huh?"

"Maybe your contacts in Chi aren't so hot, Johnny?"

"You were the smart boy," he said. "You dodged that drunken driving caper we put around your neck. I sort of wondered how you did it. There was this story about you being a big-shot from Chi and pulling in a smart mouthpiece. I checked pretty carefully on that story. Nobody knew who the mouthpiece was. Nobody seemed to really know where that story came from. The best I could make of it was that it came from a police precinct."

I inhaled a lungful of smoke and didn't say anything.

"So maybe you aren't in the rackets at all," he went on. "Maybe you're F.B.I. or maybe you're an undercover police pimp, huh?"

"You're way off base, Johnny," I said. "I come from Chi. Your information there is lousy!"

A hand seized me by the scruff of the neck and half-pushed, half-carried me into the centre of the room.

"You heard the boss ask you a question real nice," Zero snarled. "Why don't you be polite and answer him?"

A pile driver hit me in the stomach, doubling me forward. Then another pile driver under my jaw, straightened me up again. I had a vague memory of sailing across the room and then I hit the wall and slid down on it onto my knees. His ham fist grabbed the front of my shirt, hauling me onto my feet. He slapped me a couple of times and I felt my head didn't belong to the rest of me anymore.

"Why don't you open up?" he growled. "I can do this all night, pal!"

I could taste blood in my mouth. I brought my knee up sharply into the pit of his stomach and heard him grunt. I let him have a sharp right into the solar plexus with all my weight behind it and he grunted again. The next moment both his hands grabbed me and I was swung off my feet into the air.

"You shouldn't ought to have done that, pal!" he grated. Then he threw me.

I hit the wall for a second time and slid down it. The wave of pain and nausea threatened to engulf me. His toe hit me in the ribs.

"Get up!" he growled. "You're tougher than that, punk! You can take lots more of this!"

"Lay off!" Johnny said. "You'll knock him stupid in a moment and where will that get us?"

Zero stepped back, a look of disappointment on his face: "But boss, you said ..."

"Never mind!" Johnny said wearily. "He's tougher than he looks. You can horse him around for a couple of hours and maybe he'll finish up slap-happy and still not talk!"

"There's a much easier way, Johnny," Julie said smoothly.

She stepped over to where Dawn stood and with a sudden movement ripped the topcoat away from her shoulders. Underneath, Dawn was wearing not very much. The not-very-much was mostly nylon with a little lace here and there, and it looked even less.

Julie stood back and lit herself a cigarette carefully.

"I'll tell you how it is, Al," she said conversationally. "You can talk or else we'll make Zero a present of your little blonde—right now."

"Don't pay any attention, Al," Dawn said hotly. "She's ..." Then she saw the look on Zero's face as he looked at her and her voice faltered.

I got up onto my knees and it took quite an effort. I got both hands on the desk-top and levered myself onto my feet, leaning against the edge of the desk.

"You're lucky, honey," Julie said to Dawn. "It isn't every girl who gets such a hunk of man as Zero!"

"Okay," I said.

Julie looked at me, her eyes that dark, dangerous green.

"You really worry about her, don't you, lover?" she said softly.

"Give her the topcoat back," I said, "and tell that gorilla to get back into the swamp where he belongs!"

Julie tossed the topcoat carelessly to Dawn, who put it on quickly.

"All right, Wheeler," Lynch said. "Let's have it!"

"I'm a cop," I said. I told where from, that I'd been on vacation in Ocean Beach until they had pulled me in to do an undercover job.

It didn't take very long to tell. I lit a cigarette and looked at Lynch.

"I figured it was maybe something like that," he said. "I just had to be sure. Well, that solves a problem. You put the blonde up as bait, huh?"

"Sure," I said. "Then wherever you took her, we followed."

"*You* followed," Johnny said. "Nobody came after you—we watched that pretty carefully, too. And you didn't stop any place to make any signals or phone calls."

He grinned: "Looks like the Ocean Beach cops are still around Ocean Beach, waiting for Wheeler to show 'em the way!"

He was so right, of course.

"Why did you kill Salvador?" Jackson Slade asked suddenly.

I looked at him and managed to grin. It hurt my lips, but I couldn't help it.

"If you're half the big-shot in New York that I think you are," I told him, "you wouldn't even ask a question like that. I just told you I'm a cop. What the hell would I murder Salvador for? If you want to know why Salvador got his, ask Johnny!"

Slade looked across at Lynch. "Okay," he said. "I'm asking!"

"What do you care?" Johnny said.

Slade looked at him blankly: "Are you kidding?"

Johnny grinned: "I said, what do you care? Who cares about Salvador?"

"Maybe I'm nuts," Slade said in bewilderment. "You're admitting you killed him?"

"Sure," Johnny nodded. "Why not?"

"You know what you're doing?" Slade asked him. "You know what I'm going to have to do, Johnny?"

Johnny walked over to the miniature bar and poured himself another drink.

"Salvador was worried," he said. "That Wheeler's no hick—he told him I was slipping and he could take over in my place. He made it look good, too. But Salvador was a smart boy. He figured Wheeler was genuine or he wasn't. He was either a smart boy from Chi, or maybe a smart boy from the F.B.I. or the police or someplace like it. Either way, Salvador figured he was too close to me for comfort. So then Salvador makes his big mistake. He comes and tells me all about it. He says that I'm shot in the tourist business. He figures it's time for me to blow and time for Cedar Keys to go out of business."

Johnny shook his head: "Me—I can't afford to let this place go out of business. I've sunk a hundred grand into the place—I don't have a third of it back yet. So I figure if it's a choice between me and Salvador who's got to go—it's got to be Salvador. I figure I can pin it onto Wheeler if he's what he claims he is. Otherwise I can pin it someplace else."

Slade was staring at him: "Someplace else?"

He nodded: "Salvador getting his, I figure somebody's going to come down from New York. So far as the cops know, this guy might have come down earlier. Early enough to bump Salvador!'"

"If you're talking about me," Slade said, "I can prove I was in New York when Tinetti was killed."

"If you could talk about it, maybe you could," Johnny said amiably.

Slade looked at him for a moment longer, then his hand dived inside his coat—and stayed there. Julie prodded him in the back with a gun.

"Don't be silly, Jackson," she murmured.

Johnny laughed. "I got it figured," he said. "I'll tell you later on."

I got out my pocket handkerchief and dabbed the blood on my lips.

"You don't mind if I have a drink?" I asked hopefully.

"Help yourself, copper," Johnny said generously. "You don't have many left!"

I went over to the bar, walking slowly like an old man, poured myself a double whisky. I turned around, leaned on the bar and sipped the drink.

Slade sat very still, his face a dull grey. Zero ambled over and relieved him of his gun. Julie moved away from him then, a flicker of derision on her lips.

"Tell me, Johnny," I said. "What is all this?"

"All what, copper?"

"This island, this tourist business you're talking about?"

"It was all my own idea in the beginning," he said. "And it's going to be maybe the biggest pay-off ever!"

"Yeah?" I said.

He sat down in a chair and crossed his legs leisurely: "Sure! I figured it this way. The guys in the rackets—the big guys—what do they do? They spend all their lives making dough—a lot of dough—and they never really have a chance to relax any place. Any place that's really safe. So I figured if I could find them a place, they'd pay plenty for the use of it. So I looked around."

He was starting to enjoy himself. He was the big-shot tycoon explaining his success and he was loving it.

"This island's right on the outer edge of Cedar Keys," he went on. "A couple of square miles of nothing. I bought it cheap. The dough went in the plane and clearing a landing-strip. After that I started building here. Now we got everything—it's comfortable, the food's good, the liquor's plentiful. There's radio, TV; there's even a beach if a guy's really crazy on swimming."

He looked at me earnestly: "See—it pays off two ways. Not only for the guys who want a vacation, but the guys who've got to take a vacation. The boys who are hot. They come here and cool off, without worrying that somebody will recognise 'em or someone will cool 'em off. Everybody here on the island is safe—that's Johnny Lynch's guarantee and they know it. Sure, they pay plenty for it, of course. But they don't worry—they figure it's worth it."

"What about the dames, Johnny?" I asked him. "I can see you would have to have dames. But what about the dames like Lucille Randle and the others?"

He grinned: "It's like this, copper. Everything's good on the island—see? What they want, they get. So long as they pay for it. And some of the guys get tired of the regular dolls who are out here. They say they want something with some class, and what can I do about it? So I get to thinking and I get to organising. I figure there are plenty of dames with class come into the *Paradise*. If they disappear, they'll be missed—sure. There'll be a big beef about 'em, but so long as nobody can connect me with 'em and so long as they stay lost, I'm okay. And another thing—I don't have to pay 'em!"

I felt my ribs gingerly. They ached like hell, but they seemed to be all in place. "And how do they like it, Johnny?" I tried to keep my voice casual.

"I don't hear no complaints," he said. "One of 'em got sort of temperamental and tossed herself into the sea, but then you never can tell with a dame, can you?"

"I guess not," I said.

"You understand, copper," he said, "knowing this isn't going to do you any good?"

"I suppose not," I said. "But I'm still interested. It sounds like a terrific set-up."

"It costs me plenty to run," he said. "But plenty! I got to keep that plane going—the pilot costs me a small fortune alone. Then there's the regular guys here. I got two cooks, two barmen and half a dozen strong-arm guys to make sure the guests don't go haywire anytime."

"How many guests you got?"

"Right now only half a dozen. But in another couple of months there'll be maybe fifty guys here."

"Your girls won't go very far then."

"I'm bringing in a crew of the regular dolls then," he said. "It's only some of the big boys who go for the class."

"I suppose so," I said.

He swivelled around and looked at Dawn. "That blonde," he said. "She'll be worth her weight in gold!"

"And what are you figuring on for me, Johnny?" I asked. "A dive into the sea with lead weights in my boots?"

"I'm figuring on something real artistic for you, pal," he said. "You and my pal, Jackson, here."

"Like what?"

"Like you and him having a fight—and both losing."

I raised my eyebrows: "I don't get it!"

"You shoot him and he shoots you," he said. "So you're both dead—right?"

"What does that prove?"

"To the Syndicate, that Jackson bumped off Salvador, and then got bumped himself by a cop who was onto him. I'll make sure that's the way the Syndicate hears it."

"And what do you figure that will prove to the Ocean Beach cops—anything?"

He grinned again: "It'll prove to them they'll have to get up early to put one over Johnny Lynch! Their undercover cop will be a candidate for the morgue—the dame who was working with them will have disappeared. It maybe shows them they don't get anywhere trying to get something on Johnny Lynch!"

"They'll get you after all that," I said. "That's for sure!"

"I'll have alibis," he said confidently. "Like cast-iron! Let 'em think what they like. What they got to do is prove it!"

He walked over to the bar. "Anyway," he said, "I'm tired of talking to you, copper. By this time tomorrow night you'll be dead, anyway!"

"You won't get away with it, Johnny!" Jackson said hoarsely. "The boys in New York will take you apart if anything happens to me!"

"Don't worry about me, Jackson old pal," Johnny said easily. "I can look after myself!"

He looked over at Zero: "Take 'em away and lock 'em up in one of the spare cabins for the night. Separately. I'm getting tired of looking at 'em!"

"Sure, boss," Zero said. "I'll take the cop first." He looked at me, jerking his head towards the door: "Let's get moving!"

"What about the girl?" I asked Lynch. "What about Dawn?"

"Julie will look after her," he said. "Julie's good at looking after these kids with class—she's had practice!"

CHAPTER 13
Green Eyes

The cabin wasn't bad. It had electric light, a comfortable bed and a shower-room attached. After Zero had locked me in for the night, I had a shower then looked at my face in the mirror.

My lips were swollen and there was a bump under my chin. Otherwise it was much the same face I'd been shaving all these years. I got dressed again and thought about what I was going to do.

The cabin door seemed pretty solid. There was a small window and that was locked from the outside. If I busted the glass, the noise would probably bring somebody, and anyway, the window was too small to climb through.

And if I did get out, what the hell would I do on an island that was a couple of miles big? They'd probably find me inside an hour.

I sat down on the bed and lit a cigarette. I felt that Al Wheeler had been so dumb over the whole thing, he deserved to end up in Ocean Beach's city morgue. A slabhead on a slab.

My watch said it was one-thirty in the morning. Outside the window, the moonlight was still bright. I wondered how Dawn was getting on and that made me wonder about Lynch's set-up.

It was fantastic but logical—from the racketeers' point of view. A perfect set-up for a vacation and a perfect hide-out if needed. Guaranteed safety and guaranteed amusements. The Road to Rio had been shortened by a couple of thousand miles to the Road to Cedar Keys.

A key turned gently in the lock and the door swung open. I got up off the bed. Julie came into the cabin, closing the door behind her.

"Hello, lover," she said.

She was wearing a black nylon negligee and that seemed to be all. She leaned against the door, a slow smile curving her lips.

"Hi," I said.

"You know," she said, "you had me fooled for a while. I really thought you were one of the big wheels from Chi."

"Hooray for me!" I said.

"I brought you something," she said. She took one hand from behind her back and I saw the bottle.

"What man could ask for more!" I said enthusiastically.

"There should be glasses in that cupboard," she said.

I opened the bedside cupboard and she was right. I made like a barman while she stood and watched me. Then I handed her a drink and raised my own glass.

"What should we drink to?" I said. "The future?"

"It wouldn't be fair to ask you to drink to that," she said. "Would it?"

"How about the past?"

"You spoiled it with that blonde," she said. "I could have gone for you in a big way, Al, but you spoiled it."

"Talking of blondes," I said. "How is she?"

"She's sleeping," Julie said. "I gave her a bromide. I want her to wake up nice and fresh in the morning, ready to start work."

I drank the drink and replenished the glass: "How long does Johnny think he'll keep this set-up together?"

"For quite a long time, I should imagine," she said.

"It won't last more than six months!"

"Why not?"

"Too many people will know about it. They'll talk. Somebody will talk, they'll be bound to."

"I don't think so," she said. "Only the big-shots get here, Al. It's not for the little guys."

"What about the dames?"

"They won't talk—they're here for good!"

"What about the dolls Johnny's talking about bringing in when his season gets busy?"

"They'll stay here, too. That's what they won't realise until it's too late. Once they get here they stay here. There's only one way off the island for them."

"Feet first?"

"You said it, Al."

I sipped some more of the Scotch. "Well," I said. "It's all very exciting, I shouldn't be surprised."

"I thought you might like to know about the blonde," she said. "There's a new arrival here—only got in a couple of days ago. Name of Curt Mardin. Maybe you've heard of him?"

"I think so," I said. "He's a psycho, isn't he? He must be wanted all over the country."

"I think he is," she agreed. "He has that unfortunate habit of carving people like they were trees or something. People don't mind the hold-up jobs so much, but the way he treats bank-tellers and people like that ..."

"Yeah," I said.

"I think your blonde will suit Curt very well," Julie went on. "I'll introduce them in the morning."

Her green eyes glittered as she watched me, waiting for the reaction. Curt Mardin was real enough—a crazed killer wanted by the law almost everywhere. Whether he was actually on the island or whether she was feeding me the idea to get me worried, was something else again.

I shrugged my shoulders indifferently: "I should worry about the blonde. We used her as bait for Johnny, that's all. So we miss out and she gets kissed off?" I shrugged my shoulders again. "The guy I'm worrying about is named Al Wheeler!"

Her eyes narrowed: "You're lying!"

"Why should I bother? Some dumb blonde gets a piece of bad luck—it happens all the time!"

"You still don't sound like a cop!" she said.

"I'll let you into a secret," I said. "I'm not!"

"Don't let's start that again!"

I shrugged my shoulders again—it was becoming a conditioned reflex. "Okay," I said. "Skip it!"

"Of course you're a cop!"

"Of course I'm a cop," I agreed.

"What else would you be if you weren't a cop?"

"Look," I said. "The story about Chi was phony. I come from Detroit. I'm hot in Detroit—so I don't advertise where I come from. Chicago sounded far enough away. But tonight when that gorilla's bouncing me around and then you start in on the blonde, what do I say? That I'm from Detroit? And Lynch thinks I'm still stalling. He's convinced I'm a Fed or a cop. So okay—I'm a cop."

She lit herself one of my cigarettes: "'Where does the blonde fit?"

"I used her as bait," I said easily, "to find out just what Johnny's racket was. She was respectable—got class, as Johnny says. She wouldn't be interested in a hood from Detroit. So I tell her the big story—I'm an undercover cop. She can help justice. I put over the big story and she falls for it."

She hesitated for a moment: "You still think you can run this set-up better than Johnny?"

"Johnny's a dead pigeon," I said. "He doesn't know it, but his story falls apart when he bumps Slade and me off. Because I'm not a cop. I'm a nobody in Ocean Beach. So the Syndicate boys in New York will think it's a phony. And that means the end of Johnny once the Syndicate figures him out!"

"You make it sound good," she said.

"I make it sound real," I said, "because it is. You and me have got to know each other pretty well the last few days. You think I act like a cop?"

She gnawed her lower lip. "No," she said. "You don't act like a cop, Al. You never did."

"Would a cop have followed that car tonight the way I did, without having a couple of carloads of cops right behind him? The hell with it! What do you care?"

"Maybe I do care," she said. "I like Johnny's big blue eyes, but I like that crisp green lettuce better. And I'm not seeing much of it around. I miss that crackle of crinkly notes, Al!"

I poured my third drink. "Jackson Slade is a worried man," I said. "He'd be grateful for some help. If I got this set-up, I'd offer to sell it to the Syndicate boys—through Slade. Sell it cheap—for maybe a hundred grand. Or maybe fifty grand. It's still a lot of dough. Twenty-five thousand each, lover. And let the Syndicate worry about keeping the island secret!"

"What would you do with the money?"

"I'd buy us a time—first," I said. "Then I'd get into something legitimate. That's the smart way. Make enough in the rackets and get out. But nobody ever does—you know why? Because they're in too deep—they can't get out. They belong to the Syndicate or somebody else's organisation and they know too much to be trusted outside the rackets. That's why I've always been a freelance, lover. It's harder to hit the jackpot that way but when you do, it's all yours and you can move out with it!"

"You make it sound attractive," she said.

"Nearly as attractive as you," I said. I put my glass down on the cupboard-top and walked towards her. She held her glass out to me and I took it and put it beside mine.

"You're sure about the blonde?" she asked.

"I was never surer," I told her. "She doesn't compare with you, lover!"

She came into my arms, her lips fierce and demanding against mine. I reached out with one hand and switched off the light.

"You're awfully sure of yourself," she whispered.

"Should I be?"

"Yes—damn you!"

Maybe the rays of moonlight coming through the window slanted a little as the time went by. I wouldn't know. I didn't look.

My watch said three a.m. when I looked at it again. I refilled both glasses and switched on the light.

"I preferred the moonlight, lover." Julie's voice was a throaty purr.

"Okay," I switched off the light again.

"There are six guys on the island who work for Johnny," she said. "There are the two cooks and the two barmen. There's Zero and Johnny himself. Then there are the guests and they still think Johnny's okay."

"So?"

"All right, Superman. What are you going to do about them?"

"I'm only worried about four guys," I said. "Slade, because we need him—alive. Then Johnny and Zero, who we need like a hole in the head. And the pilot, who we also need alive to fly us back. The island can go right on the way it's been going on until the Syndicate take it over. All we need do is get rid of Johnny and Zero."

"You make it sound almost easy, lover."

"With a gun, it would be a cinch!"

"That wouldn't be difficult," she said.

"With two guns—one for Slade and one for me—it would be even more of a cinch!"

"How about three guns?"

"One for you?" I kissed her thoughtfully. "That's what I love about you, lover—you think of everything!"

The cabin door swung open suddenly and the light was flicked on. I blinked as the two guys stepped inside.

Julie groped ineffectually for her negligee.

"Don't worry, honey," Johnny said tautly. "I been listening for a while at the window!"

Her face went white.

Johnny nodded towards me. "That him?" he asked the other guy with him.

The other guy stepped forward and my stomach flipped.

"Sure," the other guy whose name was Roach said. "I remember him well. Lieutenant Al Wheeler he was a year back, anyway. In Pine City—he's got a quite a rep up there."

"Okay," Johnny said. "Scram back to your cabin, will you?"

"Sure," Roach said. "Sure!" He went outside, closing the door behind him. His footsteps faded away in the moonlight.

Johnny grinned at us. "That's a laugh," he said. "You ought to get a laugh out of that, Julie! This guy really is a cop. Did he sell you the idea he wasn't? Was that why you were helping him organise the guns, huh?"

"Johnny," she said. "I was just trying to make sure he was a cop, that's all. Because if he wasn't, then you making it look like him and Slade shot each other wouldn't be so good, would it? I mean if he wasn't a cop, then who was he? The Syndicate boys in New York would think he was a hood employed by you."

She took a deep breath: "You see that, don't you, Johnny? You do see it! That's why I had to make sure. That's why I had to string him along—play it this way. It was for you, Johnny, it was all for you!"

"Yeah," he said. "I'm crying. Can't you hear it?"

"Johnny!"

She stood up and walked towards him: "Johnny!"

"You double-crossing ..."

"Johnny!"

She went down on her knees in front of him: "Johnny! You've got to believe me! Johnny!"

He pulled the trigger twice in quick succession. The gun had a silencer on it and the faint hissing noise it made seemed worse than the full-blooded noise would have been.

Julie toppled backwards to lie still on the floor. The perfection was spoiled. The flawless beauty of her body was marred by the ugly bullet-holes and the slow escape of blood across her breast.

Johnny looked up at me and I waited for him to pump a couple of bullets into me.

"You got some time left you, copper," he said. "I still got my ideas for you and Slade!"

He opened the door and stepped backwards, so that he was framed in the entrance for a moment. He looked down at Julie's body, then he looked at me.

"You wanted her, pal," he said. "You got her. And you can keep her!"

Then he slammed the door shut and a moment later I heard the key turn in the lock.

CHAPTER 14
Zero's Hour

Around ten in the morning, Zero took me out of the cabin and along to the big cabin again. We went into the office—or the room that looked like an office.

Johnny was sitting behind the desk. He looked fine. He was wearing a crisp grey suit, with an immaculate white shirt and a hand-painted tie that wasn't gaudy. I felt the stubble around my chin and looked down at my crumpled suit. I felt like something that's been left out in the rain too long and gone mildew.

Johnny smiled at me. "We're going back tonight, copper," he said. "Seven o'clock. Thought you might like to know. Just you and me and Zero and Slade. It shouldn't take more than a couple of hours to get back. And I'll be in a hurry to get back—you know why?"

I didn't say anything.

He shook his head admiringly as he looked at me. "I don't know how a copper came to have such taste!" he said. "First it was Julie and I didn't think Julie was bad, either! Then this blonde you brought along. Dawn— yeah, that's it—Dawn."

I still didn't say anything.

"Without Julie a guy could get to feeling lonely," he went on. "You know how it is—you get sort of used to having a dame around. You miss 'em when they've gone. I wouldn't know where she's gone, but I got a good idea."

He grinned at me: "So I figure I need somebody to take her place. A classy dame. A looker with a swell figure and maybe a change from the way Julie looked. Then right away I get to thinking of that blonde! Yeah—she's my new girl, only she don't know it yet!"

His face tightened: "So you can think about that, pal! Think about it while you're waiting to collect that slug through your head!"

Zero grabbed my shoulder and marched me outside again. He took me back to the cabin and locked me in again. While I'd been away they had removed Julie's body. That was something.

There was still something left inside the Scotch bottle. I felt hungry and you get calories from alcohol, don't you? When the bottle was empty I thought it might come in useful sometime. I took off my belt, shoved the neck of the bottle into my sock and strapped the base of it around my calf, then pulled the trouser-leg back into place. I just hoped that when I started walking, my pants didn't fall down.

Around mid-day Zero did bring me some food. It broke the monotony. I ate, then finished off what was left of the afternoon in sleeping.

I woke up with somebody shaking my shoulder. I opened my eyes and saw Zero looking down at me.

"All right, copper," he said. "On your feet!"

I didn't argue with Zero. His name suggested a freeze and right then I was frozen. I just looked at the big guy and told him I'd be good.

"You'd better be," he said.

"I will," I said, acting like a bridegroom.

He jerked me upright. I felt the strength of this guy, although he was only using one hand. I didn't argue again.

Twenty minutes later I stepped on board the plane. The pilot was up front at the controls. In one seat sat Jackson Slade and beside him a guy I didn't recognise for a moment until he turned his head, and then I did recognise him.

Curt Mardin.

So Julie hadn't been kidding when she said he was on the island. Mardin was a psycho who liked to use a knife. It looked like being a bright trip.

Zero pushed me into a seat, then slammed the door shut and bolted it.

"What about Johnny?" I said. "Won't he be annoyed when he finds you've locked him out?"

"Johnny isn't coming," Zero said with a stiff grin. "He figures Curt can handle everything okay. He said to tell you he figured he's got better things to do on the island. He says he should worry about seeing a couple of punks like you and Slade collect theirs!"

He slumped into the seat beside me. "Okay, Vince!" he yelled. "Take it away!"

The engines gunned into life.

I sat there thinking about Dawn Blair and Johnny Lynch. I sat there thinking about the other girls on the island. With charming guys like Curt Mardin for company, I thought somebody should do something about it and that somebody looked like being me, except I hadn't exactly made a bright start.

The engines built up to a deafening roar and then the plane started to move forward slowly. What I needed, I realised, was for a flash of lightning to hit the pilot. Or if I couldn't get a flash of lightning, maybe Al Wheeler would do?

Zero sat slumped in his seat, looking straight ahead. I reached forward and loosened the belt, then eased the bottle out of my sock. I juggled it around until I was holding it by the neck.

The plane was moving along the ground fast now. In another few seconds it would be into the air. I wished I'd had a grandfather who played for the Dodgers.

I got onto my feet quickly, swung the bottle back over my shoulder, then pitched it. No inside curves, nothing fancy—just a straightforward play-ball.

Zero made a grab for me and I let him grab me. In the moment before I was pulled down onto the floor, I saw the bottle hit the pilot squarely on the back of the head and saw him start to slump forward over his controls.

The whole world went suddenly mad. I could hear the wind roaring outside the window, and the plane jerking and bumping violently across the ground. I used to get car-sick when I was a kid, but here and now in an airplane gone mad—brother, was I sick! I held onto my hat with one hand across my stomach. I was rising and falling in the seat like a greenhorn on a bronc. Right then I would have traded places.

I felt as though my breath would suddenly catch in my throat against my heart—it was there first, anyway. I tried to keep myself anchored in the seat, but it was a job. I grabbed at the seat in front and held on. Why did I have to release the safety-belt?

Then I was on my knees with Zero's hands around my throat. I felt the air being squeezed out of me, then the plane lurched sickeningly and there was a horrible noise like a plane hitting a tree.

Zero's grip around my throat came apart suddenly. I felt myself banged against the back of the seats in front and then felt myself sliding up the backs of them.

But it wasn't anywhere near as spectacular as Zero. Zero didn't have any seatbacks to stop him. He rose suddenly into the air like a guy who's conquered gravity. I saw his head hit the roof of the plane and then he started coming down again.

I heard somebody scream out in terror and the scream died suddenly in a gurgle. Then the lights went out.

I stayed where I was, listening. I didn't hear anything—the engines had stopped. I wondered if the plane would catch fire or anything. Then I heard a soft rustling noise.

I tried to stop breathing in case he could hear me breathing.

Then he spoke. His voice was soft and crooning. "C'mon," he crooned gently. "Come to mama! C'mon, I got your pal, he ain't going to give any trouble any more. I got a blade all hungry for you, copper! Where are you?"

That explained a couple of things. Curt Mardin must have killed Slade, which explained the scream which died in a gurgle—and it almost gave me a picture of Mardin crawling around in the dark, knife in hand, looking for me.

I wished I hadn't thrown that bottle!

There was the rustling noise again, only this time it was closer, not more than three to four feet away.

"You got to be close, baby," he whispered. "C'mon! You can't live that long!"

I could stay there and get stuck with his shiv or I could try and do something about it. I braced myself against the seatback and raised one foot.

"I'm right here, Curt," I said. "Just love that knife!"

He made a sort of hissing noise and at the same moment I lashed out with my right foot. It connected with something and that something seemed almost to squelch under my foot. He made a sort of bubbling noise. I lashed out again and connected a second time and then there was silence.

I got a box of matches out of my pocket and struck one with my fingers shaking silently. As the match flared I saw Mardin lying there on the floor, both hands clutched to his face. Beneath his fingers was a pulped mass that didn't seem to have any distinguishing contours. The knife lay on the floor. The match burned my fingers and I dropped it, quickly striking another one.

I leaned over and gave him a judo chop across the side of the neck and he went limp. Two matches later I found Zero.

Was it Newton—the guy who tossed the apple in the air and said what went up must come down? Whoever it was, he was dead right, of course. Zero had gone up—and he'd come down. Only thing was he hadn't planned his landing. He'd come down on top of his head and with all that weight, the weakest thing had given way. He had broken his neck quite neatly and maybe even then he was swapping experiences with Julie.

I made my way along to the front of the plane after I'd taken Zero's gun and shoved it into my hip pocket. The pilot was still out cold. There was an emergency door beside him and I forced it open, then dragged him out. I could hear vague shouts in the distance—that would be some of the staff coming to see what had happened.

I dragged the pilot well clear and left him lying on the grass.

The plane was the only way off the island and the plane wasn't going anywhere in a long time. So I needed to bring people to the island. Okay, so you light a bonfire.

I fired a shot into each petrol tank and the plane went up like the Fourth of July. When it was really burning, I remembered Curt Mardin and I can't say I felt sorry. Then I started running back towards the cabins.

I stayed behind a tree for a couple of minutes while a bunch of guys went past, heading the other way towards the plane. Then I got into my stride again.

I went to the main cabin which was empty except for the barman, who looked at me with startled eyes. I grinned back at him.

"Where's Johnny?" I asked him.

"In his cabin," he said. "He don't want to be disturbed."

"Which is his cabin?"

"Third on the right past here, but he said ..."

"I heard you the first time," I said. "Pour me a drink—I'll be back."

"But aren't you ..."

I didn't wait to hear the rest of it. I was heading for the third cabin to the right.

A light spilled from the window onto the ground outside. I stopped for a moment and looked in the window.

I saw Dawn standing there.

The silver lame was torn in half a dozen places. Her face was scratched and bleeding, her hair pulled out looking like a witch doctor's wig. There was a look on her face that said she was about at breaking point. She watched someone I couldn't see, with desperate concentration.

I moved around so I could see him. Johnny Lynch. There were scratches down the side of his face and a frozen grin stuck to his lips. His hands were at his sides, the fingers curling, ready to strike again. He took a step towards her and she instinctively stood back. He took another step and so did she, and her second step brought her back to the wall. The grin on Johnny's face seemed to widen.

I thought it was time for Wheeler to do his in-the-nick-of-time act.

I moved around to the door and tried it gently. It wasn't locked. Johnny had given orders not to be disturbed and he was the boss, nobody would disturb him—he didn't need to lock any doors.

How wrong could he get?

I opened the door and stepped inside, the gun in my hand. He turned around, a look of fury on his face that he should be disturbed. Then he saw me and the look of fury died. It was replaced by blank disbelief.

"I took a parachute," I said. "When nobody was looking I dived through a hole in the side of the plane where a rivet had come out."

He opened his mouth, but he didn't say anything.

I looked at Dawn. "Honey," I said, "is this man annoying you?"

She suddenly burst into tears. It wasn't my idea of a party.

"Get this, Johnny," I said, "and get it fast because you haven't got much time. Zero is dead and so is Curt. The plane is a wreck. You're all washed up!"

"We'll see about that, copper!" he said. I could see his self-confidence start to come back. "The island is still all mine—and they're my men on it. You don't have a chance in hell of getting out of here alive!"

"And neither do you, Johnny," I said. "Because I'm giving you the same chance you gave Julie!"

Then I put two slugs into him while he stood there sneering at me and it would have taught him a lesson never to sneer at a guy with the drop on you, only it was too late for Johnny to learn any lessons then.

I walked across to where Dawn stood, still sobbing.

"It's all right, honey," I said. "All we have to do now is take to the woods until the rescue arrives. There's a burning plane out there which they ought to be able to see in Washington, let alone Florida. Somebody's going to come enquiring and we've got to be sure to be around when they do."

She still sobbed.

I patted her shoulder gently. "It's all over now," I said. "Well, almost. I rescued you. You can kiss me if you like!"

She lifted her head slowly and looked at me: "What?"

"I said it's all over—you can kiss me now."

She slapped me across the face and it felt the way a slap from Zero had felt.

"You brute!" she said. "You got me into this! It was your idea. You ought to be shot yourself!" She lifted her hand to slap me again.

I thought once was enough—any more practice and she'd be after the heavyweight crown. I tapped her under the jaw and she collapsed into my arms. I gave her the fireman's heave and carried her out over my shoulder, the gun in my free hand.

It looked as if I wouldn't have time to go back for that drink after all.

CHAPTER 15
I'm Attachable

Commissioner Lavers scowled at me: "What happened then?"

"It was like I said," I shrugged my shoulders modestly. "We took to the woods. Then to the beach. An hour later a launch came in. They took us off. They had a radio on board—I radioed Jordan and the coppers descended on Cedar Keys like white ants onto a woodpile. They cleaned up the lot!"

Lavers shook his head wonderingly. "What a cop!" he growled. "You blackmail two thousand dollars out of Lynch—you murder Mardin and Lynch in cold blood and the Ocean Beach cops want to pin a medal on you!"

"It's understandable," I said.

"You ever do anything like that in the precincts of this city," Lavers roared, "and you won't be the Lieutenant-in-Charge of Homicide any longer. You'll be breaking rocks for a living!"

"Am I still a Lieutenant?" I said indignantly. "Before I took this vacation you promised me I'd be a Captain!"

"I thought better of it," Lavers grunted. "Came to my senses. Hanlon's in charge of Homicide now."

"What!" I stared at him.

He glared at me: "Let's face it, Wheeler. As a cop out looking for murderers and guys exceeding the speed limit, you have a certain something. An unorthodox, fumbling sort of blind luck!"

"What!"

"But sitting behind a desk, you reach the conclusion that desk is for putting your feet on. The paper work piles up and up. Hanlon doesn't have your blind, stupid sort of luck on a case, but he can handle the paper work."

"That's a fine thing to do to a guy when he's on vacation!" I said. "Stab him in the back!"

"I am doing something I have never done before," Lavers said miserably. "Sometimes I think my wife's right—I'm insane."

"I think your wife's right, too!"

He took a deep breath. "What's the use!" he said limply. "I am attaching you to my office, Wheeler. When an interesting case comes along—a difficult sort of case—you'll get it. You'll get it because with any luck it will be a murder case and you might become a corpse trying to solve it, which will take you out of my hair! You can call it a special assignment if you like."

He was still glaring at me: "And one other thing. Your seniority is still senior to that of Hanlon. I have made that generally known throughout the Department. In the Department your new appointment is regarded as a promotion."

"Well," I said, "that's better. Not much, but better."

He looked down at a letter on his desk: "There is also an idiotic letter from some cretin named Jordan in Ocean Beach, who says as your invaluable work to help them was performed during your vacation, he would consider it a personal favour if I gave you another week's vacation."

Lavers snorted: "Just because he saved my life once, I suppose he thinks I owe him something!"

"I owe him something," I said, "and I'll punch his nose the next time I see him!"

Lavers looked at his watch. "Today is Monday," he said. "Come back next Monday."

I started for the door at a run in case he changed his mind.

"Hey!" he said.

Too late!

"What did you do with the Austin-Healey?"

"It's outside right now," I told him.

He grinned: "You must give me a ride in it sometime."'

I drove the Healey back from the office to my house. I bought a crate of liquor on the way.

I got home, put a stack of Satchmo on the hi-fi and opened a bottle. I was only halfway through the first drink and Louis was only halfway through playing Fats Waller when the buzzer went.

I thought Lavers had changed his mind and I would cut his throat. I went and opened the front door and my mouth sagged open like an oyster with its throat cut.

A blonde stood there. Outside, at the gate, was a Packard convertible. She was wearing a blue shirt and cherry-red shorts. Her sun-tan disappeared under the legs of her shorts.

"Hello," she said.

"Well," I said and, "Well, well!" as an afterthought.

"I know you probably hate me," she said. "The way I went on after you saved my life and everything. I just had to come and tell you how sorry I am I behaved like that."

"That's okay," I said. "Think nothing of it."

"I'm on a week's vacation," she went on. "The folks thought I should take a vacation to let my nerves settle down again."

"Now there's a coincidence!" I said.

She cocked her head slightly to one side: "Is that Satchmo I can hear?"

"None other."

"I go for him."

"Come inside and go for him."

"You don't mind?"

I took her hand and led her into the living-room, sat her down on the couch, acquired two drinks and two cigarettes and sat down beside her.

"It so happens," I said, "that I also have a week's vacation. Why don't we spend it together?"

"Al!" Her eyes glistened as she looked at me. "That would be wonderful—we could really have fun!"

"And save money," I said. "Stay right here!"

"Would that be right?"

"Look at all the Armstrong you can listen to," I told her. "For free!"

She considered it soberly for a moment: "You've sold me! But the Armstrong is a firm condition of sale!"

"Sure," I said.

The phone rang. I got up and lifted the receiver.

"Lavers!" a voice snapped. "Sorry, Wheeler, something's come up. I need you right away!"

"So sorry," I lisped. "Misther Wheeler—he gone 'way for holiday."

"Who's that?"

"Me Wong," I said hurriedly. "Me Chinee laundry man. You got dirty linen?" I hung up quickly.

I turned around to Dawn. "There's been a change of plan," I said. "We can't stay here!"

"Oh?" She got to her feet. "Where will we go?"

"How about Ocean Beach?"

"But where will we stay?"

"There's always Palm Court," I said. "And if we get bored, we could go gambling at the *Paradise*."

I caught her in my arms as she fainted.

The End

Booty for a Babe

Carter Brown

CHAPTER 1
Blast Off!

The phone rang at 2 a.m. and I answered it, which was a mistake. I had to turn off the hi-fi and the blonde to do it. You would call it wasted effort because all I got out of it was Commissioner Lavers.

"You awake, Wheeler!" he said. "That's something."

"I am also off-duty," I said tersely. "Which is something else again!"

"Speak in the past tense," he said. "And get over to my office right away."

"You mean now!"

He chuckled evilly: "Of course I mean now! And if she doesn't live too far off the route, you can drop her off on the way." Then he hung up on me to avoid further argument.

Taking the blonde home when she least expected it left me with a phone number to cross out of my little black book for all time. It also left me with a large chunk of the blonde's mind, neatly laid out in words of one syllable.

It was two-thirty when I got into the Police Commissioner's office. He was sitting behind his desk looking like a cobweb the cleaners missed. Comes Hallowe'en, I thought, and I'm going to rent him out for scaring purposes.

He had that leer on his face that always means trouble for Al Wheeler. "This," the leer widened as he spoke, "is your big opportunity, Wheeler!"

"For what—suicide?"

"Suicide!" he looked puzzled.

"What else can you contemplate at this time in the morning," I asked him, "here?"

"Most amusing," he said. "You know, Wheeler, there are a great number of people who consider you to be just dumb."

"I'm used to it," I assured him.

"I am not one of them," he said. "I never have been. I consider you to be just plain stupid!"

"You bring me here in the small hours of the morning just to insult me?" I felt annoyed. "You could insult me in office hours couldn't you? Why change a habit?"

He shook his head: "There is reason in this. You remember when you came back from that peculiar vacation of yours at Long Beach? You remember that I attached you to this office?"

"With manacles around my feet!"

"I should have seen a psychiatrist first," he sighed. "What have you done since then, if I may ask a personal question?”

I thought about it for a long time then smiled feebly: “Well, I cleared up the mystery of who was stealing the coffee downstairs ... remember? And then there was that time you couldn’t find your briefcase and I got it back from that redhead who said you were ...”

“That’s enough!” his face was turkey-red. “I’m talking about work. Real work! I’ll tell you exactly what you’ve done in that period! Nothing!”

“Well,” I shrugged my shoulders. “It was your idea.”

His fingers drummed a call to arms on me desktop. “As I remember, I said that, as you were an unorthodox cop, I was going to attach you to this office so that when an unorthodox case came along, you could use your unorthodox methods to solve it. In the meanwhile, Lieutenant Hanlon could cope with the desk routine that you hadn’t coped with as Lieutenant-in-Charge of Homicide. Right?”

“Right!”

He smiled at me. “Hanlon is still doing a good job over there.”

“I’m glad to hear it.”

“And you’ll be undoubtedly glad to hear that at long last a job of work has turned up for you. Right now! Hanlon has been battling away at it for the last three hours and fighting a losing battle. He’s about ready to give up. So, the case is now yours.”

“Oh,” I said unenthusiastically.

That evil leer was back on his face. “Hanlon can give you all the sordid details. Just get over to the Hotel Imperial. Drive yourself over in that natty little Austin-Healey you acquired illegally in Ocean Beach! Hanlon will be only too pleased to see you, I’m sure.”

“Yes sir,” I said.

I was nearly out of the office when he bellowed.

“What was that?” I turned around and looked at him.

“Got your blaster-pistol with you?” he said, and then sniggered suddenly.

“My what!”

“Nothing,” he sniggered again. “You’d better blast-off, Wheeler, and cut straight into hyper-space drive! The boys in the outer galaxy need you!”

“In the what?”

“You’ll find out,” he sniggered. “At the Imperial!”

“If it’s not the heat,” I said soberly, “it’s the humidity.”

I wondered on my way downstairs if after all these years he’d finally blown his top. I had a nasty feeling that he hadn’t. I blasted off in the Austin-Healey like he’d told me to, and wondered who was nuts. Maybe it was me. If the blonde was right, it was me for sure.

The Imperial was holding a convention or something by the number of cars stacked out in front when I got there. There was a uniformed patrolman on the door who told me I'd find Hanlon on the third floor. And so I did.

He looked ten years older since the last time I saw him, which had been a week before. Even a woman can't do that to a man.

"The Commissioner rang me," he said. "Told me you were taking over the case, Al! Brother! Am I thankful!"

"What sort of case is it?"

"Murder."

"Complicated?"

He held his head between his hands for a moment and moaned softly. "You just won the award for the understatement of the year!"

"Lay off, will you?" I said. "First the Commissioner's making with the funny remarks and now it's you. What gives?"

"This Professor guy," he said. "Gets himself bumped off."

"How?"

"You thinking of something simple like shot, huh?" he shook his head. "A dart—made of tungsten steel. Embedded in the heart."

"Who threw it?"

"It wasn't thrown, pal. Not according to the doc. It was fired."

"By a gun?"

"Or a blowpipe—or something?"

"Any witnesses?"

"Eighty."

I did a double take.

"You heard me," Hanlon said hoarsely. "The Professor was lecturing at the time."

"On what?"

"The Elastic Dimension."

"What's that—lingerie?"

Hanlon looked at me pityingly: "As I understand it—which is not very much—it's something to do with Time."

"What sort of time?"

"Time travel."

"But that's science fiction stuff, isn't it?"

There was a long silence.

"Didn't Lavers tell you?" Hanlon asked in a quavering voice.

"Not a thing."

"What's going on here? He didn't mention it?"

"Not a word."

Hanlon pushed me gently into a chair. "This is a science fiction fans convention, brother. Some eighty of them have gathered here in the Imperial for three days talkie-talkie on things that go *whee* in the outer worlds!"

"This Professor must have been a lousy speaker," I said. "If they had to kill him to shut him up."

He smiled wanly: "For three hours I have been steadily going nuts trying to make some sense of it. Out of them! They're all nuts!"

"The fans?"

"Yeah—the fans! They talk a language I don't even understand! You tell me they're all out of outer space and brother, I'll believe it!"

"No motives, no nothing?"

He lit himself a cigarette with a hand that shook steadily. "At ten-thirty tonight the Professor is in the middle of a lecture. He suddenly keels over. Somebody finally realises he's dead. Somebody else calls a doc, then calls the cops. We arrive. We ask questions. We ask a million questions. You want the answers."

"If you got a million," I said doubtfully, "keep 'em short."

Hanlon laughed bitterly: "I can keep 'em short. Eight of 'em saw it happen—that's it. None of 'em know why. None of 'em saw anything unusual except the Professor keel over. That's it—the million answers all the same."

I lit myself a cigarette. "That's as far as you've got."

"That's as far as I've got. The Professor is still in the morgue. The eighty suspects are still in the hotel. Still in the lounge where the lecture was being given. They don't like it, but hell! I kept 'em there for want of something better to do with 'em!" He brightened up a little. "But they're all yours now, Al. I'm going home to bed and forget it all!"

The door suddenly burst open and a bright, bouncing redhead strode in, closely followed by a bellowing cop.

"You can't go in there!" the cop protested.

"Don't be a fool!" she said coldly. "I'm in here, aren't I?" She spun around and faced Hanlon. "Now look here, Sergeant! How long are we to be kept inside that lounge! There's a limit to just how much people can understand and they've reached that limit! If you don't want a riot, you'd better ..."

"I've been taken off the case," Hanlon said hurriedly. "This is Lieutenant Wheeler, he's in complete charge from now on!"

The redhead spun around and looked at me coldly. "Well, perhaps you are slightly less of an idiot than you look! More of a BEM, I'd say!"

"BEM?" I asked blankly.

"BEM," she said impatiently. "Bug-eyed monster."

"Be seeing you, Al," Hanlon said cheerfully and slipped out of the room.

The redhead took a deep breath which altered the line of her sweater. "Look here, Lieutenant, if ..."

"Shut up!" I said quickly.

"What!"

"Shut up. Answer questions—don't ask them. You're taking my job away asking questions. Who are you?"

"Flavia Romberg."

"Science fiction bug?"

"I happen to be the organising secretary of the fourteenth annual convention of the All-American Science Fictions Fans' Club," she said. "And let me tell you ..."

"Lady," I said mildly, "there are a million things you can tell me, but save 'em till I ask, will you?"

She glared at me, but at least she'd shut up for a few seconds. It was almost a victory, I thought.

"First things firstly," I said. "You can go and tell them they can leave the lounge. They can go to their rooms. They can't leave the hotel. Okay?"

"Thank you!"

"And then come back here."

"What for?"

"Questions," I said.

She bounced out of the room and the uniformed cop looked despairingly at her as she walked past.

"What's your name?" I asked him.

"Logan, sir."

"This is going to be a long night, Logan. Find the manager and while you're finding him have the room service send up a bottle of Scotch and some glasses. Ice, of course."

"Yes, Lieutenant."

That Lavers, I thought. That funny man. Have you got your blaster-pistol! The boys in the outer galaxy need you! I'd cut his throat if someone would lend me a blunt penknife!

Logan got back just after room service had delivered. The manager came in behind him. A worried-looking guy by the name of Meedlemaus. With a name like that I'd wear a worried look, too.

"This is dreadful, Lieutenant," he said. "Shocking! Why anyone should want to kill Professor Todt in, my hotel, I don't know."

"Maybe the room service was lousy," I said. "Who knows?"

He tried to be obliging and smile, but he couldn't make it.

"Never mind," I said. "We'll take all the cops away except a couple on the door. None of these conventioneers is to leave the hotel. Otherwise things can go on as usual."

"Thanks, Lieutenant," he said. "Thanks very much."

"Can you give me a room here?"

"Of course," he said blankly.

"Which one?"

"This room is vacant. I turned it over to the Lieutenant who was here first to use as his headquarters. You're very welcome to it, Lieutenant. Very welcome."

"Thanks," I said. "If I want you any more I'll scream."

He went out and I told Logan that I wanted two cops on the door to see that none of the eighty suspects left the hotel. It was an impossible order to give, but hell! People expected me to do something, didn't they?

I poured myself another Scotch and thought maybe if I drank enough I could blast off without any effort on my part at all.

There was a thunderous tattoo on the door and Flavia Romberg bounced back into the room a moment later, and I thought if she was a sample of outer space, I'd try it.

"Well," she said, "here I am!" And she took a deep breath right after she said it.

"I can see that," I said in an awed voice. "All of you here, I can see that with one long glance! Sit down."

She didn't drink, she said, which was okay by me because I had the whole bottle to myself. She hadn't met Professor Todt before the convention started. She knew he was a keen fan himself and a good lecturer. She didn't know of any reason why anyone would want to kill him.

So that fixed that.

"I think the best thing we can do is let the convention run on," I said. "This was the first day, wasn't it?"

"Yes," she nodded.

"Well, the convention might as well go on."

"Thank you, Lieutenant," she looked a little happier.

"Where were you when the Professor was killed?"

"At the table."

"Facing the audience?"

"Yes."

"Anyone else there with you?"

"Only the Professor, of course."

"That's something," I said. "That leaves me with only seventy-nine suspects!"

"I don't..." Her brow cleared. "Oh, I see what you mean! If I had killed the Professor I would have had to be in the audience to shoot him?"

"Check. And also if you'd done it at the table, seventy-nine people would have seen you."

"That sounds like logical deduction, Lieutenant. Have you ever studied Dianetics?"

"I knew a blonde called Diane once," I said hopefully. "But that wouldn't be the same thing, would it? She was quite a study—I never figured out how Kinsey missed her!"

"It wouldn't be the same thing," she said coldly. "Can I go now? It's very late."

"Or early." I poured myself another drink. "What's on the agenda tomorrow?"

"At ten-thirty there's a lecture by Wilbur Kessell."

"What's he talking about?"

"He hasn't announced the title of his lecture. We're all intrigued, of course!"

"Yeah," I said. "Me, too."

"Kessell is the biggest name here," she said.

"You don't have any three-syllabled names?"

"I mean in science fiction!" she almost snarled. "He ranks with Heinlein and Bradbury!"

"What as?"

"A writer! Really, Lieutenant, no one can be as ignorant as you pretend to be!"

"I can," I said. "It's a gift. Okay. I'll be there."

"Very well," she said. She got up from her chair and smoothed her skirt over her hips. "I shall see you in the morning then, Lieutenant. Good-night."

"Good-night," I said. She went out, closing the door gently behind her. The phone rang and I picked it up.

"Lavers," a sniggering voice said. "Having fun out there among the asteroids?"

"Go back to bed, you ... you BEM!"

"What?"

"Bug-eyed monster!" I said smugly. "This place is lousy with them!"

"We got a line on Professor Todt," he said. "All negative, Al. He comes from Missouri. Teaches Ancient History on the campus out there. Blameless life, never harmed anyone. Single, no close friends. No possible reason why anyone should want to kill him. Science fiction crank. Favourite topic was time-travel. Attended every convention that's held! And that's all."

"Thanks very much," I said. "That makes everything simple."

"What progress are you making?"

I thought about that for a moment. "I met a redhead," I told him.

"Any other progress?"

"The room service is fine."

"I am giving you all the rope you need," he said cryptically and hung up.

I arrived at the entrance to the lounge at ten twenty-five the next morning. A very tall and very fat young man beamed at me.

"Where's your badge?" he asked. "You must have your badge, you know!"

He touched the badge in his lapel, which said, "Spaceman! 14th Convention A.A.S.F.F."

"I got a badge for everything," I told him and showed him my shield.

"Oh!" he said feebly. "In that case, Captain, come right in."

"Thanks," I said, "and it's Lieutenant."

I found a seat in the front row and sat down. Flavia Romberg was seated at the table in front of the audience and there was a thin guy with a spade beard and deep-set flashing eyes beside her.

Flavia got on to her feet a couple of minutes later. "Fellow fans, it is my privilege to introduce to you Wilbur Kessell. I can only say that he needs no introduction from me!"

There was a burst of handclapping and Kessell got slowly on to his feet.

"Fellow science-fictioneers," he started in a suave voice, "it is a pleasure to meet you. I would like to discuss some of the finer points of my craft with you.... Perhaps, for a start, we could consider the mutation theories ..."

As he went on, my eyes bulged. Brother! I never even knew that such words existed! Humanoids ... planetoids ... accelerated metabolism ... anti-gravitism ...

When he'd finally finished and sat down again, a husky voice asked from the back of the audience, "Mr. Kessell! Do you really think there's life on the other planets?"

I turned around in my seat and looked at the questioner. She was honey-blonde, wearing a pink shirt and a pair of black, tapered slacks. I thought, never mind the other planets, honey, there'll be plenty of life on this planet while you're around.

"Why, certainly!" Kessell smiled at her. "I agree with Fred Hoyle. It's logical to think that as life has developed into its form as man on Earth, then life on other planets would conform more or less to the same planet."

"You think then that if there's any life on Mars, for example, it would tend to be humanoid?"

"To a degree—yes."

The blonde sat down again, apparently satisfied.

A few more questions were asked and then the convention broke up for lunch. I angled towards the blonde and walked out into the corridor at the same time as she did.

"I'm Lieutenant Wheeler," I smiled at her. "I'm investigating Professor

Todt's murder. I'd like to ask you some questions, if you don't mind?"

"Of course I don't mind," she said. "I'm thrilled, Lieutenant! You see, I have a theory about the murder!"

"Why don't we go and have a drink and let you tell me about it?" I suggested. "I have a room here."

"That would be wonderful!" she said. "Only I must he back at two-thirty. I couldn't possibly miss Yoghurt's lecture on Fact and Phantasy!"

"I'd shoot myself if I missed it!" I said. "But reminding me of that doubles my thirst." I grabbed her elbow and steered her towards my room.

As soon as I'd poured the drinks and settled her down in a chair, I sat opposite her. "You have a theory?"

She nodded vehemently. Her eyes were very blue and very wide open. "I'm sure I'm right, too!"

"You think you know who killed him?"

"Without a doubt!"

"Who?"

"The Time Theory?"

"The what theory?"

She leaned forward, her eyes glistening. "It's so simple, really, Lieutenant! You see, the Professor had made a study of Time. He really believed that time travel was possible. I think he'd come closer to the truth than he realised. So they killed him!"

"You mean ... enemy agents?"

"Of course not!" she said scornfully. "They did it—from somewhere in the future. To stop him!"

"Stop him what?"

"Travelling in time, of course. They probably have a good reason you see! We don't know what it is, naturally. But they know. And they had to stop him before he revealed the secret. So they killed him."

"It's quite a theory!" I drained my glass and absent-mindedly refilled it. "Sort of answers everything, doesn't it?"

"I'm so glad you agree," she said eagerly. "Some of the others laughed at me when I told them. But it makes sense, doesn't it?"

"The way Elvis Presley does," I agreed.

"Does he write science fiction?"

"He lives it," I said. "I think. The original rock-o-roll space ship."

"I must have missed his stories," she sighed. "I read all I can, but you know how it is, you miss some now and then."

I drained the second glass of Scotch and replenished it. "Did you know the Professor at all? Personally, I mean?"

"Oh, yes," she nodded. "I quite like him. I used to go to his lectures on Ancient History."

"How long ago?"

"I graduated a couple of years back."

"Anyone else here who knew him?"

"Well, there's Wilbur Kessell, of course. And Waldo Kipcheek."

"Waldo Kipcheek."

"You must have seen him. He was on the door, checking the badges as everyone came in."

"Fat."

"Fat," she nodded.

I lit a cigarette. "Anyone else?"

"Well, Flavia knew him, of course."

"Where from?"

"All the conventions. She organises every S.F. Fans' Convention there is."

"Oh," I said. "Anyone else?"

"I saw something yesterday," she said. "In the corridor. I'd just left my room to ... well, I'd just left it and I saw this man talking to the Professor in the corridor. They seemed to be having a violent argument about something."

"Who was he?"

She shook her head doubtfully: "I don't know. He wasn't one of the people here for the convention because I haven't seen him at any of the lectures. But he was ... well, evil-looking. If you know what I mean?"

"I get the drift," I said. "Can you get a little more accurate than that?"

"He was small. About forty, I'd say. Jet black hair brushed straight back and going grey at the temples. He was very well dressed."

I nodded: "Thanks. I'll see if I can find him. What's your name by the way?"

"Annabelle," she said. "Annabelle Starr."

"If you hear anything or think of anything that might help," I said. "I'd be glad if you'd let me know."

"Of course," she said. "Was there anything else, Lieutenant?"

"Not that I recall," I said.

I thought I could safely skip the afternoon's lecture on atomic propulsion and I dug up the hotel's detective instead. He was a lean, melancholy-looking character by the name of Dexter.

I described the evil-looking man that Annabelle Starr had described to me and Dexter nodded without any hesitation at all. "Sure," he said. "That would be Nicky Spain."

"Where does he come from?"

Dexter shrugged his shoulders. "He's got Detroit written in the register downstairs. Maybe he comes from there and maybe be doesn't. My bet would be Alcatraz!"

"Why?"

"He's got   that tough look about him. He also has a couple of family retainers."

"Who are they?"

"A torpedo and a dame. The torpedo's called Rivers and the dame signed herself Carlotta Chavez. She's got maybe twenty-five per cent Mexican blood but one look at her and you don't stop to figure out percentages!"

"What's Spain's room number?"

"Three-o-eight."

"Thanks," I told him. "You've been very helpful. See anything interesting happening you might let me know."

"Sure Lieutenant. The sooner you move out of here the happier the management will be!" He grinned: "Cops aren't good for business!"

It took me five minutes to find three-o-eight and knock on the door. But no evil-looking character opened it. The luck of Wheelers was in. A sultry-looking brunette opened the door instead.

Maybe the air-conditioning wasn't working inside or maybe she just didn't like clothes much. She wasn't wearing anything but a two-piece swimsuit which if it had been sewn together wouldn't have made a very big one-piece.

"I never knew the management built-in swimming-pools in these suites?" I said. "How's the water? Water-conditioned, huh?"

Her hair was black and long and straight. It accentuated the high cheekbones and the classical line of her face. The two-piece accented the fact that a curve can be as interesting as a line and sometimes even more interesting.

"Are you lost?" she asked in a bored voice.

"Don't tell me you're a mirage!" I said in a disappointed voice.

"For a week now I've been wandering the corridors of this hotel trying to find something just like you. And now you say I'm still lost!"

"Get lost!" she said. And closed the door in my face.

I knocked louder this time. The door opened again suddenly.

"You're beautiful," I said. But then the door was open wide enough for me to see. "Correction!" I added hastily.

He was tall and lean and looked like he should be making westerns in Hollywood. He had that sunburned, outdoors look which they pick up in Texas or Alcatraz. He was wearing a two-hundred dollar suit.

"The lady said to get lost chum," he said. "You want I should take a personal interest in you doing that?"

"I was looking for Mr. Spain," I said. "Is he in?"

"Who wants to see him?"

"A friend of Professor Todt," I said easily. "The late Professor Todt, that is."

"Stay there," he said and closed the door in my face.

It was my afternoon for doors closing in my face. I thought as long as it was in and not on, I didn't really care. By the time I'd lit a cigarette, the door was open again.

"The boss says to come in," my Western friend said.

So I went in.

Carlotta had draped herself over a sofa and was deep in a true confessions magazine. I thought she could probably write half a dozen issues on her own account.

Spain was sitting in an armchair, smoking a cigarette in a long ivory holder. He looked the way Dexter had described him.

"What do you want to see me about?" he asked.

"Professor Todt," I said. "You see, I'm a friend of his ..."

"You're a cop," he said. "Name of Wheeler. What is this—a gag?"

There wasn't room for both of us to be unorthodox.

"Lieutenant Wheeler," I said. "Yesterday you had a violent argument with the Professor. Last night he was murdered."

"He was in with those hopheads at his convention," he said. "I wasn't there."

"What were you arguing about with the Professor?"

"Relativity," he said blandly.

I sucked smoke into my lungs. "You're from Detroit?"

"Sure."

"What business are you in there?"

"Automobiles, what else?"

"I thought the name was Spain—I had it wrong? It's General Motors?"

"Second-hand autos," he said. "I'm on vacation here. This," he flicked a thumb in the cowboy's direction, "is my manager, Lazy Rivers."

"Has Miss Chavez anything to do with your relativity?" I asked him. "I mean—is she a relative?"

"Girl-friend," he said. "You got a law against girl-friends in this town?"

"Not that I know of. You knew the Professor?"

"Never met him before in all my life. He was a crank, that's all—I'm kind of interested in some of this science stuff, not the fiction part, the real dope. Rockets and that sort of stuff. He figures to be a bright guy so I ask him a question and we get kind of wrapped up, there's all about it."

"What did you do last night?"

"Stayed right here in my suite."

"Alone?"

"Lazy was here part of the time—he went out around nine. Me and Carlotta were here the rest of the time."

"Until when?"

He twitched that eyebrow again. "Around nine this morning."

"Discussing relativity, no doubt?"

"We was reading one of her magazines," he said, with his face deadpan. "She's crazy on that true confession stuff. Me, I figure dames with that sort of grief should jump off the nearest bridge."

"Then there wouldn't be any magazines like that?"

"That's what I figure!"

I knew when I was beaten. "Okay," I said. "Thanks for your time."

"Pleasure, Lieutenant," he said. "Glad to know any friend of the Professor's!"

I went out of the room and the hotel. I drove down to Homicide and dug into the files. I sent a wire to Detroit. There was nothing in our files on any of them. Maybe Detroit would have something and maybe they wouldn't. I had a feeling they wouldn't. Spain would be too smart to have any sort of record. I had to admit to myself that he was too smart for me.

Around seven that night I brought Flavia Romberg a drink in the hotel bar.

"Have you found out who killed the Professor yet?" she asked me.

"Not yet," I said.

"I hope you do soon," she said. "Otherwise it will be too late won't it?"

"Too late?"

"Tomorrow's the last day of the convention. Everyone goes home the day after."

"Not if we haven't got the murderer, they don't!"

She stared at me. "But you can't keep people here in this hotel indefinitely!"

"You watch!"

She bit her lower lip. There was plenty of it to bite. This redhead was built in generous proportions. The black tube of a gown she was wearing accentuated it.

"What do you do for a living when you aren't organising these science fiction clambakes?" I asked her.

"Nothing very much," she said. "I'm fortunate to have a rich father who indulges me in my sincere desire to do nothing but what I want to. Work is not one of the things I'm crazy about."

"You can count me in on that one," I said.

I ordered two more drinks and wondered if Flavia was interested in hi-fi.

"You like music?" I asked her.

"Crazy about it," she said. "Brahms, Sibelius, Grieg ... I even like

Stravinsky.”

“What about real music?” I said hopefully. “Armstrong, Ellington ... Brubeck?”

“You mean ... jazz!” She looked shaken.

“Sure, what’s wrong with it?”

“Nothing, for a moron!”

“I have the most magnificent hi-fi set-up at home,” I said sadly. “And just because you don’t appreciate real music, we can’t go and listen to it.”

“It so happens I have a couple of LPs in my room,” she said. “We could compromise. I’ll listen to your hi-fi if you play my discs on it.”

“Lady,” I said, “you just got yourself a deal.”

So half an hour later we arrived at my house. I escorted Flavia inside, sat her carefully on the sofa, left the hi-fi warming up, and poured us a drink. Wheeler’s house may sometimes be without food, but never without drink.

I took her discs out of their covers and looked at them. There was a little something with the hep title of *Drei Gediche Von Michelangelo*. I tried the next one:—*Klavierstuke, Opus 119 (Brahms)*. I took an even bet with myself that you couldn’t whistle it. The last one was *Danse Macabre*.

“Just put them on,” Flavia said happily.

“You sure you wouldn’t like some Peggy Lee or Sinatra instead?” I asked desperately.

“We made a bargain—remember?”

“Should I ever forget!” I put the discs on the turntable, held my drink firmly in my hand and went and sat down beside her on the sofa.

“Lieutenant ...”

“Call me Al,” I said. “Al Wheeler is the name. All redheads call me Al because it just comes naturally to them.”

“What does?”

“Al!”

Her lips tightened: “I’ll call you Al, under duress. I hate abbreviations of proper names. What does Al stand for?”

“Never you mind,” I said firmly. “A man is entitled to one secret and that’s mine.”

There was a weird cacophony coming through the five loudspeakers which I concluded was Brahms. I decided with luck I could ignore it.

“You’re not married?” I said.

She shook her head: “I don’t believe in it.”

“I always go for a girl with an outlook that’s advanced,” I said. “It saves so much argument.”

“I don’t have an outlook all that advanced!” she said coldly. “So don’t delude yourself. I just haven’t met any man I’d care to marry yet.”

"Never even been in love?"

"Cow-eyed under a full moon?" she said tartly. "No, and I'm not likely to, either."

"You're listening to the wrong sort of music," I said. "That's obvious!"

She shrugged her shoulders: "I just happen to be adult in my outlook, that's all." She turned and looked me straight in the eyes. "You are the most peculiar policeman I have ever met! Aren't you supposed to be trying to find out who killed the Professor?"

"I have to relax sometimes," I told her. "And anyway, I thought I could ask you some more questions."

"Ask away."

Anything was better than listening to her discs. "I can't figure it out," I said slowly. "How a gorgeous redhead like you hasn't fallen like crazy for some guy before now. I admit it baffles me!"

"Is this relevant to the murder, Lieutenant?" she asked frigidly.

"Al is the name. And it could be."

"I told you before, I never met anyone yet who …"

"You ever go to the movies?"

"Occasionally."

"Gregory Peck, Bill Holden, Mel Ferrer … no?"

"Fall in love with a two dimensional-image?" She laughed softly. "Al—really!"

"Your education has been sadly neglected," I said. "I see I shall have to do something about it. You know a guy called Spain?"

"Only a country, I'm afraid."

"Nicky Spain? You sure?"

"I'm sure I don't know him—should I?"

"Maybe not. You must have met Todt before though—at other conventions you organised, like this one?"

"I ran into him a couple of times."

"You said you never saw him before."

"I didn't think the other conventions were worth mentioning, I'm sorry. Do they have any special significance?"

"I wish to hell I knew the answer to that one," I said moodily. "This Todt is a nice harmless character so somebody has to bump him off. Nobody had a motive, nobody knew him!"

"I'm sure you're just joking with me," she said. "I suppose you've really made an arrest already?"

"I can't pinch all the suspects," I said. "Even Jack Webb never had a dragnet that big!"

She finished her drink so I poured her another.

"Have you talked to Wilbur Kessell yet?"

"No, should I?"

"He might know the Professor better than anyone else."

"That's something. How about this Lipcheek character? You know him?"

"Waldo? Of course. Everybody knows Waldo."

"Not me."

"He's a dear, really, I think he hates science fiction really but he's madly in love with that little blonde, you know—the one with the impossible name. Annabelle Starr. So he just follows her around wherever she goes. And mostly she seems to go to science fiction conventions."

"Around and around," I said. "Getting no place."

I poured myself another drink. The phone rang. I debated whether to answer it or not and thought maybe I should. I got it on the sixteenth ring.

"Another blonde?" a gentle voice purred in my ear.

"Sure," I said, "only you underestimate me—by five! I have six blondes here! They're all over six feet tall and weight around a hundred and eighty in their nyloned feet! They're a weight-lifting team from burlesque and ..."

"Write me a memo!" Lavers snarled. "I hate to interrupt your life's work at a time like this, Wheeler, but weren't you working on that Todt murder? Or am I thinking of two other guys?"

"I'm working on it right now," I said quickly. "Interrogating a suspect!"

"I hate to interrupt your field work," he said. "I wouldn't if it wasn't for just one thing?"

"What's that?"

"Another murder!"

I looked at the phone blankly. "For a moment I thought you said another murder."

"That's just what I did say! Get the hell back to the Imperial and do something fast! I already sent Hanlon and a team over there!"

"Who was murdered?" I croaked.

"I'll let that come as a surprise," he said. "So put your six blondes down and hurry!"

He slammed the 'phone down in my ear.

I dropped my own receiver gently back on to the cradle and as sounds gradually penetrated my tortured eardrum again I heard the spine-chilling *Danse Macabre* creeping out of the speakers.

Flavia was looking at me with raised eyebrows. "Was that trouble?"

"Nothing to speak of," I said. "Only another murder!"

It was just as well she was sitting on the couch. She didn't have far to fall when she fainted.

Three minutes to throw some water over her face and get her into the Healey. Twenty-five minutes back to the hotel. There were two prowl cars parked outside. The cop on the door even looked sympathetic. "Fourth floor, Lieutenant," he said. "Lieutenant Hanlon is up there now."

"Okay," I said. "Fine!" I looked at Flavia. "You're on your own from now."

"I'll manage," she smiled faintly

"Fine!" I said. "See you around."

I found Hanlon on the fourth floor okay. He gave me a disenchanted look. "I thought you had probably dropped dead," he said. "But the Commissioner was way ahead of me. He said you were just womanising again."

"I was interrogating ..."

"Who cares?" he shrugged his shoulders. "I just wish you'd stay on a case, Al. That way maybe I could sleep nights!"

"Who got murdered this time?"

"The hotel dick!"

"Dexter!"

"Yeah, that's the name. He's in there." Hanlon jerked his thumb towards a door. "Go take a look."

I went into the room. The expert squad were still chasing clues around. Dexter lay on the floor, on his back. His eyes were wide open and his fists clenched.

The doc stood in one corner, fastening up his little black bag. "A hell of an hotel this is!" he grunted. "Their guests knock off like flies!"

"How did it happen, Doc?"

"Same thing as before, Al. A dart—probably the same type. I can't tell till I've done the autopsy."

"It's getting to be an epidemic!" I said.

I went back to Hanlon. "Find out anything?"

"The manager—Littlemouse ..."

"Meedlemaus!"

"Maus-snaus! He wanted him down at the desk an hour back so he sends a bellhop up to his room. The bellhop finds him the way he is. Doc figures he's been dead maybe four hours."

"Since somewhere six."

"That's about it. Looks like whoever knocked off the Professor knocked off the hotel dick. That's his own room, of course. So happened that there were only a couple of people on the floor around that time, and they were both in their rooms and didn't hear anything."

"That helps!"

Hanlon brightened up a little. "Well, it's your case, Al, so I won't stick my nose in. I'll have the lab's reports sent out to you here. Okay?"

"Sure."

"There was some stuff came in for you from Detroit, by the way. I left it up in your room."

"Thanks. You organised the morgue?"

"Sure—they'll be here any time now to take it away. Anything else you want doing? Want any men left here?"

"No thanks—twice."

"Well," he tipped his hat on to the back of his head and grinned brightly. "Have fun!"

"And don't break a leg riding the elevator down!" I said.

I went up to my room. I rang room service and ordered some more Scotch. I picked up the envelope on the bed and ripped it open—the good oil from Detroit.

WHEELER, PINE CITY. NO RECORD FOR NICKY SPAIN. NO KNOWN SECOND-HAND AUTO DEALER BY THAT NAME. NO RECORD OF ANYONE ANSWERING PHYSICAL DESCRIPTION OF SPAIN ON FILE.

I lit a cigarette and held the match to the paper. That helped a lot, I thought. It was wonderful. It was something to bother Nicky Spain with, anyway.

There was a knock on the door—a discreet knock. I shifted the Service .38 to a handier position and crossed the room. I flung open the door. A guy in a white jacket, black pants and a sweat stood there.

"You rang for Scotch, sir?" he said.

"Sure," I said. "But did you have to run all the way with it?"

He stared at me, then saw what I was getting at.

"It is warm, sir," he said.

"The Scotch? You can take it right back!"

"Oh no, sir,—not the Scotch, the weather!"

He came in and put the tray down on the table. I flipped him a five dollar bill, and didn't have the heart to let the guy go without a drink. He appreciated that.

When he had gone I built myself a second drink and decided to pay Carlotta a visit.

I went down to the third floor and along to room three-o-eight and knocked. Carlotta opened the door. She'd changed out of the two-piece into a playsuit which clung to her like a child to its mother. "You!" she said.

"And coming in," I told her.

She stepped backwards into the room and I followed her in, closing the door behind me. The room was empty.

"Where's Spain?"

"He went out about an hour ago."

"Rivers?"

"He went with him."

"When do you expect them back?"

She shrugged olive shoulders. "Not for a few hours, I think. They wanted to go to a nightclub. I did not want to go, so I stay here."

"You been here all evening?"

"Since they leave about eight. Before that we were in the bar for awhile."

"Yeah," I said, for want of something better to say.

She was standing in front of me, quite close. She took a step that brought her a lot closer. The playsuit shook hands with my hopsack. Her arms came up and wound around my neck and she pulled my head down slightly so that my lips met hers. Being kissed by her was like shaking hands with an electric eel. A shock galvanised me.

It seemed like half-an-hour later when she let go of me and stepped back, taking the playsuit with her.

"What the hell was all that about?" I said in a dazed voice.

"I often wondered," she said with a faint smile, "and now I know."

"Know what?"

"About policemen, I wonder if they are human. Now I know."

"Are they?"

"I think so. Very human. You have a lot of experience, Lieutenant. A girl can tell just by kissing you. Nicky will stay out late, he always does when he goes to a club." Her voice was soft. "We could lock the door."

I shook my head. "Some other time, Carlotta. I have to go see a guy about a corpse—two corpses!"

She shrugged her shoulders and the ripple went way down past her swimsuit. "If you prefer!"

I was halfway down the corridor before I remembered she hadn't even commented when I'd mentioned two corpses. That could mean something or nothing.

CHAPTER 2
Delfs!

William Kessell was wearing a light blue silk robe and had a pipe nicely clenched between his teeth. He also sat in a comfortable chair with a book open on his knee. Everybody's seen that picture a million times. The successful author relaxes—and for sure he's reading one of his own books.

I closed the door behind me.

"Lieutenant Wheeler, isn't it?" he said. "This is an unexpected pleasure!"

"Fine!" I said. "I wanted to talk to you for a few minutes."

"Sit down," he gestured to an empty chair opposite his own. "I am intrigued, Lieutenant! Do you suspect me of murdering Professor Todt?"

I sat down and lit a cigarette.

"Yeah," I said.

He took his pipe out of his mouth so that he could smile without keeping his teeth clenched. "Well! This sounds exciting!"

"Why do I have to figure everybody I want to talk to is a murderer?" I said. "I want some dope on Todt."

"I can't help you much there," he said. "He was quite a harmless old boy, you know. Why anyone should want to kill him is completely beyond me."

"You know him well?"

He shook his head: "Not really. I met him quite regularly at the S.F. conventions. I have to go to most of them. It helps sell books. I'm one of those stupid writers, I write for money. I like money."

"Sure," I said. "What about Todt?"

"He was always there. Fanatically keen. Had a pet theory, you know."

"Something about relativity?"

Kessell laughed deprecatingly: "Well, not exactly. Todt had a half-baked theory based on Time. You know the old stuff about Time being the fourth dimension. It's about the earliest science fiction plot there was. Wells used it and a million others have since—with minor variations. Todt's theory was that Time and the universe—our universe governed by the sun, that is— were controlled by what he called the Delfs."

"The what?"

"Delfs. He claimed that these Delfs were a people from another universe, immeasurably older than ours, who had created our universe and everything in it purely for their own amusement."

"And they still let him walk around without an attendant!"

Kessell grinned: "He was quite harmless, you know. And remarkably sane in every other way. And it was only a theory and only aired in S.F. circles. And compared with many theories I've heard in the same circles, his was quite mild."

"Go on," I said.

He sucked his empty pipe contentedly: "Well, these Delfs, according to the Professor, were ageless and live for eternity. Their universe has no time and therefore no one gets any older—without time there is no ageing, of course. The Delfs just are!"

"Just are," I repeated vacantly. "Is there more?"

"Oh, lots more!" Kessell said brightly. "A whole lot more. Todt thought the Delfs created our universe for their own amusement and for their final, priceless joke they invented Time to go along with it. Todt figured if we could only find a way of distracting the Delfs' attention from our own universe, Time would grind to a stop. Everyone living at the moment Time stopped would then be immortal!"

I felt I needed a drink, six drinks.

"He also," Kessell continued remorselessly, "had a theory on how to distract the Delfs."

"Put salt on their tails?" I ventured.

He grinned his appreciation. "Not quite. The theory was that they could be distracted by confusion."

"That makes everything clear," I said. "You don't mind if I scream?"

"I'll come along with you," he said. "Todt thought that the progress made by the human race wasn't really made by us at all. It was spoon-fed to us, along with our systems of money and trade and politics, by the Delfs. If Man could invent something himself that would ruin a Delf-created system, then Todt argued the Delfs' attention would be distracted. They would be intrigued and annoyed. They would forget their administration of other things—like Time. And Time, not being administered, would stop."

I lit another cigarette from the butt of the first. "It gets screwier and screwier!"

"Todt informed me confidentially he'd discovered a distraction and he was going to announce it in his lecture," Kessell went on. "He didn't have time—somebody murdered him first."

"You don't have any idea what this distraction was?"

"No, unfortunately."

"Maybe he was going to show them Marilyn Monroe?"

"I doubt it," Kessell grinned again. "That idea could make sense—Todt never would have thought of anything as logical as that."

I grunted. "Apart from the Delfs—you know anything else about Todt?"

"He was harmless. He lectured at a small university some place. He kept his theories for the S.F. conventions, so the people in his hometown probably thought he was sane all through!"

"Thanks," I said. "Do you have any theories about why he was murdered?"

"Sure!" he said.

"Let's have it."

"If his distraction would work," Kessell said slowly with a deadpan face, "and the Delfs found out what he was up to ... maybe they killed him to stop him!"

I got on to my feet and scowled at him. "Very funny!"

"You asked me!" he chuckled.

I went out of his room and down the corridor. I was going to have a drink—six drinks. Delfs! I got up to my room and poured the first drink and drank it. I was pouring a second when there came a knock on the door. I yelled to come in and the door opened.

Nicky Spain walked in, a polite smile on his face.

"You were looking for me earlier, Lieutenant?"

"Yeah—where were you?"

"The Golden Goose. You want witnesses?"

"What time did you get there?"

"Around eight, I guess."

"Where were you before that?"

"Downstairs in the bar. For about an hour."

"And before that?"

"In my room."

"With Carlotta Chavez and Lazy Rivers—of course."

"Of course," he said blandly.

I started to drink my second drink. "How's the second-hand automobile racket these days?"

"Booming."

"But not in Detroit, huh?"

"I don't follow you, Lieutenant"

I sighed: "You aren't a second-hand auto dealer, not in Detroit, anyway. You never have been."

"I'm sorry," he said. "I meant that as a joke. I thought you realised that."

"I'm just a dumb cop," I said, "liable to throw the book at a witness who gives false evidence."

"What did I witness?"

"The hell with that! Where do you really come from?"

"All over. I move around the country a great deal. I have a permanent residence in Palm Springs, but I'm only there a couple of months of each year."

"What do you do for a living?"

"I am an investor."

"In what?"

"Anything that looks profitable. Anything at all I think can make money."

"You have the dough to invest?"

"Half a million capital," he said. "If you have any spare cash, Lieutenant, I'd be happy to turn it over for you and make a quick profit!"

"Five bucks," I said. "What does it get me—a piece of the Empire State Building?"

He took a cigar out of his top pocket and unwrapped the cellophane carefully. "I heard about the house detective. A terrible thing!"

"Yeah—he's dead."

"Any ideas why, Lieutenant?"

"No."

"Oh. I wondered ... the second murder coming so quickly after the first ..."

"Don't let it keep you awake nights," I told him.

"Definitely not." he smiled. "I let Carlotta do that."

He walked out of the room closing the door gently behind him. I thought he was a nice guy and he'd look even nicer stretched out on a slab in the morgue. And if he kept on giving me unorthodox answers I'd see to it that was where he wound up!

And I poured myself another drink.

And another tap on the door. Flavia walked in.

"I didn't have time to thank you for playing my discs," she said. "I enjoyed it very much, Al."

"Fine," I said.

"Have you ... found out anything about the second murder yet?" she asked anxiously.

"Only that it happened."

"It's dreadful, simply dreadful!"

"It breaks my heart too."

"Am I intruding?"

"On what? Sit down—pour yourself a drink."

She did both.

"You know about the Delfs that will get you if you don't watch out?" I asked her. "That Time is myth and if we can stick Marilyn Monroe out into space somewhere the Delfs can get a good look they'll be so distracted that Time will go kerplunk! And we'll all live forever, except the guys who get run over in California!"

She smiled: "Who told you all about this?"

"Kessell."

"Poor Professor Todt!" she said. "He really believed it all you know."

"You think it was a Delf got worried that Professor was on the ball and knocked him off. Threw a dart all the way from somewhere the other side of the Milky Way?"

She laughed: "It sounds wonderful doesn't it?"

"I can see the Commissioner dying laughing," I said. "After he shot me first."

"Can I help in any way?" she asked seriously.

"Sure you can. I'd like to look at your records of the people attending the convention."

"Right now?"

"What better time?"

"I'll get them and bring them up."

She went out again. The phone rang and I answered it.

"Lavers. What progress?" a voice barked in my ear.

"Wheeler. None!" I barked back then hung up smartly.

I thought if anybody deserved the Delfs it was Commissioner Lavers!

Flavia came back ten minutes later carrying a portable filing cabinet with her. I could tell it was portable because she was carrying it. She put it on the table and I flipped the lid open and started to take out the papers inside.

"Do you mind if I stay and watch you work?" she asked.

"Why not? You can refill the glasses when they get low."

After an hour or so, I'd read all the dope she'd got on S. F. fans attending the convention. Names, home addresses, occupations, and whether they were attending their first convention or not.

"Would you know anybody that Todt was going to lecture at this convention?" I asked Flavia.

She shook her head: "No, the only name we plugged, was the only one that would mean anything—Wilbur Kessell."

"Then the first-timers at the convention would have no idea the Professor would be there?"

"I don't see how they could."

"Working on the theory that the murder was premeditated," I said, "That means we should be able to subtract the names of the first-timers."

I went through the papers again and weeded out forty-two. That narrowed the suspects down to thirty-eight. We still had enough for a ball game.

"Who else would have known the Professor, other than yourself?" I went on and answered my own question before she had a chance to get a word in. "Kessel would. Annabelle Starr did, and that probably means Lipcheek did, if he follows Annabelle around. We've got Spain and his dame and his tough boy. You—but you don't count. You were standing beside the Prof when he was killed so you couldn't have done it and you had the best alibi a girl can have for the time Dexter was killed."

"What's that?" she asked interestedly.

"You were with me," I said complacently. "Which proves that cops have their usefulness at times!"

I went through the thirty-five names again. "Who's this character Rocko Jones! Never missed a convention in the last ten years!"

"He's an S.F. fanatic," she said.

"He'd know the Prof okay?"

"Well, I would say. Rocko hasn't missed a convention in ten years either. I don't think he lives for any other reason than S.F. conventions."

"If I felt that way I would cut my throat!" I muttered.

"You're just biased about something you know nothing about!"

"From ear to ear!"

"You're not human—just humanoid!"

"Is that insulting?"

She sighed heavily. "It needs a moron's language to talk to a moron!"

"Pour me another drink," I said. "Just don't stand there having yourself a ball!"

She poured me another drink. I didn't see anyone else in the file who looked interesting. I made a note of Rocko Jones' room number, then put everything in the file and shut it.

"Thanks," I said "That was very helpful."

"A pleasure, Lieutenant."

"Al is the name."

"Thanks, Lieutenant Al."

"You should be in vaudeville," I said. "Or a cage!"

"I have been," she said sweetly.

"What?"

"In a cage."

"At what zoo?"

"It wasn't a zoo! Some people call them penthouses."

1 raised an eye-brow. "And he wouldn't let you out? Can't say I hold that against the guy."

"It wasn't that. I just don't like being possessed."

"Lady," I said, "this conversation is strictly for the birds!"

"Well," she said finally. "If you've finished with the file I'll take it back."

"Fine."

I poured myself another drink.

She hesitated for a moment. "There wasn't anything else you wanted any help with?"

"Not a thing, thanks."

"Oh."

She still didn't make a move to go.

"You lose something?" I asked her.

"No," she said. She turned around and walked towards the door. "Maybe I never had it."

After she had gone I had another three drinks and tried to forget about murder, the fact that I was a cop and wasn't getting any place towards finding the murderer.

I forgot all about blondes, brunettes and redheads for a time. The only thing I couldn't forget was those damned Delfs.

Brother, they really got me!

I might have rated as an unorthodox cop, but as a Time and no-motion exponent I was at a standstill. Maybe guys like Kessell and Todt could figure it—and brother they could have it!

Right then I had that feeling again. Maybe if I opened a window I'd see the moon heading back towards the horizon from which it had come. Maybe a crowd of Delfs would be playing pinochle on a cloud—with one Al Wheeler as the stake.

I tried the whisky bottle again, but it offered little solace.

I had one for the long bed, and then went to bed. The ceiling spun a couple of times and I sat up quickly. It steadied down again and I watched it carefully for a while until I was sure I had it under control then I lay my head back onto the pillow again.

Boing!

It was getting monotonous. I closed my eyes tight and tried to ignore it. Sometime, I must have fallen asleep.

CHAPTER 3
The Solid Gold Buck!

The ceiling was still whirling around and around.

"Cut in the artificial gravity!" a curt voice said.

A moment later the ceiling stopped spinning. I found myself sitting down. I looked out of the porthole beside me and saw a small orange rapidly falling away behind us.

"Earth," the voice said succinctly.

I thought I recognised the voice. I turned around and had a look at its owner. I was right, it was Flavia Romberg. She was wearing a tunic of some shimmering metallic material which fell from her shoulders to the top of her thighs. She was wearing a sort of plastic-bubble helmet.

"What are you wearing that thing for?" I asked her.

She took it off quickly. "Silly of me! I forgot I was wearing it."

"Where are we going?"

"To see the Delfs of course."

"How far is it?"

"About three billion miles as the spaceship flies. We'll cut into hyper-drive in a minute."

"Into what?"

"A time-warp, silly! Anyone would think you'd never taken a short cut across the universe before!"

"Yeah," I said. "Imagine that."

The ceiling swung violently again and everything blurred.

When things settled down again, I looked out of the porthole and saw nothing. A sort of darkness. I hastily looked back inside the spaceship.

Flavia smiled brightly at me. "Out of the time-warp now. Only half a million miles to go!"

"Do I have time for a cigarette?"

"Is that supposed to be funny?" she asked coldly.

"Isn't all this supposed to be funny?"

"This is S.F.!" she said, her voice a clarion-call. "And science fiction is never funny!"

Then the ceiling spun again and everything, even including Flavia's long, tanned legs that contrasted so nicely with the metallic shimmer of her tunic, wavered and became blurred.

When things cleared again the spaceship was motionless. "What are we waiting for?" I asked hoarsely.

"The Delfs," she said. "What else?"

"How can we stay still in Space like this?"

"It's Time!" she said excitedly. "It's stopped."

"Huh?"

"The Delfs have been distracted, don't you see? That was the whole reason for bringing you along on the trip. The Delfs have never seen an unorthodox cop before. They wouldn't believe any human could have an I.Q. of minus eight and still live. They all want to come and look at you!"

I tried to figure out whether that was a compliment or not. I gave up. "How long before the Delfs arrive?"

"You can't say that, silly!"

"Can't say what?"

"How long—there isn't any time now—it's stopped."

"Yeah," I said vaguely.

"It doesn't make any difference now," she went on determinedly. "If they come in five minutes or five hundred years. Don't you see! Time has stopped!"

I looked at the watch on my wrist. Sure enough it had stopped. "What do the Delfs look like?" I asked her.

"Like Delfs—what else?"

"I should ask a question like that!"

We sat in silence for no time at all.

"Here they come!" she said suddenly.

There was a noise like oysters moving in their shells, only louder. The porthole opened and in came three of them. They had furry bodies and they walked on six stalks. They had fifteen arms on each side of their bodies and each arm ended in a flower which spread its tendrils enquiringly. They had heads like squashed oranges and their eyes were on eight-foot long stalks. They had three eyes apiece. They made a shrill shrieking noise which I presumed was conversation.

Flavia looked at them disgustedly. "Shoo!" She waved her arms at them. "Shoo! Go on! Get out of here!"

They shrieked shrilly at her but they got. I mopped my face with a damp handkerchief. "Delfs!"

"Delfs!" she said scornfully. "They weren't Delfs—only bug-eyed monsters!"

"What do Delfs look like?"

"You'll see when they come."

We sat around for no minutes more. Then there was a ringing noise.

"Here they come!" Flavia said excitedly.

I looked out of the porthole again. Seven little dwarfs came bouncing along through nothing towards the ship. The ringing noise was getting louder and louder.

"Hi-ho, hi-ho," the dwarfs sang lustily. "It's off to limbo we go ..."

I turned away and looked at Flavia blankly. Her tunic had disappeared and in its place she was wearing some clinging garment that swathed her from head to foot. Its colour was snow-white....

"I get it!" I said. "It's Grumpy and Sneezy and Dopey and ..."

"Mirror, mirror on the wall," she said in ringing tones, looking straight at me, "who is ..."

The ring in her voice grew louder and louder, drowning out the words. The whole scene blurred and dissolved gradually, breaking up into fragments of cotton that rang and rang and ...

I opened my eyes and saw sunlight streaming in through the window. The phone on the table beside the bed still rang insistently. I picked up the receiver and held it to my ear.

"Who you got in there with you!" a curt voice demanded.

"Sneezy and Grumpy and Dopey and ..."

"Dopey!" the voice snarled. "Who the hell do you think you're talking to, Wheeler!"

"I'm not sure," I said doubtfully. "Maybe you're Snow White or maybe a Delf or maybe just a bug-eyed monster."

"Bug-eyed ...!" His voice strangled itself for one peaceful moment, then came back at top force. "Listen, Wheeler! This is Lavers speaking, as if you didn't know! I've just about stood enough! You get down to my office right away!" He slammed the phone down like always.

I staggered out of bed and looked at myself in the mirror. I didn't have to ask that mirror on the wall real loud. It told me more than I wanted to know just by looking. For sure, I was the foulest in the land!

I crept into the shower, then had a shave, brushed my teeth and got dressed. I thought about breakfast, shuddered and tried to forget about it. I drove the Healey up to City Hall.

By the look on Lavers' face when I got into his office, he thought that somebody had returned the garbage.

"Still feeling witty, Wheeler!" he thundered.

"I'm not feeling anything," I told him and sank into a chair. "I'm numb!"

He scowled at me. "I hate to bother you over a trifling matter like two murders, but what progress are you making ... Dopey!"

I winced: "Well, it's kind of complicated, Commissioner and ..."

"What progress!"

"Not much. There's no motive for anybody bumping off the Professor except maybe the Delfs ..."

"The what!"

"They're something he dreamed up."

"He dreamed up? Where from?"

"Outside our universe. They control everything and he was trying to figure out a way of distracting them so Time would stop and then ..."

"Are you sick?"

I shook my head feebly. "Nothing more than a combination of hangover and nightmare—I hope. These science fiction boys and girls have got me going nuts and that's the truth! Bug-eyed monsters—Delfs—time-warps—planetoids. They're out of this world, and that's nothing but the truth!"

"Apart from leering at blondes and getting drunk," he said heavily. "Have you done anything else?"

"If I could get a line on motive," I said, "Then maybe I could get somewhere."

"You'd better hurry," he said grimly. "Their convention finishes today, doesn't it?"

"Tonight."

"They all expect to go home tomorrow—the whole eighty of them. I don't know who's going to pay their hotel bills if we force them to stay! The City can't afford it—not and pay salaries to people like you and me as well!"

He scowled down at his desk. "Hanlon's been doing some of the routine work I knew you'd forget. Professor Todt wasn't quite so lilywhite as we imagined."

"What did he do—park in front of a fire-hydrant once?"

"There are times ..." Lavers shook his head. "That's not true—it's all the time. Every time I see you, talk to you, I want to stave in your head with a blunt axe!"

He rustled the papers on his desk. "Professor Todt took his degrees only twelve years ago. He was then a reformed character apparently."

"What did he have to reform about?"

"He had a record. He did two years in the State Penitentiary in Illinois. Con-man, swindler would be a more accurate word for it. Took a bunch of farmers for a ride to the tune of twenty-five thousand dollars."

"How?"

Lavers swallowed twice. "They must have been hick farmers. Believe it or not—a fake rain-making machine!"

"Oh, no!"

"One for Ripley. But they bought the rights to the machine for thirty thousand. They got shrewd before they paid over the dough and beat him down to twenty-five. Todt was picked up three months later living a life of luxury in Palm Springs. But when he came out of the pen he reformed. Worked his way through college and got his degrees. The quiet life on the campus until the day before yesterday."

"I'd better check the list of S.F. fans again and have a look at the farmers," I said.

"I can't see any of them waiting twelve years to get him," he said. "But maybe the Professor wasn't quite so strongly on the straight and narrow as he appeared to be."

"Thanks," I said. "Anything else?"

"Yes."

He opened his drawer and took something out. "When they took his clothes off at the morgue and checked them, they found a secret pocket at the back of his jacket. This was in it." He tossed it across to me and I caught it automatically.

It was a gold-coloured coin. Big like a silver dollar.

"What is it—paint?"

Lavers shook his head: "That's the genuine article—solid gold."

"What the hell would he want with that?"

"That's your problem."

"Yeah," I said unenthusiastically.

"We've got until tomorrow morning around eleven at the latest," he said. "Then we'll have to let these people go home. You've got another twenty-four hours, Wheeler, to produce some results. And if you don't you're going back to a precinct, and not as a Lieutenant. I've let you hang around here doing nothing, waiting for something like this to turn up. If you can't handle it, I don't think it fair for me to waste any more of the City's money in keeping you here. Okay?"

"If I say no," I said gently, "does it make any difference?"

"None!"

"Then it's okay. If I get fired from being a cop I can always make a living selling rain-making machines in Illinois!"

"You kill me!" Lavers said. "And ten minutes of your twenty-four hours have gone by already.”

I looked down at the gold coin in my hand. “I'd like to hang onto this for a while—okay?”

“Okay,” he said. “But try and hock it and I'll ...”

“I know,” I said. “You always do.”

I left the Commissioner's office, left City Hall and went down to the Homicide Bureau. Hanlon was sitting in his office looking nice and bright and fresh and unworried.

“How are things with you, Al?” he smiled happily at me. “Having fun with the blaster-pistols?”

“If I had one with me right now I'd have fun with it,” I told him. “I'd disintegrate your body and use your head as a doorstop! And that would be the first time it ever had a use!”

“Lavers has been talking to you again,” he said smugly. “I can tell!”

I sat down and lit a cigarette. I took the gold coin out of my pocket and tossed it up in the air and caught it again, a couple of times. “You see this?” I asked him.

“Sure—what do you make of it?”

“Maybe he was saving up for his old age.”

“He was quite a guy with that rain-making machine,” Hanlon grinned. “No wonder his wife quit.”

“Wife?”

“Sure, didn't you know about her?”

I made an effort and didn't scream. “Tell me more,” I said. “I admit I'm only the guy who's supposed to be handling the case, but stretch a point, huh?”

Hanlon didn't even blush. “He had a month's vacation two years ago—got married in New York. Girl by the name of Mabel Hertz. The marriage lasted most of two weeks. When he went back to the campus, he went on his own. Nobody at the university knew he was married. It was one of the things we stumbled on—you know how it is. His wife swore a complaint against him the first week they were married that he threatened her life. She was going to charge him then changed her mind. New York had a record of it. He must have been quite a guy.”

“Whatever happened to Mabel?”

“There you got me.”

“No divorce?”

“Not that we can trace.”

“With a name like Mabel, she probably changed it,” I said. “She probably calls herself Myrtle now.”

“We'll probably never know,” Hanlon said. “Anyway the newspapers will have let her know she's a widow. She might turn up hoping he left her something."

"If she's a dame—and I take it she is even if her name's Mabel—she'll catch the first rocket."

"That's the way I figure it, Al."

"And maybe she'll be dead right to come."

"You mean ..."

"The solid gold buck!" I flipped the coin up into the air again. "Any more vital information you might have forgotten to tell me?"

"Not that I recall."

I got onto my feet. "Okay, junior!"

"Expecting to make an arrest soon, Al?" he asked as I reached the door.

"Sure," I said. "Any time now. Once I cut the hyper-drive and I'm finished with the time-warp, there's nothing can stop me!"

"Uh?" he said in a dazed voice.

"In S.F. circles, brother," I told him. "You'd be known as a square!"

CHAPTER 4
Love In The Afternoon

I got back to the hotel in time to have lunch. I was beginning to feel a little better. The food was taking care of my hangover.

I walked into an elevator and Nicky Spain came in behind me followed by Carlotta and Lazy Rivers.

"Caught your murderer yet, Lieutenant?" Spain asked politely.

"Not yet," I said.

"This guy," Rivers said, leering at me. "He couldn't catch a cold!"

I looked him up and down. He was wearing another two-hundred dollar suit. "Didn't they teach you any manners," I said to him, "not even the last time you were in Alcatraz!"

His face darkened but before he had a chance to say anything the elevator stopped at their floor. Spain got out first, followed by Carlotta. Rivers started forward and I saw the glint in his eye. His foot stomped down heavily where my instep should have been, but I saw it coming a moment forward and moved my own foot quickly. I stomped down my own foot on his instep and he yelped with the pain. Instinctively he bent down to massage it. I put the flat of my hand against his face and pushed sharply. He staggered backwards out of the elevator and landed flat on his back.

The elevator-boy gaped at me, open-mouthed.

"Up!" I said gently, and a moment later the doors slid together smoothly and the elevator took me up to my own floor. I remembered after a quick Scotch as a hair of the super-sonic dog from outer space, that I had wanted to talk to Rocko Jones, so I went to look for him. But I didn't get there. I bumped into Annabelle Starr. Literally. I came around a corner in the corridor fast as she was coming the other way. We collided and I grabbed her to save her falling over. Well, that was my story, anyway.

"Why don't you ..." She stopped suddenly and smiled. "It's you, Lieutenant!"

"Yeah," I said, "and it's you, too. The world is full of coincidence!"

"Isn't it?"

I still held her tight.

"Thank you for saving me from falling over."

"It was a pleasure."

"But I'm all right now." She looked down at my arms encircling her. "So you can ..."

"You can never be sure," I said earnestly. "When the reaction sets in you might keel over," I snapped my fingers. "Just like that!"

"Oh!" she looked at me interestedly. "How can I tell when the reaction starts?"

"I'll show you," I said. "Close your eyes." She closed her eyes obediently. "Relax!"

She relaxed and sagged gently against me. I kissed her firmly on her full lips and after a while she stopped relaxing and took a positive interest in the procedure. Maybe we would still have been there only the elevator opened and half a dozen people got out and then decided they didn't have any place to go anyway. So they just stood around and looked at us.

I stopped kissing her. She still leaned against me, her eyes closed.

"How do you feel?" I asked her.

"Weak," she said. "Trembling at the knees, agitated pulse."

"You see!" I told her triumphantly. "Reaction!"

I looked over her shoulder at the circle of interested faces about a foot away. "All right, folks," I said crisply. "Show's over! No more matinees this week. Drop around in the evenings, you might be lucky and get a repeat!"

They broke up slowly and wandered away. All except one of them. I recognised him vaguely. Lipcheek. The fat boy.

"What are you waiting for—an encore?" I asked him.

He smiled pleasantly: "I was just interested," he said. "I wondered why you were kissing my girl?"

"The same reasons you kiss her," I said. "Only I guess mine are more virile!"

Annabelle broke away out of my arms and looked at him coldly. "What do you want, Waldo?"

"The last lecture of the convention is due to start in ten minutes," he said.

"Wilbur Kessell. I thought we'd better get down there and get a decent seat."

"You go on down," she said, "I won't be long."

He hesitated for a moment, then shrugged his shoulders. "Okay. Don't be long, though."

He walked over and pressed the elevator button. "How's the investigation going, Lieutenant?"

"Just fine," I said. "I'm discovering something new all the time."

The elevator doors opened. He turned away. "On second thoughts, I think I'll …"

I put my hand on his chest and pushed. He gave the appearance of walking backwards rapidly into the elevator. The boy gaped at me, open-mouthed. "Down!" I said gently and the doors snapped shut.

I turned back to Annabelle. "Now—where were we?" I put my arms around her. "Somewhere about here, as I remember?"

"Not in the corridor," she said. "Or if it has to be in the corridor, shouldn't we charge an admission fee?"

"I have some beautiful Scotch in my room," I said. "We could go and have a drink."

"I should go to the lecture …" she said doubtfully. "Waldo will be keeping a chair for me."

"Let him sit on both of them," I suggested. "He'll be more comfortable that way. Anyway, I've got a lot of questions to ask you and I hate to remind you that as a Lieutenant of Police, I …"

"All right," she said, "we'll have a drink."

We got up into my room and as soon as I'd closed the door I took her into my arms again. She broke clear by the simple expedient of giving me a jolt in the solar plexus with her clenched fist. For a fragile-looking blonde she certainly packed a punch.

"Questions," she said, "and a drink."

"You've changed since a couple of floors back!" I protested.

"Just give girl time to get her breath," she said. She sat down and crossed her legs. The hem of the black sheath she was wearing rode up over her knees. They were nice knees, they had dimples.

"You know," she said, "you could pour us a drink and still look at my legs."

"You should pull your skirt down," I said severely, "and stop seducing policemen from their duty!"

"I can't," she said composedly. "This dress is built on the Jayne Mansfield model—it's built to stand up in, not sit down in."

"Then why don't you stand up?"

"Because you'll grab me again if I do."

"That's a reason for sitting down?"

"Please," she said. "All you have to do is get the bottle and a glass, tilt the bottle so that the Scotch runs out into the glass, add a little ice and ..."

"I get the picture," I said gloomily. "All you want is a drink."

"I really shouldn't be here at all," she said. "Waldo will be worried."

"You're worried about Waldo being worried!"

I poured the Scotch, gave her a glass and sat opposite her, nursing my own glass. "You couldn't take a guy like Waldo seriously, could you?"

"What's wrong with Waldo?"

"Well, he's fat and he's a slob and ... well ..."

She looked at me critically. "You're not so hot in the daylight, you know, pal! Your face looks like somebody trod on it and those muscles will all run to fat pretty soon and you've got an irritating conceit ..." She shrugged her shoulders impatiently. "Oh, I'll admit there's a certain huskiness that may have some appeal, but the general picture," she shook her head, "it's not good!"

"Well, okay!" I said. "And if it comes to that! Take away your blonde hair, your beautiful face and your terrific figure and you're not so hot, any-way!"

She smiled: "Now you're kidding me!"

"I never kid a beautiful blonde," I said. "Or I never kid them about their beauty, anyway. The rest is a matter of luck and judgment."

She sipped her drink. "What about these questions?"

I took the golden buck and handed it to her. "Ever seen that before?"

She looked at it curiously. "No—what is it?"

"Solid gold. Todt had it on him when he was killed."

She shuddered and handed it back to me quickly. "It gives me the creeps, thinking about that."

"Yeah," I said, "it's tough!" I put the dollar back into my pocket. "I found the evil-faced guy you told me about. Name of Nicky Spain."

Annabelle looked interested. "Did you find out what they were arguing about?"

"Sure."

"What was it?"

"Relativity."

"What!"

"That's what Spain says. I can't argue with him."

There was a knock on the door. I opened it and Lipcheek pushed past me into the room. "Here you are!" he said. "Well, we've missed the lecture now! I couldn't keep the seats any longer so ..."

I tapped him on the shoulder. He turned around and glared at me.

"This is my room, chum," I told him. "I don't like people busting into it.”

"I came to …”

"You can skip the sordid detail,” I said. “I’m busy—out!”

He glared at Annabelle again, glared at me and then went out. “If you’re thinking of marrying him,” I told her, “my advice is don’t.”

"Who asked your advice?”

"It’s just for your own good. He’ll go to work in the morning and sneak back around eleven to see how long the iceman takes to deliver the ice! Comes the baker’s delivery and he’ll be inside the van with a pair of binoculars just to make sure the only thing you get is bread. The washing-machine breaks down and he’ll electrocute himself trying to fix it rather than take a chance on letting a serviceman into the house. If there’s a fire he won’t call out the firemen in case a helmet does something to you … if …”

She finished her drink and stared frigidly at me. “I thought you wanted to ask me some questions?”

"So I did. Another drink?”

She held the glass out. I took it and refilled it, gave it back to her. “Thank you,” she said. “Of all the self-opinionated, conceited, smug little jerks I have ever met …”

"That’s what I’ve been trying to say!” I broke in quickly. “Waldo Lipcheek is rock bottom! Even a clam would open up and scream if it saw Waldo on a clear day!”

For a moment I thought I was going to get her Scotch back—in my face, but suddenly she started to laugh. “You are the most impossible Lieutenant I ever met!” she said, her shoulders still shaking.

"And how many lieutenants have you met?”

She didn’t answer right away. Finally, “You’re the first.”

"Well, there you are! You know absolutely nothing about Lieutenants. Not cop lieutenants, anyway.”

She smile shyly. “But I’m willing to learn, Lieutenant”

"Then you’ve come to the right Lieutenant,” I said.

"I thought I had,” she whispered.

She came to the right lieutenant, physically, then. I put one arm around her, nestled her against my chest. She sighed.

"You forgotten about Waldo?” I said.

"He’s fat and he’s a slob,” she murmured.

"Honey, you say the sweetest things,” I said.

I walked over to the window and closed the blinds carefully.

"What are you doing?” she asked.

"Love in the afternoons,” I said carefully, “is for guys like Hemingway!”

I walked back across the darkened room to where she sat. For a moment she just looked at me without saying anything, then she handed me her glass. "You'd better put that down somewhere," she said in a small voice, "otherwise I might spill it."

I put the glass down on the table and turned back towards her. She came out of the chair and into my arms, her hands gripping my forearms. "How did you know?" she whispered. "How did you pick me so easily?"

"Honey," I said. "A girl who looks the way you look has to be impulsive otherwise she'd let her hair grow straight, wear dark glasses and get a job in a public library!"

"You know something?" she whispered. "That's the nicest way I've ever been called a tramp!"

CHAPTER 5
Lazy Rivers Flow Deep

Around six I left the room with the mingled scent of Scotch and 4711 cologne still hanging around and went down to pay a call on my old friend Nicky. Annabelle had left some fifteen minutes before. I never had asked her all those questions. One of the troubles with asking questions is that you have to think them up first. It's the toughest part of being a cop.

The door opened and it was Carlotta. This time she was wearing a jade green robe and from the way it fitted, nothing underneath. A black dragon arched across the front of it, spitting fire just under her left shoulder. If I ever got that close to her I'd do the same, I figured.

"You!" she said, which is a hell of a conversational gambit.

"I want to learn to play the Spanish guitar," I said. "Nicky home?"

"He's here."

"That's fine." I walked past her into the room.

Nicky was also clad in a robe—a scarlet silk robe—and he was smoking a cigar and sitting comfortably reading a book with a glass perched on the arm of his chair. He looked like one of those business tycoons you see in the ads. You know the guy—he owes everything he's got to the simple fact that come hell or high weather he always smokes the same brand of cigarettes. The ones that are good for your throat or good for your chest or good for social prestige or good for practically anything except smoking.

Rivers had his back to me, and was staring out of the window as I came in. He turned around and his eyes glittered as he looked at me. "The tough cop!" he said.

"Relax, jailbait," I told him. "I'm here to talk to the grown-ups!"

Spain shut his book carefully, took another pull on his cigar and looked at me. "You wanted something, Lieutenant?"

"Yeah." I took the gold buck out of my pocket and tossed it in the air a couple of times. There was a strangled exclamation from Rivers. I looked at him. "You say something?"

He shook his head. "No," his voice slurred slightly. "I coughed."

I tossed the coin to Spain who caught it automatically and looked at it. "Very interesting, Lieutenant," he said carefully. "What is it?"

"I thought you'd tell me."

"I'd say it was silver dollar except that it's gold in colour." He hefted it in his hand thoughtfully. "Looks like real gold!"

"It is."

His eyebrows lifted: "Really?"

"Todt had it with him when he was murdered," I said. "The idea hit me that maybe it was the gold buck you were arguing about with him and not Einstein after all."

He shook his head. "No, Lieutenant. Relativity was the subject. You know he had a fixation about a people he called the Delfs?"

"Don't give me that again!" I said hastily. "I know all about it—Time being stopped by a distraction—the whole works!"

"I was just trying to point out the absurdity of the whole theory to him," Nicky said smoothly. "We got a little heated in argument, that was all ..."

"Yeah," I said. "That's what you told me before. Okay."

There didn't seem any point in sticking around there much longer. Spain looked bland, Carlotta bored and Rivers hostile.

"Okay," I said and left.

I got back to my room and found somebody waiting for me. A redhead in a nylon shirt and dark skirt.

"Hi, Flavia," I said.

"I wanted to have a talk to you," she said. She sniffed deeply. "How long have you been using 4711?"

"Ever since my best friends told me," I told her. She sniffed again. "The convention's over. There are eighty people here who want to leave tomorrow. What are you going to do about them?"

"That's quite a question," I said. "And it makes me feel sick trying to figure out an answer. I need a drink. Will you have a drink?"

"Yes," she said.

I made us a drink. I took out the solid gold buck and showed it to her. "Make anything out of that?"

She looked at it curiously: "Is it real?"

"Real gold? Sure!"

"Where did you get it?"

"The Prof had it hidden away in his coat, in a secret pocket no less!"

"Why?"

"That's what I'm trying to find out."

"Maybe he really was crazy?"

"Maybe he was," I said wearily. "But not that crazy he could split himself in half and have one half give a lecture while the other half shot a tungsten dart into the first half and killed both of them!"

"I don't think sarcasm is very funny," she said.

"I'll make a note of it," I told her.

"What am I going to tell the rest of them?"

"That I'll let 'em know in the morning what's happening."

"All right—if you can't do any better than that."

"I just can't."

The 'phone rang and I answered it. It was Hanlon and he sounded apologetic. "Al, I'm sorry. We had a report here yesterday which should have been turned over to you and wasn't."

"Let's have it."

"About Rivers."

"Yeah?"

"Real name is Jonathan Judd Rivers. He's got quite a record. He's a third-time loser, one more and they put him away for good."

"What was he convicted for?"

"Robbery with violence, assault, resisting arrest, carrying an unlicensed gun, using it ... mugging ... extortion ... you name it, we got it!"

"Thanks. Anything else?"

"No, Al. I'm sorry you didn't get that any earlier. How are things going?"

"Fine," I said, "just fine! I expect to make an arrest any time this century—if the murderer confesses. Anyway, Time is only a distraction, so there's no hurry."

"Huh?"

"Your trouble is you're just a square!" I said. "A Delf left on the shelf—a humanoid on a planetoid with no hyper-drive left to arrive. A bug-eyed monster without a sponsor! A..."

"Are you feeling okay, Al?" he asked worriedly.

"No," I said. "But don't worry. I'm not likely to get better!" I hung up then before I started telling him about pixies at the bottom of my Scotch bottle.

Flavia looked at me concernedly. "This is beginning to get you down, Al!"

"Not me," I said, "but it's playing hell with the Delfs!" I drained the glass and poured myself another drink. "You got any more troubles?"

"Only personal ones."

"You keep 'em, honey," I said. "I got plenty of my own!"

"It's Wilbur Kessell," she said slowly. "He wants me to have a drink with him tonight—in his room. And the look in his eyes when he invited me ...

do you think I should go?"

"That boy and girl business doesn't concern you, does it?" I said. "Sure—you go. You can have yourself a time talking S.F. and devil take the extraterrestrial!"

"You don't care if I do go?"

"Frankly," I said, "I don't care if you go to Mars and get a job there sweeping the canals! I have, I repeat, enough troubles of my own—quote, unquote!"

"Thanks, Al," she said stiffly. "You're a great help!" She went out, slamming the door behind her with what I considered unnecessary violence.

I had another drink and thought about things. I thought that so far I might just as well be starting all over on the case. I also thought that Lavers kept thrusting this unorthodox business down my throat and maybe it was about time I started being unorthodox.

And what better time was there to start being unorthodox than right now?

I rang down to the reception desk and told them to tell one of the cops on the door to come up. He arrived five minutes later. A thin, unhappy-looking character by the name of Steinbeck. I asked him if he was any relation to John and he said he had a brother called John who was a plumber. I let it lie there.

I told him to bring Rivers up to the room, then wait outside. Another five minutes and Rivers arrived. He walked in, his hands thrust deep into his pockets with a scowl on his face. Steinbeck delivered him, then went outside as he'd been told. I told Rivers to sit down and then lit a cigarette, taking my time over it.

"What do you want with me?" Rivers asked.

"I'm arresting you," I said easily.

"What!" He sat bolt upright. "What the hell for?"

"Murder," I said, "two murders, to be precise."

"You're crazy!"

"I don't think so."

He half rose out of the chair then changed his mind and sank back again. "You're nuts! I got an alibi!"

"You know how much an alibi is worth—particularly an alibi supplied by Spain and Carlotta?" I snapped my fingers. "Not that much!"

"You won't pin this on me!"

I sighed gently: "You keep on talking but you aren't saying much, are you?"

"What do you mean?"

"You know cops," I said. "You ought to by now—you, a third-time loser! You got a record so long it would take six hours to play on a phonograph!

How will that sound in court? I don't know whether you killed Todt and then Dexter or not. I don't care very much. I got to make an arrest—you're it!"

"I'll get a mouthpiece!" he shouted. "I'll get the best mouthpiece in the country! I'll ..."

"Finish up in the chair! You got no chance of dodging this one, Rivers! No chance at all. We can make it look good and we will. Who's going to believe a third-time loser? You're just the sort of break a cop always looks for in a tough case. You're the fall guy because you're a natural for the job!" I shook my head. "I could almost feel sorry for you, Rivers!"

He lit himself a cigarette and his fingers shook slightly as he did so. "Cops!" He threw in a lot of nasty adjectives after the word.

"Have yourself a ball," I said. "But it doesn't make any difference, Rivers. We need a patsy for this one—and you're it!"

"Now wait a minute!"

"What for?"

He moistened his lips. "Look, Lieutenant. I'm only a stooge for Nicky, see? He gets into some funny deals at times and he needs a strong-arm around. Me, I'm just the strong-arm. I don't know nothing!"

"That's your trouble," I said. "You don't know nothing. That's what makes you just the guy for us!"

He tried again: "Nicky is the big shot! I'm just the stooge for him!"

"Sure," I said, "and you're just the stooge for me, too. You're the stooge who's going to take the rap!"

"Nicky has this big deal with the Professor character," he said. "I just come along because Nicky says to."

"Maybe you bump off the Prof just because Nicky says so?"

"No!"

I poured myself a drink. "I'm taking you in tomorrow morning, Rivers. Don't try and leave the hotel tonight—you won't make it!"

"Listen!" he pleaded. "You can't do this to me!"

"There's nothing to stop me, pal!" I told him. "Now get out of here— you're wasting my time!" I raised my voice. "Steinbeck!"

The cop came in and looked at me enquiringly. "See that Mr. Rivers gets back to his room and see he doesn't try and leave the hotel tonight."

"Yes, Lieutenant."

"Wheeler!" Rivers said desperately. "You can't ..."

"Now," I said to Steinbeck, who nodded, then grabbed Rivers' arm and escorted him out of the room.

I sipped my drink and waited.

Steinbeck came back. "Anything else, Lieutenant?"

"Sure," I said. "I want the girl, Carlotta Chavez. Bring her up here now."

Five minutes more and Carlotta arrived. She was wearing a scarlet top with a scoop-neckline and it looked like the scoop had been made with a dredge! She also wore a skin-tight pair of pants that came down to mid-calf. She shimmered as she walked. She had a cigarette in a long holder and a sullen look on her face. She looked like a schoolboy's version of a secret agent. I waved Steinbeck away and told Carlotta to sit down.

She sat down and puffed at her cigarette.

"Rivers cracked," I said easily. "He's a three-time loser. The next time he gets convicted of anything at all he goes into the pen and he stays there till they bury him. A guy with that sort of thing on his mind is open to persuasion."

She lifted her eyebrows slightly: "What has that to do with me, Lieutenant?"

"I thought you'd like to know," I said. "He bust wide open, told me the whole thing. Why the three of you are here, what Nicky was arguing about with Todt. The murders …"

"I don't understand," she said.

"He told me how you killed Todt under Nicky's instructions," I said. "He's made a full statement—he only signed it five minutes ago."

She laughed shortly: "You must have the vivid imagination, Lieutenant!"

"Will you skip giving me that phony Mexican accent?" I asked her. "Just because suntan makes you look that way, you don't have to speak it!"

"All right, wise guy!" she said.

I grinned at her: "I'll let you into a secret. All I'm interested in is getting a case against somebody—anybody. I clear my own alley then as long as my case will stand up in court. Rivers is scared to death and I don't blame him. Maybe it's true that you killed Todt and the hotel detective and maybe it isn't. I don't care. Rivers has made a statement saying it's you and that's good enough for me."

Her face tautened: "It's a lie! I did not kill either of them!"

"You'll have to do better than that," I said.

"Lazy is mad if he says I killed them!"

I yawned: "Excuse me for a minute." I got up and went outside, closing the door behind me. Steinbeck looked at me expectantly. "You want me, Lieutenant?"

"Sure. In a couple of minutes I want you to come in and say the squad-car's waiting downstairs. Then come out here again. And when I send the dame back downstairs I want you to go with her and get Spain. Bring him up here with you and make sure that he and the dame don't get a chance to talk."

"Okay, Lieutenant." He looked blank. "What's with this squad-car?"

"It's part of a game of imagination that I'm playing," I said. "It's about as real as that plumber brother of yours who writes books!"

I don't think that helped him much, either.

I went back inside to Carlotta. She was sitting there gnawing her lower lip and looking worried.

I sat down, picked up my glass and sipped some Scotch. Then I lit a cigarette.

"I don't know who you think you're kidding!" she said abruptly, "But I can tell you that ..."

There was a knock on the door and Steinbeck came in. "The squad-car's waiting downstairs, Lieutenant," he said.

"Thanks." I got onto my feet and looked at Carlotta. "Okay—let's go."

"Go? Where?"

"To Homicide, of course. I told you, I'm booking you on a double murder charge."

"But you can't!"

"Don't let's waste time," I said impatiently.

"Please!" she said frantically. "You've got to listen to me. I'll tell you what I know, but it isn't much! Please, listen!"

I waved Steinbeck outside again. "I'll give you two minutes, but it had better be good."

"I don't know much about it at all," she said. "But I don't see how Nicky or me, or even Lazy could have killed either of them. Nicky nearly went crazy when he heard the Professor was dead. He had a big deal with the Professor and I know that's what they were arguing about—the Professor put up his price when we got here, but Nicky was going to pay it. He didn't like it, but he was going to pay it!"

"What for?"

She shook her head helplessly. "I don't know what it was. Nicky said something about the Professor was a nut and anybody who refused a hundred and fifty thousand was crazy!"

"Refused what!"

"That's what Nicky said. I asked him what the money was for and he wouldn't tell me. He said I wouldn't understand and he didn't want me worrying about business matters anyway."

"What else?"

She shrugged her shoulders helplessly: "I don't know anything else, so help me, Lieutenant!"

"Okay," I said. "I'll check on that. Consider yourself lucky, Carlotta—I'm not going to book you tonight. But don't try and leave the hotel."

"I won't!" she said tearfully.

"Steinbeck!"

The cop came in on cue. "Cancel that car," I said with a straight face, "and take Miss Chavez back to her room—and bring Mr. Spain up here."

"Sure, Lieutenant."

After they'd gone I poured myself another drink. It looked like being a long night.

But it was broken right then by the 'phone ringing. I picked it up.

"Wheeler?"

"Lavers."

"Right. What progress?"

"Listen, don't you ever sleep?"

"What's that got to do with it?" he snarled.

"If you don't—maybe I could write a science fiction piece on it. About a cop who doesn't sleep, who goes on day after day, night after night ..."

"Shut up, Wheeler."

"Yes, sir."

"I was checking. Is there something against a Police Commissioner checking on his men?"

"Not a thing, sir."

"Okay. I'm going to bed."

He hung up. It certainly looked like being a long night.

CHAPTER 6
The Reign Of Spain

Nicky Spain looked slightly irritated when he came into the room. "Is this necessary, Lieutenant?"

"Yeah," I said. "Sit down."

He sat down and unwrapped a cigar from its cellophane tomb with loving care. "Yes?"

"Just a few facts," I said. "There's such a thing as a material witness, Nicky. There's also something that's known as withholding vital evidence. I can book you as a material witness. I've got written statements that prove you've been withholding vital evidence. That can bring quite a term in the pen."

He lit his cigar. "Just what are you talking about?"

"I'm talking about the deal you were trying to negotiate with Professor Todt," I said harshly. "The deal that was worth a hundred and fifty thousand dollars to you! The deal he upped his price on at the last moment so you had an argument about it in the corridor. The deal that seems to give you one hell of a good motive for his murder!"

"Oh," he said.

I looked at him carefully: "I'll tell you something else," I said almost gently. "These two murders have got coast-to-coast publicity. The gimmicks have been too good for the press to miss. Mysterious murder at a science fiction fans' convention. And that means the heat is on. We've got to find a murderer. I only have to book you as a material witness to get you down to the Homicide Bureau. Down there you'll be questioned—the boys are keen. It could be a painful business."

"And is that your intention—to take me down there?" he asked tautly.

"It depends on you, Nicky," I said. "You can be smart and talk now. Or you can talk down there. You please yourself, only make up your mind quickly. I don't have much time."

He puffed his cigar. "I am an intelligent man, Lieutenant—that, I suppose, is obvious!"

"I wouldn't bet on that," I said. "But don't let me interrupt you."

"I'll tell you about the deal," he said. "I see that I don't have any choice. You are using the unscrupulous methods that most police use to extort information and ..."

"Stop!" I said. "You're making me cry! The deal! I want to know the deal—you can skip the lecture on cops. I've heard that before."

"All right," he said.

I even poured him a drink and handed it to him. He inclined his head in thanks, which was very nice of him indeed.

"Do you know what alchemy is, Lieutenant?" he asked abruptly.

"Rings a vague bell," I said. "Sort of medieval science, wasn't it?"

"That's correct. The alchemists were the forerunners of the scientists. They had certain beliefs, all of them erroneous as we now know. One of those beliefs was the existence of the philosopher's stone. The major power of that stone was the transformation of base metals into gold."

"What's this got to do with the deal with Todt?"

"Quite a lot."

He tapped ash from his cigar onto the floor. "You have heard of Todt's obsession with these imaginary beings, the Delfs?"

"Don't let us go through that again!"

"I'm afraid we have to—briefly. As you know, his theory was that if only the Delfs could be distracted, then Time would stop and if that happened, Todt's theory of the Delfs controlling our universe would be proved." Spain smiled thinly. "Todt didn't stop to consider what would happen to the world if Time did stop, he was only concerned with proving his theory. The Delfs could only be districted by some apparently impossible achievement by Man. That is, if Man did something from his own efforts unaided by the Delfs, and if it was spectacular enough, it would distract them."

"I've heard this routine before."

"Todt had been a metallurgist," Spain went on. "The transmutation of base metals into gold was—according to him—one of the earlier jokes of the Delfs. It was an impossibility. He thought about it. If he found a way to do it, it was to him, the distraction the Delfs would fall for. A paradox, you understand, Lieutenant?"

"No," I said helplessly.

"The Delfs fostered the idea as a joke," Spain said patiently. "Because it couldn't happen. So if Todt made it happen—made an impossibility possible—that was the distraction he needed."

I finished the drink and thought maybe I'd better not have any more. Spain looked sober and look at the way he was talking.

"He was successful," Spain said soberly. "It may sound crazy to you, Lieutenant, but he was successful. I suppose only a man like Todt—intelligent and a near-genius but warped on this idea of his about Delfs—could have displayed the imagination and ingenuity needed to perfect such a machine."

"You mean he turned base metals into gold!"

"As I remember you're carrying an example around in your pocket, Lieutenant? It looks like a solid gold dollar. It is. It was a silver dollar when it was put into the machine. I have seen it happen."

I laughed coarsely.

"Laugh if you wish," Spain said. "I flatter myself I am as shrewd as the next man—a good deal shrewder in fact. I tell you I saw it happen. Not once, but half a dozen times. The machine wasn't perfect by any means. And silver was the only metal that could be changed into gold. But it worked."

"It's your story," I said.

He drew on his cigar again: "You realise what a machine like that could mean to whoever owned it? An endless fortune. It would have to be used carefully, of course. But the machine was literally priceless in its value. I made Todt an offer and he said he wasn't interested. He was only interested in causing his diversion so Time would stop."

Nicky made a tired gesture with one hand. "Try arguing with a madman! I did for weeks. Last week he seemed to be changing his mind a little. He was more interested. I think he was going to admit to himself that his Delf theory was wrong. He'd used the machine—created his paradox, his diversion, but nothing had happened. Time hadn't stopped. So I figured that even Todt was beginning to realise that his theory about the Delfs must have been wrong."

"He was going to accept your offer of a hundred and fifty thousand?"

"He was thinking about it. I think he would have done, if he'd lived."

"Did he have the machine with him?"

"Sure," Nicky nodded. "That's what frightened me. I thought maybe he might be crazy enough to demonstrate it to the convention! I lost my temper arguing with him in the corridor that day. I wanted to clinch the deal right then."

"How big is the machine?"

Nicky shrugged and held his hands out, about three feet apart. "About so big."

"We haven't found it."

"Of course you haven't," Nicky said bitterly. "That's what he was murdered for—the machine. Whoever murdered him got the machine, you can bet your last dollar on that!"

"Why would it be necessary to murder him? They could have got the machine without doing that."

Nicky grinned tiredly: "That one's pretty obvious, isn't it, Lieutenant? Todt could always build another machine—another ten or a hundred machines if he wanted. But dead, that machine he'd already built becomes the only one in existence. Killing him was insurance against the value of the machine depreciating."

"I see your point," I admitted.

"Was there anything else, Lieutenant?"

"Do you have any ideas who might have the machine right now?"

He shook his head: "If I did, Lieutenant, I wouldn't tell you. I want that machine!"

"Okay," I said. "Maybe I won't book you as a material witness after all. You can go."

"Thank you," he said stiffly.

After he'd gone I sat and wondered. Steinbeck came in and asked me did I want him to do anything else. And I told him not to forget to send me a copy of his next book and that was all I wanted him to do for me right now.

I thought I'd go visiting people for a change instead of having people visit me. So I called on Waldo Lipcheek who was sitting in his room drinking coke out of a bottle with a straw in it. I'd never believed that grown-ups drank soft drinks outside of the advertisements. So after I got into his room I just looked at him, fascinated.

He unhooked his lips from around the end of the straw and frowned at me. "What's the matter, Lieutenant? My slip showing or something?"

"You really drink that stuff?" I said. "Not laced with rum or anything?"

"Or anything," he said. "Shouldn't I?"

"There's no law against it as far as I know," I said. "I suppose if you're thirsty there's some excuse for it."

"I happen to like the flavour," he said. "Is there something riotously funny about that?"

"I guess not," I said.

"Did you want to see me about something—or just to pitch the breeze about drinking habits?"

"I wanted to see you about something," I admitted.

"I'm here."

I suppose that was a hint.

"What do you know about Annabelle Starr?" I asked him.

He raised his eyebrows: "After this afternoon I would have imagined there was nothing you didn't know about Annabelle Starr!"

"You imagined wrong," I said.

"Yeah?" he raised his eyebrows in sheer disbelief.

"Tell me what you know about her?" I said.

He sipped some more coke. "She's blonde," he said. "Her vital statistics are 37-25-37. I happen to know because I bought her a dress once. She's intelligent,"

"What else?"

"Do you need to know anything more about a blonde with such vital, vital statistics?" he asked smoothly.

I walked over and grabbed the lapels of his coat, hauling him onto his feet. "Look, buster!" I said. "I'm investigating two murders. I need all the information you can give me!"

"Take your hands off me!" he said breathlessly.

"I'll take 'em off when I'm good and ready," I said. "And if that doesn't suit you, just what are you going to do about it?"

He started to take a half-hearted swing at me. It was so slow it was painful. I let go his lapels and hit him not too hard a short jab into his midriff and felt my fist sink into the soft fat.

He fell backwards into the chair again and sat there gurgling.

"We were talking about Annabelle Starr," I said.

He kept on making the gurgling noises.

"What does she do for a living? Where does she come from? Are you going to marry her? Is she going to marry you? That's the sort of information I want from you, fat boy, and you can give it or I can beat it out of you!"

"I'll have you broken!" he whimpered. "I'll lay charges of assault! I'll complain to the Commissioner, the District Attorney ..."

"Why don't you go straight to the White House and quit horsing around?" I said. "Annabelle Starr—or do I have to get really tough?"

"No!" He shrank back in the chair. "I'll tell you all I know about Annabelle."

"That's better," I said. "A whole lot better. Let's hear it."

He picked up the coke bottle and sucked on the straw again. "Well—I've known her for maybe a couple of years. She comes from New York. We both do. She works in an advertising agency and so do I. That's how we first met. I'm ... well, I'm crazy about her. I want her to marry me, but she won't—not yet that is.

"She's a nice, sweet kid. She's got this bug about S.F. She goes to all the conventions and I go along too because it gives me the chance to be near her, that's all. That's about all I know about her, and for me, that's enough."

"Love's sweet young dream!" I said.

He flushed: "Okay. So I'm not hard and tough the way you are. I'm a fat boy who gets pushed around a little because I'm easy going. But I'd look after her—I want to marry her. You don't want to marry her, do you, Lieutenant? Not even after this afternoon, you don't want to marry her, do you? I bet you never even thought about it!"

He had a point there.

"Did you ever see Professor Todt before?"

"A couple of times at other conventions, that's all. I never even talked to him."

"Did Annabelle?"

"Sure. She went to the same university he lectured at, so she knew him. Not awfully well, of course, but she'd say a few words to him each convention."

"You ever hear his theory about the Delfs?"

Waldo grinned suddenly: "Sure! Everybody did. It was his hobby-horse and brother, he sure rode it to death!"

"That's my guess," I agreed. "He did just that."

CHAPTER 7
A Redhead Aflame

I went back to my own room again and poured myself a drink. I had to drown the vision of a bottle of soft drink and a straw. I also had to work out what I was going to do the next day.

I had it just about worked out when I had a caller. I yelled out, "Come in" and in she came.

Flavia Romberg.

She was wearing a negligee of some black, rustling stuff that was cut low enough in front to give her a cold and wasn't opaque enough for her to stand in front of any light-source with confidence.

Flavia stood in front of the light-source and looked at me. I looked at Flavia and somehow she looked different. A redhead aflame.

"Have you made up your mind about what you're going to do about everybody tomorrow?" she asked.

"Sure," I said. "I'm letting them go home. At twelve in the morning they can quit Pine City as they will."

"Oh!" she seemed surprised. "Why are you letting them go? Do you know who the murderer is?"

"No," I said. "But I'm just naturally a soft-hearted slob!"

"I wouldn't say you were soft-hearted. The rest follows all, right!"

"You know something?" I said coldly. "You wouldn't be at all attractive if you didn't just happen to be a woman!"

"Do you think I'm attractive?"

"I hadn't realised your possibilities until I saw you in that outfit," I said.

"This old thing!" She twirled around disdainfully. "I'd almost forgotten I had it."

"Would you like a drink?"

"Yes, please."

"Good. Fill my glass again, will you?"

She glared at me for a moment then refilled my glass and poured herself a drink.

"Don't get up," she said as she handed me the glass. "Something might break!"

"Thanks," I lifted the glass. "Here's to redheads in old things. May they never buy any new!"

"Do you find me attractive?"

"I've been trying to convey that impression," I said. "Maybe my choice of words hasn't been too good. I think you are a wow! The greatest! The mostest! I think you're a ball! Do I make myself clear?"

"You're definitely helping."

"But it's a wasted effort," I said. "You don't care about that birds and bees stuff—that man and woman stuff. To you Gregory Peck conjures up a vision of a tame canary and Clark Gable is an architectural term!"

She looked at me soberly for a moment then shook her head. "No," she said. "I've changed. You worried me. You shook my girlish confidence. I hung around you like a limpet and you paid me as much attention as you would a non-alcoholic drink! But now your reactions are positive, my confidence is restored again!"

"That's fine," I said. "If you come a little closer I could restore your confidence even further!"

She didn't come any closer.

I snapped my fingers a couple of times. "Don't be shy, Flavia!" I said. "This is an experience that every girl has to face up to, sooner or later. And though I say it myself, I am just the guy to get your experience from!"

"You certainly are unique!" she said wonderingly. "I just don't see how you can walk around under the weight of all that ego!"

"Switch the lights out before you come," I told her.

"All right," she said.

She sort of shimmered over to the light-switch beside the door and turned it off. The room was plunged into gentle darkness. I put my glass down on the floor beside the chair and waited expectantly. I heard soft movement towards me.

"Lift up your face," she said huskily, "and close your eyes."

"Honey," I said. "Our first kiss!"

I lifted up my face and closed my eyes. And the next moment she gave it to me—a bowl of near-melted ice-cubes that flowed everywhere—through my hair, down the front of my shirt—into my eyes and all over.

Dimly, while I spluttered, I heard her laugh and then the sound of the door opening and closing. I staggered across the room and pawed around the wall until I found the light switch. Then I stripped off my wet clothes and had a shower. After that there seemed only one thing left to do—go to bed. I had three quick nightcaps for the night and then got in between the sheets.

Maybe it was the room or maybe it was the company I was keeping. The trip in the space-ship to meet the Delfs had been bad enough. This time I found myself cranking the handle of a massive machine vigorously whilst a steady stream of gold poured out of a pipe the other end and made a heap on the carpet.

I kept on cranking and the pile of gold on the carpet got bigger and bigger and bigger.

Flavia came into the room. She was wearing a tunic that reached from her shoulders to the top of her thighs. It was made out of spun gold.

"That's good, darling," she said. "Keep on turning!"

"It's no effort," I told her. "How are things going?"

"Fine!" she said. "I just checked our bank balance with the bank this morning. We've eight hundred and fifty million million in credit!"

"Is that all!" I said, disappointed. "I thought we would have been over the thousand mark by now. I've done nothing else but turn the handle all week!"

"Darling!" she said quickly. "You're forgetting our other assets."

"Assets?"

"You know—the things we've bought!"

"What things?"

"Don't tell me you've forgotten the things we own already!"

She ticked them off on her fingers: "There's the Taj Mahal, the Bank of England, the Panama Canal, Marilyn Monroe, Gregory Peck, the Kremlin—we got that cheap because it needs a new duco, remember? And then ...” she laughed and clapped her hands together. “I nearly forgot ... the United States of America!”

“That’s better,” I said. “I’m glad we have assets—my arm is getting tired!”

“It certainly is a wonderful machine,” she said. “Keep on turning!”

“When do you think we’ll have enough?” I asked, changing arms quickly so that the machine didn’t stop for a second.

“In about fifty years,” she said. “Don’t forget I have expensive tastes.”

“Fifty years! But I’ll be old by then.”

“Don’t worry about it, honey. So will I!”

“But I do worry about it!”

“Darling!” her voice became severe. “You know how I can’t stand ugliness. And you did agree it was all right to pull down New York and rebuild all the buildings in gold instead of that ugly steel and concrete, didn’t you? We haven’t even finished the Empire State Building yet.”

“What are we calling it when we’re finished?”

“The AlFlavia, of course, silly!”

“Sounds pretty good, huh? Something like UNO, eh?”

“We paid them off a long time ago,” she said. “That was why we bought the Kremlin. Don’t you remember that after we’d given away the first ten tons of gold free there weren’t any Communists left? Don’t you remember that beautiful speech Mr. Krushchev made? The one that started off, ‘Capitalists of the World unite! You have everything to lose if the gold standard goes?’ Even the Hearst newspapers printed it!”

“I forget these things,” I said. “And my arm is aching.”

“Change arms.”

“I just have.” I looked at her hopefully. “Don’t you think I could rest for a minute?”

“Don’t be absurd, darling!” she said coldly. “There isn’t any time to rest. We must have more gold!”

“But ...”

She turned to a gold chair and picked up something. A heavy whip I noticed, made of knotted gold links.

“I must rest!” I said desperately.

“You can’t!” she snarled. The whip curled through the air and cut into my shoulders. “We need more gold!” The whip hit me again. “More gold, more gold, more gold ...”

I found myself sitting bolt upright in bed, whimpering. It was morning. I crawled out of bed and into the shower. Half an hour later I had some coffee sent up and drank a couple of cups. Then I left the hotel, picked up the Healey and drove down to City Hall.

Lavers’ eyes popped when he saw me. “I don’t believe it,” he said hoarsely. "Only five after nine and Wheeler is already working!"

"It only happens once," I told him, "so treasure this moment, Commissioner!"

"You must have booked somebody," he said hopefully. "To get up this early in the morning?"

I told him what I'd found out so far. I told him about Spain and the machine that Todt had invented. When I'd finished he didn't say anything for a moment then he exploded.

"That's the silliest thing I ever heard!" he yelled. "It's ridiculous nonsense! A machine for the transmutation of base metals into gold!"

"Maybe," I said. "But Spain believes in it. He claims he saw it working—and we have the solid gold buck!" To enforce my point I took the gold buck out of my pocket and flipped it into the air a couple of times.

"You sure you aren't out of your mind?" he asked me hopefully.

"Maybe you need a long rest, Wheeler. I can get you a nice padded cell cheap for a couple of years. Maybe you've been overworking ... no, that's not possible. Maybe your mind just gave way—it couldn't have much to hang onto at the best of times!"

"If you've finished being funny," I said as politely as I could. "Maybe you'll listen to me for a moment!"

"What have I got to lose—except my sanity!"

I lit myself a cigarette. "Spain is a hard-headed guy who invests his dough in anything that will make him a quick and substantial profit. If he says he saw the machine—he saw it."

Lavers opened his mouth to bellow again.

"Wait a minute!" I said quickly. "I'm not saying the machine really turns silver into gold. I'm only saying there is a machine that apparently does, in existence."

"There are fairies at the bottom of my garden, too!" Lavers said in a choked voice.

"You should do more gardening then," I told him. "If you aren't careful they'll probably choke your roses! I'm saying that I believe this machine exists. Spain offered a hundred and fifty thousand bucks for it. And Todt was dickering with him on the price. There we have a reason for murder, huh? A hundred and fifty thousand is a lot of dough. I believe that Todt was murdered to get him out of the way and so that the murderer could get hold of that machine. And if he's got it, what has he got it for? One reason—to sell it to Spain."

Lavers picked up a pen from his desk and plunged it into the desktop where it stood quivering. "Go on!" he said in a hoarse voice.

"I want to let them all go this morning," I said. "But I want a squad of men down there to search their luggage as they go. That will mean the machine stays wherever the murderer has hidden it inside the hotel. Spain isn't dumb, he'll have guessed the reason why Todt was murdered, and I figure he won't move out of the hotel. He'll stay there hoping the murderer will contact him about the machine. Even if he does move out, we can have him followed. As long as we keep tabs on Spain, we'll be keeping tabs on the murderer, who'll have to contact Spain sooner or later."

Lavers picked out the pen from his desk and plunged it into his blotting-pad. "If the murderer's got a machine like that why should he sell it to Spain? Why not to anybody? Why not use it himself?"

"We agree that nobody could invent a machine to turn silver into gold," I said. "It's a chemical impossibility. Okay. So the machine is a fake. The only guy who believes in it and is prepared to pay big money for it is Spain. So the murderer has to contact Spain to make a sale."

The Commissioner grunted non-committally. "So?"

"So we search all their baggage at noon when they leave the hotel and make sure the machine doesn't go. I shall also make sure I let Spain know it hasn't gone. We keep tabs on Spain. I can do that inside the hotel. I'll need some men outside the hotel to make sure that if Spain, or Carlotta or Rivers leave the hotel they're followed. This way all we have to do is wait for the murderer to come to us."

"I hope you're right," he said. He blistered the air for a few seconds. "You'd better damned well be right!"

"I'm right," I said modestly. "I'm a genius."

Lavers lit himself a cigar. "How did Todt ever sell Spain the idea in the first place?"

"Remember what Todt was before he became a Professor? He was a con-man. Remember the rain-making machine he sold the yokels? This is another rain-making machine only on a bigger scale!"

"I still don't see ..."

"You will," I told him, "if you listen. Todt reformed, took his degrees and settled down to a life on the campus. But during the last couple of years there must have been some urgent reason come up that gave him his need for dough—a lot of dough. And that's how the machine came into existence."

A wreath of blue smoke surrounded Lavers. "Go on!"

"I think Todt was smart. The only way he knew to raise a lot of money was by another confidence trick. And he laid the ground for the machine with his theory about Delfs!"

"Not science fiction again!" Lavers groaned. "I can't stand it!"

"Sure—science fiction. He stumped the conventions giving out with his crazy theory in large lumps until everybody knew it and he was an established character. He also had a colossal natural asset in the fact he was a genuine professor!"

"I don't follow you?"

I lit a cigarette and waited until my lungs had finished their spasm. "How do most people think of a professor? A highly educated man in the academic sense with no understanding of world things like the importance of money and strip-tease artists. They think of a vague, absent-minded genius who is likely to come up with anything and never realise its true value. To ordinary people it's quite possible that somebody like Todt might invent the aeroplane one day and the atomic bomb the next, simply because he's a professor.

"And the biggest suckers for that line of thought are the guys who pride themselves on being hard-headed business men. Guys like Nicky Spain, in fact. Todt spent nearly two years laying the ground for this, remember? He established himself as a nut. He ranted his crazy theory. What more logical way could he have found of proving his theory than by inventing something that was theoretically impossible, just to distract his Delfs? And the value of what he'd invented was only secondary to trying to prove his Dell theory by it!"

Lavers chewed the end of his cigar some more. "So that takes care of Todt—maybe! He's knocked off so somebody else can get hold of the machine and sell it to Spain for a hundred and fifty thousand bucks. What about the house detective? Dexter?"

"He found out something he shouldn't," I said. "The time I talked to him he looked like a smart guy. So maybe he found the machine or he heard something—something that would have blown the whole thing sky-high! So he had to stay in line and keep his mouth shut, and the only way that could be guaranteed was if he became dead suddenly, and permanently."

The Commissioner took the cigar out of his mouth and looked disgustedly at the frayed end, then dumped it in the ashtray. "Okay," he said reluctantly, "I'll buy it, but I don't like it."

"I don't like it, either," I said. "But it's the only thing I can think of."

"So you let 'em all go at noon?"

"And wait for one of them to come back."

"What if nobody comes back?"

"I always wanted a chicken-farm," I said eagerly. "I have a theory about eggs. Everybody worries about 'em getting smashed. I'm going to smash the lot—deliberate policy—smash 'em, freeze 'em, cut 'em into chunks and wrap 'em in cellophane and what have you got?"

"What have you got!"

"Quick-frozen omelette!" I said. "Make a fortune!"

I saw the look on his face and got out of his office a moment before he made a third homicide.

CHAPTER 8
A Lot Of Carlotta

I stood in the hotel lobby at noon and watched them go. The girls and boys with dreams of hyper-space drive and the universes beyond the universe in their eyes, all going back to the sordid reality of being clerks and housewives and worrying about the rent and taxes again.

I could almost feel sorry for them.

By one o'clock the exodus seemed to have been complete. But there were some omissions. Some notable omissions. Nicky Spain, Lazy Rivers and Carlotta Chavez hadn't been among the departing guests. Neither had Wilbur Kessell, Annabelle Starr or Waldo Lipcheek. Neither had Flavia Romberg.

I checked the list of people attending the convention I had got from Flavia, with the hotel register. All the others had gone. Theoretically, then, the ones that had stayed were the suspects. Minus Flavia—she had been with the Professor facing the audience so she couldn't have fired that dart into him. But maybe she had an accomplice who did? I hadn't thought about that angle before. Maybe it was time I did.

I went up to her room and knocked on the door. She called out for me to come in. So I went in. She was wearing that robe that didn't really, and was eating what looked like breakfast.

"Breakfast?" I confirmed my suspicions.

She nodded: "Is that against the law, Lieutenant?"

"No." I sat down in the nearest chair and lit a cigarette.

"Only it's lunchtime now and you persist in calling that meal breakfast; you'll end up confused. You'll be a meal behind for the rest of your life. Why don't you call it lunch and solve the whole problem?"

She poured herself another cup of coffee and gave me the sort of look that's normally reserved for out-of-order drains.

"Did you come in here to talk mealtimes?"

"I noticed it was past noon," I said. "The covered wagons have pulled out down the trail—the S.F. convention has ended. But Flavia lingers on. I wondered."

"Why?"

"It's a habit cops have," I told her. "It stops them foaming at the mouth sometimes."

"My time is my own," she said indifferently. "I like it here in Pine City. I think I'll stay a few days."

"Hoping to pull off a big business deal?"

She looked up at me blankly: "Big business deal?"

"It doesn't matter. We'll say you like the climate then?"

"You could say that."

"Yeah."

I tried to blow a smoke-ring towards the ceiling and ended up coughing.

"Why don't you trade in those lungs?" she suggested. "That way you could get to breathing here and there."

"I would," I said, "if I could find anyone to take them. That robe you're wearing—what's it made of?"

"A mixture," she said, "of nylon and silk. Why?"

"I just wondered."

"Why?"

"I just wondered why you wear it."

"Why do most people wear a robe?" she said icily. "To cover themselves with, that's why!"

"That's what I meant," I said. "I can't figure out why you wear that one!"

"Why don't you get out of here and leave me alone?"

"Since you ask," I said, "I can't think of one good reason. Not one!" I got on to my feet. "Have dinner with me tonight?"

"Where?"

"I still have my room."

"Should I bring along another bowl of ice cubes?"

"Sure!" I said. "Keep 'em close to you—they'll melt before you get up there."

I went out. I was running out of wisecracks—witness the last! I went on till I got to Wilbur Kessell's room and knocked.

Wilbur was in. He looked up and smiled as I came into the room. "Hullo, Lieutenant. Still sleuthing?"

"You call it that," I said. "You like Pine City, too?"

"You mean why am I staying here?" He looked down at the sheets of paper beside his typewriter. "I'm halfway through a story, I don't like to shift until I've finished it. And there's no hurry for me to get home. The hurry is the story—I promised it to *Astounding* a couple of weeks ago."

"Find it hard to turn them out?"

"Sometimes. This is one of the times. Only now I think I've got it right and I want to finish it before I change my mind."

"Yeah," I said, "guess I can take a hint. See you around, Wilbur."

"Sure, Lieutenant," he nodded, then bent over his typewriter again and started to hammer the keys.

Next stop was Annabelle Starr's room. She raised her eyebrows as I came in. "I thought you thought I was dead?" she said coolly.

"I've been busy."

"The classic excuse of the male!"

"Two murders," I said, "unsolved. Breathless Lieutenant with Police Commissioner breathing hotly down his back for an arrest—you know how it is."

"No," she said, "I don't. All I know is that Lieutenant sweeps girl off feet one afternoon. Not seen since. Leaves girl with feeling that was all Lieutenant wanted and rest is brush-off. What are we talking, by the way? Telegraphese or pidgin-Chinese?"

"No brush-off was intended," I said. "I really have been busy. Sorry, honey."

"I have survived," she said.

"You haven't left with the rest?"

"I still have four days of my vacation left," she said. "I might as well spend it here as go back to New York and mope around my apartment."

"I guess so," I said. "How about Waldo?"

She sighed: "Waldo stays where I stay. He is the original leech."

"You should marry him and put him out of his misery!"

"Advice to the lovelorn, Lieutenant? Or Stage Two of the brush-off?"

"Neither," I said. "I was just talking for the sake of talking."

"It's a bad habit," she said. "Was there anything else on your mind?"

"Not a thing," I said. "See you around."

"Why not?" she said. "It's a free country."

I thought enough was enough. I went up to my room, up to the bottle I knew was still there, and had myself a drink. The 'phone rang half an hour later.

"Wheeler," I said into the mouthpiece.

"Lieutenant?" the voice was soft and husky. "This is Carlotta Chavez speaking."

"Sure," I said. "Go ahead."

"I have something to tell you," she whispered, "something that will interest you, I think."

"Go ahead."

"Not over the 'phone, Lieutenant. Could you come down to my room, right away? It is the one next door to Spain's, to the right."

"I'll be right there," I said.

And so I was. I knocked on the door and went in, closing the door behind me. The shades were down and the room was in semi-darkness. It took a moment for my eyes to get used to the gloom.

"Over here, Lieutenant," the husky voice said.

I looked and saw she was stretched out on the divan, wearing a robe. The robe was mostly unbuttoned. Her legs were long and lithe and sunburned.

I walked over to the divan and stood there, looking down at her.

"Okay," I said, "where's the fire?"

She smiled. "Fire, Lieutenant? The only one I know is the one that burns in my heart!"

"Anti-acid tablets will fix that!" I said. "What's this hot piece of information you've got for me?"

She patted the divan beside her. "Sit down," she said, "and I will tell you."

I sat down on the edge of the divan. She took a deep breath and the undone buttons became a little more so. "It is that I am bored, Lieutenant! I lie here thinking and you know what I am thinking about?"

"Pancho Villa? Or the Dodgers maybe?"

"I am thinking about you. Such a man of muscles! And I think it would be nice if you visited me for a little while, Lieutenant." She pouted her full lips at me. "I think you would be a man to make love exciting!"

"Me and Marlon Brando," I agreed. "What else?"

She smiled. "You need something else besides love, Lieutenant?"

"What if Nicky Spain should bust in half an hour from now? It would be kind of embarrassing, wouldn't it?"

"Nicky won't bust in. I make sure of that. He had too much to drink with his lunch and now he sleeps."

She sat up and linked her hands behind my neck and then lay down again, pulling me with her. "Let us not worry about Nicky, amigo!"

There was no good reason for me to worry about Nicky Spain. Carlotta was showing me an awful lot of good reasons why I shouldn't worry about Nicky Spain.

Yet I was worrying about Nicky Spain.

I gently disengaged her hands from around my neck and straightened up. Straightened right up on to my feet.

"Fascinating as your proposition is, amigo," I said, "I have things to do. Lots of things to do. So—if you will excuse me?"

She stood up quickly.

So quickly that I was taken by surprise. She ripped off the robe in one swift movement and started to scream. She dug her fingernails into one tanned shoulder and ripped. And she screamed. At the top of her voice. She had healthy lungs, they must have heard her down in Homicide.

She was still screaming when something heavy, like the sky, descended on the back of my head. I got a brief glimpse of more stars than were ever thought of, even at an S.F. Fans' Convention.

But only for a brief moment before everything went black.

When I came around I was sitting in a chair. I felt the back of my head carefully. There was a bump on it the size of a baseball. Lavers and Hanlon stood there, glaring down at me.

"You ought to have more sense!" Lavers said wearily.

"More sense than what?" I asked him.

"More sense than to tangle with a dame like that—and in a hotel, too!"

"Tangle with her? All I know is that someone slugged me on the back of the head!"

His eyes were bleak as he glared at me. "Can't you ever keep your mind off women?"

"What's that got to do with who slugged me?"

"Her rescuer," Hanlon put in. His voice sounded embarrassed. "Saved her from a fate worse than death. There she was, in nothing, and nasty scratch marks on her shoulder."

"Yeah?"

I jerked upright in the chair, remembering. Somebody hammered an iron stake into the back of my skull, but I almost didn't notice it. "I remember. She wanted me to play games with her and I wouldn't! So she pulled the old act. Scratched her shoulder and screamed!"

They both looked at me sourly.

"It's true! How come the guy who slugged me got there so fast, anyway? I'll tell you—it was a put-up job! That's why! Who was it? Rivers—or Spain, I'll bet my last dollar!"

"The girl said the guy scrammed out of the room when she started to ring the police," Hanlon said expressionlessly. "She had never seen him before. Her description would fit a million guys!"

"You see! It was a put-up job to get me out of the way. You know why! So that Spain could get out and clinch his deal for the machine. You've got guys watching the hotel—where did he go?"

Hanlon lit himself a cigarette. "He didn't go anywhere. I've got men watching all the exits. The only one who went out this afternoon was Kessell. And all he did was buy a new typewriter ribbon. Sorry, Al."

I snapped my fingers. "You know something—I'm crazy! Of course Spain didn't go out! He didn't have to. We know all the suspects are still staying on in the hotel. He went to talk to one of them—inside the hotel! We should have had men inside the hotel, not outside!"

Lavers lit himself a cigar. "There was a guy from the *Gazette* around, Al. A photographer. He got a picture—the dame with nothing on, screaming like mad, and you sprawled out on the floor. He got it before we got here."

"Doesn't that prove it was a frame-up, if nothing else does?" I said. "How did he just happen to be around?"

"The *Gazette* isn't sympathetic to the present City administration," Lavers went on dismally. "That picture will be on their front page tonight!"

"So what?"

"There'll be a scream that'll be heard coast to coast! A cop assaulting a woman! I don't like it, Al. It's not good. The Mayor and the D.A. will have heart attacks when they see it."

"I should worry about the Mayor and the D.A.!"

"You should!" he said grimly: "I'll have to! I don't have any choice, Al. You're suspended right here and now. I'm putting Hanlon back on to the case. You'd better get your stuff out of here!"

I stared at him. "You're crazy!"

"Look, Al," he said heavily, "maybe it was a put-up job. Maybe it happened the way you say it happened. But the dame's made a statement and she's got a lawyer pressing on it. Maybe it's only a bluff, but he's proceeding, and with that newspaper picture as evidence, it's going to look pretty lousy. I don't have any choice. You're suspended until the case comes up."

"What case?"

"Yours—for assault. This mouthpiece is smart, he's not pressing for anything more than that. Unprovoked assault. And you're going to have a hell of a time disproving it."

The iron stake was being hammered more firmly into my skull. I lit a cigarette and it tasted like the ashes of yesteryear. "Okay," I said, "I'm fired again."

"You'd better get your things together and get out of here," he said. "I'll have Hanlon move in."

"He can move in someplace else," I said. "I like it here—I'm staying!"

"Here, in the hotel?"

"Sure. I'm not under arrest, am I?"

"No."

"Then I can pay for this room and stay here, can't I?"

"You'll embarrass us, Al," he said. "I wish you'd move out."

"You're embarrassing me!" I said. "Suspending me is a very embarrassing thing to do!"

He grunted and looked at Hanlon, who shrugged his shoulders hopelessly.

"Okay, Al," Lavers said. "If you want to be awkward!" He walked out of the room, slamming the door shut behind him.

Hanlon looked at me miserably, seemed to say something, then changed his mind. He also went out, closing the door gently behind him.

CHAPTER 9
Annabelle Has Hidden Talent

I had a drink after they'd gone. Just one. It didn't seem to make any difference to the stake being driven into my head, but it did give me some energy. I thought I needed some energy.

I went down to Nicky Spain's room. I knocked on the door and then I opened it. Rivers was halfway towards the door, and behind him I could see Spain sitting in a chair, reading a book. He looked at me calmly. "I'm not at home," he said to Rivers.

Rivers grinned at me. "You heard the boss—he ain't in. Beat it!"

I stamped down on his instep, putting my weight on the foot, pinning his foot under mine. His face whitened with the pain and I hit him a couple of short jolts into his solar plexus which hurt a whole lot more because he couldn't ride with them, not with me pinning his foot.

He started to sag a little, so I took my foot away and hit him once more. He went down on to the floor then and lay there, looking up at me with his eyes filled with almost equal quantities of pain and hate.

"Scream, why don't you?" I said. "Scratch yourself all over and scream. It's the routine around here, isn't it?"

"Touch him again and I shall shoot!" Spain said quietly.

"Shooting a cop is about the most stupid thing any guy can do!" I said.

"You're not a cop," he said. "You're different! You're a cop who's going to be facing an assault charge! I imagine that your superiors won't appreciate that, will they, Wheeler?"

Lazy Rivers dragged himself on to his knees. He looked as if he wanted to crawl away somewhere and die. I hoped he would. And where the hell would that get me?

"If you don't leave this room right now, Wheeler," Spain said coldly, "I shall be forced to ring for help to have you thrown out."

"I wanted you to know just one thing, Nicky," I told him. "I'm going to get you. I'm going to find some nice, king-sized rap and pin it on you before this case is finished!"

"Lieutenant," he permitted himself a sneer, "you scare me!"

I went out of his room and back to my own.

If I kept on playing it this way I could get myself a job on *Dragnet*.

Two hours later the evening edition of the *Gazette* was delivered to my room. Lavers had been so right. There was I on the front page. It was a nicely angled photograph—shot through the half-open door of the room, showing me lying on the floor and Carlotta screaming. The picture of Carlotta was blurred enough not to send the League of Decency into action, but clear enough to see the scratches on her shoulder, and also that, unless she got into something quick, she was liable to catch a cold.

There was a story to go with the picture. The only comment Commissioner Lavers had made for the paper was that I had been suspended from duty until further notice. The *Gazette* was screaming for my hide to be nailed to a wall of City Hall. I read it through and then had a drink.

I had a caller later on. Annabelle Starr. She was wearing a strapless, backless, not-much-front, tight-fitting gown and all it did for her was to emphasize she was a woman. The sort of woman you can see once every leap year if you're lucky. So I was lucky?

She came in and closed the door behind her. "I read the paper, Al," she said. "It's not true, is it?"

"It's what an art dealer would call a frame," I said. "But I can't prove it."

"Maybe," she said, a tight smile on her lips, "I could work this Chavez dame over a little? She might soften up?"

"No," I said. "But thanks for the thought."

"Is it really true—that you've been suspended?"

"Really true."

"What are you going to do?"

"Get drunk, I think."

"Why don't we go out and get drunk? Why don't you take me out and we both get drunk?"

"It sounds like a fine idea," I said.

"I'll give you ten minutes to knot your tie," she said. "And I'll meet you in the bar downstairs."

"Okay—that's a date."

I met her in the bar some ten minutes later. We had a couple of drinks and then we were on our way. At least, we started out with that idea. We reached the glass doors that led into the foyer and I stopped suddenly. I saw Spain, Rivers and Carlotta walk across the foyer and out of the main entrance.

"What are we waiting for?" Annabelle asked coldly. "A fanfare of trumpets?"

"I just remembered something I haven't done, honey," I said. "Will you make like an angel and go back and have one more drink on your own? I'll be ten minutes, no more, no less."

"When they ask for votes for the 'Escort of the Year'," she said tersely, "frankly, you don't get mine!" But she went back to the bar and bought herself another drink.

I rode the elevator to the third floor and went along to Spain's room. The door was locked. There was a 'phone down at the end of the hall. I rang the desk and told them it was Lieutenant Hanlon speaking and to send up a master key to the third floor right away.

A desk clerk appeared a couple of minutes later and I put on my look of authority and relieved him of the keys. I was glad he was a guy I'd never seen before, so he didn't question me taking the keys, and not Hanlon.

As soon as he'd gone I opened the door of Spain's room and let myself in. How big was a machine for turning silver into gold? I figured it would need to be bigger than a matchbox. It would need to look impressive—worth a hundred and fifty thousand bucks.

I went right through the apartment, but I didn't find anything that looked that impressive or looked remotely like a machine for the transmutation of base metals into gold.

I dropped the key off at the desk and picked up Annabelle from the bar. "I'm glad you found the time to come back," she said. "I was just considering slitting your throat."

"You're too late," I said. "It's already been done—or don't you read the *Gazette?*"

We went to a nightclub called the Flamingo because, if you put a match close to your breath after drinking their liquor, you'd burst into flames.

We got a booth at the far end of the place. The Flamingo catered for people with or without money, for cops—in fact anybody who could reach the cover charge.

Annabelle seemed to like the atmosphere—and the martini specials. She had four and started to glow. I figured a match held near her breath and she'd burst into flames. I hoped not. I'd never had a burning woman in my arms.

"Al," she said after a time, "You're not getting drunk—like you promised."

"The whisky's been watered," I said.

"Really, Al?" she said. "You really are a smart policeman to know that!"

"You don't have to be a cop to know those things, baby," I said.

"I like cops," she purred, slurring the words a little.

"I am no longer a cop," I said. "I told you that."

"I still like cops," she said. "And I say that silly old Commissioner should see a psychiatrist!"

"He has."

"And what happened?"

"He fired me," I said.

The music started and Annabelle lurched to her feet. "Dance," she said.

"Think you can?" I said.

"I'll show you!" she replied. "Come on!"

We drank and danced our way around to the early hours of the morning, and then I suggested some good liquor and quiet hi-fi was the answer, so we went back to my house.

I stacked some of Jackie Gleason's mood music on the turntable and let the speakers pipe it around the room. I left one shaded table lamp burning, opened a new bottle of Scotch, poured the drinks, then took the drinks and Annabelle over to the sofa.

Basic organisation means so much to a technique.

Dames are funny things. Right then, she decided she wanted to talk.

"What about the Professor, Al?" she asked. "What's doing about the murders?"

"You should ask Lieutenant Hanlon about that," I said. "He's in charge of the investigation."

"I can't believe you've really been suspended!"

"Ask the Commissioner," I said. "He should convince you—he convinced me without any trouble at all!"

"It's terrible!" she said. "To think that dreadful woman framed you like that!"

"It breaks my heart, too!"

"Can't you do anything about it?"

"Like what?"

"I don't know—there must be something you can do about it surely!"

"I can't think of anything, honey."

She sat there deep in thought. "I know—maybe I can do something!"

"Forget it, honey. Let's concentrate on Jackie Gleason and you and me!"

"No, Al, I'm serious!"

I reached for a cigarette and lit it. "Forget it!"

"Just maybe I might be able to fix that hex from the mixed-up Mex!" she said.

I winced. "Don't let that alcohol confuse you!"

"No, really, Al, I mean it!"

"Like doing what?"

"I've got an idea," she said. "You wait a minute!"

She got up and walked to the phone.

"What are you going to do now?" I asked her.

"I have a friend," she sang happily. "He is a good friend!" She dialled a number and then asked to speak to Mr. Lipcheek.

"Waldo!" I said. "What the hell's Waldo got to do with this?"

"Quiet!" she said. Then her voice changed to the gentle coo of the dove. "Waldo, darling, I want you to do something for me. Of course it's important! I want you to ring the Chavez woman ... yes, of course, I mean her! Ask her to come up to your room for a drink. Tell her you're lonely

... no, I'm perfectly sober!"

She went into detail and my eyes started to pop.

"You can't!" I started to say.

She put her hand over the mouthpiece. "You shut up, Al Wheeler! Let genius work!"

Then she went on giving Waldo explicit instructions. When she'd finished she hung up and dialled another number.

"The *Gazette*? Give me the Editor, please!" She smiled happily at me. "I should have worked on a newspaper, I have a natural talent!"

"You can say that again," I said. "And also for the clothes that set it off, too!"

"The Editor?" she said. "Listen carefully. Send one of your photographers along to the Hotel Imperial right away." She gave him Waldo's room number. "Tell him to walk in and be ready to take a photograph.... What's it all about? He'll find out when he gets there.... By the way ... how often can a girl get assaulted?"

She hung up and walked back to the sofa. "Now that's organised," she said, "you can tell me some more about my talents." She switched off the table lamp as she passed it. Gleason's strings let loose an appropriate chord.

CHAPTER 10
I'm Hit By A Tornado

The *Gazette* thought it was worth bringing out a special edition the next morning. They had another photograph on their front page. It was identical with the photo they had published the previous afternoon with one exception.

The guy in the photograph was Lipcheek this time and not me. And he wasn't stretched out on the floor. He was just standing there with a look of blank amazement on his face.

The *Gazette* was caustic.

They wondered just how often a girl could get assaulted. They wondered if getting assaulted was Carlotta Chavez's regular occupation. They wondered a lot of things, and they were generous to a certain Lieutenant.

They even apologised to me. They said I had obviously been framed as she had attempted to frame an innocent house guest the following night. They gave Carlotta the kiss of death, in fifteen paragraphs.

I sat up in bed and drank another cup of coffee. I thought that Annabelle was quite a girl in more senses than one. Quite a girl!

The 'phone rang sharply and I lifted the receiver.

"Okay, Wheeler!" a familiar voice said. "Hanlon's out and you're in again. I don't know how you did it, but you did it! You aren't suspended—you never were!"

"Thanks, Commissioner," I said. "And if I may offer a gentle word of advice?"

"I suppose I asked for it," he said in a resigned voice.

"Next time, before you do something impetuous," I said pleasantly, "why don't you stick your head in a bucket of cold water?"

There were gurgling sounds on the other end of the line.

"Five minutes should be enough," I added, and then I hung up thoughtfully before he got his breath back.

I went through the routine of shower, shave and getting dressed. Then I went along to see Annabelle.

She was eating breakfast and reading the special edition of the *Gazette* when I got there. She was wearing a robe and she looked blonde and beautiful. I thought it was too early in the morning to have thoughts like that, so I had a cigarette instead.

"You are a genius!" I told her.

"It worked?"

"Like a charm. I am now reinstated. I never was suspended according to the Commissioner."

"I'm glad," she said.

"I'd better go see Lipcheek and thank him," I said.

"I'll see you later then," she smiled at me.

"Well there's no need to rush," I said. "I've got a reputation."

She smiled. "For what, Lieutenant?"

"Al," I said.

"Al, then," she said. "Tell me about your reputation."

"I never let a good deed go by without recognition," I said.

"A regular Boy Scout?" she smiled.

"Always prepared," I said. "Come here."

"Oh, no," she said quickly, blushing a little.

"Come here, woman!" I said loudly. "There's never been a Wheeler who didn't appreciate certain things."

"But, Al ..."

"Come here!"

She tried to look meek and mild. I gathered her in my arms and kissed her—hard. When we came up for air, she said, "Al! I didn't know—anyone could be so appreciative!"

"Honey, you haven't lived!" I said.

"Al."

"Uhuh?"

"Don't you think you should go see Lipcheek?"

I'd forgotten about him. "Hell," I said. "Why did I ever become a cop!"

Lipcheek was fully dressed when I got to his room.

"Just wanted to thank you for the organisation last night," I told him.

"That's okay," he said briefly.

"It's got me off the hook—I appreciate it."

"That's okay," he said listlessly.

"Well," I was beginning to feel awkward. "Thanks, again."

"Sure," he said coldly. "Any time. I'm a sucker for things like that. My ex-girl asks me to help the guy who made her my ex-girl and I do it! Maybe I'm just stupid!"

I couldn't think of an answer to that one, so I beat a retreat out of his room and then went along to Spain's suite. I was wondering whether Nicky would be happy to see me.

Lazy Rivers opened the door to me and I could tell right away from the look on his face that he wasn't happy to see me.

"I want to see Spain," I said.

"He's busy right now."

"I happen to be a reinstated cop, chum," I said pleasantly. "So when I say I want to see Spain—I see him. And if you don't move out of the way I'll arrest you for obstructing traffic!"

I stepped into the room and he moved out of the way with a horrible scowl on his face. I got about three paces into the room when a screeching, scratching tornado hit me.

"It was you!" she screamed. "You did it! You tricked me, into going to his room! You fixed it so that cameraman was there! You ...!"

I held her off at arm's length. "Why, Carlotta!" I said. "You sound like you've got troubles!"

She made a frantic effort to kick me, but missed. I got tired of holding her, so I tossed her at Rivers, who caught her clumsily and got his shins kicked for his pains.

"Here," I said, "fold her up and put her away somewhere. If she runs around loose in the frame of mind she's in, she might hurt somebody!"

Spain was sitting in an armchair placidly reading his copy of the *Gazette*. So far he hadn't paid any attention to what had been going on.

"Good morning, Nicky," I said.

He folded the paper carefully, then lit a cigar.

"Good morning, Lieutenant."

"Did you make your deal yesterday?"

"Deal?" he raised his eyebrows.

"The one you wanted to make privately," I said. "Without me around. The one you organised Carlotta into making sure I wasn't around for," I smiled at him. "The grammar may not be so hot, but you get the point, I'm sure?"

"I'm afraid not," he said regretfully.

I lit myself a cigarette. "You still want that machine Todt invented. Obviously the murderer has it. Obviously the murderer contacted you with a view to making a deal. Obviously you didn't want to be seen. So you organised Carlotta to get me out of the way while you made your deal yesterday."

"Do you really think so, Lieutenant?"

There was an empty armchair so I sat down and made myself comfortable. "Did you know that Todt had a record?" I asked him.

He puffed his cigar. "Record?"

"Criminal record. He did a couple of years before the war."

"Really?"

"He was a conman," I said. "He sold some yokels a rain-making machine that didn't."

"Oh?"

"Maybe he intended to sell you a gold-making machine that didn't."

He shook his head slowly. "I saw the machine working."

"It's amazing the number of people who've seen a diamond-making machine working," I said. "And paid good money for it. But when they try and work it, it doesn't work somehow. The suggestion is that when the seller works it there's a certain amount of sleight of hand involved."

"Do you think I'm naive?" he asked coldly.

"Sure," I said. "All smart businessmen are. They have a blind side. All their lives they have a subconscious hope that some day they'll find a jackpot in solid gold. If they didn't, the conmen wouldn't survive. You know something? Around eighty per cent of conmen's victims aren't poor old grey-headed mothers—they're smart, up-to-the-minute businessmen— like you!"

He bit onto his cigar. "Did you come here to say anything, lieutenant?"

"I've said it," I told him. "If you've made a deal for this machine, pal, that's your bad luck—it's your dough. But also if you've made a deal you know who you're dealing with. And that means you know who knocked off the Professor and the house detective. And if you don't reveal their names, that makes you an accessory after the fact."

I got onto my feet and walked towards the door.

"You could think that one over," I said. "Ask Rivers about how things are in the pen. If anybody can tell you, he sure can!"

I smiled at Carlotta as I walked past and she looked as if she was about to explode. I thought it would be a waste of suntan if she did.

It was late enough in the morning to have a drink. I walked down the stairs to get some exercise, through the foyer towards the bar.

Meedlemaus, the manager saw me and came hurrying over.

"Lieutenant, please!" he said in anguished voice. "How much longer!"

"How much longer what?"

"Does it go on! The hotel will be ruined! I shall be ruined. Two murders—they were bad enough! But then those two photos in the newspaper! All morning I have people ringing up asking for a room. They giggle—they say they want a room with the brunette attached! Our reputation!" He raised his eyes and looked at the ceiling. "Before, our reputation it was spotless. It was an hotel anybody could stay at. People even used to bring their children!"

I patted his shoulder gently. "Never mind, Meedlemaus. We'll move out after the very next murder!"

"Next murder!" He clutched my sleeve desperately. "You are not expecting another murder, Lieutenant!"

"We expect them all the time," I said. "You should have the hotel's atmosphere checked—have you ever thought about that?"

"Atmostphere?" he said blankly.

"I think it's conducive to murder," I said. "There's something in the air—some elusive quality that excites people to strange thoughts …"

I reached out and put my fingers around his throat and squeezed gently. He shuddered. "Sometimes," I whispered, "I feel it myself!"

I let go of him and he backed off, his eyes bulging. "Tell me," I whispered. "What is your room number?"

He kept on backing until he backed into a marble column. He jumped convulsively then turned around and ran for his office. I went on into the bar.

Flavia Romberg was already there, wearing a black sweater and a tight, black skirt. She sat perched on a stool with her legs crossed. I sat on the stool beside her and ordered Scotch.

"I read the paper this morning, Lieutenant," she said.

"I am now reinstated," I told her.

"Congratulations."

"Thanks."

She sipped her drink. "I never used to drink till I met you. Now I find I like it—is that bad?"

"It depends on what sort of liquor you're drinking," I said, "and who you drink with."

"Oh."

I looked at her. "Would you do something for me?"

"If it's what I think it is," she said cautiously, "the answer is no! I'll get my experience in my own good time thank you!"

"This is strictly business," I said. "Flavia, I'm surprised at you!"

"Well," she said, "I've given up being surprised at you!"

"All I want you to do is to make a phone call."

"I might do that for you. What do you want me to do—explain something to your girl-friend?"

"I want you to help me trap a murderer."

"Really?" she brightened up a little. "That sounds exciting!"

"When we've had the drink," I said, "we could go up to my room."

"My suspicious nature is aroused," she said. "Why can't we make the call from the foyer?"

"Because we could be seen," I said. "I shall finish this drink and go on up to the room. You follow in about five minutes and make sure nobody sees you coming into my room, will you?"

"Of course," she said. "A girl always does. I have my reputation to think of."

"Your reputation as what?" I asked interestedly.

"Just finish your drink!" she said. "Before I pick up this stool and break it over your head!"

I did as I was told, then rode the elevator upwards. I waited around in my room for nearer ten minutes than five, then Flavia came in.

"All right, mastermind," she said. "What do I do?"

"You ring Spain," I said. "You don't tell him who you are—we'll put a handkerchief over the mouthpiece so that he can't recognise your voice. You tell him you can get the machine. You know who has got it and where it's hidden. You ask him if he's interested in buying at a cut price. If he says he is, you make a date with him—for tonight."

"Where?"

"The roof garden on top of the hotel," I said. "Tell him you'll be up there at ten tonight and if he comes up, you'll make yourself known to him."

"It sounds easy enough."

"Sure—it is."

She walked over to the phone and picked it up. I gently took it out of her hand. The girl on the switchboard answered a moment later. "This is Lieutenant Wheeler speaking," I said.

"Yes, Lieutenant."

"I'm going to make a call in a moment to Mr. Spain—I want you to put it through after we've finished talking."

"Certainly, Lieutenant."

"I want you to make it appear the call is coming from outside the hotel. If he should ring you back afterwards and ask you to trace the call, I want you to play along with it—ring him back afterwards and tell him it came from a pay booth and that's all you can find out. Okay?"

"A pleasure, Lieutenant!" she sounded excited. "Getting close to the murderer?"

"I hope," I said. "Put the call through now, will you?"

I gave the phone back to Flavia and stood beside her. I put my arms around her waist and bent my head close to her.

"What's the idea!" she snapped.

"I just want to hear what he says!" I smiled at her. I suddenly remembered the handkerchief and just got it over the mouthpiece when Spain answered the phone.

"Spain!" His voice was curt.

"I believe you are interested in purchasing a machine," she said. "One that was developed by the late Professor Todt?"

There was a moment's silence then Spain said harshly. "Who is this speaking?"

"That isn't important," Flavia said smoothly. "What is important is that I can get that machine for you—cheaper. At a much cheaper price than it is being offered to you now."

"How do you know?"

"I know a lot of things," she said. "I know who has the machine and where it is hidden. If you're interested in making a deal with me, I'll meet you tonight and discuss it further."

"Very well," he said without any hesitation. "Where?"

"On the roof garden," she said, "at ten."

"How will I know you?"

"Don't worry about that. I know you—I'll come up and make myself known."

"All right," he said, "at ten."

"Till then," she said and put the 'phone down onto the cradle. Then she turned and faced me. "How was I?"

"Good," I said, "terrific!"

"Thank you, sir."

"Thank you, madame."

"What happens now?"

"Well," I said, "we find some way of filling in our time until ten o'clock tonight."

"And what then?"

"We go onto the roof garden."

"How do you suggest we fill in our time?" she asked. Then she must have seen the look in my eyes because she backed up hastily.

"Oh, no! I shouldn't have asked!" She ran for the door and I was going to chase her but the phone rang.

Flavia made her escape out of the door while I answered the phone.

"Lieutenant Wheeler?" It was the switchboard girl.

"Sure."

"Your party checked back. I told him it was an outside call and I'd check. I rang him back and said it was made from a public pay booth."

"Thanks a million," I said.

"It was a pleasure—Lieutenant!"

"You sound like a blonde."

"I am," she said. "Name of Joanna Wright. Vital statistics—37-26-37. I like Austin-Healeys and hi-fi, Lieutenant. My phone number is easy—just lift the phone any day of the week except Thursday—Thursday is my day off."

"Now there is a magnificent coincidence," I said. "You like Healeys and hi-fi! It so happens that I have ..."

"I know," she said demurely, "I've heard about you ... Lieutenant!" And then she hung up.

There were some things I had to do before ten that evening, I remembered. And I might as well do them now. I rang Kessell first. With a handkerchief across the mouthpiece of the phone.

"You're being double-crossed, punk!" I said. "Spain's got a date with somebody at ten tonight on the roof garden. He's being offered the machine at a cut rate!"

"Who's that?" Kessell asked blankly.

"You want to get wise," I said. "You don't have a deal any more. This somebody knows where the machine is stacked and they're figuring on hijacking it and selling it to Spain at a cut-rate."

"Who's speaking?"

"Just a pal. Just somebody who doesn't like the somebody who's trying to cut in on your deal. Don't forget, pal. The roof garden at ten tonight is the time the deal gets made with Spain!"

I hung up then. I rang Lipcheek and gave him the same story with pretty well the same results. Then I rang Annabelle Starr and gave her the story and got pretty well the same results.

So then there was nothing to do but wait till ten o'clock. Flavia had got out of my clutches and I felt she had probably barricaded her door by now.

So I went downstairs into the foyer—and along to the switchboard.

CHAPTER 11
The Roof's The Limit

Joanna Wright was a blonde whose vital statistics looked just as they had when she had enumerated them over the phone. She wore a white, nylon blouse and a tight grey skirt. Her eyes were a vivid blue and they had the look of a girl who knows how to add up two and two into a penthouse if the occasion arises.

I leaned as far as I could across the counter that separated the switchboard from the wolves like me and smiled into those deep blue eyes. "I'm Al Wheeler," I told her.

She smiled back at me. "I know," she said. "I've seen you around."

"According to all the labour laws in this State there must come a time when you stop working. When does that happen tonight?"

"At five o'clock," she said.

"Then we've got a date?"

"I'm sorry, Lieutenant," she said. "I already have a date for tonight. But tomorrow night ..."

"It has to be tonight," I said. "I don't have to book you as a material witness, do I?"

"Well," she said. "This date I have tonight is a big butter-and-egg man from out of town. I wouldn't bother with him if it wasn't for the mink I hope he's going to buy me before he goes back to the farm. I could tell him I was working and that would be almost the truth, wouldn't it?"

"You said it, honey." I agreed. "I pick you up here?"

"I think it would cause talk," she said. "The Manager is against it."

"Why?"

"On principle."

"What principal?"

"That if anybody dates the switchgirls it should be him. Supposing I come up to your room around five-thirty and we could take it from there?"

"That sounds wonderful," I said.

It must have been the glazed look in my eyes. "When I say take it from there, I mean we could go out some place," she added. "I wouldn't like you to misunderstand me, Lieutenant."

"I never understood a girl yet," I said. "Except that one time I was out with a redhead in a bowling-alley and she said, 'Let's roll!'"

"I shall bring my Alsatian with me," she said.

"I have an armoury of muzzles," I assured her. "I am the most provided-against-any-eventuality-wolf you ever met!"

"And I am a girl with a long line of experience," she said. "I have my defences from the short right hook to the electrified girdle! One grab and—sizzle!"

"Honey," I said, "I would get the same reaction with you whether you had the battery connected or not."

"Your call should be through any moment now, Lieutenant," she said crisply.

I looked over my shoulder and saw Meedlemaus bearing down on us rapidly. "Thank you," I said curtly.

The manager stopped and glared at me. "Phone call, Lieutenant?"

"Why, no," I said courteously. "I just stopped off here to take a shower!"

He thought about making something out of that. I bared my teeth at him in mirthless grin. "Did you ever consider statistics, Meedlemaus?"

"Statistics?" It threw him off his stride.

"Sure," I said. "In Homicide we got them down to a fine art. There's one and seven-eighths people murdered in this city every day."

I glanced at my watch and saw it was ten after one. "We can even narrow down the time of day to expect a murder. We can narrow down the place."

"Really?" he said, goggle-eyed.

"Right now," I added casually. "The next murder's expected at one-fifteen." He glanced at his watch, involuntarily. "And the place is right here," I said.

"There have been two murders in this hotel already. The hotel has become what you might call murder-prone!" I looked hard over his shoulder. "That character who's just come in—is that a gun in his hand!"

Meedlemaus jumped convulsively and spun around. He saw there wasn't anyone behind him and took a deep breath. He turned back to say something and I looked at my watch carefully. "One-thirteen," I said idly.

He didn't stop to argue.

"Five-thirty, honey," I said to Joanna. "I shall count the minutes!"

"I'll be there, Lieutenant," she said. "And if Meedlemaus really does get himself murdered, I'll bring you a cigar!"

I went and had some lunch. After that I went up to my room and slept till four o'clock. Then I had a shower and got dressed very carefully in the near-new grey tropic weight. Then I went along to Flavia's room.

She opened the door cautiously. "Oh it's you!"

"Don't sound so enthusiastic," I said. "You make me feel like a zombie!"

"That's logical," she said.

I didn't press the subject any further. I stepped into the room and she retreated behind a chair. "If you try anything," she said firmly, "I'll scream!"

"As if I'd even think of it!" I said severely. "Look—I'm here to tell you what to do tonight."

"I'll do no such thing!"

"I'm talking about Spain and the roof garden," I sighed.

"Oh?" she brightened up a little. "All right."

I lit myself a cigarette: "I can't be seen with you—that would give it away. So I'm taking a blonde to dinner on the roof garden." I saw her face stiffen. "Simply for camouflage," I added hastily. "To make it look as if I'm just there to enjoy myself—get it?"

"I get it," she said coldly. "You have the most original ideas on camouflage I ever heard!"

"I want you to come up onto the roof garden a couple of minutes after ten," I said. "Go straight to Spain and tell him it was you who rang him. Tell him you'll deliver the machine to him before morning for seventy-five thousand dollars."

"Do you think he'll take me seriously?" she asked. "It sounds plain crazy to me."

"I think he'll take you seriously," I said. "I don't think he can afford not to. He'll ask you a lot of questions and you just refuse to answer any of them. All you want to know is whether it's a deal or not. My bet is he'll say it is a deal. And once you've got that fixed, you leave him. And this is important. When you leave, come straight back to your room."

"Why?"

"Never mind why. But it's vital that you do that."

"All right—if you say so. What happens then?"

"I don't know," I said. "But you won't have to worry." And crossed my fingers when I said that.

I went out of her room leaving her with a puzzled look on her face. I went back to my own room and rang room service.

When Joanna arrived at five-thirty, everything was highly organised. She came into the suite and stared at the array of bottles on the table. "I didn't know you were having a party?" she said.

"Just you and me," I said.

"What about the other twenty people you'll need to drink all that?"

"I thought we'd try and see how long we can do without them."

She must have been a quick-change artist. The nylon blouse and grey skirt was gone. In their place was an evening gown. Its colour was a wine-red. It was off-the-shoulder. It emphasised that cleavage had its place outside of television. It emphasised that whoever had made it hadn't wasted an ounce of material. There was just enough of it. Or not quite enough of it. It depended on your point of view. My view was that there was too much of it altogether.

I poured a couple of drinks and handed one to her.

"Here's to us," I said.

"To a not-very-much closer acquaintance," she said cautiously.

"I don't understand you," I said. "You're like all blondes. You have a fast line of talk but once you get alone with a man you suspect the worst. The fact that you're quite right doesn't make any difference! The word," I said with quiet emphasis, "to describe such a blonde is piker!"

She shook her head in admiration. "That's what I like about you, Lieutenant," she said wonderingly. "It's your innate modesty. You think one drink and free meal buys a girl's all!"

"I am offering drinks unlimited," I pointed out. "And you are sabotaging my technique before it has time to get started."

"Drinks unlimited!" she said. "You sure your name isn't Rockefeller?"

"Okay," I said. "No technique!" I picked up the phone and asked for room service. "Send up a deck of cards," I said.

"Goody!" Joanna said enthusiastically. "I'm crazy for gin-rummy!"

I looked at the wine-red gown. "I guess I'm just crazy!" I said glumly.

Came nine o'clock and I was owing her ten thousand bucks. I never did have any luck in gin-rummy. All the bottles bar one were still unopened. The one that was open was three-parts full. It was what you would call an immoral evening. There was me—in my room, alone with a blonde, drinking and gambling. I thought I was going to get me a soapbox and preach the evils of drinking and gambling—particularly gambling. They're the sort of things that distract a man and woman from the fundamental things of Life, which—as somebody else once pointed out—are free!

Joanna shuffled the deck then tossed it onto the table. "You know something—I'm hungry!"

"Food is a thought," I admitted.

"Make you a bargain. You owe me ten grand, right?"

"Where did you learn such language?"

"I've been around!" she fluttered her eyelashes. "You buy me something to eat and we'll call it square."

"That's a deal," I said. "We'll eat on the roof garden—how's that?"

She wrinkled her nose. "I work in this crummy hotel. I like to see some place different in my spare time."

"Sorry," I said, "it has to be the roof garden."

"I'll surrender," she said. "I'm too famished to argue!"

So we went up to the roof garden.

It was nice. On a fine night like this night, you could eat with the sky as your ceiling. On wet nights they pulled out awnings so they didn't run at a loss. It was twenty storeys off the ground and you could see the bright lights all around for quite a distance.

The headwaiter gave us a table on the edge beside the parapet, and if you craned your neck slightly you could see the street way below and the head-lights of the bugs moving up and down it.

I had one look and decided that was enough. We ordered the meal and some liquor to go with it, and then I had a look around. Half a dozen tables away sat Kessell with an attractive-looking redhead, and I wondered if she was a science fiction fan or a supporter of the longer-established forms of recreation. It was an interesting thought until I saw Joanna watching me coldly. I looked further afield.

At another table was Spain, immaculate in a dinner-jacket, Rivers likewise, and Carlotta in a gunmetal gown that had even less to it than Joanna's. And right in the corner, eating steadily, were Annabelle Starr and Waldo Lipcheek.

So the family was all here.

We ate. We had got to the coffee stage when I looked at my watch and saw it was five to ten. I called the waiter over and got the check.

Joanna raised her eyebrows: "What's the hurry?"

"We have a date in ten minutes or so," I said.

"Really?"

"I'll explain later," I said.

Ten o'clock came and a couple of minutes after. Then Flavia came onto the roof. The guy who made her gown was the meanest of them all. How she had enough room to walk and breathe in it at the same time, I couldn't figure out.

She stopped for a moment, looking around, then headed straight towards Spain's table. A moment later she was sitting down and deep in conversation with him.

I swallowed the last mouthful of coffee. "Okay," I said to Joanna. "Here we go!"

"You're the fastest eating man I ever did eat with!" she complained.

"It's a matter of life and death and all points south," I said as I steered her towards the door.

Three minutes later we were in Flavia's room. Joanna sniffed strongly. The room had a definite perfume of *Nuit d'Amour.* There were also some nylon thingamajigs on the floor. Flavia must have got dressed in a hurry.

"Since when have you been wearing lace-trimmed panties?" Joanna asked guardedly.

"This is not my room," I said cheerfully. "This is Flavia Romberg's room. The redhead who came onto the roof garden a couple of minutes before we left."

"I saw her," Joanna said coldly. "May I ask just what we're doing in her room?"

"You may. We're waiting for her to return."

"A threesome! Is that your idea of fun?"

"This is business, honey," I said. "Business!"

"Whatever it is," her voice would have chilled an iceberg now, "I don't think I want any part of it!"

She headed towards the door.

"Where are you going?" I asked her.

"Home!" she said, and slammed the door behind her.

Well, I consoled myself with the thought that if you've got two dames to fit into one evening, at some stage of the evening you must lose one. As long as you don't lose both you can consider yourself lucky. And the blonde had been expendable. The fun and games were over for the rest of the night now. Unhealthy as it was, I was going to have to do some work.

I picked up the 'phone and got through to Homicide. I spoke to Hanlon and told him what I wanted done and how important it was. "It needs to be a good man," I said, "or we might as well quit right now."

"Okay," he said. "In that case I might do the job myself. I always did want to see an unorthodox cop in action."

"Fine!" I said. "You can ring me here," I gave him the extension number of the 'phone I was using. "But ring fast—otherwise we might be too late!"

"Okay," he said. "If this is a gag of yours, Al, I shall personally slug you over the head with that silly little red sports car of yours!"

"If it's a gag," I told him, "I'll give you my full permission to do it!"

I hung up, lit a cigarette, then settled down in an armchair to wait for Flavia's return.

CHAPTER 12
The Price Of Experience

Flavia came in maybe fifteen minutes later. She closed the door carefully behind her, looked at me, then looked around the room carefully.

"What's the matter?" I asked her.

"There seems to be something missing."

"You lose something?"

"Not me," she shook her head, "you!"

"Me?"

"Didn't you have a king-sized blonde in tow the last time I saw you?"

"Oh, her! She was just to throw dust into Spain's eyes and the rest of them."

"The rest of who?"

"Skip it!" I said quickly. "Anyway, the blonde's gone home."

"Oh!"

I offered her a cigarette, which she refused. I asked hopefully if she had a drink in the place and she hadn't. I lit a cigarette for myself: "How did things go with Spain?"

"Supposing you tell me just what I'm supposed to be doing?" she said.

It seemed fair enough. She was sticking her neck out and she didn't know it. She was entitled to know it. So I told her the whole story. About Todt and his wacky theory and his wacky machine. How I figured it as a confidence trick on the grand scale. About the suspects and just why I'd got her to pretend to make an offer to Spain to get hold of the gold-making machine and sell it to him at cut price. I even told her about the other 'phone calls I'd made after she had rung Spain in the morning.

Flavia changed her mind about a cigarette. And about a drink. She rang room service and told them to send up a bottle of Scotch. "If I'm not mistaken," she said, "that makes me what is generally known as a fall-guy, doesn't it? Or is it a fall-dame?"

"Check!" I said. "That's why I told you to come straight back here. That's why I'm here. Because the rest of them saw you go over to Spain's table up on the roof garden. Whoever has the machine knows that you've made an offer to Spain to get it for him and sell at a cut rate. So they'll come and see you—probably with mayhem in mind—but surprise, surprise! They'll find me here!"

"I'd like it better," she said, "if I had any faith in your ability to protect me."

"For those kind words!" I said.

There was a discreet knock on the door. I pulled the .38 Police Special out of my shoulder holster and backed off to one side of the room where I wouldn't be seen by whoever was the other side of the door. "Answer it!" I whispered to Flavia.

She gulped a couple of times, then moved slowly towards the door. The knock sounded again. "Room service," a polite voice said. I holstered my gun—the Scotch had arrived.

I poured the drinks—Flavia's hands were shaking too much. We had one drink. We had a couple. We had three. I checked with my watch. It was an hour since Flavia had returned to the room.

"Whoever it is, they aren't in any hurry!" I said.

Flavia was halfway through her fourth drink. "I think I'll get into something comfortable," she said. She unzipped the gown and stepped out of it, then put a robe over the lace-edged minimum she was wearing underneath.

I put my hand to my face and pressed my eyeballs firmly back into position. I wondered what had hit Flavia—or maybe it was the Scotch.

She sat down on the sofa and crossed her legs so that the robe fell apart above her knees. "Come and sit down beside me, Al," she said.

There was a blue streak across the room and then I was sitting down beside her.

"I've been thinking," she tucked her arm through mine and moved closer. She moved so close that if I'd been a ghost she would have been sitting were I was sitting.

"That experience we were talking about," she said.

"What experience?"

"Mine. The one I haven't got. If we're going to wait around here all night, now might be a good time to get it!"

"You mean—that boy and girl stuff?"

"I'm not talking about mechanical engineering!" she said tartly.

"Well!" I said. "Well!"

"I haven't got any experience," she said softly. "But I'm willing to learn, Al!"

Her lips pouted up at me: "There's something called a kiss, isn't there?"

I was going to demonstrate but the 'phone rang.

"Who's that?" Flavia sat up, looking startled.

"I'll get it!" I told her.

I went across to the 'phone and picked up the receiver.

"Al? Hanlon here."

"Yeah."

"A blonde's just gone into Spain's room."

"Anybody else with her?"

"Just the blonde."

"Okay. Let me know when she comes out again."

"Check. How are things with you?"

"Torrid, brother, torrid!"

I went back to the sofa. Flavia sat upright, pulling the robe close around her. "Who was that?"

"A friend of mine."

"What did he want?"

"Just wondered how I was."

"At this time of night!"

"He's a very good friend."

She frowned at me. "How did he know you were here?"

I lit a cigarette: "I must have told him."

"Why?"

"What about all this experience you're hungering after?"

"That can wait!" she said curtly. "I want to know why you tell somebody you're in my room at this time of night!"

I sucked smoke into my lungs. "You know how it is, honey. Duty calls and a guy must answer if he doesn't want to get fired."

She got up from the sofa and went over to the table and poured herself a drink. "What's happening around here?"

"I'll tell you," I said. "I had a theory and I just wanted to test it, that's all."

"What theory?"

I walked over and helped myself to a drink. "This is really theory number two," I explained. "Theory number one was that you contacted Spain and let all the suspects see you do it. So then if we waited here, the one who had the machine—the murderer—would pay you a call. That one hasn't worked so far."

"And theory number two?" she asked in a tight voice.

I sipped the drink. "Theory number two was that if you happened to be part of the set-up, waiting here was a sure-fire way of knowing I wouldn't be roaming around anywhere else in the hotel, so that would make it the safest time for your partner or partners to contact Spain and clinch the deal."

"Al! Are you crazy?"

"Not more so than any other time," I said. "I think."

She stared at me. "You can't think that I am part of the ..."

"As a clincher," I went on, rudely interrupting her, "you could make really sure of having my interest over these hours by putting on a robe like the robe you've got on, inviting me to sit beside you on the sofa and then asking softly for some boy-girl experience with me as the demonstrator—couldn't you?"

She laughed harshly. "I suppose you think I killed Professor Todt? Stood beside him in front of all those people and killed him!"

I took a stab into the dark. "I don't think you did that," I said. "I don't think you'd want to kill your husband!"

Her face drained of colour. "Husband!" she said hoarsely.

"You are the Mrs. Todt who disappeared a couple of weeks after he married you in New York," I said. "Aren't you?"

"The photograph," she whispered, "how did you see the photograph?"

The 'phone rang again and I picked it up. "They're just leaving," Hanlon said softly over the 'phone. "Spain and his two boys, and the blonde as well. They rode the elevator upwards."

"Stay with it, pal. I'll see you down in the foyer," I said.

I replaced the 'phone and turned around to face Flavia.

"You aren't going anywhere, Lieutenant!" she said tightly,

To emphasise her argument, she was holding a gun in her hand pointed right at me. And at that small distance, if she pulled the trigger I had a nasty feeling the result would be fatal.

"You can't get away with it, honey," I said. "There's no point in trying. Why don't you ..."

"Shut up!" she said.

The remains of my drink was within reaching distance. I reached out and grabbed it.

"If you saw the photograph before the house detective was killed," she said, "why have you waited all this time to do something about it?"

"Simple, honey," I lied. "We wanted to make sure we got everybody concerned."

"Todt was a sentimental fool!" she said bitterly. "I didn't know he'd kept that photograph. A street photographer took it the day we got married. Dexter found it and kept it to himself—I thought. He wanted to blackmail me. I paid or he turned it over to you. I paid him all right," she bared her teeth in a nasty imitation of a smile.

"It was you who killed Dexter?"

"That's right," she said. "But I didn't kill my late unlamented husband!"

"I'll believe that," I said. "Whose idea was the machine?"

"Todt's," she said. "But I was his inspiration, you could say. He lied to me when I married him; told me he really had dough. I was sucker enough to believe him, and I stayed with him a whole fortnight until I found out the truth."

"He wanted you to come back afterwards?"

She patted her hair complacently. "He was crazy for me. He'd do anything. I told him he'd have to have dough before I ever came back to him! Real dough!"

"So he got the idea of the fake gold-making machine?"

"Check. And I followed him around the conventions to make sure he kept working on it. It was a question of finding the right type of sucker to buy it as well. Fortunately Spain came along after awhile. Then the whole thing was set. Only Todt didn't know it. But," she laughed harshly again, "I had no intention of going back with him afterwards. He wasn't my style!"

"And there was me all set to teach you that elementary boy and girl stuff!" I sighed. "Brother! Was I wasting my time!"

The 'phone rang again. I looked at Flavia.

"Answer it," she said. "But give the right answers. Tell whoever it is that you're quite okay and not to bother ringing you again tonight."

"Okay," I said, and picked up the 'phone.

Hanlon's voice was urgent. "Where the hell are you? I'm down in the foyer now. They're coming through."

"I'm quite okay," I said. "You go on home and don't worry about me again tonight."

"Huh?"

"Don't bother ringing me again tonight," I said. "I'm highly organised."

"Have you gone nuts?"

"And tell room service to send up another bottle of Scotch."

I hung up and looked across at Flavia. The gun still pointed at my belt buckle steadily.

"You can just relax now, Lieutenant," she said. "You're not going any place for quite a time!"

"You're the boss," I said.

I went over and sat down on the sofa. "You sure you don't want me to try that boy and girl stuff again while we're waiting around here?"

Her lower lip curled: "If anybody needs the experience, I'd say it was you, Lieutenant! Your technique is straight corn. Put you in the middle of a Midwestern field and nobody could tell the difference between you and the rest of the corn. Except your ears stick out more, maybe."

"I wish you wouldn't keep building my ego," I said. "It's bad for me."

There was a discreet knock on the door.

"Answer it," Flavia said softly. "Maybe it's room service and maybe it's your pal. Hope that it's room service—if it's your pal, you get shot first!"

I walked over to the door and opened it. A waiter stood there with a tray. "A bottle of Scotch, sir?"

"Thanks," I said.

I saw Hanlon standing to one side, behind the waiter—a gun in his hand and his eyes two great question marks. I shook my head slightly, then gave the waiter a buck and took the tray.

"Just put it down on the table," Flavia said. "And thank your lucky stars that your friend wasn't very smart."

"What use is it on the table?" I said. "Here, catch!" I threw the tray towards her. The bottle and the two glasses, the bowl of ice-cubes, all left the tray and made their own independent tracks towards her. She must have felt like a guided missile target.

The gun exploded and there was a boing as the slug hit the tray. Then the bottle caught her on the side of the head and she staggered forward onto her knees, dropping the gun to the floor.

I picked up the gun as Hanlon exploded into the room.

"What's happening?" he asked.

"Too long to explain," I said. "Have the others left?"

"Sure—a couple of minutes ago in a Buick. I've got the number."

"Okay! Grab her," I said.

I picked up the 'phone and got through to Homicide. I repeated the number of the Buick as Hanlon gave it to me and put out a statewide alarm. I wanted it tabbed—not picked up. And I gave them the extension number to ring me back as soon as they got a report on it. I told them to send a car over and pick up Flavia Romberg from us. The desk sergeant croaked when I told him I wanted her booked for Dexter's murder.

When I came around, Flavia was sitting up on the sofa, her head in her hands. "You'd better put something else on instead of that robe, honey," I told her. "You're going down to Homicide in a minute!"

"Yes," she said dully.

She got up and slipped out of the robe. Hanlon noiselessly whistled his approval. Then she slipped into a demure, high-necked dress and went over to the sofa and sat down again.

I brought Hanlon up to date on the story.

"So she's in it with the blonde?" he said.

"Check."

"How can Spain be sucker enough to buy it?"

"Who buys the Brooklyn Bridge at least twenty times a year?" I asked him. "How many guys are in business selling the Empire State Building, non-existent oil wells in South America and tall timber growing on land they don't own?"

"Okay, okay," Hanlon said. "So there's a sucker born every minute."

"And the biggest suckers are the smart boys," I said, "because they never quite lose their dream of one day getting a gold mine for nothing."

"Yes, Professor," Hanlon nodded.

"And don't call me Professor," I said. "Remember what happened to the last Professor around here!"

There was a knock on the door and the two Homicide boys came in. "Take her away and book her for Dexter's murder," I said. "I'll be down later."

"Okay, Lieutenant," one of them said. "Come on, babe. Let's move."

Flavia got up from the sofa and walked towards the door. When she got level with me she turned suddenly and threw her arms around my neck. It was a kiss that literally sizzled. Then she let go and stepped back a pace. There was a curious smile on her face.

"Maybe you should have been a Professor," she said. "We would have been married then. Don't you think you missed something, Lieutenant?" Then she continued on her way towards the door.

When the door had closed behind them, I noticed Hanlon staring at me, open-mouthed.

I shrugged my shoulders modestly. "I don't know what I've got when it comes to beautiful women!" I said. "But whatever it is—I'm loaded!"

"I wasn't thinking about that," he said. "I was just thinking you're the first cop I've ever seen with four lips!"

I dug hastily for a handkerchief.

CHAPTER 13
Rivers Overflows

The first call came five minutes later.

"We picked 'em up, Lieutenant," the desk-sergeant said. "They're heading north along Highway 55."

"How far away are they now?"

"Just past the North Beach turnoff, Lieutenant."

"Okay," I said.

I put down the 'phone and told Hanlon.

"About eight miles away," he said. "What are you going to do?"

"If they look like they're making a run out of the state we'll have 'em picked up," I said. "But I don't think they are. I think they'll stop some place and dump that machine. I've got a two-way radio fitted into the Healey, we'll tail them."

"How the hell did you ever get a two-way radio into that midget?"

"I got one of Dick Tracy's wrist-radios, stupid," I said. "It's attached to the steering-column."

"How does it work?"

"Fine!" I said. "Except when you get backlash."

"Backlash!"

"Then you get a car full of Mumbles, B.O. Plenty and ..."

"I think," Hanlon said, "that stinks!"

"Okay," I said. "Let's go."

We got downstairs, then out into the street and into the Healey. The radio was fixed in the back seat the Healey people have made specially for midgets. "You operate the thing," I said. "And I'll drive."

"Okay," Hanlon said.

Five minutes later we were out on Highway 55. I opened up the Healey to eighty-five, taking the outside lane and hoping that no truck decided to pull over suddenly.

"They're still on the highway," Hanlon said. "About fifteen miles ahead of us."

"Just a minor point," he said. "Did you get take-off clearance from the control-tower?"

"You keep on talking like that and I'll put it into top!" I told him.

Five minutes later Hanlon croaked: "We're gaining—they're only six miles ahead now. There's also a report about somebody low-flying along the highway. I told them not to worry—it's only us."

Another five minutes and then Hanlon said: "They've turned off the highway two miles ahead. A right-hand turn—there's a neon Pepsi sign on the corner."

"Grab a couple of bottles as we go past," I told him.

"Slow down," he said hoarsely, "or we'll be part of that sign."

I saw the sign coming up ahead. I held the speedo steady on eighty-five, seeing the sign coming along on wheels towards me. Then I pumped the brake-pedal twice, shifted down into third, keeping my foot on the gas and brake pedals at the same time.

I got into second a moment before I made the turn and was changing up into third as the Pepsi sign leapt at us, hung hovering in front of us for a fraction of a second, then went whipping past us. I shifted back into top and raised the headlamps on to full beam.

"And to think," Hanlon muttered, "I used to worry about being shot dead!"

The radio was chattering voice and static.

"They can't be more than a half a mile ahead," Hanlon said. "We're the closest to them now. You want any patrol cars to follow us in?"

"Tell them to wait ten minutes and then come in for instructions," I said.

I saw the glint of a tail lamp up ahead, cut the headlamps down to normal beam and slowed. We still came up on the tail lamp and then it winked once and disappeared.

I held the speed of the Healey down to fifty. We went past a gravel driveway between two gates and saw the tail lamp stationary in front of the house.

"That's them all right," Hanlon said. "I picked up the number."

I went about a mile further down the road, made a U-turn and started back. "Tell them where it is," I said. "And tell them to send a couple of patrol cars up in another ten minutes."

"I guess you know what you're doing!" Hanlon muttered.

I switched off the lights of the Healey and slowed down to thirty. I parked the car about a hundred yards short of the gravel drive and we walked the rest of the way.

We stopped at the gates. The Buick still stood there, its lights out. Lights showed from inside the house.

"What do we do now?" Hanlon asked.

"We sneak up on them, I hope," I said.

So we snuck.

There was a back door to the house that wasn't locked. We got in, through the kitchen and into the main hallway. Light spilled from the half-open door down the hall and there was the sound of voices.

We tip-toed down the hall, Wheeler going first because he hadn't been quick enough to get behind Hanlon.

The sound of voices grew louder as I got nearer the door. There was a faint humming noise coming from the room. The humming noise stopped abruptly as I got up to the door. I lined myself up so I could see inside.

There was a table with an impressive-looking black box on it, an electrical lead ran from the box to a power point on the wall. Grouped around the box were Spain, Rivers, Carlotta and Annabelle Starr.

"It doesn't work," Spain said tautly.

Annabelle was holding a large brown paper parcel in her hands. "You just didn't do it right," she said. "It probably needs some practise."

"Then we'll practise," Spain said.

"You practise all you want," she said coldly. "I'm going."

"No, you're not," Spain said. "Not until this thing's turned silver into gold, you're not!"

"I'm going," she said.

Rivers moved in front of her. "The boss says you stay—you stay!" he said.

She faced him for a moment, her face white and strained, then she relaxed. "All right!" she shrugged her shoulders. "In that case, I might as well have a cigarette."

She opened her purse and put her hand inside. "I've got a pack in here somewhere," she said. Her hand came out, but not holding a pack of cigarettes. There was a zipping noise and Rivers' knees buckled and he fell on to the floor.

She turned to face the other two, her back towards the door. "I'm going," she said. "Try anything and I'll let you have what Rivers just got!"

She started to back towards the door. She kept on backing until she backed right into the nose of my Police Special. "Drop it, honey!" I told her. "To coin a phrase—this is a pinch!"

Hanlon stepped past me into the room, his gun covering the other two. There was a faint thud as Annabelle dropped it. Hanlon stooped and picked it up.

"Interesting!" I said. "A zip-gun. I wouldn't have thought Annabelle was a juvenile delinquent, but you never can tell. Only she fired tungsten darts instead of .22 slugs."

"That's how she got Professor Todt?" Hanlon asked.

"Sure—without making so much noise that the people around her heard it. She should have been a Delf, she's so smart!"

Spain took out a cigar and slowly lit it. "Let you into a secret," I told him. "You could stay with that machine from here to eternity and it wouldn't even make you a frankfurt!"

Carlotta seemed to be speechless for the first time in her life. Then she recovered. "I am not in this!" she said. "I only come with him because he is—how you say?—my boy-friend!"

"And you only come with us because you are—how you say?—withholding evidence?" I smiled at her. "Don't worry about it, amigo, it shouldn't bring you any more than one to three."

And then it was all over.

We sent them back to Homicide in one of the patrol cars and Hanlon and I took the Healey.

I drove along at a cautious seventy on the way back.

"How did you pick the two girls?" Hanlon asked me.

"I didn't," I said honestly. "The suspects came down to four, really. Wilbur Kessell, Lipcheek, Annabelle and Flavia. I knew she couldn't have killed the Professor, but that didn't guarantee she was mixed up in it. And she was too anxious to help—she kept sticking her nose into the case. Annabelle did the same. She fixed Carlotta and got me off the suspension hook. Why? My theory was she thought it was safer to have a dumb cop like me on the case than maybe get somebody smart put on to it, like you."

Hanlon nodded thoughtfully: "That makes sense!"

"Relax, Sherlock!" I snarled at him. "I'd figure Flavia as the brains of the outfit though. Annabelle used Lipcheek because he was stuck on her. He'd do what he was told without asking any questions. Poor Waldo's going to be a lonely guy."

"And so is Wheeler," Hanlon said smugly. "This is one case where he doesn't get left with a beautiful dame because he's booking all three of 'em." He threw back his head and laughed contentedly. "You're slipping, pal!"

"A Wheeler never slips in the important things of life," I said. "Sure, we might gum up a couple of murder cases, arrest the wrong party a few times and shoot an innocent bystander here and there. But get left without a beautiful dame at the end of the case! Hell! That's getting orthodox!"

It took a couple of hours to get through the formalities at the Bureau. One thing I like about women—they stick together. Both Annabelle and Flavia talked their heads off about how it was all the other's fault. Either way they put enough in their statements to make the D.A.'s job even easier than it is.

I quit around five in the morning. Lavers even smiled at me. "I knew you'd come good, Al!" he said. "Never doubted it for moment!"

"Even when you suspended me?"

He coughed gently. "Well, that's another thing. But I want you to know that I appreciate your efforts in this case, and I'm going to prove it!"

That was something. At long last maybe I was going to get made Captain. I smiled thankfully at him. "Thanks, Commissioner!" I said humbly.

"Think nothing of it," he said. "Here! Have a cigar!"

I took the cigar. "You were saying?"

"I just said it," he looked at me blankly.

"Something about showing your appreciation, Commissioner—remember?" Hell! He was the shortest-minded character I'd ever met.

"I just did, didn't I?" he thundered. "I'll have you know I pay fifty cents for those cigars—each!"

I took the cigar out of my pocket and looked at it.

"I don't want to take all the credit for this thing, Commissioner," I said. "Here!" I broke the cigar in half and handed him one half. "Would you see that Lieutenant Hanlon gets this?"

His face went a dull beetroot colour and he opened his mouth wide to say something. I shoved my half of the cigar into the void and his teeth clamped down on it automatically. "I couldn't take bribes even from a Commissioner, Commissioner," I told him. And then I went out quickly before I got fired again.

It was six-thirty when I got home. I thumbed through the directory until I found the number, then rang.

She answered on the tenth ring. "What happened?" her voice was drowsy. "The sky fall in or something?"

"Al Wheeler," I said. "Today is Thursday—your day off—right?"

"Oh!" she said coldly. "You finally quit that woman's room in the hotel?"

"Right when I booked her for murder," I said.

"Really?" She sounded interested. "What happened?"

"You come over and have breakfast with me," I said, "and tell you all about it."

"It's a deal!" she agreed. "You aren't kidding me about that dame?"

"She's booked for murder," I said. "If you don't believe me, ring Homicide and check. You call a cab and I'll start frying some bacon and eggs and things."

"Okay," she said, "I'll be over in half an hour. Was that why you got rid of me last night? So you could book her for murder?"

"What other reason could there be for getting rid of a beautiful blonde like you?" I asked her.

"You sound better in the mornings," she said. "Half an hour then, Al?"

"I'll count the seconds, Joanna-honey," I told her.

I hung up. I put some nice sentimental Sinatra on to the hi-fi, pulled the drapes to shut out that horrible sunlight, primped the cushions on the sofa, and then went into the kitchen to make breakfast.

I thought it would take me a long time to tell Joanna the full story. Maybe I should get another four meals lined up ready as well as breakfast—but

then we probably wouldn't be eating all the time.
  That Hanlon!
  What did he think we Wheelers were?
Orthodox?

The End

Eve, It's Extortion

Carter Brown

CHAPTER 1
Eve?

Commissioner Lavers had made an improvement around his office. The improvement's name was Annabelle Jackson and hush my mouth, she came from the South. Her vital statistics, at a casual glance, were thirty-seven and three-quarters, twenty-six, thirty-eight and maybe an eighth.

From the time the improvement appeared, I started appearing more regularly in the office. I thought it was only fair for me to take notice of the improvement. If I didn't, then the Commissioner probably wouldn't make any further improvements and maybe he had in mind getting me a secretary as the next improvement.

Well, I can dream, can't I?

I was sitting on the edge of Annabelle's desk, looking at her and thinking about mint juleps and hay rides under a harvest moon, when she gave me that slow smile of hers.

"You know, Lieutenant," she drawled. "You got me tricked."

"Call me Al," I said. "And I haven't. You haven't been out with me yet. You haven't had a ride in my English sports car, you haven't even heard my hi-fi."

She shook her head. "I don't mean that way. I mean why are you around here every day? Don't you have a job?"

"You don't know what you're saying, honey-child," I told her indignantly. "Didn't Commissioner Lavers tell you about me? Didn't he tell you that Lieutenant Wheeler is his right-hand man? And also his left. I sometimes even deputise for his feet. I'm his expert. The unorthodox cop ready for any emergency that's too big for the rest of the force to handle."

She shook her head again. "All he said to me was that if a big slob by the name of Wheeler got into my hair, to dust him off."

"He said that?"

"Cross my heart, honey." She traced two straight lines across her chest.

I was speechless, wondering whether I should sue Lavers for defamation of character or tell Annabelle about the murder cases I'd handled—both of them—when the buzzer thing sounded on her desk. She flicked a switch and a tinny replica of Lavers' voice spoke.

"Is that no-good, idle Wheeler out there?"

"Yes, sir," Annabelle said dutifully.

"Send him in here. Is he sober?"

I leaned across and answered for Annabelle. "As a Police Commissioner," I said. "And I resent that idle crack."

"Bee around the honey-pot, eh?" Lavers said. "Well, come a-buzzing in here." There was a click and the thing went dead.

I looked at Annabelle sourly. "He must have been watching Steve Allen on television."

"Is he good?"

"Who? The Commissioner?"

"Steve Allen."

"Sure—he's very good."

"I'll have to watch television," she said thoughtfully. "Some night when I don't have a date—whenever that will be."

The thing buzzed again.

"Ask Wheeler," Lavers said loudly, "how he'd like a nice blue uniform and a traffic detail."

"I think he's getting impatient," Annabelle said.

"What do I care?" Then I remembered what a traffic detail is like.

Two seconds later I walked into the Commissioner's office and closed the door gently behind me. He had company. A short guy, bald and smoking a cigar.

"This is Mr. Moss," Lavers said. "Lee Moss. He's an old friend of mine— I can't remember why. Lee, this is Lieutenant Wheeler—Al Wheeler."

We shook hands.

"You tell Wheeler about it," the Commissioner went on. "Get him out of my hair. It's about time he did some work around here, anyway. Stop him terrorising my secretary."

"I don't terrorise your secretary," I said. "I can't even get to first base with your secretary. She won't even listen when I play my banjo and sing *Dear Old Southland.*"

"Take him away and talk to him, Lee," Lavers said. "Before my ulcers burst and make a mess of the carpet."

"Maybe we could go some place and drink a cup of coffee, huh?" Moss grinned at me.

"Sure," I said. "We can sit on Annabelle's desk and ..."

"Take him out of the building, Lee," the Commissioner said. "And if you manage to get him run down by a car, we won't book you."

Ten minutes later we were in the nearest bar, drinking Scotch.

"I'm with United," Moss said, and lit himself a cigar.

"Baseball?"

"Insurance."

"You look like an honest man, too," I said. "To tell you the truth, Lee, I have all the insurance I need. In fact, more than I need. You can't take it with you and I don't have anybody to leave it to, except maybe a blonde in South Dakota and I hear she's got married recently—to a wrestler—and if you think I want a wrestler tramping on my grave you've got another …"

"A claims investigator," Moss interrupted loudly. "I don't sell insurance."

"I'm sure glad to hear that, Lee," I said. "You see I don't really want insurance …"

"We've been through all that."

"Okay," I said. "I was just making a point."

He sucked his cigar and snorted. "I didn't believe the Commissioner when he said he had a screwball Lieutenant attached to his office, but now I see what he meant."

"You don't have to pay me compliments," I said. "What's with the claims investigation department?"

"You know how it is sometimes. You get a feeling about things."

"Sure," I said, "I know. I get it all the time—with blondes, brunettes, redheads—even grandmothers sometimes."

"Yeah," he said heavily. "But I'm talking about the feeling you get about an insurance claim. I've got the feeling about one right now."

"Tell me about it," I said. "That's why I'm here."

He took another puff on his cigar. "Guy by the name of Farnham—Henry Farnham. Got knocked down by a car and killed the night before last. Hit-and-run driver. No witnesses, no nothing except a corpse in the middle of the street. Happened just on dusk—he'd just left a bar, was on his way home, crossing the street."

"Was he drunk?"

He pulled a face. "No more than usual, according to the guy behind the bar who'd been serving him. He used to go there and drink every afternoon."

"What smells about it?"

"He had a life policy with us—for thirty thousand dollars. He was a deadbeat, a bum, but his insurance payments were always met—by his wife."

"And she gets the money?"

"She gets all of it. She works as a waitress. She kept up the insurance payments—she admits it."

"You think she knocked her old man down?"

He shook his head sadly. "I checked. She was working all day. She was serving in a hamburger joint at the time he was killed."

"Then why do you have this feeling?"

"She didn't have to do it—somebody else could have done it for her."

"Any ideas who?"

"No," he said sourly. "But I still got that feeling right in the pit of my stomach."

"What do you want me to do?"

"Have a look at it," he said. "People don't pay any attention to an insurance investigator, but they get nervous when a cop comes around."

"You want me to talk to the widow?"

"I'd be grateful if you'd just nose around and see if you can get the same smell in your nostrils as I've got."

I remembered he was a friend of the Commissioner's. "Sure," I said. "You have the address?"

"408 Oakley Street," he said. "The apartment's on the second floor. Her name is Eve."

"Flatfooted and frowsy?"

"Brother," he grinned. "You're in for a surprise."

"I can always use one," I said. "I have a feeling I'm not going to get one from Annabelle."

"Turn up anything and you can always reach me at United."

"Okay," I said. "You're sure this feeling of yours isn't just heartburn?"

"It's never been wrong yet," he declared, patting his paunch lovingly.

"Then I'll take your word for it. Or your stomach's word for it."

I left him outside the bar and went back to the office.

Lavers looked at me from under his eyebrows. I make the point because his eyebrows are a second cousin to those of an abominable snowman. As a matter of fact, it wouldn't surprise me if the Commissioner is a first cousin to an abominable snowman.

"Well?" he barked.

"You really want me to nose around this hit-and-run's widow?" I asked him.

"Sure I do," he said. "Moss is an old friend of mine, and he's been helpful to the Department in his time and probably will be again."

I listened for the sound of muted drums and the band playing the Marine Anthem in the background.

"And furthermore," Lavers went on. "It's about time you did something. You've been cluttering up my office for the last month and I'm sick and tired of it."

"Yes, sir," I said.

His fist banged down on his desk. "And further furthermore, with you out of the office my secretary might have a chance to get some work done."

"Yes, sir, Mr. Commissioner," I said.

He pointed towards the door. "Go!"

I went.

I went into the outer office again and saw Annabelle's beautiful head bent over her ugly typewriter. I walked over to her desk and smiled down at the part in her hair—it didn't smile back at me.

"It may interest you to know," I said casually, "that the Commissioner has just assigned me to the most baffling case in the history of this Department."

"Don't tell me, Lieutenant," she said without looking up, "that somebody's really lost a needle in a haystack?"

"Very funny," I said. "Did you know the part in your hair isn't straight? There are an awful lot of blonde hairs straggling all over the place—particularly the ones with dark roots."

"Very funny," she said. "Why don't you go some place, Lieutenant—and drop dead."

I moved away back to my own desk. "I am about to start my investigation, Miss Jackson," I said. "Will you please keep a note of any phone calls whilst I'm gone?"

"Certainly, Lieutenant," she smiled at me. "What shall I tell the finance companies—the usual story?"

CHAPTER 2
Who Bit the Apple?

Oakley Street was the dump I had expected. A four-storey brownstone which was about two years away from being a tenement. The front door was wide open and a couple of kids were playing on the steps.

I went past them and up two flights of stairs. There were two apartments to each floor. I pressed the buzzer of 408 and waited.

Some thirty seconds later the door opened.

"Mrs. Farnham?" I asked.

"That's right," she said.

I saw what Moss had meant when he said I was in for a surprise. I was looking at it right then. She was brunette and tall with it. She had coal-coloured eyes and a wide mouth. She was wearing a black sweater and a skirt. The sweater had a low scoop neckline that was stretched tight against her skin. You could say the whole sweater was stretched tight. I thought if they ever ran a "Miss Bustline" competition in Oakley Street, she'd win—without even taking a deep breath.

I remembered this was business.

"I'm Lieutenant Wheeler," I said and showed her my shield which proves I'm a cop, or I just slugged a cop and took his shield. She believed the first theory.

"Oh," she said. "Have I done something?"

"I'm making inquiries into the death of your husband," I said. "I wonder if I could ask you some questions."

"Of course," she said. Then the after-thought. "Won't you come in?"

I followed her into the apartment and took off my hat. She was the sort of woman you took off your hat for automatically. The apartment was neat and clean and spartan.

"Won't you sit down?" she said.

I sat in an armchair and a couple of springs made themselves known to me. She sat down opposite me.

"I'm afraid I can't tell you much, Lieutenant," she said. "You see, I wasn't there when it happened and …"

"I know," I said. "A hit-and-run driver, wasn't it?"

She nodded. "And Henry was drunk—as usual."

"He was an alcoholic?"

Her lower lip curled slightly. "You could call him that—if you wanted to be polite. He was a lush, Lieutenant. He was no good. A stinking, no-good lush."

"I get the picture," I said.

Her shoulders sagged a little. "I'm sorry, Lieutenant. It doesn't sound very nice—not coming from a widow, does it? But I've worked for the last three years to support him and …"

"Even paid his insurance premiums?" I suggested.

"That's right," she nodded. "I paid everything."

I took out a pack of cigarettes. "You mind if I smoke?"

"No," she said. "I'll have one, too."

I got up and offered her a cigarette, then struck a match. She put her hand on mine to guide the match. Her fingers were cool and impersonal.

"I work as a waitress," she said. "In a joint that slings hash. If I sound bitter about Henry, Lieutenant, you should try working in a hash joint sometime. If you're under forty and don't look like the side of a house— you're on the menu as far as the men are concerned. They make passes at you when you walk by … while you're serving them … the whole time you're in reach. And if you don't just smile, they complain to the management and you get fired."

"Tough," I said.

She exhaled gently and looked at me. "I suppose you're used to hearing people's problems?"

"Not many have a problem that money can't solve," I said. "Particularly a lot of money—like thirty thousand dollars."

"What are you trying to say, Lieutenant?" Her voice was indifferent.

"In your own words, your husband was a no-good lush who you feel no grief for. And with him dead, you collect the insurance money—thirty thousand dollars, I understand. A tenth of that sum has been a good reason for murder."

"You think I killed him?" She raised her eyebrows a fraction. "That I ran him down in the street? Sorry to disappoint you, Lieutenant, but I was working at the time—a dozen people can tell you …"

"I know," I said. I leaned back in the chair and shifted the pressure of the springs to a couple of new spots. "These are only routine questions, Mrs. Farnham. Routine questions because the question of the amount of insurance money demands a routine investigation."

"I see," she said.

I stubbed my butt out in a cheap glass ashtray. "Did anything unusual happen during the last week or two? Anything out of routine?"

"I don't think so," she said. "I worked—he drank. It was as simple as that … There was the locater, of course."

"Locater? From a finance company?"

"A woman," she said. "It was on my day off. Henry owed a thousand dollars in Detroit that I didn't even know about. We left there twelve months ago and moved here to Pine City."

"Which day did she call?"

"Wednesday."

"Your husband was killed on the Friday?"

"That's right."

"What was the locater's name?"

She thought for a couple of seconds. "Bright," she said. "A Miss Bright, from Laurence Cole and Company. She said it about three times, so I guess I remembered it without any trouble."

"And nothing else out of the ordinary happened?"

"Nothing else."

"What about your husband? Did he seem any different?"

"Henry was exactly the same. At night when I came home, he'd be drunk—sleeping it off. When I went to bed, he'd wake up and whine at me until I gave him enough money to drink himself through the next day. In the morning when I went to work, he'd still be asleep."

I got to my feet. "Well, thank you, Mrs. Farnham. Sorry I had to bother you."

"That's all right," she said. She walked with me to the door and opened it. "I don't remember seeing you at the precinct, Lieutenant."

"I'm not from the precinct," I said.

"Oh?" Her eyebrows raised again just a fraction. "Where are you from?"

"Homicide," I told her.

I went out of the apartment and down to the Austin-Healey, then drove back into town. I checked in the office and found Laurence Cole and Company were in a building three blocks away. It was lunchtime almost. Laurence Cole and Company could wait till the afternoon.

Annabelle was busy typing, so I sat on her desk and tried to peek at the neckline of her blouse without any success. Girls like Annabelle have a natural protective movement in everything they do, even typing.

"I was thinking of buying you lunch, honey-child," I said.

She looked up with a warm smile on her face. "I think that's really nice of you, Lieutenant," she said. "Anything I hate is buying myself a sandwich. I'll have a salami on rye, thank you."

"I said lunch, not a sandwich."

She looked up again. "Oh—you mean, together?"

"You're catching on."

"No, thank you, Lieutenant."

"Did your mother tell you about guys like me?" I asked her bitterly.

"No," she smiled warmly again. "But my father was one."

I gave up and took myself to lunch—which was cheaper but lonelier.

Around two-thirty I arrived at the offices of Laurence Cole and Company. It wasn't a very big office. It seemed to employ maybe half a dozen people.

There was a receptionist who must have been cute around the time Lindbergh flew the Atlantic for the first time solo.

"I'd like to see Mr. Cole," I told her.

"He's engaged," she said. Her voice sounded like a cheesegrater.

"Honey, I wouldn't worry if he was married," I said, and showed her the shield. "Lieutenant Wheeler, Homicide."

"Oh," she said. Her voice was a little subdued. That's what I like about being a cop. You can be rude to people and they aren't rude back—unless their name happens to be Lavers.

Half a minute later she told me Mr. Cole would see me right away. I found myself in a private office and Mr. Cole getting up from his chair to shake my hand.

"Sit down, Lieutenant," he said. 'What can I do for you?"

"I'm making some enquiries," I said. "A man named Farnham was killed in a street accident. I understand one of your staff contacted his wife a couple of days before the accident?"

He nodded. "We read about it in the papers, Lieutenant. Our business to know these things, of course. I believe there is quite a considerable sum of insurance money to come to the widow. It looks as if our client in Detroit may collect his money yet."

"Well," I said, "I'm glad the street accident was so convenient for you."

His face paled slightly. "I didn't mean it that way, Lieutenant. I just meant …"

"Sure," I said. "The locater who saw Mrs. Farnham was a Miss Bright, I believe?"

"Yes," he said. "Edna Bright. The best I have on my staff. She sticks at a job until she finds the person she's trying to locate and if I could only say that for the rest of them, I'd be a happy ..."

"Could I speak to her?"

"She's out right now."

"When will she be back?"

"Hard to say, Lieutenant. She's out on a job—another locate, of course. She should be back here some time between five and six."

"I'd like to talk to her," I said. "Maybe she could ring me when she gets back?"

"Of course, Lieutenant. At what number?"

I gave him my home number. Why should I wait around in the Commissioner's office when I could listen to my hi-fi set-up and drink at the same time?

I left Laurence Cole's office and headed to the nearest bar, had a couple of drinks and then drove home. It was around four-thirty when I left the Healey outside and got myself organised inside the house.

Ten minutes later I lay back in an armchair, the ice making a nice tinkling sound inside the glass whenever I revolved it, and the hi-fi piping out of its five speakers. I had Les Paul and Mary Ford on thirty-three and a third, with Mary singing *Go 'Long Blues*. I was with her every note of the way.

I got the Blues fast. Me, Al Wheeler, the guy who used to be known as unorthodox and here I was, handling the most orthodox hit-and-run case I ever heard of. And to cap that, an orthodox Southern belle by the name of Annabelle was giving me the run-around.

I decided I was getting old.

I got a mental picture of how it would be almost anytime now. I'd have the Funeral March playing on the hi-fi, supporting the Boy Scouts' motto of Be Prepared. I'd be sucking at an empty pipe and drinking spinach water because the doctors had banned tobacco and alcohol.

The only woman who ever came close to me would take my arm to help me across the street. I would have thin grey hair and a gnarled face—and a housekeeper. She'd have a face made of granite and wear a black dress which would rustle while she walked. Every evening about this time she'd bring in my supper—a plate of steaming hot gruel.

The phone rang ...

I managed to heave myself into an upright position. I drew the shawl tighter around my bowed shoulders, then shuffled across the room. I picked up the receiver with a palsied hand and quavered, "Grandpa Wheeler," into it.

"Oh, I'm sorry," a husky, vibrant voice said. "I thought I'd find Lieutenant Wheeler there."

"My grandson," I quavered. "I'll get him for you."

I took a deep breath and the years fell away like a heavyweight paid to take a dive. "This is Al Wheeler," I said in a voice I hoped was equally vibrant.

"This is Edna Bright speaking, Lieutenant," the voice said. It did more than just speak. It fingered each vertebra of my spine slowly. "Mr. Cole told me you wanted me to ring you."

"I wanted to ask you some questions, Miss Bright," I said. "You spoke to Mrs. Farnham last Wednesday."

"That's right," she said. "But really, I don't see …"

"This is official business and necessary, Miss Bright," I said. "I would ask you to come in straight away so we can hear your answers."

"Well, if you put it like that I most certainly will, Lieutenant," she said. "Which precinct?"

"I'm with Homicide."

"You want me to come to the Bureau?"

"No," I said loudly. I gave her my own address. "Come to that address—I'll be waiting for you."

"Very well," she said coldly, then hung up.

I cradled the receiver and did some fast organising. A stack of records on the turntable, plenty of ice and Scotch, along with two clean glasses.

I started the turntable moving and Sinatra whispered the *Wee Small Hours of the Morning* from the five speakers. That disc, of course, was going back onto the bottom of the pile—normally, if a guy plays his cards right, it's a clincher.

Dames, as some other guy once said, are sentimental. Get them crying into their liquor and your only problem is to see they don't dilute their liquor too much with tears.

I thought it might take her a little while to arrive and I had a thirst. So I poured myself a drink while Frankie-Boy gave with *Mood Indigo*. I've always wondered why a million fathers didn't band themselves together into a league for Frankie's abolition after he made that disc.

I drank the drink and poured myself another. She seemed to be taking a long time in getting here—or maybe it was me who was just impatient.

It's amazing the effect a dame's voice can have on you. Right then I wasn't feeling like a grandfather any more—more like a grandchild—a grandchild who had an advanced education at a co-ed school, that is.

I began to worry that she might have got lost—gone to the wrong house or something. She seemed to be taking a hell of a time to arrive. I thought it must have been hours since she called on the phone—then the door buzzer went.

She had a face and figure to match her voice. She was blonde and wearing a thin silk dress that the evening breeze moulded around her. I gave a long soundless sigh.

"Lieutenant Wheeler?" she asked in that husky voice.

"That's right," I agreed.

"I'm Edna Bright." She had a slightly puzzled look on her face as she stood there. "This is a private house, isn't it?"

"Mine," I said, "or it will be in thirty years when the mortgage is paid."

"But I thought … I mean, you said this was official business and …"

"Sure," said. "Come in, won't you."

"I suppose so," her voice was still doubtful, then she brightened up suddenly. "It's all right, of course, I nearly forgot … your Grandfather lives with you, doesn't he?"

CHAPTER 3
The Ice-Cold Blonde

She sat opposite me, sipping the Scotch. Her legs were crossed and the hem of her dress rode slightly above her knees. She had the best legs I've seen since before they cleaned up burlesque in Newark.

"Your Grandfather is out at the moment, is he, Lieutenant?"

"He's gone to bed," I said. "He retires early—has his plate of gruel at five-thirty every night—then off he goes to bed."

"Gruel? What on earth is that?"

"I don't know," I said quickly. "He has it, not me."

She took another sip of her Scotch. "You wanted to ask me some questions, Lieutenant?"

"There's absolutely no hurry," I assured her.

I walked over and switched on the turntable. A couple of seconds later music poured out of the wall and I smiled at her.

"Like it?"

"You have a speaker in the wall?"

"Five in that wall," I said. "When I can afford it I'm going to put another three in that wall."

"What for?"

I stared at her. "For high-fidelity reproduction, that's what."

"I thought five speakers would make it loud enough as it is."

I sat there, thinking about that.

"Anyway, Lieutenant," her voice became business-like. "What about these questions you want me to answer?"

"Okay," I said. "Are you doing anything tonight?"

She laughed. "I won't believe you're a police officer at all in a moment."

"Neither will I," I said. "I'm prepared to forget that sordid fact so long as you are."

"Please be serious."

She was sitting on the divan. I moved myself and my drink across and sat next to her. She moved away fractionally.

"I am being serious," I assured her. "Deadly serious. Are you doing anything tonight?"

She looked at her watch carefully. "As a matter of fact I am, Lieutenant. I'm due to meet my boyfriend in town half an hour from now—and he gets very irritable if I keep him waiting."

I felt like Grandpa again.

"Okay," I said. "I'll ask the questions."

"Now you're talking like a police officer," she said. "I like you better that way."

I started to feel like Great-Grandpa.

"You made a locate on Henry Farnham," I said. "Take it from there."

"All right," she said. "It was one of the easiest locates I've ever made. We had word from Detroit that it was believed the Farnhams had come here to Pine City about twelve months ago. I checked in the phone directory—there were six H. Farnhams listed, and the fourth one I tried was the right one. How Joe Williams ever missed it, I don't know."

"Joe Williams?"

"He's the other half of the leg-team at Laurence Coles," she said. "The two of us do the outside work—the tracking down. Mr. Cole does a bit here and there, but not much as a rule. Joe was given the Farnham job the week before and he couldn't find them. Mr. Cole was annoyed with him and gave me the job."

"I see," I said.

"Well," she continued, "I rang the buzzer and Mrs. Farnham opened the door. She had a wrap on and that was all." Edna's mouth was pursed with disapproval. "At three in the afternoon."

"Go on," I told her.

She took her third cautious sip of Scotch. "She seemed somehow disappointed to see me. She couldn't have known I was a locater, so I didn't get it. Not that it made any difference. I told her what it was about and she laughed."

"She thought it was funny?"

She shook her head. "I don't mean she laughed that way. It was a bitter laugh, really. She said that if anyone could get five dollars out of her husband, let alone five thousand, she'd like to know how they did it. And then she said I could find him in the nearest bar if I wanted to talk to him.

"I didn't want to talk to him, of course. I'd made the locate and the lawyers take it from there. I was satisfied so I left. I felt a bit sorry for her, married to a worthless character like Henry Farnham. But then it wasn't any of my business."

"Did she seem surprised when you told her about the money owing in Detroit?"

"Yes. She seemed staggered by it. Almost as if she couldn't believe it."

I offered her a cigarette and she shook her head. I lit one for myself. "And that's all there was to it?" I asked.

"That's all, Lieutenant."

"Okay," I said. "Thanks."

"Not at all," she said. She got up from the divan. "If you'll excuse me, I have to get back to town and …"

I got onto my feet. "Sure," I said. "And just to show there's no hard feelings, I'll drive you in."

"That's very kind of you," she said. "Are you sure you can leave your Grandfather?"

"He sleeps like a babe," I said. "That will be no trouble at all."

Five minutes later she was sitting beside me in the Healey and we were on our way.

"How come a girl who looks the way you do is a locater for a finance company?" I asked her.

"What do you mean—*a girl like me?*"

"The last thing you look like is a locater."

She smiled. She dimpled when she smiled, I noticed.

"That's my secret," she said. "I don't look like a locater. I think that's the reason I do better than Joe Williams—he looks like a locater."

"And what does he look like?"

"Cynical—hat pushed back on his head full of wisecracks. The way you'd expect a locater to look. People see him coming half a mile away and dodge."

We came into the city proper.

"Where can I drop you?" I asked.

"The Camille restaurant, if you don't mind," she said.

Four more blocks and we were there. I pulled into the curb and stopped the car.

"That was very kind of you, Lieutenant." She hesitated for a moment, then added, "Would you like to come in and meet my boyfriend? We could have a drink, perhaps?"

"Sounds like a wonderful idea," I said.

We went inside the restaurant. There was a bar just off the entrance so you could go in and have a drink before you entered the restaurant proper.

We sat on uncomfortable chrome stools. "What will you have?" I asked her.

"A coke, thanks," she said.

I sat there and stared at her.

"I've had all the alcohol I can take for one evening, thanks very much," she smiled. "Just a coke, please."

The bartender looked at me enquiringly.

"A Scotch on the rocks," I said, then lowered my voice. "And a coke."

"The Scotch for the lady, sir?"

"For me."

He served the drinks and I very carefully gave him the exact amount.

I raised my glass, "Here's to your beautiful blue eyes. And I do hope your boyfriend didn't break a leg on his way over here."

But she wasn't paying me any attention. She was staring over my shoulder, her eyes as bright as her name.

"Here's Vince now," she said. She slipped off the stool and ran to meet him.

I waited patiently while she made with the explanations of me, then the two of them joined me.

"Lieutenant," Edna Bright said, "I'd like you to meet Vince Schaeffer. Vince, this is Lieutenant Wheeler."

I looked at him for the first time. He was big with glossy black hair and an olive complexion. Handsome—very much so—in a Latin way.

"Haven't seen you in a while, Vince," I said.

"A long time, Lieutenant." His voice was flat.

Edna looked from one to the other of us. "You two know each other?"

"We've met," I agreed.

"Sure," Vince Schaeffer nodded. "We've met."

I finished my drink. "If you'll excuse me, I think I'll be getting along."

"Sure, Lieutenant," Vince said. "See you around."

"I hope not, Vince," I said.

"Goodbye, Lieutenant." Edna sounded worried. "Thank you very much for driving me back into town."

"My pleasure," I told her, and walked out of the bar.

I thought I might as well join Grandpa in an early night—but the hell with the gruel.

Lavers called me into his office the next morning before I even had time to take a good look at Annabelle.

"You talk to that woman yesterday?" he asked.

"Check."

"What gives?"

"I don't know."

"Don't be evasive."

I lit a cigarette. "So help me, Commissioner, I don't know. I would say she's a smart girl. Too smart to stay married to a lush all her life."

"You think Moss could be right—that it's murder?"

"I don't know yet," I said. "If Henry Farnham was deliberately run down, she didn't do it. She's got a cast-iron alibi. So if it was murder, then somebody else did it for her."

"Got any ideas on who?"

"There's a girl by the name of Edna Bright."

"Who's she?"

"A locater for a finance company. She called on Mrs. Farnham a couple of days before the death—to make a locate."

Lavers snorted contemptuously. "You aren't going to tell me they got to know each other so well that in two days' time Edna murdered the husband for half the insurance money?"

"Maybe they knew each other before Edna made the locate."

"Did they?"

"I don't know—I'm going to find out."

"What else?"

I settled back in my chair. "Edna Bright is an honest, upright, hundred per cent clean-living American girl."

"You mean, she wouldn't play patacake with you on the sofa?"

I looked pained. "Commissioner—you put things so crudely. And it goes beyond that, anyway. She gives that impression. And the impression sticks. It stuck with me last night all the way until I met her boyfriend."

"Who's he?"

"Vince Schaeffer. Remember him?"

"I thought he was still in San Quentin."

"So did I," I said. "I hope he's not supposed to be, because if he is I failed in my duty."

"That's routine with you," Lavers growled. "He was doing a three to five, wasn't he?"

"He tried to knock over a bank," I agreed. "But one of the tellers knocked him over. He—Vince, that is—was carrying a gun."

"It sounds as if you might be getting somewhere with it."

I stubbed my cigarette in his favourite ashtray and he growled, but only half-heartedly.

"There's another locater—by the name of Joe Williams."

"Don't tell me he located her?"

I gave him my enigmatic grin. "You remember the celebrated Sherlock Holmes dialogue, Chief? Holmes: 'Then we come to the interesting incident of the watchdog.' Watson: 'But the dog didn't bark.' Holmes: 'That's what makes it interesting!' Or something like that."

"All right—I'll buy it."

"Williams didn't make the locate. He was assigned to the job before Miss Bright but when he didn't make the locate, the firm gave it to Miss Bright. She had no trouble, she told me—she dug through the phone directory, came up with maybe half a dozen H. Farnhams and started with the first. She found him, all right; or she found his wife, anyway."

"What does Williams say?"

"I don't know—I haven't asked him yet."

"What the hell are you sitting here for? Go out and ask him."

"You want me to stay with this thing?"

"It's giving you something to do—and I'd like to convince Moss one way or the other."

"Leave it to Wheeler," I said. "Be no trouble, Chief."

"It's had better not," he said nastily. "The traffic detail needs more men every day."

I didn't press the point. I withdrew from his office as fast as my feet would carry me.

But I didn't go and see Williams right away. I drove over to the Fourth Precinct, which would have handled the routine of Henry Farnham's demise.

Captain Graut ran the precinct. I knew him vaguely from a long time back. I got shown into his office and he grinned at me and asked me to sit down.

"The Commissioner's white-haired boy," he said. "How are you, Wheeler?"

"Is that what they're saying?"

"That's the good word from Homicide to the traffic detail. Lavers loves Wheeler so much, he has to have him around his office the whole time!"

"The only reason he does that is so when he wants to kick me, he doesn't have to go over to Homicide to do it," I said. "He doesn't like the idea of going over to the Bureau around five times a day."

Graut looked as if he didn't believe me. "What's the pitch, anyway? We done something we shouldn't?"

"Not so far as I know," I said. "I'm interested in a hit-and-run victim. Name of Henry Farnham. Happened last Wednesday. Your boys would have handled it."

He nodded. "Sergeant Kane handled it."

"I'd like to talk to him."

"Sure. He's on duty now—I'll get him for you." He pressed a buzzer on his desk. "Something wrong with it?"

"I don't know," I said. "Homicide got a lead on it in a roundabout way. The Commissioner gets the idea here and there that I should earn my living. So I'm going around asking questions here and there."

"Okay," Graut smiled thinly. "So I'll mind my own business."

Sergeant Kane came in a couple of minutes later. He was a big fat guy who looked sleepy, but his eyes weren't. I told him the pitch.

"Sure, I remember the Farnham business," he said. "He was a lush. Left a bar around five in the afternoon, got knocked over in the middle of East Street. Hit-and-run job."

"You ever find the car?"

"Sure—one of those happy coincidences that sometimes impress the general public," he grinned. "It was stolen—no wonder the guy didn't stop. Reported stolen at five-thirty. Six o'clock when the licence-plate number is being given out over the radio—one of our guys in a prowl car finds he's parked right behind it."

"Nobody tells me these things," I said.

"This is the first time you asked," Graut said.

"I wasn't thinking of you," I said. "You sure the car was stolen—the guy wasn't putting on an act to dodge the hit-and-run indictment?"

"We checked him pretty thoroughly," Kane said easily. "A guy by the name of Jones—unusual, huh? Salesman for office equipment. He said he parked the car around three-thirty outside the office of Fabrics Incorporated and went in to see their general manager. Said he was there with the general manager until five, then they had a couple of drinks at a bar and when he went to collect his car, it was gone—so he reported it."

"And that checks out?"

"With the general manager, his secretary, with two other guys who work there and were called in for half an hour. The barman who served them the couple of drinks recognised them. Jones is in the clear, all right."

"How did you know it was the car that killed Farnham?"

"Blood on the bumper bar—and some fragments of cloth. The analysis proved the cloth came from Farnham's suit—the blood group matched as well."

"The car's stolen some time after three-thirty, knocks down Farnham around five and is found abandoned at six," I said. "Fast work."

"I'll bet the guy who stole it ditched it smartly after he had knocked down Farnham," Kane said. "Wouldn't you?"

"I guess I would," I agreed. "I was wondering if he stole it for just that reason."

"Huh?" Kane said blankly.

"Skip it. You tell his widow?"

He nodded. "Sure. Works as a waitress in a dump. Found her serving there."

"How did she take it?"

"Like she expected something like that to happen sooner or later. She's some looker, that wife of his. I guess being married to a lush wouldn't be much fun for her, anyway. She didn't burst out crying. She was honest that way."

"And there were plenty of witnesses to say she was serving there at the time the accident happened?"

"There sure were, Lieutenant."

"Thanks," I said.

"What did we do wrong?" Graut asked.

"I told you before," I said patiently. "Not a thing."

"You didn't come down here to say that."

"I came down to ask some questions, Captain," I said. "I've asked them. That's all there is to it."

"What's the pitch, Lieutenant?" Kane asked interestedly.

"There's thirty thousand bucks insurance attached to it."

He whistled softly. "And you were thinking the wife might have knocked him off, huh?"

"I wasn't thinking anything—I was just asking questions. What make and model was the car?"

"A '54 Plymouth," Kane said. "Why?"

"Just that when somebody steals a car, they are sometimes inclined to take a model that they know—or a make that they know, anyway. Needn't mean very much."

They both waited. They had nothing to wait for, but they wouldn't believe it.

"No witnesses to the accident?" I asked.

"None," Kane said. "The guy serving in the bar didn't even know it had happened. There was no scream or anything."

"Sounds like it was almost planned, doesn't it?"

"A lot of 'em happen that way, Lieutenant. With no insurance money attached."

"I guess so," I said. "Which bar was he drinking in?"

"Place called the Roulette. Guy serving there owns it. Name of Deems—Hank Deems."

"Not his fault, I suppose," I said. "Thanks. How much money did Famham have on him?"

"About fifteen bucks," Kane said. "Give or take fifty cents."

"Had he had much to drink?"

"Deems said he was loaded. The alcoholic content was pretty high, the doc said. High enough to say he was drunk for sure."

"How much did Deems say he had to drink?"

"A bottle of rye. And he bought another couple of bottles to take home with him. Funny thing—we found 'em in the gutter, neither of 'em were smashed."

"How did the rye taste?"

The grin faded from Sergeant Kane's face. "That ain't funny, Lieutenant."

"I guess not," I agreed. I got to my feet. "Well, that about winds it up, thanks."

"That's okay," Kane said stiffly.

"We still have the two bottles of rye, Lieutenant," Graut said. "Would you like to see them?"

I grinned at the two of them. "I sure would."

Kane turned around, his face wooden and headed for the door.

"And bring three glasses back as well," I added.

He stopped and turned around again and the grin slowly spread across his face. "I guess we had you wrong, Lieutenant."

"That's what all the girls say," I told him.

Kane produced the bottle and the three glasses. It was good rye. I mentioned the fact when we were drinking our third glass of it and they agreed.

"How is it, Lieutenant?" Graut asked me. "Working for the Commissioner?"

"Just so-so," I said. "I find the responsibility unnerving. He'd make so many mistakes without me around."

"Seems to me he still does make a hell of a lot of mistakes," Graut grunted.

"I can't be around all the time," I said quickly. "You know how it is."

Kane grinned at me. "You've got the reputation of being unorthodox, Lieutenant. The way I hear it, the Commissioner figures you for a screwball who sometimes gets lucky. He can't afford to fire you because he needs your luck sometimes and he can't afford to let you loose in Homicide in case you blow up the city by mistake. So he keeps you real close where he can watch what you're doing all the time."

"Sergeant," I said stiffly. "You don't want to pay any attention to rumours like that just because they happen to be the truth."

CHAPTER 4
The Happy Family

Laurence Cole seemed quite pleased to see me. It was a change for anyone to be pleased to see me, except the finance companies.

"How's your investigation going, Lieutenant?" he asked.

"Coming along," I said. "I spoke with Miss Bright last night."

"She's a nice girl, Edna," he said. "Isn't she?"

"Sure," I said. "Been with you long?"

"Maybe six months. Used to work for a similar company to mine in Los Angeles."

"Good record with them?"

"The best."

I offered him a cigarette and had one for myself. "I understand you have another locater working for you—name of Williams?"

"Joe?" He nodded. "That's right."

"Good man?"

He spread his hands in a fanning motion. "Joe's all right most of the time. Why?"

"Just that Miss Bright mentioned he missed the locate he was assigned to before she got the job."

"That's correct, Lieutenant," he said. "Joe missed out on it, so I gave Edna a try and she came up with it. It can happen—even Edna misses some of them."

"Sure," I said. "I'd like to talk with Joe Williams, if I may?"

"He's out at present—won't be back until this evening."

"That's a pity," I said. "I'd have liked to talk to him earlier."

"He almost always has a couple of drinks in the bar of the Camille at lunchtime," he said. "If you like, Lieutenant, I could go along there with you and we'll probably spot him."

"Don't bother," I said. "Thanks all the same. I'll pick him up here tonight."

"As you wish, Lieutenant."

I got to my feet. "Thanks for your time and co-operation."

He licked his lips. "Lieutenant?"

"Yeah?"

"Don't think I'm presuming, but, well, I was telling my wife about your visit yesterday and she was fascinated. She's always been crazy about how the police work—you know—she watches *Dragnet* on television and …"

"Sure," I said.

"I was wondering," he smiled hesitantly. "I was wondering if you had nothing better to do this evening whether you'd consider coming over to our house to dinner and meet my wife. She'd be thrilled and it would—well, you know. Do me some good, too." He grinned feebly. "I'm in the doghouse right now."

"I'd like to do that, Mr. Cole," I told him. "Thanks for the invitation."

"You'll come?' He sounded pleased. "Thanks a lot, Lieutenant. How about seven-thirty?" He gave me the address and I wrote it down.

"I'll be there."

I got to the bar of the Camille just before one. There were a couple of dozen people there. I sat on one of the chrome stools and ordered a Scotch. I asked the barman who served me if he knew Joe Williams, and he said he did. I asked him to point the man out to me when he came in.

I was halfway through the Scotch when someone sat on the vacant stool beside me. I looked around and saw it was Vince Schaeffer.

"Wanted to thank you, Lieutenant," he said.

"For what?"

"For not shooting off your mouth to Edna last night."

"She doesn't know?"

"Not a thing, Lieutenant. I came out of the pen six months back—clean. Did three and a half years and told myself that was the last time. I got a job and I'm going to marry Edna pretty soon now."

"Congratulations," I said.

His mouth twisted in a grin. "No cop ever believes an ex-con's going to tread the straight and narrow—I know that, Lieutenant. But you gave me a break last night and I appreciate it."

"Fine," I said. "You're well-dressed, Vince. Got a good job?"

"Sure," he said. "I'm a salesman."

"Selling what?"

"Life insurance."

"I got all I want, Vince."

"Yeah," he grinned. "I haven't got around to selling to all the cops I know yet." He slid off the stool. "Just wanted to say thanks, Lieutenant."

"That's okay," I said. "Who you working with, Vince?"

"United."

He walked out of the bar and I finished my Scotch, then ordered another. It was ten minutes after that when the barman leaned across and said, "That's Mr. Williams now, sir. Just come in—down at the other end of the bar."

"Thanks," I told him.

I walked down to the other end of the bar. "Mr. Williams?" I said.

"Sure, buster," he said. "What can I do for you?"

I showed him my shield. "Lieutenant Wheeler," I said. "I'd like to talk to you."

"Okay. Go ahead and talk. Buy you a drink?"

"Thanks," I said. "Scotch."

He ordered the drinks. Edna Bright's description of him had been pretty accurate. He looked tough. He had his hat pushed back from his forehead and his suit could have done with a pressing.

The bartender served the drinks and Williams paid for them.

"Okay," he said. "What's doing, Lieutenant? I park my car somewhere I shouldn't?"

"I'm making some enquiries about the death of a man named Henry Farnham."

"I've heard the name," he said. "Got run down by a car, didn't he?"

"That's right."

"Tough." He finished his Scotch with a practised swallow.

I finished mine and ordered another two, so that I didn't owe him anything.

"Your co-partner in locating, Edna Bright," I said. "She made a locate on him, I understand. Found his wife a couple of days before the wife became a widow."

He grinned ruefully. "Don't remind me of that, Lieutenant, I missed that one and she hasn't stopped crowing over me yet. Neither has Laurence Cole and Company."

"How come you missed it?" I asked. "Miss Bright seemed to think there was nothing to it."

He grimaced. "I'll tell you something, Lieutenant, I'll deny if you repeat it in the office. That day was as hot as hell. Sure, I got the addresses of all the H. Farnhams out of the directory the same way Edna did. I covered five of them. My car was being repaired that day, so I was on foot. On the fourth try I was a limp rag. It was around three in the afternoon," he grinned, "so I said the hell with it and went into the nearest bar. When I got back to the office around five, I said I couldn't make the locate."

"And then Mr. Cole gave it to Miss Bright?"

"That's right. Laurence Cole doesn't like me very much, but I'm about the cheapest male locater he can get—so he keeps me, but he doesn't trust me."

"Bad luck Miss Bright making the locate, wasn't it?"

"I said I checked the address, of course, but there was nobody home. Cole said why didn't I go back and I told him he'd given the assignment to somebody else before I got the chance. We had quite a little scene over it, dear Laurence and me."

"You don't like him?"

He shrugged his broad shoulders. "I like a man to be a man. Cole isn't. Don't get me wrong, Lieutenant. He's got all the natural male instincts, all right—ask Edna. He chases her from one end of the office to the other. But he's educated himself up to being a bum. Because he's snide he figures every other guy must be the same way, so he treats you as if you are." His voice was bitter. "And after a while you get to be that way, of course."

He stopped suddenly and picked up his glass. "Anyway, you didn't come around to have me tell you my troubles. What's so important about the locate on Henry Farnham?"

"Only that he got run down and killed," I told him. "And he's worth thirty thousand dollars insurance money dead and nothing at all while he was alive."

He whistled softly. "That isn't hay, is it? You think the wife might have knocked him off?"

"She's got a cast-iron alibi," I said. "It's only a routine check to see if there's anyone else in the picture who might have done it."

"Even if I don't make a locate on a guy," he grinned, "I don't get so mad I hunt him down and run over him."

"I'll believe that," I said.

"Anything else, Lieutenant?"

"Miss Bright," I said. "She lives up to her name?"

"The girl wonder," he said, and the bitterness came back into his voice. "The genius. The feminine locater absolute."

"She's good?"

"She's good. Very good. Girl scout. But she misses a few, all the same."

"I suppose everybody does."

"Sure, some of these people are smart. When they really owe dough, they make it hard for you. Change their names, their occupations—everything that might lead you to them. That's why I figure Edna isn't really so smart. Get anybody who really owes dough and might have some left, and Edna never makes a locate. Sure, she'll find the pikers all right—the guys like Farnham who couldn't find ten bucks ... but the big stuff—she never gets within a mile of them." He grinned again. "Or maybe I'm just prejudiced."

"Maybe," I said. "Thanks for your information anyway, Mr. Williams."

"Call me Joe," he said. "Everybody does."

"All right, Joe," I said. "I called in at the office this morning to see you and Cole said I'd probably find you here at lunchtime. I said I'd call back at five to see you, because I didn't want him with me when I spoke to you. You might tell him I caught up with you, so I won't be at the office tonight."

"Sure, Lieutenant. Be a pleasure."

"Fine," I said.

He looked at the empty glasses. "Have another drink?"

"Not for me, thanks," I said. "I have to be going. Thanks for your time. How's your auto now? On the road again?"

"It's going okay," he said. "It isn't exactly a Cadillac, but it's running all right."

"What do you drive?"

"A Chev, '50 vintage."

"Be seeing you," I told him.

I walked out of the Camille bar and went some other place cheaper to have some lunch. I thought the set-up at Laurence Cole and Company was interesting. Any of the three would cut either of the other two's throats for the sheer pleasure of it.

After I'd had lunch, I went pack to the office. Annabelle was talking on the phone when I arrived so I sat down at my desk opposite hers and lit a cigarette.

"Sure, honey-chile," she drawled intimately into the phone. "I know just how you feel. I sure miss you, too. I don't know how I'll get through till six tonight without seeing you. You be sure and have a big kiss and hug ready for me now." She pursed her lips and made a smacking noise into the phone. "That will just have to last you, honey-chile, till tonight."

She put the phone down with a fond smile on her face, then looked up and saw me looking at her.

"I was just talking to someone," she said lamely.

"Your mother?" I raised my eyebrows.

"He's got four oil wells and he just doesn't know what to do with all that money, I do declare," she said. "I think it's a girl's duty to show him."

I scowled at her and the more I scowled, the more contented became the smile on her face.

"Is the Commissioner in?" I asked.

She shook her head. "He went out before lunch, Lieutenant. Said he won't be back this afternoon."

"Oh," I said.

"But you don't go getting any ideas, honey-chile," she said firmly. "I used to win the hawg-callin' contests in Alabamie when I was a chile. If ah scream in this office, they'll hear me down in Los Angeles."

I picked up the phone and rang United Insurance and got through to Moss.

"Lieutenant Wheeler," he said. "I was wondering when I'd hear from you."

"I've been rolling around," I said. "And you know what they say—a rolling Wheeler gathers no Moss."

I laughed heartily into the phone until I realised there was just dead silence at the other end.

"Have you found out anything, Lieutenant?" he asked finally. There was no hope in his voice that I had.

"Not much," I said. "But I'd like you to check something for me, if you would."

"What is it?"

"You've got a sales representative there, by the name of Vince Schaeffer. I'd like to know how much he has earned—average earnings per month, that is—since he's been with you."

"All right," he said abruptly. "I can do that. I'll call you back."

"I'll wait for the call," I said.

I hung up and concentrated on Annabelle. She was wearing a thin wool sweater and a tight skirt. She was typing busily.

"You know something?" I said. "Every girl who has an oil millionaire should also have a hi-fi set-up in her apartment. Perfectly reproduced music to suit your mood whenever you want it."

She opened her mouth to say something but I held up my hand commandingly.

"You don't realise what you're missing until you've heard a really good hi-fi set-up," I said. "Out of the natural generosity of my heart, I'm prepared to give you a demonstration. It just so happens that I have a hi-fi set-up at home and I'd be pleased to take you there one night and play some discs for you. Then you can make up your mind."

"Honey-chile, ah need a mink first." Then her left eyebrow twitched. "And ah figure ah'll get it soon. Hush my mouth."

"The only thing I can say," I said coldly, "is three cheers for Abraham Lincoln."

There was a strained silence after that, broken only by the furious clatter of Annabelle's typewriter. The phone rang at my elbow and I picked it up.

"Moss here," he said. He sounded more interested. "I have that information you want."

"Fine," I said.

"You probably know that we pay our sales representatives on a commission basis," he said. "So much per cent of what they bring in. The good ones are almost rich and the medium ones do all right ..."

"And what's Schaeffer?"

"Lousy. His average earnings since he's been with us wouldn't be more than two hundred dollars a month."

"Fifty a week. You'd wonder how he lives on that."

"He can't eat too often," Moss agreed. "I had a talk to the sales manager about him. You know Schaeffer at all?"

"We've met."

"The sales manager says he's always well-dressed and seems eager to get on. He doesn't have much success, but the sales manager thinks he might as he gets used to the idea of selling and develops more confidence."

"He had enough confidence to try and knock over a bank about four years ago."

There was that silence again at the other end of the line. "What did you say?" Moss asked hoarsely.

"You didn't know he was an ex-con?"

"Of course I didn't. And neither did the sales manager—I'm sure of that. Schaeffer must have given the personnel department a phony story and they slipped on their checks. Well, he won't work for us any longer after today."

"Do me a favour," I said. "Don't do anything about it—not yet, anyway. I have a theory that perhaps he isn't doing much work for you, anyway."

"What do you mean by that?"

"An ex-con, if he's smart and still crooked, needs a front. An explanation of how he manages to live and pay for his groceries with honest money. I think he's only using your company as a front. So he won't do you much harm."

"He's connected with the Farnham business?" He was getting interested now.

"I think so," I said. "But I don't know yet. I'll let you know when I have something more definite."

"I told you that stomach of mine was never wrong."

"From what I saw of it," I said carefully, "I think it's big enough to admit a mistake if it's made one."

There was a sharp explosion in my ear as he hung up. Annabelle's typewriter still clattered furiously. It didn't look as if it would be worth my while to stay in the office the rest of the afternoon. So I collected my hat and walked towards the door. When I got there, I turned around.

"Annabelle?"

"I'm very busy, Lieutenant."

"If I had four million barrels of oil just sold, would you come out with me then?"

She looked up. She tapped her chin thoughtfully with one tapering fingernail. "I'm not sure," she drawled. "But I think I'd probably give you a place in the line."

CHAPTER 5
The Noble Spirit

Laurence Cole lived at Grenville Heights, which is a Cadillac and three-car garage suburb. The house was two storeys and imposing. A wide, flag-stoned drive ran up to a two-car garage which was open, showing a Cadillac and Buick side by side. They were both this year's models.

I ran my little Healey up on the drive and got out. There must be dough in this locating business, after all. The time was 7:25 and for once in my life I was punctual. There was nothing to stop me being punctual. My love life was a vast expanse of arid desert, populated only by mirages where Jayne Mansfield and Marilyn Monroe fought bitterly for my favours.

I pressed the buzzer and inside I heard a series of chimes peal like hepped-up cathedral bells. The door opened a few moments later and a maid stood there. She was just a maid—she looked like an old maid.

"Lieutenant Wheeler," I said.

"Yes, sir," she said. "You're expected. Won't you come in?" I followed her into the hall and she took my hat.

"Mr. and Mr. Cole are in the bar," she said. "Will you please follow me?"

I followed her down the wide hall and then she turned under an open archway. Three steps led down into a vast living room. At one end was the bar.

Laurence Cole hurried towards me, his hand outstretched. "Glad to see you, Lieutenant."

"Nice place you have here," I said, and shook hands with him.

I remembered Williams' description of him as a boss and took a closer look. Williams could be right, I thought. Cole was around thirty-five, his hair thinning at the top and it had already receded a fair way back from his forehead, giving him a high-domed appearance. But his eyes were maybe just a little too close together, and beneath the thin line of moustache the lips were thin and tightly compressed.

"Come and meet my wife," he said.

I walked with him across the room to the bar, where his wife stood waiting.

"Natalie," he said. "This is Lieutenant Wheeler."

"How do you do, Lieutenant," she said.

She was probably five years younger than he was. A tall, thin redhead but not so thin she didn't have just enough curves in the right places. The curves were accentuated by the short evening gown she wore. It was strapless and cut very low in front and even lower at the back, by the way the line curved downwards under her arms she must have once been very nearly beautiful, I thought. Even now she had plenty of what it takes, but there was a strong hint of petulance in the line of her mouth, and her eyes lacked lustre. She looked bored and discontented.

"What will you have to drink, Lieutenant?" Cole asked, as he moved around behind the bar.

"Scotch, thanks," I said.

"The same again for me, Laurence," his wife said. Her voice was low in timbre, almost harsh.

"Of course, dear," he said.

He poured the drinks and handed them around.

"Had no trouble finding the place, Lieutenant?"

"No trouble," I said.

"That's fine. How's your investigation going?"

"Slowly," I said. "They always do."

"Williams told me you saw him at lunchtime, after all." There was a note of disappointment in his voice.

"I saw him," I said. "I happened to be close to the Camille bar around one o'clock, so I thought I'd take a chance on finding him and I was lucky."

"It's a fascinating business you're in, Lieutenant," he said. He turned his head slightly. "You remember, dear, I was telling you about the investigation the Lieutenant's making? We made a locate on a fellow named Farnham and ..."

"I wish you wouldn't harp on about your business, Laurence." She wrinkled her nose with disgust. "You know what I think of it."

Cole looked at me apologetically. "My wife doesn't approve of the business I'm in, Lieutenant. She thinks locating is vulgar."

"Sordid is the word I'd use,"' his wife said. "Making money out of other people's misfortunes."

"A lot of people do that." Cole forced a smile on his face. "Even doctors, if you want to look at it that way."

"There's no parallel," she said. "Doctors heal people—that's what they get paid for. You only add to their misfortune."

She looked at me. "It isn't as if Laurence has to do it, you know, Lieutenant. We have plenty of money."

"Oh," I said.

She made a gesture which embraced the house, the two cars in the garage and the Scotch in my hand. "I provide Laurence with a decent background, but he still insists on running that miserable little business. It hardly makes enough money to pay the staff. If he wants a hobby, I can't think why he doesn't take up something respectable, like golf."

"If his golf is anything like mine, it isn't respectable," I said. "When they see me coming on a course, they take up the greens and relay them after I've gone. They figure it's cheaper to do it that way than have me take them up for them."

Cole laughed too loudly and his wife didn't laugh at all. We had another drink and then moved into the dining room, where a maid served the dinner. It was quite a dinner. The wife sat and ate without saying a word. For a dame whose favourite TV show was *Dragnet*, she wasn't talking much to a real live cop.

"Could Williams give you any information, Lieutenant?" Cole asked after a while.

"Not much," I said.

"That's a pity," he sighed. "None of us seem to be able to help you much, do we?"

"You might be surprised, Mr. Cole," I said.

"Oh, really?" He tried not to look too interested.

"Little things have a habit of adding up," I said. "Joe Williams seems to be a very bitter man."

"He's got a grouch against life," Cole nodded agreement. "He thinks he's being victimised by society because he can't do better than work as a locater for a hundred dollars a week. If he only stopped feeling bitter and started feeling a little more friendly and sympathetic towards other human beings, he probably would do a lot better for himself."

"Why, Laurence." His wife put down her knife and fork to stare at him. "I never knew you were a philosopher."

He looked at her. "It's a philosophy that can apply to a lot of people. It's my experience that what most people lack is the milk of human kindness."

Natalie Cole turned towards me, her eyebrows upraised. "And this from a man in the locating business," she said. "It would be funny if it wasn't so pathetic."

I cleared my throat and concentrated on Cole. "Miss Bright is the better locater of the two, I imagine?"

He made an effort to stop glaring at his wife and looked at me. "Quite definitely," he said. "That girl is smart."

"And good-looking, too," his wife added. "In a tawdry sort of way. But then, I suppose in the locating business you can't be too particular."

"She makes twice the number of locates that Williams does," Cole went on, carefully ignoring his wife.

"I wonder why you keep him?" I said.

"I've been wondering about that lately," he said. "If he doesn't improve and show some results pretty soon, I shall have to get rid of him. I think he spends half his days drinking in the nearest bar and not even trying."

"While you spend all your days chasing Miss Bright around the office," his wife said, "and making plans to take her out at night if you can sneak out of here with some excuse."

The maid came in and cleared the plates away, then served coffee. There was silence until she'd gone out again. Mrs. Cole poured the coffee and handed the cups around.

"You'll forgive my wife, Lieutenant," Cole said carefully. "Her nerves are a little upset."

"Why don't you tell the Lieutenant why, darling?" she asked him sweetly. "Tell him that it's putting up with your tantrums and intrigues and unfaithfulness and …"

The phone rang sharply, cutting across her torrent of words.

"I'll get it," Cole said. He went out into the living room and came back a couple of minutes later.

"I'm terribly sorry," he said, "but that was Williams. For once in his life he's working. He thinks he's just made a locate on a man we've been trying to find for months, but he needs some help. If we find him, we think he's got the money to pay his debts, and our commission will be considerable. You will excuse me, Lieutenant?"

"Sure," I said.

He turned to his wife. "I'll get back just as quickly as I can and …"

"Of course," she said tartly. "And give her my love, won't you, Laurence."

Cole turned his back on her and walked out of the room. I heard one of the cars start up and thought the drive was wide enough for him to get past the Austin-Healey.

I finished my coffee.

"Thank you," I said to Mrs. Cole. "The dinner was beautiful." I started to get to my feet. "I guess I should be going."

"There's no hurry, Lieutenant. Why don't we go into the bar and have a drink?"

I almost did a double-take. I looked at her. Her lips were parted in a smile and she looked as if she meant it.

"Well," I said, "I never refuse a drink."

"Would you like some more coffee first?"

"No, thanks."

She pressed a bell-push set in the wall and the maid appeared a few moments later.

"You can clear away the coffee cups, Martha," Mrs. Cole said. "I shan't need you any more tonight."

She got up from the table and I walked with her through to the living room and down to the bar.

"Scotch, as I remember, Lieutenant?"

"Thank you, Mrs. Cole."

She shook her head. "We don't have to be so formal. My name is Natalie."

"Mine is Al," I said.

"I hate abbreviated names," she said. "What's your full name?"

"It doesn't bear repeating," I said. "I'm sensitive on the point. Al, if you please."

"All right, Al," Natalie laughed. "I won't pry into your dark secret."

She poured the drinks—about twice the measure to the glass that her husband had poured.

I thought up a suitable topic of conversation. "That *Dragnet* is some show."

She looked puzzled. "Is it?"

"Why, sure it is."

"Oh," she said. "Do you watch television, Lieutenant?"

"Whenever I get around to it."

"I must take a look sometime," she said.

It was my turn to look puzzled. "I thought *Dragnet* was your favourite show?"

"I never watch television," she said. "I prefer music. Something I can listen to and close my eyes while I listen."

"You should hear my hi-fi set-up," I told her.

I told her all about the hi-fi set-up. I cut it down, kept it brief. It didn't take me any more than about half an hour. By that time we were onto our fourth Scotch.

"It sounds fascinating," she said. "I never realised there was so much to sound reproduction. I'd love to hear it sometime."

"You must come over one night," I said. "That is, you and your husband."

There was a faint, burnished glow in her eyes. "That jerk," she said bitterly. "What would we want him along for? Once he had located the speakers, he'd lose interest."

"It's the usual invitation to make," I said lamely.

"But I'm not a usual sort of person—am I?"

"I'd go along with that," I said.

She looked at me thoughtfully. "You know something, Al? I like you."

"That's fine," I said. "I like you."

"We should have another drink to celebrate that fact," she said. "Tell me something, Al. This room—doesn't it remind you of a bar?"

"Sure," I said. "But a very expensive bar."

"But still a bar," she said. "I have a sitting-room all of my own upstairs. And it's comfortable. You get to the top of the stairs and you turn left and it's the second door on the right."

She started walking towards the door. "You'll find a tray under the bar," she said. "Bring the Scotch and some more ice and a couple of glasses, Al." She disappeared through the archway. I stood there, looking after her—wondering. But then I thought the motto was—when in doubt, do as the lady says.

I found the tray, got some ice out of the built-in refrigerator and crushed it in the machine, then put it into a bowl. I selected two glasses and put them on the tray with the ice. The bottle of Scotch was half-empty. I scouted around and found a full one with the seal intact. Then I carried the tray carefully out, through the archway and into the hall, then up the stairs. I turned left at the head of the stairs and knocked on the second door to the right.

"Bring it in, Al," she called out.

I pushed open the door with my foot and carried the tray in. There was a small table directly ahead of me. I concentrated on putting the tray down without spilling the bottle of Scotch. When I'd successfully achieved my objective as the Air Force guy said talking about his favourite blonde, I straightened up and took a look around.

The sitting-room was neat, compact and very feminine. A door led off, presumably into the bedroom. There were a couple of armchairs and a divan in the sitting-room.

Natalie Cole was stretched out on the divan and she looked different. Right away I could see what the difference was. She'd taken off the gown and was wearing a negligee that seemed to consist of transparent ruffles that frothed so much, she looked as if she was sitting in a foam bath.

She smiled at me. "I thought I'd get into something more comfortable, Al."

"It may be comfortable for you," I told her, "but it's blood pressure to me."

"You'd better drink something for it then," she smiled.

I poured a couple of drinks and took them over to her. She shifted her legs slightly. "Sit down here, Al," she said, as she took the glass.

I sat down there. She sipped her drink and watched me over the top of her glass. The burnished glow in her eyes was no longer faint—it glowed like a beacon.

"This is wonderful," I said, "and I'm enjoying every minute of it. But supposing your husband comes back?"

"He won't," she said confidently. "He's pulled that gag about a locate or whatever he calls it in the middle of the evening about once a week on an average for the last year."

"If you're sure?" I said doubtfully.

She smiled at me. "I'm sure, Al. Laurence's trouble is pretty obvious, isn't it? He married money when he married me. And he let me dominate him. No woman wants to dominate a man, Al. They only do it out of desperation."

"Is that a fact?"

"You know it is," she grinned. "I'll bet no woman has ever dominated you. Laurence's trouble is that he isn't big enough to ignore my money. It worries him. So he runs that dirty, snide little business of his and thinks it makes him independent of me."

I drank the rest of my Scotch.

"And furthermore," she went on, "he picks up any cheap little blonde he can find and takes her out in preference to me." She shook her head slowly. "It hurts a girl's pride, Al. I've had about as much as I can take. One of these days soon—and I do mean soon—I'm going to catch up with him and one of these blondes, and then—blooey!"

"Divorce?"

She nodded. "And not a cent of mine will he get. Meanwhile, after these last two wasted years of my life, I have finally come to a decision."

I could read her mind, but I let it come as a surprise.

"Why should I be faithful to a man who doesn't love me and isn't faithful in return? Why shouldn't I enjoy myself?"

"You're answering your own questions so far," I said.

"Don't spoil the routine!" She gurgled with laughter. "You're my idea of a man, Al. I like you—like you a *lot*—but I guess you know that."

"I guess so," I said.

I got to my feet and walked away from her.

"The noble spirit," she sneered. "The honour of the Homicide Bureau is at stake. She belongs to another man, sir, faithless heel that he is. So my lips can never touch hers, I must go out into the cold, cold snow and never see her again. What a line of corn that is!"

"Noble spirit hell," I said mildly. "I was looking for the light switch."

Natalie Cole laughed. She lay there laughing while I eventually located the light switch and flicked it off. She was still laughing as I fumbled my way back to the divan. Then I reached it.

She stopped laughing, suddenly.

CHAPTER 6
Hangs a Tail

Annabelle turned around to take off her hat and knocked a box of pins off her desk. They scattered onto the floor with a terrible thudding noise.

I pressed my hands tightly to my head. "Why don't you bring a brass band in with you in the mornings? They could play *Dixie*."

She turned around with a look of surprise on her face. "Why, honey-chile," she said. "You sound as if you had a night out last night?"

"I had an *evening* out," I said. A blissful smile spread across my face as I remembered. "But it was as good as a night out."

Her face registered disapproval. "Don't gloat," she said coldly. "Whoever the poor girl was she has my sympathy. She probably trusted you."

"She certainly did," I agreed. "And I proved to her that her trust wasn't misplaced."

"I'll bet you did," she said coldly.

"Did it ever occur to you, magnolia blossom," I said slowly, "that there are some girls who don't consider it their duty to ward off passes? That some girls like passes and expect passes? And surprisingly enough, it's those girls who wind up with oil wells and the others who wind up married with ten children."

"And what's the matter with children?"

"Nothing," I said. "So long as they're not mine, I love 'em."

"You're a no-good heel, Al Wheeler, I do declare." She took a deep breath to show me she meant it.

The door swung open and Lavers came bustling through on his way to his office. "Want to talk to you," he bellowed without stopping.

"So loud?" I asked him. But it was too late—he was already in his office.

"The Commissioner doesn't sound happy," Annabelle smiled at me dreamily. "And if you ask me, ah figure it's *you* he's not happy with."

"You know something?" I said. "When I look at you critically like right now, I get to thinking. Apart from a good figure, a face that won't give people nightmares and a phony Southern accent, you have nothing. Absolutely nothing."

"Why, you—you!"

"Wheeler," came a bull-like roar from Lavers' office.

"Magnolia and oil wells," I said. "That's you, honey-chile. And if you represent the deep South, for the first time in my life I understand what Erskine Caldwell is trying to say."

I walked quickly into Lavers' office, but not quite quickly enough. As I reached the door, a steel ruler bounced off the back of my skull. It was enough to send the piledrivers in my head screaming back into full production. I got inside Lavers' office, closed the door quickly behind me and tottered across the room. I just made the visitor's chair and sank into it gratefully.

"Who told you you could sit down?" Lavers roared.

"Don't shout at me, please," I said. "Not this morning. And if I don't sit down I shall have to lie down. You wouldn't want me cluttering up your floor, would you?"

He stared at me for a moment, then grunted. "You've been drinking again."

"Still," I said. I thought that should close the subject.

"What about Henry Farnham? Moss tells me that apart from you being a maniac—which I already knew—you're developing into an objectionable maniac. You insulted him over the phone yesterday afternoon."

"I didn't," I said. "I told him a physiological truth about himself, that's all."

"You didn't tell him to go and ..."

"I told him his stomach was big enough to admit a mistake. Isn't that the truth?"

Lavers' lips twitched for a moment. "I guess it is. What about Farnham?"

"It's developing," I told him. "There's an interesting bunch of characters in that locating company and they've got themselves attached to a couple of interesting characters outside the company as well."

"That's fine," Lavers said. "I can hardly wait till you write a psychological study of them for me. What about Farnham?" His voice started rising again. "Was he murdered or not?"

"I don't know."

"You don't know."

"I'm inclined to think he was," I said. "But I don't have any proof of that—yet."

"When do you think you might have some proof? Next week? Next month—next year?"

I pressed my hands to my head again.

"Look, Commissioner," I said. "Moss is your pal—not mine. It's his idea that it's murder—not mine. I'm doing the best I can."

"You've had three days."

"Two."

"Today's the third, isn't it?"

"I want a couple of men."

"What for? To hold your head?"

"One to watch this girl Edna Bright for a couple of days, and one to watch Vince Schaeffer."

He thought about it for a moment. "All right then, I'll tell Homicide."

"Let's not worry Homicide," I said. "Let me take them from the Fourth Precinct."

"Why?"

"I don't want Homicide trampling all over everything," I said patiently. "There's a Sergeant Kane who seems to be a nice sort of character. How about detaching him and one other? Tell him to make his own choice."

"Graut will like that."

"The hell with him. You're the Commissioner, aren't you?"

He nodded. "That's right, so I am." Then his head jerked up. "Of course I'm the Commissioner, and don't forget you're just a Lieutenant. And Graut happens to be a Captain."

"It shows the pull he must have, doesn't it?"

"Political," Lavers said absently. His head came up again. "Stop putting words in my mouth. All right—I'll get you this Sergeant Kane and another. But you'd better come up with something fast, Wheeler, or you'll have that traffic detail, I promise you. Some place where it rains all the time, I'll make a point of it."

I still held my head, so he got onto the phone to Graut and arranged for the transfer of Sergeant Kane and one other to be selected by Kane. I could tell by Lavers' tone of voice that Graut didn't like it. The hell with him. Lavers slammed the phone down.

"All right," he grunted. "They're on their way—practically. They're assigned to you, Wheeler. I want no part of them. And as I said before, you'd better come up with something fast."

"Yes, sir," I said. "Anything else?"

"Drop dead," he snarled.

"You don't know what you're saying," I told him. "I'm so close to it, it doesn't matter any more."

I tottered out of his office and back to my desk. The typewriter opposite clattered furiously for about ten minutes, then stopped suddenly.

"Do you want coffee, Lieutenant?" Annabelle asked frigidly.

"Thanks," I said. "Black and hot."

"No cream and strychnine?"

"It's a thought—don't tempt me."

"One thing you can be sure about, Lieutenant Wheeler," she said coldly. "I wouldn't tempt you to anything."

While she was out making coffee, Kane came in, followed by another guy. Lavers must have been listening for them, because his door jerked open as they walked into the outer office.

"Sergeant Kane?" Lavers asked.

Kane came to attention. "Yes, sir."

"Who's with you?"

"Sergeant Johns, sir."

"You're both attached to this office until you hear different. You take your orders from Lieutenant Wheeler. I don't want anything to do with you—you're his responsibility, not mine. Understand?"

"Yes, sir," Kane said blankly.

"Good." Lavers' door slammed shut again.

Kane looked at me. "Hi, Lieutenant."

"Sit down," I said. "Grab yourselves a couple of chairs." They did that and Kane introduced me to Johns, who was a morose-looking character who probably nourished an ulcer.

I told them briefly the story. They knew about Farnham's death, of course. I told them about Edna Bright and Vince Schaeffer. Kane had seen Vince in a line-up once and remembered what he looked like—so he got Vince. And Johns got Edna. I told them it was a straight job of tailing. I wanted to know where they went and what they did and who they saw. And I wanted them to report back to me. I gave them my home number and the office number as well.

Sergeant Kane nodded. "How long do you want us to work at it, Lieutenant?"

"During the day," I said, "and early evening. I have a feeling they get together most nights so when they do, one of you can knock off. Unless it looks really interesting you can both knock off around seven, anyway. It's what they do in the daytime I'm interested in."

"There's a switch," Kane grinned. Annabelle came in with my coffee.

"Annabelle," I said. "Meet Sergeants Kane and Johns. Gentlemen, meet Annabelle Jackson, the pride of the South."

They said hello to each other.

"Sergeants Kane and Johns have just been attached to this office for a few days," I explained to Annabelle.

Her jaw dropped. "You mean, they need three of you to do nothing now?"

Johns started to laugh, then thought better of it. Kane didn't—he kept on laughing.

"Okay," I said. "Don't just stand there, Annabelle. They drink coffee, too."

"Maybe they even appreciate it," she said, "which is more than some people I know."

I got Kane and Johns started on their tailing jobs around ten-thirty. My hangover was beginning to feel a little better, but not very much. I took it out and gave it two Scotches, then a gentle lunch. After that it felt so good it disappeared.

It was two in the afternoon by then and I thought maybe I should go and do some work. What? I thought maybe it was time I called on the widow again.

I drove the Healey down to Oakley Street again and parked outside number 408. I climbed up the two flights of stairs and pressed the buzzer. Nobody answered. I pressed it half a dozen times and still nobody answered. So, remembering my training in deduction, I figured she was out.

I remembered she used to sling hash before her old man got knocked over. She probably still did—she had to eat and there wouldn't have been any insurance money yet.

I went back to the Healey and thought I'd call again in the evening. That meant if I was going to work in the evening, I might as well relax in the afternoon. Oakley Street depressed me so I thought I'd trade it for something better. I drove into town and went into the Camille bar for a drink.

I'd had a couple before I noticed him down at the end of the bar again. I ordered a third drink and took the glass with me.

"Hi," I said. "The long arm of coincidence or maybe we just drink in the same place."

"Good afternoon, Lieutenant." Williams gave me an exaggerated bow. "You want to ask me some more questions?"

"No, I was just buying myself a drink and I happened to see you, that's all."

"Always delighted to drink with the law," he said thickly.

"Fine," I said. "Not locating this afternoon?"

"Giving it a rest," he said. "The glamour-puss is out on a job and I'm just killing time waiting for her to fall down on it—and then Cole will give it to me."

"You reckon?"

He nodded. "Sure. This is a big one. Accountant from New York skipped with over fifty thousand bucks. Maybe I shouldn't tell you this, Lieutenant, you being a cop, but you're a nice guy—you can keep a confidence, huh?"

"Try me," I said.

He leaned close to me. "Sometimes when that happens, the people whose dough it is are more concerned with getting it back or even getting some of it back, than they are with putting the guy in jail. Maybe you don't approve but if it was your dough, what would you do?"

"The same thing," I assured him. "The same thing."

"That's right," he nodded again. "I knew you was a reasonable guy as soon as I saw you. Well, this accountant—Blount is his name—Edgar

Blount. There's a lead come into the office that he's in town at one of the hotels. So little Miss Blondie gets the job. But she won't make the locate—she never does make the big ones. And when she comes crawling back, Cole will give me the job, see? That's what I'm waiting for."

"I see," I said.

He finished his drink and waved wildly to the barman to refill it.

"Yeah," he said. "I can afford to stick around and do nothing. Got a date tonight. What's the time, Lieutenant?"

"Half-past three."

"Plenty of time."

"Doesn't Mr. Cole complain about you not making any of these locates, Joe?" I asked. "You can't make them if you spend your day here."

He waved his arm violently. "Don't you worry about little Joe and Larry Cole, Lieutenant," he chuckled. "We're pals." He extended his hand in front of him unsteadily and held the first two fingers close together. "That's me and Cole—see? We're like that."

"That's fine, Joe," I said. "Then you've got nothing to worry about."

"Not a thing," he said. "Not one sweet little thing."

I finished my drink and put the empty glass down on the bar counter. "I should be going," I said. "Have fun on your date tonight."

"I sure will, Lieutenant," he said. "I sure will."

I didn't feel in the mood to play nursemaid to Joe Williams, and he looked as if he was going to need one before very long. I went out of the Camille and drove home. I put some Andre Kostelanetz on the turntable and relaxed, listening to the strings.

I relaxed for a whole ten minutes and then the phone rang. I made an effort and answered it.

It was Sergeant Johns. "That you, Lieutenant?"

"That's me," I assured him.

"I picked her up about twelve," he said. "Had a break—she was in the office until then. She's been around the hotels most of the afternoon."

"Anything special?"

"I think maybe so," his voice was diffident. "I'm at the Plaza right now. She's been going through the hotel registers in each place and talking to the desk clerks—showing 'em a photograph. At times I've been starting to feel I'm watching a cop at work. Anyway, she seems to have hit the jackpot this time."

"So?"

"So she phones from the public booths in the foyer. She picks one that's got another booth alongside which is empty. So I get into the next booth with my ear against the wall."

"And then what?"

"I can hear most of what she says. She's talking to somebody she calls Vince—that would be Schaeffer, I guess. And she says, 'I've found him all right, Vince. He's here at the Plaza, under the name of Edgar Jones.' Then Vince must do the talking, because she's quiet for a time. Then she says, 'All right. I have to go back to the office first. I'll meet you at seven, in the foyer.' Then she hangs up."

"What then?"

"She gets outside and picks up a cab and I'm close enough to hear her tell the hack to take her back to her office. So I let her go and ring you. Anything in it, Lieutenant?"

"Could be," I said. "It sounds very interesting, Johns."

"Glad to hear it," he said. "What do you want me to do?"

"Quit," I said. "For tonight, anyway. Go on home and I'll see you in the office in the morning."

"Thanks, Lieutenant," He sounded pleased with himself as he hung up.

I went back and listened to some more Kostelanetz. Half an hour later the phone rang again. This time it was Kane.

"He's made about three calls all day," Kane said. "In different parts of the city. All business companies he's called on—I've got a list."

"Skip that for the moment," I said. "Where is he now?"

"He's got an apartment on Stanmore Street. He got home a quarter of an hour ago and he's still there. You want me to keep tag on him and see if he goes out again?"

"No," I said, then told him what Johns had already reported. "I want you to be in the foyer of the Plaza at six-thirty," I said. "Tag along as close as you can without getting under their feet. Unless they look as if they're going to do something exciting when they leave, you can quit then and go home."

"If they're going to do something exciting, they'll probably go back to his apartment," Kane chuckled.

"I meant something exciting to a cop."

"We got human instincts, haven't we, Lieutenant?"

"Okay," I said. "Come into the office in the morning and tell me about it—unless something urgent crops up before then. I'll be out for part of the evening, but I'll probably be home around ten."

CHAPTER 7
Spurs Across the Carpet

It was just after seven when I pressed the buzzer outside her apartment again. This time I heard footsteps. The door swung open and the smile of welcome died on her lips when she saw me.

"It's a hard life being a cop," I said. "You're mostly never welcome."

"I'm sorry, Lieutenant," she smiled. "Come in, won't you?"

I followed her into the apartment. She was wearing a tight-fitting white sheath with a low neckline. She'd come out of mourning with one abrupt holler.

She turned to face me when we got into the living room, her hands clasped in front of her. "What can I do for you this time, Lieutenant?" She didn't ask me to sit down.

"Just a couple of questions," I said. "This time. The day that Edna Bright called on you—remember?"

"Yes," she nodded, "I remember."

"How was the routine? I mean—she introduced herself as a locater? That right?"

She smiled and shook her head. "No—I guess you haven't been chased hard for money, Lieutenant. They don't do it that way. She just smiled and said, 'Mrs. Farnham?' And I said yes. Then she asked was my husband in and I said no. When did I expect him in and I said not until the evening. That's about all I would have got probably until a writ arrived, but she took pity on me, I think. She told me she was a locater and who she worked for and what it was all about. And I told her about Henry drinking and ..." She shrugged her shoulders. "And we were almost crying on each other's shoulders. Me, because of Henry, and her because I think she's a fundamentally sympathetic type. Then she left. That was all there was to it."

"She didn't offer to run a car over him and split the insurance money with you?"

Her eyes widened as she looked at me and one hand touched her throat. "What a horrible thing to say, Lieutenant."

"Just a thought. You look very beautiful tonight, Miss—sorry, Mrs. Farnham. Going out?"

"Is it any business of yours, Lieutenant?" Her voice was icy cold.

"I guess not," I said. "I just wondered. You strike me as being much too smart a woman not to cash in on that insurance sooner or later."

She looked at me, her face expressionless. "I don't know very much about the law, Lieutenant," she said. "But I feel sure that I'm not forced to stand here and listen to you insult me."

"I guess not," I said. "And I've run out of insults, anyway." I turned around and walked towards the door.

"Lieutenant?"

"Yeah?" I looked at her.

"The insurance company hasn't paid the amount owing. That wouldn't be because of your ideas, would it?"

"I wouldn't know," I said. "Maybe they have ideas of their own on the subject."

She bit her lip for a moment. "I never knew how defenceless a woman can be on her own," she said in a low voice. "Not until I became a widow. People—people like you, think they can come into my home and insult me. Say wicked things to me. Even worse, they ..." Her voice cracked then and she started to sob.

I took an instinctive step towards her.

"Get out," she said fiercely. "For Heaven's sake, leave me alone."

So I went, closing the door gently behind me.

Just before seven-thirty I got back into the Healy. I thought the visit to the widow had been short and unsweet. I drove home.

There was somebody waiting on the doorstep. His bulk stood out in the moonlight like the Taj Mahal.

"Lieutenant?"

"Sure, Kane. What's the pitch?"

Kane shuffled his feet. "If you're going inside, I'd rather tell you inside."

"Okay," I said.

We went into the house and I switched on the lights, poured a couple of drinks.

"Thanks," Kane said gratefully when I gave him the glass. "I don't know how to start this, Lieutenant."

"Try the beginning," I suggested.

"Okay," he sighed, "I'm in the foyer of the Plaza before six-thirty, like you said. The dame comes in on her own. She goes up to the desk and I hear the clerk tell her that Mr. Jones is in, and then he rings up to the room for her and tells the guy she's there. Then he tells her Mr. Jones is expecting her and she's to go on up. I watch her across to the elevator and then I see it goes up to the third floor and I figure I'd better get up there, too. So I ride the elevator to the third and get out.

"The corridor's empty and I start walking along it, and the next moment—bingo! Somebody slugs me on the back of the head and the next thing I know, I wake up in the elevator. The elevators in the Plaza are automatic. Some dame gets in on the ninth floor and finds me, thinks I've fainted. So there's the old dame, a couple of bellhops, and a floor manager all giving me air.

"When I can get to my feet, I get across to the desk and think I'll take a chance." Kane grinned ruefully. "What does a chance matter then, anyway? So I tell the clerk I came looking for a friend of mine—a Miss Bright who was calling on a Mr. Jones—and does he know if she's with him. And he tells me she went up maybe a quarter of an hour ago and he'll ring and check if she's there. But Jones' phone doesn't answer. I let it ride at that and come out here to your place. I figure I've messed it up enough already."

I poured him another drink. "Bad luck," I said. "Looks like Vince let her go in first, then watched to see if she was followed. When he saw you tailing her, he followed you up in another elevator and took the first chance he got of slugging you, then dumped you back into an empty elevator."

I walked across to the phone and rang the Plaza. I asked to speak to Mr. Jones and the desk clerk told me he was sorry, but Mr. Jones checked out half an hour before. I told him thanks and hung up.

I told Kane and his face sagged. "Looks like I sure made a mess of that one," he said.

"I think it might have happened, anyway."

I picked up the phone again and rang Cole's number to ask him if Edna Bright had reported her locate on Edgar Blount, the guy who'd picked himself the original alias of Jones.

Natalie answered the phone.

"Lieutenant Wheeler," I said formally. "Could I speak to your husband, Natalie?"

"Al, darling," she said. "How wonderful to hear your voice again."

"Take it easy," I winced. "He'll hear you."

"He's gone out tonight—again," she said. "He can't hear me. Why don't you come on over, honey? I've been missing you all day."

"I'd like to, honey," I said. "But I can't. I'm a cop—you know how it is."

"I don't," she sighed. "But I'll believe you. I'll see if I can find *Dragnet* on the TV and find out what keeps you so busy. Call me soon, Al. Tomorrow—in the daytime—he'll be at the office."

"Sure," I said. "I'll do that."

I put the phone down and turned around in time to catch the broad grin on Kane's face the moment before it vanished.

"Cole's out," I said.

"Yes, Lieutenant," he said.

I realised that Cole was only a name to him.

I picked up my glass and finished my drink.

"Let's go looking," I said. "I don't think we've got much chance of finding, but let's go looking."

Twenty minutes later I parked the Austin-Healey outside the apartment block where Schaeffer lived and we went inside. He opened the door a few seconds after I pressed the buzzer.

"Hello, Lieutenant," he said. He was wearing a T-shirt and a pair of slacks, looking nice and casual.

"Hi," I said, and pushed past him into the apartment with Kane following close on my heels. There was a living room, a bedroom, a kitchenette and a bathroom. I went through the lot, then back to the living room.

"What's the idea?" Schaeffer asked.

"I thought you might have company, Vince," I said. "I see you haven't."

"No," he said. "Is that a crime—to have company?"

"I was just interested. Where have you been tonight?"

"Me?" He shook his head. "Nowhere."

"You sure?"

"Of course I'm sure. I got home about four-thirty—I haven't been out since."

I remembered that a bright character by the name of Wheeler had told Kane he needn't bother to keep tabs on Schaeffer after four-thirty—all he had to do was be at the Plaza before six-thirty.

"Okay, Vince," I said. "I won't argue. Not got a date tonight?"

"With Edna, you mean?" Vince shook his head. "No—she's working tonight. So she told me, anyway. I don't think she'd two-time me about that."

"I'm sure she wouldn't," Kane said coldly.

"Fine," Vince said. "You know Edna?"

Kane pursed his lips tight as his face got redder. "Okay, Sergeant," I said. "I think we can go."

We went to the Plaza Hotel desk. I showed my shield to the desk clerk, who yawned.

"I'm interested in a man calling himself Edgar Jones," I said.

"Yeah?" he said.

"He checked out a while back."

"That's right."

"Leave any forwarding address?"

"Nope."

He examined the fingernails of his left hand, his right hand resting negligently on the desk. I picked up a pen and stabbed him carefully with the nib.

He yelped and jumped about six inches into the air.

"That's better," I told him. "Now I can be sure of your concentration."

He gulped. "Sure, Lieutenant. He checked out seven-fifteen in a hurry. Had his bags packed, came racing in here and paid his bill, then scrammed. I don't know where he went."

"Did he take a cab?"

"I don't know, Lieutenant," he was almost apologetic. "I was stuck here behind the desk."

"Okay. How long was he here?"

"Eight days."

"Have any visitors in that time?"

"Not until tonight. A Miss Bright and …" He looked at Kane, his eyes widening. "Say, aren't you the guy who …"

"That's right," Kane nodded.

"Nobody else?" I asked him.

The clerk shook his head. "No, sir—nobody else."

"Okay," I said.

We went back to the Healey.

"If he's with Edna Bright, then maybe she's hiding him out at her apartment?" Kane suggested.

"If she's half as Bright as I think she is, she won't be doing that," I said. "She'll have him on a plane to somewhere by now. And there won't be a damned thing we can do about it."

"We go take a look?"

"I suppose so," I said.

We found her apartment about half an hour later. There was nobody home. We went down to the car again.

"What now, Lieutenant?" Kane asked.

"I'll drop you home," I said. "See you in the morning."

"What are you going to do?" he asked. "Anything I could help with I'd be glad to—I mean …"

"Thanks," I said. "But I can get to bed by myself, Sergeant."

We drove to his place in silence. I dropped him, then headed homeward. It was just after ten when I arrived. I felt so sour, I didn't have any discs to match my mood to put on the turntable.

I didn't even feel like a drink, which shows how bad Wheeler felt. I just sat and chain-smoked for about an hour, then thought I'd make myself some coffee and go to bed.

The door buzzer went and I answered it.

When I saw who it was, I didn't believe it.

Annabelle Jackson stood on my doorstep, smiling demurely. She wore a crimson evening gown that was cut so far south that if the northern troops had ever seen it, they would have surrendered without a struggle.

"Hello, Lieutenant," she said, almost shyly. "I know it's late. I hope I'm not interrupting you or anything? I just wondered about that hi-fi set-up you've got. You know you said that if …"

"Sure, Annabelle," I said. "Sure. And you're not interrupting a thing, I was just sitting doing nothing. I'd be glad for you to hear the hi-fi."

"Thanks, Al," she smiled. She turned her head. "Come on in, Hubert."

"Hubert?" I said.

"You know," she smiled and lowered her voice. "My friend with the oil wells. He said he'd like to hear some hi-fi before he had to put into my apartment and ..."

So help me, spurs jangled along the concrete path and the next moment Hubert appeared. He was a tall, lean guy with a drooping moustache, pin-striped suit, homburg hat and black boots with spurs that jingled, jangled, jingled.

I watched him coming towards me and turned to Annabelle.

"Is he for real?"

"Sssh," she whispered fiercely. "He'll hear you. He's the best shot in Texas, you want to be careful you don't insult him. He'll probably challenge you to a duel."

"What with—spurs?" I said. "You think I'm a cockerel or something?"

"You know what I think of you," she said.

Hubert came into the house.

"This is Lieutenant Al Wheeler, Hubert, honey-chile," Annabelle said. "And this is Hubert Marshal, Al."

"Marshal of what?" I asked, and Hubert chuckled in a deep bass.

"Sure like an hombre with a sense of humour," he said, and punched me painfully in the ribs.

By the time I'd got my breath back, they were both sitting down in the living room. Correction, Annabelle was sitting down and Hubert was opening the bottle of Scotch I'd left on the table.

"Pour us all a drink," I said.

"Sure aim to, partner," he said. "That's what I like in Pine City. You sure got hospitality. Not like Texas, of course, but it's pretty good all the same."

"Play something for us, Al," Annabelle said. "Let's hear it."

"Okay," I said limply.

The Kostelanetz was still on the turntable. I switched it on and brought the volume up to nearly full bore on the five speakers. Violins hummed around the room, cellos vibrated the floor, a double-bass set the ceiling quivering.

After five minutes Annabelle put her hands over her ears. "Al, turn it off," she shouted. "Please!"

I switched it off. The room was terribly quiet except for the floorboards settling down again.

"Poured you a drink, partner," Hubert said, and handed me an empty glass.

I looked at it, then at him. "You did what?"

"Shucks," he chuckled. "Guess I must have drunk it myself."

"I'll pour myself one," I said. "If you don't mind?"

"You go right ahead, partner," he told me. "Don't you worry about me."

I poured myself a drink. Annabelle sat sipping hers and the colour started to come back into her face again.

"What did you think of the hi-fi?" I asked her with a leer on my face.

"In the South," she said tersely, "a lady isn't supposed to use the language she'd have to in describing an experience like that."

"Shucks, honey," Hubert said. "I thought it was doggoned wonderful. I'm a-gettin' me ten o' those afore I go back to Texas."

I stared at him. "Ten? What for?"

"I got a lotta fences around my ranch," he said. "It's still a purty big sort of property I got out there on the range." He chuckled again. "Well, that is so long as they don't find no more o' them pesky oil wells on it!"

"You want music everywhere you go?"

"Not me, partner," he grinned. "I'm what them sawbones call tone-deaf. But I figure ten of them things would save me a small fortune in fencing. Yessir, just string them things around and any time one of the beeves looks like strayin' off my property." He grinned triumphantly. "I'll just switch the old hi-fi on and scare the hell out o' that steer!"

"Hubert," Annabelle said fondly. "You're a genius."

"Guess I am," he said modestly.

Annabelle got to her feet. "Well, thanks, Al. We have to go now."

"Sure," Hubert said. "Gotta git the little lady back to her own barn with night a-rollin' by."

"I thought she lived in an apartment," I told him. "But I guess there's no telling when they come from the South."

Hubert looked at me suspiciously. "Now, you wouldn't be insinuatin' anythin' about the little lady, partner?"

"Who—me?"

"I sure am glad to hear that," he said. "I don't like sheddin' blood on a vacation. Kinda spoils things, but I got mah honour, partner. Tell you what—I ain't a hundred per cent sure about that remark of yours. You apologise anyway to the little lady an' we're still partners, partner."

I closed my eyes and counted five. When I opened them again he was still there.

Annabelle tapped her foot impatiently. "I'm waiting, Al."

I put my hand inside my coat where I had the Police Special in a holster. I took it out in my hand and rammed it into Hubert's stomach. He recoiled backwards with a shrill cry of terror.

"Al!" Annabelle said shrilly. "Put that gun away,"

"I'm prepared to fight a duel right now," I said. I slipped the gun back into its holster. "You call the draw, *partner*."

Hubert's face was chalk-white. "Please don't take that thing out again," he pleaded. "I'm allergic to guns …"

I took a couple of steps towards him and grabbed hold of one end of his moustache in each hand and yanked. He mewed pitifully and then the moustache came away in my hands. I could see the trace of spirit gum adhering to his upper lip.

"Hubert," I told him, "you'd better saddle up and ride out o' here afore I gits the Sheriff."

"Sure," he muttered. "I'm on my way."

He started towards the door at a run and then one of his spurs caught in the carpet, sending him flat on his face. He scrambled to his feet again and kept on running.

"So long," I called after him, "partner."

The sound of his running feet disappeared into the distance—a jingle, a fainter jangle, a jingle fainter still—and then nothing.

I looked at Annabelle. She bit her lip and then the tears started to edge out of the corners of her eyes and down her cheeks.

"Where did you get him?" I asked her. "In a raffle?"

She sat down and dissolved into a flood of tears. I waited until the dam was nearly empty and then I handed her a drink. She took it and drank it in one. She seemed to get a little better.

"I knew you never believed in the man with the oil wells," she sniffed. "So I thought I'd prove he was real."

"Where did you get him from?"

"An amateur dramatic society I used to belong to once. His name really is Hubert Marshal. And he'll never forgive me for this—never."

"Listen," I said. "If we're talking about who's going to forgive who, I'm at the top of the line."

"Oh, you," she said.

I sat down beside her and held her hand. She didn't seem to mind.

"You know something?" I said. "It's gone. Disappeared without a trace."

"What?"

"The Dear Old Southland. The accent, honey-chile. Where are the magnolia blossoms of yesteryear?"

"Oh," she said. "That."

"Yeah, that."

"I was born in San Diego," she said. "But a lot of men think a Southern accent is fascinating, so I got me a Southern accent—it seemed to fit my name, anyway."

She turned around suddenly and glared at me. "Anyway, you big lug. You should be glad a girl takes all this trouble to make you notice her."

She wrapped herself around my neck with such violence that I went over backwards on the divan, without breaking a hold. A little thing like that didn't disturb Annabelle—she kept on kissing me.

I managed to break the half nelson she had on me and got onto my feet.

"Honey-chile," I said, "I shall be back in a moment—but an occasion like this should have some organisation behind it. 'Don't spoil your neck-ing for the sake of a clean collar,' my old man used to say. I shall be back—fast."

I hurtled across to the turntable and organised music—music sweet and soft which would gradually pick up in tempo as the discs dropped onto the turntable. I poured us two quick drinks and took them back to the sofa with me.

Annabelle took hers, drained the glass and tossed it carelessly over her shoulder.

"Hey," I said. "Those are good peanut-butter glasses."

"We girls from the South," she said with a gleam in her eyes, "are tem-pestuous."

"And we guys who live around here," I said, "just love you that way."

I drained my glass, tossed it over my shoulder and got back into the clinches. Or should I say, was dragged back?

We would have still been there, but the phone rang. I went through four holds quickly with Annabelle and I won. I managed to get off the divan, weaved across to the phone and lifted the receiver.

"Whatever it is, it had better be good," I said.

"Al?" The voice was almost a whisper.

"Yeah," I said. "Who's that?"

"Natalie. I … You must come. You must help me."

"What's the trouble?"

"It's … Laurence."

"He found out about last night?"

"He's dead," she whispered.

"Dead?"

"And they say I did it!"

"Who does?"

"The police."

"I'll be over right away," I said.

"I'm not at home."

"Then where are you?"

"At Mrs. Farnham's apartment."

I put the phone down slowly. Annabelle looked over the top of the divan at me. "Hurry back," she said. "We've only had the preliminaries."

"I'm sorry, honey-chile," I said. "But this is as far as we go—for the moment. Somebody just got themselves murdered."

CHAPTER 8
Lavers' Old Lady

There were a couple of prowl cars parked outside and a couple of uniformed cops keeping back the curious crowd. I parked behind one of the prowl cars and flashed my shield at the cops who let me through.

When I got to the apartment there were two more uniformed cops outside. I showed my shield again and asked them who was handling the case.

"Lieutenant Portus from Homicide," one of them told me. Portus was one of the new boys from Homicide. I hadn't met him before.

"Okay," I said. I went to walk in, but the cop didn't move out of my way.

"Sorry, Lieutenant," he said, "but Lieutenant Portus gave strict orders that nobody was to go in."

"Okay," I ground my teeth. "I'm a reasonable guy—tell him I'm out here."

He looked doubtful. "He said not to disturb him."

"If you want to go on eating regularly, you'll disturb him right now," I told him.

He took my word for it and went inside the apartment. He came out again a couple of seconds later. "The Lieutenant says it's okay for you to go in, Lieutenant."

"Thanks for nothing," I said, and went into the apartment.

In the living room were two uniformed cops. In one chair sat Natalie Cole and in the other sat Eve Farnham. There were also a couple of plainclothes guys.

"Al." Natalie got to her feet. "Thank Heaven you got here, I—"

"Shut up," one of the plainclothes men said coldly. She subsided limply into her chair.

The character who had told her to shut up came across to me slowly. A big cop, this one. A really big cop. His eyes were cold and his face moulded finely the way a sledge-hammer is.

"I'm Portus," he said, "from Homicide."

"Congratulations," I said. "I'm Wheeler, from Commissioner Lavers' office. What the hell's going on here?"

He nodded towards the bedroom. "Want to take a look?"

I looked at him for a moment. "Yeah," I said. "I'd like that."

"Help yourself," he told me.

I walked past him into the bedroom. There were the science boys all over the room—dusting, photographing, fingerprinting. On the floor, a surprised look etched on his face, was Laurence Cole. He was wearing a pair of shorts and nothing else. He must have fallen from the bed. One hand had dragged a sheet with him and the corner of it was still clenched in his fist.

There was a doctor looking him over.

"How did he get it?" I asked.

"In the back of the head," he said curtly. "Real close—powder burns there. Two slugs. Died right away."

"Must have been some consolation to him," I said.

"This is the sort of thing that makes me glad I'm a bachelor," he grunted. "When I see what happens to a man who gets mixed up with two beautiful women."

"You should write a soap opera," I told him. "You're wasting your time."

He grunted and went on with his job. I had a look around and then started back towards the living room. There was nothing else in the bedroom for me—the science boys could have it.

Portus looked at me as I came out. "Okay?" he said.

"What's the story?" I asked.

"I'll file my report in the Bureau," he said curtly.

I looked at him disbelievingly. "I'm a cop," I said. "From the Commissioner's office. What happened?"

"I spoke to the Commissioner," he said, "maybe ten minutes ago—when the dame said she knew you. He figures you aren't from his office any more. He gave me definite instructions about you, Lieutenant."

"He did?"

"Sure," Portus said. "He said I was to tell you to get over to his house right away. And secondly, he said, on no account was I to let you talk to anybody concerned in the case. Most of all, he said, Mrs. Cole."

"I don't get it," I said.

"The way I figure it," Portus said slowly. "You knowing the dame so well and her knocking off her old man, the Commissioner don't think it would look good for the Department if you spoke to her … Lieutenant."

There should have been something bright I could say, but right then I couldn't think of anything. I stared at him for a moment, then swung around and walked out of the apartment. I didn't look at Natalie on the way out. I was frightened what I might see on her face.

I drove over to the Commissioner's house, which was a hell of a long way away. Or it seemed so that night. When I got there I parked the Healey on his drive behind his sedate sedan, and walked up onto the front porch.

The house was a blaze of light. I thundered a tattoo on the front door and it opened abruptly a moment later.

"What are you trying to do?" a harsh voice asked. "Wake the dead?"

"Or the Commissioner," I said. "That's practically the same thing, isn't it?"

"You sound rude enough to be a reporter," she said.

"Sorry," I told her, "I'm only a cop."

"And I'm only his wife. You want to see him—he's talking into the phone nineteen to the dozen right now and—"

"The name is Wheeler," I said. "Al Wheeler."

"Oh," she said softly. "Then you'd better come in."

She stood back and I walked into the hall, taking off my hat. "I've heard a lot about you," Mrs. Lavers said. "But all I can say is it doesn't show on your face."

I was going to tell her fortune for her, then I caught the twinkle in her eyes. "Confidentially," I said. "It's all true."

"If I was thirty years younger," she said, "I'd find out just how unorthodox you really are."

"If you were thirty years younger," I said gallantly, "you'd be in kindergarten."

"I see what they mean," she murmured. "You're dangerous, Lieutenant. Definitely dangerous."

There was a familiar bull-like roar from somewhere further inside the house. "Where the hell is that coffee you promised me!"

"Keep a civil tongue in your head, Lavers," she called sharply. "Or I'll take a poker to you. It's coming. And there's a visitor here to see you."

"I don't want to see any visitors."

"This one you do. It's your unorthodox cop."

"Wheeler!" His voice rose another shattering octave. "Come in here, Wheeler."

I looked at Mrs. Lavers and she looked at me. "You think he means me?" I asked.

"I'm quite sure he means you. Would you like a cup of coffee, Lieutenant?"

"Please," I said. "I'd also like a plane ticket to New York, if you happen to have one."

"It's just his liver," she said. "He will eat chillies and rubbish like that. I keep telling him a man of his age shouldn't eat that stuff, but he will do it."

"I have a nasty idea this is more than his liver," I said.

"Well," she smiled. "If he gets too much for you, I'll take a poker to him."

"Thanks, pal," I said. "How did he ever manage to catch a gorgeous girl like you?"

"I didn't run very fast," she smiled. "Now, go along with you." I went along with me. I didn't like the idea very much and I also didn't like Lavers very much. Was it Napoleon who said the best defence was attack? Who the hell cares who it was, it was good enough for me.

I walked into the living room, where Lavers was sitting in his dressing-gown beside the phone. His face was purple.

"Wheeler!" he exploded.

"What the hell do you think you're doing to me?" I shouted. "Treating me like a rookie cop, telling some stumblebum of a jumped-up Lieutenant out of Homicide to brush me off!"

Lavers' mouth sagged open as he stared at me. Then it closed spasmodically and opened again.

"You should get your head read—or shrunk," I said coldly. "Maybe you're getting too old—going soft between the ears. Who the hell do you think you are to take me off a case I've been working on the last week?"

His mouth opened and closed again. Then he made a braying sound—and then he got his voice back again.

"Too old," he repeated softly. "Going soft between the ears. Should get my head shrunk." Then his voice really came back.

He heaved himself onto his feet. "Who the hell do I think I am? I think I'm the Police Commissioner of Pine City, that's who I think I am! And I think that Lieutenants of the Force take their orders from me—all Lieutenants!"

His wife came hurrying in with a tray carrying the coffee and cups.

"Now, remember your liver," she said. "If you shout again, I'll take that poker to you. I promise you by the grey hairs on my head that I will."

She had a thick crop of grey hair that framed her face attractively, so I figured she meant it. She poured the coffee out while Lavers glared at her in silence. She gave me a cup, then gave him a cup.

"I'll hear you," she said as she went out of the room. "And I've warned you for the last time."

Lavers just sat there glowering until she'd gone.

"All right, Wheeler," he said softly. "So you've been investigating the death of Henry Farnham. For one whole week. Was he murdered or wasn't he murdered? In the course of that investigation you report to me that some people working in a locating business may be mixed up in the Farnham case. And tonight we have proof that they are ... Cole is murdered in the widow's apartment—with the widow present—by his wife.

"The widow phones Homicide and Portus goes down there. And he's greeted by a murderess who demands that Lieutenant Wheeler must be present. That he's a very dear friend of hers. That she refuses to say a word to Portus and will only talk to you. When Portus refuses to let her ring you, she gets hysterical and says she *must* speak to you. You're the only man who will try and protect her. That you're her lover!"

I sipped my coffee cautiously.

"So Portus does the right thing. He knows you're attached to my office, as everyone on the Force does. He knows you work under my personal direction. So he rings me and asks me what he should do. And I tell him."

"But ..."

"Shut up."

I shut up and sipped some more coffee.

"How do you think it would look in the newspapers?" he said softly. "Jealous wife murders husband in arms of lover? Red-headed killer demands protection of Police Lieutenant lover?"

His voice started to rise again. "How do you think that will look in the morning newspapers?"

"Remember the poker," I said quickly.

He lowered his voice again. "The whole Department could never lift its head again. We'd be finished—all of us. And you come in here demanding to know what the hell I think I'm doing to you."

I could see his point. And I'd employed a lousy strategy. No wonder Napoleon finished up on St. Helena.

"For your information, Wheeler," he went on and the bluster had gone out of his voice and it sounded so cold without it, I wished it would come back. "For your information, I'm busting you. Busting you right out of the Department. No suspensions this time. No nothing. As of now, you're through."

I thought about that for maybe half a minute. I finished my coffee, put down the cup; lit a cigarette.

"I don't think so, Commissioner," I said gently.

His face started to flame again. "You what?"

"How would it look?" I asked. "Red-headed killer demands protection of Police Lieutenant lover ..."

"That's why I'm busting you," he looked bewildered. "I just said that."

"That's why you're not busting me," I corrected him gently. "How does a busted cop earn a living?"

"That's your worry—not mine."

"He doesn't," I said. "But this busted cop does have something he can sell. The inside story of the killing. I'd think one of the evening papers would pay me quite a lot for it. *I Was Natalie Cole's Lover*, written by Al Wheeler, ex-Lieutenant of Police."

I leaned back in the chair and smiled at him. "I should think it would be worth a couple of thousand dollars, at least."

He slapped his hand across his face, pinching the jowls of his cheeks tight and closing his eyes. He sat like that for more than a minute. Then he slowly took his hand away from his mouth and opened his eyes.

"All right, Wheeler," he said slowly. "What do you want?"

"I'm still a Lieutenant of Police?" I asked. He nodded slowly. "That's fine, Commissioner," I told him briskly. "I want to be reinstated on the case as your personal representative. I want you to let Portus know that right now—with full power to act as I think fit. I might need Kane and Johns still—I'll let you know about that later." I sat there for a moment. "That's about all I can think of for the moment."

"So help me, Wheeler," he said hoarsely, "I'll get you for this if I bust myself doing it."

"You were going to ring Portus?" I suggested.

He pulled the phone over closer to him and dialled a number. "Lavers," he growled into the phone. "Put me through to Portus. I don't give a damn what he's doing, I want to speak him now."

Maybe ten seconds went by and then he spoke again. "Portus? This is Commissioner Lavers." He swallowed hard. "You are to forget my previous orders concerning Lieutenant Wheeler. He is acting as my personal representative in this case and with full authority. I want you to give him your fullest co-operation. Is that understood?" He grunted a couple of times after that, then slammed down the receiver.

"Thanks, Commissioner," I said.

"Just understand one thing, Wheeler," he said softly. "I'll save your hide to save the Department's hide. But rather than save a murderer's hide, I'll let the whole Department go under."

"I understand that very well, Commissioner," I said. "And that isn't the idea, anyway. It never was."

"And another thing," he said. "You may be unorthodox. But you have been too unorthodox. From now on you're going to be one of two things. Either an orthodox cop or an ex-cop. You can make your own choice."

"I can't understand it," I said, shaking my head. "I really can't understand it."

"Just what are you talking about?"

"Mrs. Lavers," I said. "How a wonderful girl like her could marry a—well, it baffles me."

His face got that cherry-red colour again as his fist slammed down on his desk. "Now listen, Wheeler!" He gargled for about ten seconds, then shook his head helplessly. "What's the use? I'm only building my own blood pressure."

I gave him an encouraging smile. "That's so true, Commissioner. Why don't we talk about the case?"

He looked at me curiously. "What do you intend to, do?"

"I'm going to find out who really murdered Cole," I told him. "Because one thing is for sure—it wasn't his wife."

CHAPTER 9
She'll Fry For Sure

It was one in the morning when I reached Homicide. There was a Sergeant Riley on the desk who grinned when he saw me.

"Look out, boys," he made a pretence of calling out. "Here comes the Commissioner's boy. Get those cards off the table!"

"You old fake," I said. "Sitting there pretending to be a cop. Where's Portus?"

"He's in with Lieutenant Hanlon right now."

"Thanks," I said.

"Hanlon said not to disturb them."

I grinned at him. "I'm the Commissioner's boy—remember?"

I knocked on the door of Hanlon's office and then walked in. Hanlon's like me—still waiting to be made Captain. He's been Lieutenant-in-Charge of Homicide for almost a year now.

He looked up from his desk with a frown of annoyance on his face. It didn't clear any when he saw me. Opposite him, Portus sat like a granite statue, a cigarette dangling from his lips.

"It's you, Al," Hanlon said.

"Check," I agreed. "What gives?"

"We booked Mrs. Cole on a first-degree rap maybe twenty minutes ago."

"Yeah?"

"It's open and shut, Al," he said. "Mrs. Farnham was a witness to the whole thing."

I lit myself a cigarette. "Tell me the whole story," I said.

"Maybe you'd rather hear it from Mrs. Cole first?" Portus suggested.

I looked at Portus, then looked at Hanlon. "How did he get into Homicide?" I asked. "Somebody leave the back door open?"

"Can it, Al," Hanlon said uncomfortably.

"Let's have the story," I said. "I hate to quote my influence around here, but the Commissioner …"

"Okay," Hanlon said. "Tell him the story, Portus."

The hunk of beef sitting in the chair shrugged his shoulders. "We got a call just after eleven. The dame sounded almost hysterical. She said that somebody had been murdered in her apartment and the killer was still there. We got her name and address and we didn't wait to ask questions— we took a couple of prowl cars around there as fast as we could."

"With their sirens screaming and you sitting in the back seat with a determined look on your face," I added. "Hell's teeth, Portus, I don't want a ball-to-ball description. Like the man says in *Dragnet*—give me the facts."

Portus sucked in a deep breath, but his face didn't change its expression. "When we got there, we found Mrs. Farnham in a robe. Inside was Laurence Cole's body in the bedroom—you saw that, didn't you?"

"Yeah."

"And sitting on a chair having hysterics is this Mrs. Cole. I try to calm her down a little, but she won't listen. So then I ask the Farnham dame what happened. And she tells me the story. This guy Cole runs a locating business ..."

"I know all about Cole," I said. "What did she say happened? How was he killed?"

"Sure, Lieutenant," Portus said flatly. "I was forgetting that you knew all about Cole—and his wife. She says that after her husband was dead, this guy Cole calls around to see her. He tells her that her old man's debt of five thousand bucks is now her responsibility. She tells him she'll pay when she collects the insurance money and Cole says the people it's owed to won't wait that long. They want to take her to court right away and if she hasn't got the money, they'll send her to jail. And she was dope enough to believe it. So she gets worried and Cole tells her he'll see what he can do."

I stubbed out the cigarette and lit another one. "Then what?"

"Then he comes back again the next day. He tells her he could fix it. He could tell the people concerned that Farnham was dead and he'll be able to collect the five thousand in due course from his estate. He won't mention the fact that Farnham was married. That is, he won't so long as Mrs. Farnham plays ball with him."

"How?"

"You saw the way he was dressed, Lieutenant," Portus sneered slightly. "I wouldn't think I had to paint a picture for you of all people."

I didn't say anything to that. The time would come when I could fix Portus. Right now it wasn't so important.

"So that's what happens," he went on. "Tonight he comes over to her place and just before eleven there's a ring on the buzzer. Mrs. Farnham puts on a robe and goes to the door, thinking it must be someone who's got the wrong apartment. She opens the door and Mrs. Cole bursts in, then walks right past her into the bedroom and sees her husband.

"Mrs. Farnham is following her up, but she isn't quick enough. Mrs. Cole pulls a gun out of her bag and puts two slugs through her husband and he's dead before he hits the floor. Mrs. Farnham picks up an umbrella and hits her over the head with it—knocks her out cold. Then she realises that Cole is dead, so she rings us.

"By the time we arrive Mrs. Cole has got hysterics, like I said before. Says she's not going to talk to anyone but you. Says you know her, you'll protect her. Says that you and her …"

"I got the drift of that before," I told him. "And you rang the Commissioner, then you let her ring me. I can take it from there."

"Some character, this Laurence Cole," Hanlon said.

"Yeah," I nodded. "Where's Mrs. Farnham now?"

"Still at her apartment," Portus said. "The doctor gave her a sedative and a neighbour's spending the night there. We cleaned up the room before we left, of course."

"Yeah," I nodded again. "I'd like to talk to Mrs. Cole." They looked at each other.

"It's kind of late, Al," Hanlon said hesitantly.

I looked at Portus. "Will you tell the Lieutenant-in-Charge of Homicide what the Commissioner said, or will I?"

Portus cleared his throat. "The Commissioner said you were acting as his personal representative in this case with full authority." The words seemed to stick in his throat. "He said you were to get the fullest co-operation."

"I don't know how you do it, Al," Hanlon said softly. "I really don't."

"I threatened to expose all the slobs he's got masquerading as Homicide Lieutenants if he didn't give me the case back," I said. "I can talk to Mrs. Cole?"

"You talk to who you want, Al," Hanlon said tiredly. "I can't stop you."

"Thanks for nothing," I told him.

I walked out of his office and slammed the door behind me. Three minutes later a police matron unlocked the cell door and let me in.

Natalie got up off the bunk and fell into my arms.

"Al," she said. "I could have bitten my tongue off when I realised what I'd said. And when I heard what that horrible Lieutenant said to you, I thought I'd busted your career wide open."

"You hadn't, Natalie," I said. "So don't worry about it."

"It's like a dreadful nightmare," she said. "And I can't wake up from it."

"You'll wake up from it okay," I assured her. "Tell me what happened."

She moved away from me slowly and sat down on the bunk again. "Laurence went out," she said dully. "You knew that—I told you he was out when you rang."

"Sure," I agreed.

"About ten o'clock I had another phone call. But I couldn't recognise the voice. It said that my husband was with another woman and if I wanted to collect some divorce evidence, there was the golden opportunity. He was with Eve Farnham, the voice said, and gave me the address. If I went over there straight away I'd catch both of them."

I gave her a cigarette and lit it for her.

She inhaled deeply. "Thanks, Al. You remember last night, I told you I'd made up my mind to divorce Laurence as soon as I had the opportunity of catching him. It seemed almost like Fate, I thought.

"I rushed out of the house and took the Buick and drove over there. I saw the Cadillac parked outside and I knew the voice hadn't been kidding me. As soon as she opened the door, I walked past her into the apartment. He wasn't in the living room, so I went on into the bedroom. And I found him. He went green when he saw me. Then the Farnham woman came into the room and asked what the hell I wanted."

She took another deep drag on the cigarette.

"I said I had all the evidence I wanted. Laurence got up and started swearing at me. He called me a spying Jezebel or something equally stupid. Then something hit me over the head and that's the last thing I remembered.

"When I came round, the Farnham woman was standing over me with an umbrella in her hand. She said she'd hit me with it if I tried to get away before the police came. I was still dazed, Al. I didn't know what was happening. Then the police came in and she told them I'd burst into the apartment, gone straight into the bedroom and pulled out a gun and shot Laurence. So she'd hit me with the umbrella and called the police."

She tried to smile and didn't make it. "I was still bewildered. At first I thought it must be some sort of crazy joke, but then they took me into the bedroom and showed me his body and I got hysterical then when I realised he'd been murdered."

She looked up at me appealingly. "Al, it must have been the Farnham woman who shot him. It must be, I didn't kill him—I swear it."

"Sure, honey," I said gently. "I believe you."

"What will they do to me, Al? They charged me with first degree murder."

"They won't do anything for a while," I said. "They have to fix up a court for your trial—and that takes time. Meanwhile, you'll have to stay here, I'm afraid—but you won't find that too bad when you get used to it. And I'll be checking on the thing. I'll have you out of here within a couple of days."

"Will you, Al?" She looked at me, a wild hope appearing in her eyes. "You really mean that?"

"Sure," I said, trying to sound confident. "It's only a question of pinning the murder where it belongs. You take it easy, kid."

"I'll try," she said.

I lit myself another cigarette. "This voice on the phone—you couldn't recognise it?"

"No," she shook her head. "It sounded muffled. I had to strain my ears to hear what it was saying."

"Was it a man or a woman, do you think?"

She looked miserable. "I couldn't even be sure of that, Al."

"It doesn't matter very much," I said, trying again to sound as if I meant it. "You said you walked straight through to the bedroom and saw Laurence—and then Mrs. Farnham came into the room and asked you what you wanted and you said you had all the evidence you needed. Where was she standing then—in relation to you, I mean?"

Natalie thought for a moment. "Beside me."

"And when Laurence started swearing at you, you turned your head and looked at him?"

"Yes," she nodded eagerly, "I did."

"So you weren't looking at her—you couldn't see her?"

"No, I couldn't. That's when she must have picked up the umbrella and hit me with it."

"Did you take a gun with you?"

"No," she whispered. "I never owned a gun in my life, Al. I wouldn't know how to use it if I had one."

"Did they show you the gun?"

She shuddered. "Yes, they did."

"Had you ever seen it before?"

"Never."

"Did Laurence own a gun?"

"Not that I know of."

I nodded. "Okay, that gives me something to work on, anyway. I'll go now, honey. You try and get some sleep. Have you contacted a lawyer yet?"

"I hadn't even thought about it," she said. "You know one?"

"Jerry Schultz is a pal of mine," I said. "I'll get him to come in and see you in the morning. Don't worry now."

"I'll try not to, Al," she said. "And thanks a million."

I went back up to Hanlon's office. He and Portus were still there.

"The gun," I said. "You have any leads on it?"

"Thirty-two Mauser," Hanlon said. "Serial number filed off a long time ago. Sort of gun you can buy for fifty bucks—with nobody asking questions or remembering you bought it."

"Fingerprints?"

"They checked," Portus said. "Only one set of them—matches Mrs. Cole's."

"Anything else?"

"You think we need anything else?" he asked.

I thought maybe he could be right about that.

"Okay," I said, then left the office. Sergeant Riley grinned at me as I came up to his desk.

"Never a dull moment," he said.

"Never a dull moment," I agreed.

"That dame will fry for sure," he said cheerfully. "I've never seen a more open and shut case."

I went out without answering him.

CHAPTER 10
Blonde Fury

I got into the office at nine the next morning. Kane and Johns were there waiting for me. I could see by the look on their faces that the grapevine had reached them. It would have reached every precinct in the city—it was too good a story not to travel fast.

Lavers hadn't arrived yet and neither had Annabelle. She was gone when I finally got home around two-thirty that morning. I had forgotten about her being there until I got home. I had a feeling that last night was the beginning and end of a beautiful romance between Annabelle and me.

I sat down behind my desk and looked at the two sergeants.

"You heard the good news?" I asked them. They both nodded silently, watching me carefully.

"I'm still assigned to the case," I said.

"We heard that, too," Johns said.

"I think we've got some unfinished business with Edna Bright and Vince Schaeffer," I said. "I need help to finish it, but I'm not ordering either of you to stay and work with me on it. If you'd rather go back to the Fourth Precinct this morning, that's okay with me. But if you'll stay on the case and work with me, I'll appreciate it, of course. You make up your own minds about it."

They looked at each other, then looked back at me.

"If it's all the same to you, Lieutenant," Johns said carefully, "I'd rather go back to the precinct."

"Sure," I said. "How about you, Kane?"

"I think I'll stay with it," he said.

"Then I might as well get on my way," Johns said.

"So long, Sergeant," I said.

"Goodbye, Lieutenant." He went out of the office, closing the door carefully behind him.

I looked at Kane. "What makes you want to stay?"

He grinned. "The grapevine stinks most of the time, anyway, Lieutenant. And when I pulled that dumb act in the Plaza, you didn't even ball me out.

Drove me home even. I figure one good turn …"

"Thanks," I said. "Maybe we don't need Johns, anyway."

"What do you want me to do, Lieutenant?"

I pulled the phone and the directory over closer to me and looked up a couple of numbers. I rang Vince Schaeffer first and the phone rang and rang, but nobody answered. I tried Edna Bright's number next. On the fourth ring it was answered.

"Hello?" her voice said. "Yes? Who is it? Hello."

I put the phone gently back on its cradle.

"Edna Bright's still in her apartment," I said. "I want you to tail her when she leaves. Take my car—it's parked outside." I tossed him the keys. "Follow her wherever she goes. If she goes to any place except her office, let me know as quickly as you can. I'll be here."

"Sure, Lieutenant." He shoved the keys into his pocket and went out of the office.

I lit myself a cigarette. Ten minutes later Annabelle came in. She walked over to her desk and started to take off her gloves.

I watched her. She was wearing a light print dress which stayed close to her curves. I thought if I had a million barrels of oil, I'd trade them for Annabelle.

Well, half of them, anyway.

She got her gloves off, then took out a mirror from her purse and began to primp her hair.

"Good morning," I said.

She went on primping her hair.

"You're not talking, Annabelle?"

She looked over at me. "I was mad at you running out on me last night," she said in a small voice, "till I read about the murder being genuine in the newspaper this morning. Then I met Margie Farrell as I was coming in."

"Who's she?"

"A stenographer with the Bureau. She told me the story that's going around the grapevine." Her voice grew even smaller. "Is it true?"

"What part of it?"

"About you and Mrs. Cole? About what she said to Lieutenant Portus when she asked could she ring you?"

"Yeah," I nodded. "That's true."

"Oh," she said, and sat down at her desk.

Then the door opened and Lavers came into the office, walking slowly. "Good morning, Miss Jackson," he said and went on into his office, ignoring me completely.

Annabelle put a sheet of paper into her typewriter and started to pound away. I thought my hunch about the end of a beautiful romance had been dead right. It looked like being a beautiful day all round.

She gave me a cup of coffee when she made coffee around eleven. She stood as far away from my desk as she could and put the cup down on the edge, then walked away quickly.

At eleven-thirty Lavers called her into his office to take some dictation, and at eleven forty-five my phone rang. I grabbed it off the cradle quickly.

"Kane here, Lieutenant."

"What gives?"

"She left the apartment half an hour ago and got into a car. A '54 Dodge. She drove it and I tailed her in your Healey." A note of awe crept into his voice. "You have a hell of a time keeping that thing on the ground? I did."

"There's a couple of ships' anchors in the back," I told him. "If you throw those out before take-off, most times you can keep four wheels on the ground. What about Edna Bright?"

"She stopped ten minutes ago out here where I am now. Out on the lakeside. I parked your car and tailed along. She went into a cabin, so I watched for five minutes but she didn't come out, so I thought I'd ring you. I'm in the general store here."

"Where exactly?"

"Riverview—it's a little place maybe a couple of miles further on from Lakeside itself. You turn off the highway to Lakeside 88 and keep on following that road. You can't miss the general store—it's the only thing here."

"Okay," I said. "You stay where you are till I get there."

I picked up a cab outside the building and showed the driver my shield, then told him to get out to Riverview as fast as he could and not to worry too much about red lights. I lived to regret that statement, but at least I lived.

I tottered out of the cab at the general store and paid the guy. "Seems like a shame to take the money, Lieutenant," he said.

"Okay," I said hopefully. "Give it back to me."

"I mean," he said, putting the money away quickly, "I enjoyed the ride."

"I only wish I could say the same," I told him.

Kane came out of the general store to meet me as the cab drove off. He pointed down the road. "That's her Dodge parked there," he said. "She hasn't come back, so she must still be in the cabin. Your car's around the other side of the store." He gave me the keys.

"Okay," I said. "Let's take a look at the cabin."

We walked down a path that skirted the edge of the lake and passed a couple of shacks. There was no one else around.

"Place seems dead," I said to Kane.

"Off-season," he said, "and the middle of the week. Few people come out here on weekends."

"You got a gun with you?"

"Sure," he said. "You figure I'm going to need it?"

"You might," I told him.

The path turned away from the side of the lake and wandered through the trees. We followed it another fifty yards, then ahead of us was a shack.

Kane held my arm a moment. "That's it. I didn't get too close before in case she saw me."

"Fine," I said.

"What do we do, Lieutenant?"

"We go in," I told him.

I slipped the thirty-two out of its holster into my hand. "You get around to the back through the trees. I'll give you a couple of minutes and then I'll go in through the front door. When you hear the door open, you come in through the back door. Okay?"

"Sure," he grinned. "We're taking an awful lot of trouble over one dame, aren't we, Lieutenant?"

"She mightn't be alone," I said.

"Yeah," his face sobered. "I should have thought of that."

"Get going," I told him.

I watched him skirt through the trees well to one side of the shack until he disappeared from view. From where I stood, I was covered by a clump of trees from being seen from the shack, unless somebody inside used a pair of glasses. I thought I would like a cigarette and then I thought the arc of the match might attract somebody's attention inside.

It seemed an awfully long five minutes. When my watch told me it was up, I got as close to the shack as I could, using trees for a cover—until I was within twenty yards of it. I covered the remaining distance at a fast run and stopped with the door in front of me.

When you go into a place where somebody might be waiting for you with a gun in their hand, the thing to do is not stop to think about it. Otherwise you resign and become a car-park attendant.

I turned the handle of the door and slammed the door inwards so that it swung through an arc of one hundred and eighty degrees and ended up crashing into the wall.

Then I was inside the shack.

Three startled faces stared at me. Vince Schaeffer swore, then his hand dived into his pocket and came out holding a gun. I didn't stop to argue with him about who he was going to shoot with it. I pulled the trigger of the thirty-two and the slug took him high in the shoulder, spinning him off-balance.

I hadn't had time to watch the other two as well. The next moment a purse smashed down on my wrist and the thirty-two bounced out of my fingers onto the floor.

Schaeffer steadied himself and the gun in his hand swung in a tight arc until it was pointing at my stomach.

"This is for you, copper," he snarled.

I stood there helplessly, watching his finger tighten around the trigger in the split second before the gun went off. I thought it was one hell of a way to die …

Two shots sounded in quick succession and Schaeffer arched backwards, the gun spilling out of his hand. He screamed once, thinly, then his legs buckled under him and he crashed onto the floor.

I saw Kane standing behind him, the smoking gun in his hand. "Thanks, pal," I told him.

"A pleasure, Lieutenant," he said. "I should have got through that back door quicker, but the lock jammed and I had to force it open."

"Don't apologise, pal," I said. "You did fine."

Edna Bright dropped to her knees beside Schaeffer and then began to sob wildly. "He's dead," she moaned.

"You killed him!" The third member of the trio was crouched on the floor, shivering convulsively, his hands pressed tightly over his eyes. I tapped him gently on the shoulder and he jumped like a guy who hadn't paid his taxes—and he hadn't.

"You can come out now," I told him. "It's all over."

He slowly took his hands away from his eyes and looked at me.

"You should have stuck to your figures," I said. "I can see you weren't cut out for a life of crime."

He got onto his feet slowly and saw Schaeffer's body on the floor, then he began to shake again.

"Mr. Edgar Blount," I said. "Or should I say Edgar Jones? That was a hell of an alias to pick on."

"I've been a fool," he said. "A crazy fool." He looked at Kane and then at me. "You are police officers?"

"Check," I agreed.

"I'm glad you came," he said. "I think they were going to kill me."

"I wouldn't be surprised," I said. "Once they were sure they had all the money."

"How did you know that?"

I lit myself a cigarette and it tasted sweet. "She saw you in the afternoon— the first time," I said. "She told you she was a locator and you were Edgar Blount." He nodded. "She said maybe she could do a deal with you. She wouldn't report that she'd made the locate and she could get you out of Pine City and hide you out till the heat was off, then get you into another state—for a price."

"A thousand dollars, she said then."

I grinned at Kane. "You never find an honest man making such sucker of himself as some of these guys do."

I looked at Blount again. "Then she came back in the evening. She told you the cops were hot on your trail and they'd be at the hotel any minute. Her friend had just taken care of one, and you had to check out right away."

"You must have been watching."

"More or less." I grinned at Kane, who looked sheepish. "So they got you out of the hotel into a car and she drove you down here."

"That's right."

"She told you they'd be back this morning and whatever you did, not to show your face outside the shack."

He shivered. "I didn't, it was cold here, too—no blankets—couldn't go out and collect wood to make a fire. I just sat and shivered all night. I don't think I had more than an hour's sleep."

"Tough," I said. "The two of them came back this morning and told you the price had gone up. You were too hot for them to handle otherwise. They wanted—twenty-five thousand?"

"Thirty thousand," he said bitterly. "I told them I only had thirty-two thousand plus a bit left over out of the original fifty. Before I came to Pine City, I stopped off in Vegas. I didn't have any luck there. I guess my luck ran out when I stole the money."

"If only everybody saw it that way," Kane said wistfully.

I sucked smoke into my lungs. "Let's get back to the story."

"The man got here first," Blount said. "Vince was his name? When I told him I only had thirty-two thousand left, I saw the grin on his face and I realised he'd only said that amount in the hope I'd tell him what I really had. He said two thousand was enough to start somewhere fresh. Better than going to jail, he said."

Kane shook his head slowly. "Vince was a guy who'd know. Ask any of the boys in San Quentin."

"I told him I wouldn't pay it," Blount went on. "And then he started to threaten me. He took out his gun and said he could shoot me and no one would even hear the noise of the shot. And when I said what about the body?" Blount swallowed painfully. "He just laughed and said he'd toss the body into the lake and the gun with it, and if anyone ever did find the body which was unlikely, they'd think I'd committed suicide."

I dropped the butt on the floor and trod it out.

"I guess I …" Blount flushed. "Well I guess I'm just not the type for violence. I told him I didn't have all the money with me. Only about five thousand. The rest was in a safe deposit in Pine City. He said we'd wait till the girl arrived. And when she came they talked, and it was agreed that she would take the key and go and collect the money."

Edna Bright had stopped crying. She got onto her feet slowly and automatically dusted the hem of her skirt with one hand.

"I gave them the key," Blount said, "and they opened my bags and saw the five thousand there. Then the girl sort of looked at him and said why didn't they both go in and collect the money from the safe deposit and then they wouldn't have to come back here. The man said what about me and she laughed and said what was wrong with the lake. And then the man looked at me." He shuddered again. "I could see it in his eyes—he was going to kill me. They were going to take all the money and then they were still going to kill me!"

His voice had got hysterical. "Take it easy, son," Kane said. "A couple of years in San Quentin will do your nerves the world of good. Nothing to worry about—just do as you're told and dig that rock."

Blount held out his soft, delicate hands in front of him and stared at them numbly.

"Answer me a couple of questions, Blount," I said. "What time did you get out here last night?"

"Around nine."

"What time did the girl leave?"

"When the man came for her."

I stared at him. "You mean, Vince Schaeffer came out here to get her?"

"Yes, that's right," he nodded.

"What time did he arrive?"

"About eleven—a little after."

"And what time did they leave?"

"Just after midnight."

I looked at Kane and his face was as bleak as mine must have been.

"You're sure about those times?" I asked Blount, desperately. He nodded his head vigorously. "I'm quite sure, Lieutenant. I kept looking at my watch last night. I thought the night would never end."

Edna Bright gave a brittle laugh. "Trying to fix us with the Cole murder, Lieutenant? You're out of luck."

"And so are you, honey," I said. But there was no satisfaction in it.

I lit another cigarette and looked at Kane. "Go on up to the general store and phone Homicide to send somebody out to take care of this. Better take Blount with you. You can wait there till they arrive and show 'em the way here."

"Sure, Lieutenant," Kane nodded, then pushed one beefy hand into the small of Blount's back. "Okay, Dillinger," he said. "Let's walk."

"I'll be glad to," Blount muttered. "This place will haunt me for the rest of my life."

They went out, closing the door behind them. I picked up my own gun from the floor and slipped it back into the holster. I picked up Edna's purse from the floor, then put Schaeffer's gun down on the table beside me, in easy reach. I flipped through the contents of her purse and saw there wasn't any gun there.

"When you've quite finished with that purse," she said coldly, "would you mind if I had it back?"

"Sure," I tossed it over to her and she caught it clumsily. "I'm sorry you didn't kill Laurence Cole," I said. "I had you and Vince tapped for the Farnham killing."

"That was an accident," she said.

"Not any longer," I said. "Not since Cole got murdered last night. And I had you figured for it. You made the locate on Eve Farnham. She tells you about her husband being a lush with no money, only an insurance policy. I figured you went away and thought about that and came back with a proposition. Or maybe she made the proposition first. Either way, I had you figured for it.

"Joe Williams told me that you were good on the locates that didn't matter, but on the big stuff you weren't so hot. He didn't know the truth. You made your big locates—and Vince stepped in to help you strong-arm a deal with whoever it was. They paid you blackmail money and you never reported the locate. A real sucker like Blount must have looked like a gift from the Indians."

"You're so smart," she said tonelessly.

I bowed my head in acknowledgement. "Thanks, I hand it to you. You certainly fooled me in the first place with that wide-eyed innocent approach. And you played it smart. You knew that sooner or later I'd find out you were going around with Vince Schaeffer, so you deliberately introduced me to him as the guy you were going to marry and he thanked me for not letting you know he was an ex-con."

"We were married," she said. "We were married six months ago."

"And you kept separate apartments?"

"It was safer that way," she told me. "Most nights we'd spend together—in one apartment or the other."

"And Vince had his job with United as a front," I said. "It was a nice organisation. You got a little too ambitious when you went after Blount."

"We were going to pull out after him," she said. "We had about ten thousand we'd made out of the others altogether. But with his thirty thousand, we could really go places. We were going to South America—Vince was half-Spanish. His mother came from Buenos Aires and he knew the town and some people there. We were going to buy a club or a restaurant, or something like that."

I nodded. "Last night when you went into the Plaza the second time, you knew you were being followed by Sergeant Kane?"

"I thought I was being followed," she said, "but I didn't know who by. I didn't think I was followed into the hotel, but I had a feeling I'd been followed the first time I went there. We played it safe—Vince hung back and waited to see if was. When he saw—Kane? Is that his name?"

I nodded again.

"When Vince saw Kane follow me up in the elevator, he took another one. Kane got out just ahead of him and Vince saw there was nobody else in the corridor, so he knocked him out and put him into an empty elevator, then came along to Blount's room and warned me. We got him out the back way, then waited to see what happened to Kane. We watched him leave the hotel and when we were sure he'd gone, we sent Blount back in to check out. Then we brought him out here—or I did. But you know the rest of that story."

"Yeah," I nodded, "I know the rest."

She sat on a rickety chair and crossed her legs. She opened her purse and got out a pack of cigarettes and lit one. Then she looked up at me and her eyes looked like two separate calculating machines.

"Would ten thousand dollars interest you, Lieutenant?" she asked softly.

"Could be," I said. "For what?"

She looked down at Schaeffer's body for a brief moment.

"I always believe in cutting my losses," she told me. "Vince is dead. Nothing I do now can hurt him. You could tell the story in court that he was the evil influence. That he forced me into it by threatening me with personal violence. He was an ex-con with a bad record. A jury would believe the story without questioning it, if you told it. You could say it was true that I didn't know his record until after I'd married him, and it was too late to go anything about it then."

I looked at her legs—they were nice legs and the rest of her was nice to look at.

"If you did that," she went on, "I'd give you the ten thousand dollars—before you went into court, of course."

"You'd trust me?"

"If you gave me your word, I don't think you'd go back on it. If you told that story, what do you think I'd get?"

"Maybe nothing," I told her. "Probably nothing. A jury could easily return a verdict of not guilty in your case. Vince being dead already."

"Then you'll do it?" she asked, and her voice trembled with eagerness.

"You know something, honey?" I said. "I would do it—and for free—but for one thing."

"What do you mean?" Her face was suddenly ugly with rage.

"It was you who suggested picking up Blount's money from the safe deposit and leaving Blount cooling his heels on the bottom of the lake."

She called me a nasty word.

"Honey," I said. "When I get through in that witness box, you'll pick up a seven to fifteen as a minimum. And when they let you out of Fulton, you'll be an old woman."

She lashed out with her purse in a blonde fury. I caught her wrist and twisted it so that the purse dropped onto the floor.

"It's dames like you," I sighed, "who make me lose my faith in dames!"

CHAPTER 11
Her Bullets Curve, Too

It was four o'clock when I got back to the office. Annabelle looked up at me over her typewriter. "The Commissioner wanted to see you as soon as you came in," she said and went on with her typing.

Welcome home, I thought. The massed bands playing and the crowds cheering.

I knocked on the Commissioner's door and went into his office.

"Sit down, Wheeler," he said.

I sat down obediently and looked at him.

"I hear that Schaeffer was shot trying to shoot you, that an embezzler was saved from being murdered and he now faces a charge, that Edna Bright faces about six counts from extortion to being an accessory after the fact to an embezzlement."

"That's right, sir."

"But none of them killed Cole last night?"

"No, sir."

"Don't you think you'd better give up trying, Wheeler?"

"No, sir."

His lips twisted. "With your genius for inventing," he said, "I felt sure you'd manage to pin it onto one of them somehow."

"I didn't."

"Bad luck, isn't it, Wheeler?" he said. "You won't believe that any woman who bestows her favours on you could become a murderess."

"Does it matter what I believe?"

"I don't suppose it does," he aid. His voice was tinged with irony as he went on. "I wanted to congratulate you, Lieutenant, on your devotion to duty."

"Thank you, sir," I said, poker-faced. "Is that all for now?"

"Quite."

I went out to my desk again. I'd sent Kane back to the Fourth Precinct, not because I wanted to but because I didn't have anything else for him to do. And also, if he stayed around me too long, some of the taint might rub off—and I didn't want that to happen to him.

I glared at the top of Annabelle's head which was bent over her typewriter, then suddenly remembered with a nasty jolt that I'd promised Natalie to send Jerry Schultz down to see her that morning.

I rang his office and found he was in.

"How are things, Al?" He sounded merry and bright.

"I meant to ring you this morning, Jerry," I said. "To ask you to do me a personal favour."

"I already have," he said.

"Huh?"

Jerry chuckled. "You're talking about Mrs. Cole, I presume? One of the matrons rang me and gave me a message to ask if Al Wheeler had been in touch with me about defending her. So I said of course he had and I was on my way. I saw her, talked with her, told her what a wonderful cop you were and she didn't have to worry about a thing. In fact, I lied in my teeth as usual."

"Jerry," I said. "I love you."

"I can always use a client," he said. Then his voice sobered. "Just between you and me, Al, you think she did it?"

"No!" I shouted down the phone.

"Okay, okay," he said. "Don't blast my eardrum that way, Al, I don't think she did, either—you get a feeling about these things after twenty years of criminal practice. But I'd take an even bet that we're the only two people in town who believe she didn't do it."

"So?"

"Find out who did, pal," he said seriously. "Because if they ever put her in the box, it'll be a one-way trip to the chair for her. I never saw such a case for the D.A. He doesn't even have to try."

"You should have been a gravedigger, you're so cheerful," I snarled, and hung up.

Annabelle's head was still bent over her typewriter. I thought I might as well sit in a morgue as sit in the office. I thought I'd go and have a drink, but even that didn't really interest me. I thought I'd take a walk instead. I hadn't been for a walk since I was in sixth grade. From then on it's always been prowl cars and then the Healey.

I walked a couple of blocks, then I wondered how Laurence Cole and Company were getting on without Laurence Cole and their pin-up locater. I was within a few blocks of the office, so I thought I'd take a look.

When I got there the door was open, but the general office was deserted. I walked in and yelled. "Anybody home?" Which is almost the most stupid-sounding thing you can say out loud.

"In here," a voice answered from within Cole's office.

I walked over and pushed open the door. Joe Williams looked up from behind Cole's desk and smiled wanly. "Hi, Lieutenant." I went in and pushed the door shut behind me. The desk was strewn with papers. "You look like you're having trouble?"

"I'll say." He ran a hand through his hair. "What with Cole murdered, his wife held for the murder, and then Edna Bright tossed into jail this afternoon." He shook his head. "It's all too much for me. I went down to see Mrs. Cole this afternoon and she wants me to run the office for the time being, so I'm trying to sort out the mess. But I don't think I'm winning."

"Why don't you take time out and I'll buy you a drink?"

"Sounds like a wonderful idea," he said enthusiastically. "I'll come back here afterwards."

He collected his hat and locked the outer door and we went down in the elevator. The nearest bar was half a block away and we made quick time.

"Here's luck," Williams said as he lifted his glass.

"Sure," I said. "We all need it."

He took a long pull on the glass and smacked his lips. "I could certainly use that. You know, the only thing I've got for laughs since last night is what Edna Bright turned out to be—not a locater but an extortionist!"

"Goes to show," I said.

"Brother." He shook his head. "You never said a truer word. Sort of scares you, you know, Lieutenant? You wonder what everybody would turn out to be if you could get a sort of inside look at them."

"Praise be we can't," I said.

We finished our drinks and he ordered another two.

"You saw Mrs. Cole this afternoon?" I asked casually.

"Sure—right after her lawyer—she's got the best, too, Jerry Schultz. Know him?"

"I've heard of him."

"If anyone can swing it, that Schultz can." He shook his head in admiration. "That guy is one smart cookie, all right."

"Yeah," I said. "How was Mrs. Cole?"

"She seemed okay," he said. "Quite bright, you know, for a dame with a murder rap hanging over her head. If she did knock him off, I hope she gets away with it. Laurence Cole was nothing more than a low-grade louse."

"How come?"

"He was always chasing other women. And always snooping around the office. Hell, he'd even play private detective and snoop after you when you were out on a locate. He caught up with me in a bar a couple of times and raised hell. I nearly socked him the second time."

"But you didn't?"

He looked at me for a moment and then the grin broke out all over his face. "Okay, Lieutenant," he said resignedly. "You got me tapped, I didn't. I was too scared of losing my job."

"Aren't we all, Joe," I said.

We had a third drink.

"You know," Williams went on. "He was a funny guy. He married a dame with a load of money, but he kept that business going for peanuts. He was always on the make, that Cole. He was always trying to chisel a buck."

"Huh?"

He looked at me enquiringly. "What's that, Lieutenant?"

"You said something?"

"I did?"

"Something about Cole."

"Oh, yeah—I said he was always trying to chisel a buck."

"That's what I thought you said. Thanks, Joe."

"For what?"

"The drink. I must go now." I drained my glass and put it on the bar counter. "See you around. Thanks again."

"Anytime, Lieutenant." He looked at me blankly. "Anytime at all."

I left the bar and walked back to the office. Why the hell hadn't I thought of that before? It took a character like Joe Williams to tell me. Laurence Cole was always trying to chisel a buck. It was as simple as that.

I walked back to City Hall, but I didn't go back up to the office. It was getting close to six in the evening. I picked up the Healey and drove downtown, then had a meal.

It was just after seven when I arrived in Oakley Street again. I pressed the buzzer of her apartment and she opened the door.

She looked slightly colossal. She was wearing an ivory-coloured sweater and a tight black gabardine skirt, as black as her hair and as tight as her sweater. Her already wide eyes widened a little more.

"Lieutenant Wheeler," she said. "Again?"

"Some more questions, Mrs. Farnham," I said. "Can I come in?"

"I suppose I can't stop you," she said.

I followed her into the living room.

"I'm representing the Police Commissioner in this case," I said. "If you'd care to check that with Lieutenant Portus or Hanlon at Homicide— or the Commissioner himself."

"You sound much too impressive to be kidding me, Lieutenant Wheeler," she smiled. "So go ahead—ask your questions."

"The night Cole was killed …"

"I'm not likely to forget that," she said in a low voice.

"I've heard Mrs. Cole's story, of course," I said. She smiled again.

"Of course." I forced myself to smile back. "You and Cole were in the bedroom when the buzzer went?"

"Yes."

"You went out and opened the door. Mrs. Cole pushed past you through the living room, then into the bedroom and saw her husband there?"

"That's correct."

"What happened then?"

She turned away from me and walked over to the window and stood there, looking down at the street.

"She saw him and she opened her purse and pulled out a gun." Her voice trembled. "Before I could stop her, she fired two shots and he was dead. I picked up the nearest weapon I could find—an umbrella—and hit her over the head with it and …"

"I know the rest of it, Mrs. Farnham."

She turned back towards me. "Was that all you wanted to know, Lieutenant?"

"Not quite all," I said. "I wondered if you'd help me in a little experiment?"

"Very well."

"Thanks," I smiled at her, "It won't take long. Do you mind if we go into the bedroom?"

"What for?"

"I assure you I won't get within a yard of you, Mrs. Farnham."

We went into the bedroom. From the open door, the bed was in the corner, the pillows against the far wall. I went over and lay down on the bed and looked up at her, framed in the open doorway.

"No," I said. "We'll just act this over briefly. Just so I can get it clear in my mind."

She clenched her teeth. "You already said that."

I pulled the thirty-two out of its holster, made sure the safety catch was on, and tossed it to her. "Catch," I said.

She caught it awkwardly and looked at it with distaste written on her face. "What do I do with it?"

"You're Mrs. Cole," I said. "And I'm Cole, Okay? You appear in the doorway, you open your purse and then you've got a gun in your hand."

She pointed the gun at me.

"Now," I said. "What happens? What do I do?"

"You get up," she said. "You sit up, that is."

I sat up obediently.

"And then I come closer."

She came a couple of paces closer to me. She crouched forward slightly. A couple of feet at the most separated our faces as we looked at each other.

"Then?" I said softly.

"She fired."

"Two shots?"

"Yes—two shots."

"The safety catch is on," I said. "You can pull the trigger."

The gun was only a foot away from my face and I was looking down the barrel. Her finger tensed on the trigger and then pulled it twice. It clicked uselessly.

"And now I'm dead?"

"And now you're dead," she agreed tonelessly.

I took the gun from her limp hand and slid it back into my holster.

"That Mrs. Cole," I said. "She was a genius."

"I don't understand you, Lieutenant," she said. "What do you mean?"

"She fired a gun so that the bullets didn't go straight once they left the barrel. They went around in a circle. And she did it twice."

She just looked at me.

"Cole was shot in the back of the head," I said, getting to my feet. "The *back* of the head, Mrs. Farnham."

She recoiled a pace and naked fear showed in her eyes for a moment; then she quickly put her hand to her head.

"I'm confused," she murmured. "I don't know what happened or what didn't happen any more. After what I've been through in the last two weeks, I think I'll go mad."

I walked up close to her so that we nearly touched.

"You aren't confused, Mrs. Farnham," I told her. "You aren't confused at all."

"Please," she said. "I have a bad headache. Would you please leave?"

"You were married to a lush," I said. "You said so. A no-good bum whose only value was the insurance he was carrying. He was worse than useless alive—but he was worth thirty thousand bucks dead."

She turned and walked out of the room, back into the living room. She sank into a chair. "Leave me alone."

I sat on the arm of the chair and looked at her.

"This Cole," I said. "He had a rich wife whom he hated, so he ran a second-rate locating business to give himself what he thought was independence. He was always out to chisel a fast buck. He didn't trust anybody—not even his own staff. He'd follow them around sometimes to see if they were working or not.

"He was following Edna Bright the day she located you. He maybe even saw you. He had just as sharp an eye for a good-looking woman as he did for a fast buck. And then when Edna Bright told him about your conversation, she'd have mentioned the fact that your husband was a lush and also the amount of insurance he carried.

"So he got to thinking that maybe he could make himself a fast buck and get to know a beautiful woman as well. He called on you."

"I said that," she almost shouted. "I told the police he called and threatened me. Forced me to …"

"*Forced you*, Mrs. Farnham?" I laughed. "That sounds a little humorous. He called on you, all right—he told you he was the big-shot of the locating business. And you two looked at each other and saw the same type of person as you were yourselves, sitting opposite. And he worked the conversation around to your husband and the insurance money and then, maybe almost before you knew it, you were planning a murder.

"But the murder had to be an accident because otherwise there wouldn't be any insurance money. And you had to have a cast-iron alibi. So it was fixed that Cole would run him down and when it was all over, the insurance money would be halved. And then Henry took the long trail and nobody even thought of Cole having anything to do with it, so everything looked fine."

"This is just a pack of insane lies," she said, and went to get out of the chair.

I held her wrist and forced her back into the chair.

"I haven't finished yet," I said. "Sure, everything looked fine for Cole. He'd have his monetary independence from his wife as soon as the insurance company paid out. And he had you as well. And he didn't have to wait for an insurance company's okay on you. So he visited you at night.

"And that was when you began to hate him. That mean, snide streak in him was becoming a mile wide. And you thought of having him around your neck for the rest of your life … even worse than Henry had ever been. At least a lush drinks himself into a stupor. And also, you were going to have to give him half the insurance money."

She buried her head in her hands and started to cry.

"He'd told you about his wife," I went on. "His red-headed, hot-tempered wife whom he thought was only waiting for the chance to get enough evidence to divorce him. And that gave you an idea. You invited him over that night. You excited him, telling him how much you were longing for his kisses—anything to make sure he would come.

"And when he was here, you made some excuse to leave the apartment. You went down to a pay booth and rang Mrs. Cole, and told her that her husband was with a Mrs. Farnham and gave her the address. You disguised your voice so she wouldn't recognise it later.

"You had a gun ready in your purse. You left the purse on the table over there. You made sure that there was plenty of evidence for her when she arrived. You heard the buzzer and you told Cole it was a neighbour or something—made some excuse so he wouldn't panic.

"You opened the door and in came Mrs. Cole. She went past you to the bedroom and saw her husband. Cole started to swear at her, to revile her. You took the gun out of your purse and crept up behind her and hit her over the head, knocking her unconscious.

"Cole would ask you why you did it and you would say you couldn't stand scenes and tell him to carry her into the bathroom and you'd bring her around. You'd be standing in the bedroom then and he'd have to walk past you to get to her. And as he knelt down to pick her up, you put the gun against the back of his head and fired two shots, killing him instantly. You caught him off-balance and as he fell backwards to the floor his hand, in in a last spasmodic twitch of life, clutched the sheet and pulled it from the bed.

"Then you carefully wiped the fingerprints from the gun and held it by the barrel, with a handkerchief between you and the metal, and pressed it into Mrs. Cole's unconscious hand so that a good set of prints registered, then you let it drop onto the floor. Then you rang Homicide and reported the murder. You picked up an umbrella and stood over her until the police arrived."

She tore her wrist free from my grip and got onto her feet suddenly. "It's not true," she gasped. "It's lies! All lies. You're all in it! You want to kill me and I don't know why!"

Then she laughed and cried. "Why?" she moaned. "Why do you want to destroy me? What have I done that you all hate me so much?"

"I'm going, Mrs. Farnham," I told her. "But I'll be back. You know what I've just said is the truth—and I know it. I'll be back and I'll get a confession from you. You'll crack, Mrs. Farnham, You'll bust wide open at the seams. I'll find evidence to back it. I'll check on Cole. I'll find people who saw him coming in here at night, leaving at night—people who maybe saw you down at the pay booth on the corner an hour or so before the murder. I'll find them, Mrs. Farnham—all of them."

She ran into the bedroom and threw herself down on the bed, burying her face in a pillow and sobbing wildly. I leaned against the door jamb and looked down at her.

"And you know what they'll do with you? They'll put you in the electric chair."

I turned around and walked out of the apartment, closing the front door gently behind me. I walked down the stairs into the street and I hoped I was right—that she would crack. If she didn't, things could be very tough indeed.

I stopped to light a cigarette and looked around me. I looked at the meanness of the street, the squalid apartment houses that lined both sides, and I wondered how it would be?

How it would be married to a hopeless alcoholic who plunged you into debt beyond any hope of ever getting clear? How it would be having to earn a living slinging hash in a dump that always smelled of frying onions and stale fat? And all you had to look forward to the rest of your life if you were lucky, was working in the same dump.

For a moment I could feel sorry for Mrs. Farnham.

CHAPTER 12
The Dame Was Persecuted

The police matron opened up the cell door for me. I stepped inside and she swung it shut again, then backed off a discreet distance where she couldn't hear what I was saying, but she could see what I was doing. A dame in a cell is chaperoned twenty-four hours a day.

Edna Bright was sitting on the bunk. She looked up at me listlessly. "What the hell do you want?" she asked.

"Some information," I said.

She laughed shortly. "That's very funny. Coming from you, if had it, I wouldn't give it to you. What did you ever do for me, you jerk?"

"I gave you a ride into town to meet Vince once," I said.

"I should have cut your throat on the way," she said.

I took out a pack of cigarettes. "Smoke?"

She brightened. "Yes, I can't get those things."

"I know," I said. I lit the cigarette for her. "I have an edge with that police matron over there. I'm a cop. She can turn a blind eye for a little while. Some day I might be able to do her a favour."

She puffed hungrily at the cigarette. "What are you talking about?"

"Cigarettes," I said. "I've got two full packs in my pocket and a couple of packs of matches. She won't see me pass them over. So long as you're careful when you smoke them, she won't know."

"Thanks," she said, and held out her hand.

I looked down at it with mild interest.

"Come on," she said impatiently. "Let me have them."

"For free?"

"What do you want?" Edna grinned. "A dance of the seven veils?"

"I'll trade," I said. "The information I want for the cigarettes."

"Always an angle," she sighed. "You must have been born a cop. I bet you wore a shield on your diapers."

"Most kids do," I told her.

She grinned. "All right, Lieutenant, I'll trade. What do you want to know?"

"Where were you the afternoon Henry Farnham was run over and killed?"

She thought for a moment. "I was out making a locate on some guy who didn't have the money, anyway. So I went back to the office to report it— look good for Cole, you know?"

"Remember what time you got back to the office?"

"Be somewhere around four. No, four-thirty."

"Was Cole there when you got back?"

"Sure," she said.

I lit a cigarette for myself. "Then he went out?"

"No," she shook her head. "I went into his office to tell him about the locate and after I'd finished, he offered me a drink and made a couple of fast passes at me like he always did."

"You sure?"

"Of course I'm sure. You should have experienced some of Larry's passes—once felt, never to be forgotten."

"Okay," I said. "What time did you leave that night?"

"Somewhere around a quarter to six. It wasn't any earlier."

"And what about Cole?"

"He was still there when I left."

"You're absolutely sure about this?"

She scowled at me. "Look, if you don't want to believe me, then don't, but I wasn't the only one in that office. Ask some of the others."

I shook my head slowly. "I believe you. I don't want to, but I believe you."

"Well, that's something," she said. "How about my cigarettes, then?"

I took the cigarettes and the matches out of my pocket and dropped them on her lap. "That's about the lousiest trade I ever made," I told her.

Edna hastily concealed the cigarettes and matches under her bunk.

"Sorry, Lieutenant," she said. "You ever go past the women's penitentiary, be sure and look me up." She lifted her hand with the first two fingers tight together. "I'll be the one next to the warden." She winked. "Right next to the warden."

I signalled to the matron to let me out and she did. She walked part of the way with me.

"Bribery and corruption, Lieutenant," she said with a twinkle in her eyes. "I'm ashamed of you."

"For information," I said. "And the information I got wasn't what I wanted."

"She lied to you?"

I shook my head. "She told the truth."

The matron stared at me. "I don't follow, Lieutenant."

"It gets more complicated as it goes along," I told her. "Never mind."

I walked out of the Bureau and into the Healey. It was nine in the bleak evening. I didn't know what to do—I didn't feel like going home. I deliberately hadn't counted five along the women's cells from Edna and called in to see Natalie. I didn't have the heart to face her with nothing to tell her.

I sat in the Healey and lit a cigarette. I thought of the act that I'd put on for Eve Farnham's benefit and I squirmed. No wonder the dame had hysterics and thought she was being persecuted. She was.

My memory jolted. She'd lied about the shooting—the bullets that went around in ever-decreasing circles instead of going straight. She'd lied. She'd lied in her teeth. Why?

The cigarette burned down between my fingers, and I tossed the butt out of the window when it started to burn my fingers.

I started the motor and put the Healey into first and nosed out from the curb. I changed into second and eased past a cab, just catching a green light. Suddenly I was getting the right idea. I changed up to third at forty and the ideas began to beat through my head like a burlesque dancer's bumps to *Bolero*.

Vaguely I heard a siren in the distance which seemed to be coming closer.

This time, I thought, I have to be right. I can't afford to be wrong. I've got to hurry slowly on this thing.

The siren grew louder and louder. I looked out casually and saw a prowl car riding along beside me. The guy beside the driver waved frantically. I waved back and smiled.

His face contorted hideously and he waved again. So I waved back to him. The next moment the prowl car swung in towards me and I stamped on the brake pedal and the Healey stopped sharply.

The prowl car slithered sideways across the road with a scream of tortured rubber, bounced off the curb and slithered the other way. Then it suddenly nose-dived to a stop, the back slewing around so that it finished up broadside on across the road. I let the Healey run on gently and stopped a couple of inches from the side of the sedan.

I got out and walked over to them and glared at the guy who had waved at me. "What the hell do you think you're doing?" I asked him and the driver who was sitting there, hands clenched around the wheel, staring fixedly ahead of him.

The cop with the rubber face twisted it up again in all directions and made gurgling sounds.

"You damned nearly ran me off the road," I said. "Cutting in like that!"

Rubber-Face gurgled some more and finally found his voice.

"You," he said. "You—you got the nerve to come up and ask what we're doing!"

"Waving to somebody like that," I said. "No point."

"Waving?" He quivered. "I was telling you to pull over, you dope."

"Pull over?" I looked at him enquiringly. "What for?"

He slapped himself across the mouth. "Look, bub," he said heavily, "there's a thirty limit through the city. You was doing seventy. That's over a hundred per cent more than the limit. So we chase you. We blow our siren at you. You still go on—still doing seventy. We pull up alongside you—I wave you into the curb. And what do you do?" He seemed to be strangling himself. "You wave right back!"

"I was thinking of something else," I said. "Sorry."

The driver suddenly gave a convulsive jerk and let go of the wheel. He looked around at Rubber-Face cautiously.

"Did we stop?" he asked in a hushed voice.

"Yeah," Rubber-Face said. "And this is the guy we nearly killed ourselves for."

Then he looked at me lovingly. "Oh, brother," he said. "I'll get your licence suspended for life, I'll get you in jail for this, I'll get you …"

I looked at him closely. "Take that chewing-gum out of your mouth," I said. "You know it's against the regulations."

I leaned my arms on the sill of the door and looked into the car. "You've got a couple of buttons undone, do them up." I transferred my stare to the driver. "And you, the way you handled that car, you shouldn't be allowed out on a scooter."

"I …" he started to say.

"You men aren't from the traffic detail," I said. "They don't keep suicidal fools like you there. What precinct are you from?"

"Sixth," Rubber-Face said automatically and then his face went crazy again. "Hey," he yelped. "Who the hell do you think you are?"

I took out my shield and held it three inches from his nose. "Lieutenant Wheeler," I told him. "Attached to the Commissioner's office as his personal representative."

Rubber-Face and the driver looked at each other in what could only be described as pregnant silence.

"Lieutenant," the driver said in a hushed voice.

Rubber-Face writhed his mouth into something that looked like a figure 8. "Personal representative for the Commissioner."

"You should get your head read," the driver told him bitterly. "That is, if they can find your head."

"Was it my idea to drive him into the curb?" Rubber-Face said passionately. "Was it me who bounces the car all over the road and ends up facing nowhere?"

"But ..." the driver said desperately.

"All I did," Rubber-Face cut in hurriedly, "was wave to him." He gave me a hideous smile. "And he waved right back, isn't that right, Lieutenant?"

"I think there must have been a misunderstanding somewhere," I said gravely. "You go your way and I'll go mine."

"Amen, Lieutenant," Rubber-Face said fervently.

I got back into the Healey, reversed and drove around the prowl car. Both cops stiffened their backs and looked straight ahead as I went by. The last I saw of the prowl car in the rear-vision, it was steadily reversing into the path of an oncoming truck.

I didn't have the strength to look any more. I heard the whine of air brakes and a torrent of abuse from the truck driver which carried right back to the Healey.

I went home the rest of the way at a steady thirty.

I got home and thought for a couple of hours. I mapped out a plan. I didn't listen to the hi-fi. I didn't even have a drink. And I went to bed early. It was the most boring night of my life.

Next morning I was in the office at nine-thirty, but not Lavers' office. This one belonged to United Insurance. I got shown into Moss' office and he scowled at me.

"You want something?" he asked.

I gave him the big smile—the magnetic Al Wheeler goodwill builder. It left him cold.

"I'm very busy, Lieutenant," he said. "Very busy."

I pulled out the visitor's chair and sat down determinedly. "Mr. Moss," I said, "I am here firstly to apologise—to your stomach."

"What's this?" he asked suspiciously. "Another of your ideas of something funny?"

"I once said that your stomach was big enough to make a mistake. It's not. It never has made a mistake."

He looked at me for a long moment, then grunted and dug his fingers into his top pocket. "Have a cigar, Al," he said.

"I'll stay with a cigarette, thanks," I said, and carefully held a match for him to light his cigar.

He grunted his thanks. "You think I'm right about the Farnham killing?"

"I'm sure you're right," I told him. "It was murder."

"You know something?" he said. "I was just about convinced that you were right about my stomach, after all."

"Let's get together on this thing," I said. "You haven't paid her yet?"

He scowled. "No, but it's getting awful close. A couple of days more and we'll have to pay her."

"You won't," I said. "Not if you help me."

"You on the level about this, Wheeler?"

"I was never more serious in all my life," I assured him.

Moss picked up his phone. "No phone calls," he said to the operator. "I'm out. To anybody. If they want to know where I've gone, say I was taken away—under police escort." He banged the receiver down. "Talk to me, Lieutenant, I'm all yours."

It was eleven-thirty when I left his office and made my way towards City Hall and just after twelve when I got there. Annabelle was a head bent over a typewriter that didn't look up.

I sat down at my desk and twiddled my thumbs slowly. At a quarter to one, Annabelle put the cover on her typewriter and went out to lunch.

I still thumb twiddled. At a quarter past one Lavers came out, looked at Annabelle's empty desk, then reluctantly turned and looked at me.

"Lunch," he grunted. "Be late back. Not before four. Tell her." He pointed at the empty desk, then went on his way.

I waited another ten minutes to make sure he hadn't forgotten something and come back for it, then I removed myself and my hat into his office. I closed the door carefully and locked it.

I smoked one of the visitor's cigarettes from the box on his desk and listened. Around a quarter to two, I heard Annabelle's swift footsteps. She came over to Lavers' door and tapped a couple of times and then was apparently satisfied he was out. I heard her go back to her desk and a couple of minutes later, the typewriter started to clatter again.

I gave it fifty seconds, then lifted the phone and dialled her extension. She answered on the first ring.

"Miss Jackson, Commissioner Lavers' secretary."

"Lavers," I growled huskily into the phone.

"Yes, sir?" She sounded an eager beaver.

"Something's come up."

"Yes, sir?" Still the eager beaver.

"This is most important. It's vital."

"Yes, sir." She fairly quivered with eagerness.

"Lieutenant Wheeler is right about the Cole murder," I said solemnly. "The whole Department, and I don't exclude myself, Miss Jackson, were wrong."

"Oh?" she gasped.

I took a deep breath. The rasp in my voice was beginning to crack my vocal chords. "He's a much maligned man," I went on. "The story deliberately fabricated about him and Mrs. Cole was a malicious falsehood."

"Oh," she said warmly.

"Now, listen carefully," I said. "He needs help in unmasking the murderer. He needs a girl—someone not known as a police woman—to co-operate with him. I am asking you, Miss Jackson, in the name of Justice, to collaborate with him."

"Oh, I will, Mr. Commissioner," she said joyously. "I will."

"I knew I could rely on you, Miss Jackson," I said. "There may be a certain element of risk attached to it."

"I don't care," she said. "Anything for Al Wh … I mean, Justice, sir."

"Excellent." I had a fit of coughing and buried it in my handkerchief.

"Did you say something, sir?" she asked anxiously.

"I was saying," I wheezed, "that when Lieutenant Wheeler returns to the office, he will tell you what you have to do. I want you to be entirely guided by him. Do exactly as he says without querying any instructions."

"Yes, sir."

"And … Miss Jackson?"

"Sir?"

"I have an idea that I left a file on Macaron in the D.A.'s office. While you're waiting for Wheeler, slip downstairs and see if I did."

"Macaron, sir?"

"Sebastian Macaron the terrorist."

"Oh yes, sir."

"Good luck," I added gruffly. "To both you and Wheeler."

I hung up and waited, listening. I heard her phone hit the cradle and the next moment her footsteps receded as she ran out of the office.

I quickly unlocked the door and stepped out into the outer office. I closed Lavers' door and locked it carefully behind me and put the key in the keyhole.

I tossed my hat on my desk and made a fast run for the water cooler. My throat was scraped raw. I drank three glasses and felt a little better.

I heard her high heels come tap-tapping down the corridor and I leaned negligently against the desk. She came into the office and her eyes lit up when she saw me.

"Al," she said and threw herself into my arms.

"Why, little magnolia blossom," I said. "You've come back into mah life!"

"The Commissioner rang," she said breathlessly. "Told me everything. How wrong everyone's been about you. Al, I've been as bad as the rest of them. Can you ever forgive me?"

"Of course, honey," I told her grandly. "Don't give it another thought."

"But I've been so horrible to you."

"I know," I said sadly. "I've been breaking my heart—quietly. I haven't cried out loud, except when I've been alone. But into each life, I told myself, some rain must fall, and if too much was falling in mine I would just have to give a great big smile."

She almost glared at me. "You don't have to be corny about it. I'm trying to say I'm sorry."

"You're sorry," I smiled pathetically at her. "Just like that you say you're sorry and this heart of mine which is cracked in four separate places, mends itself right away."

"All right."

"I'm not complaining, you understand," I said. "I'm just telling you part—a small part—of what you've done to me. I'm not the sort of character who sits and thinks about things like this—sits and adds up just how much a person owes him in damages, but if I was that sort of person I'd know the score—just how much you owe me right now. But I'm a decent sort of guy—I'll give you the chance to pay off."

"What do you want me to do, Al?"

I very nearly said the wrong thing. I managed to choke back the words before they reached my mouth. "Get your gloves, purse and anything else you need," I said. "We'll go and have a drink and I'll tell you all about it."

"Wonderful."

"I hope you're a better actor than Hubert," I said.

"Why?"

"Because I have a nasty feeling the penalty for failure might be much more severe for you than it was for him."

She giggled. "Poor Hubert. Somehow the story got around the dramatic club and every time he comes in now, someone always starts whistling *Give Me My Boots and My Saddle!*"

CHAPTER 13
You Slay Me

We were waiting outside her apartment for her when she came home from the restaurant. I looked at my watch. Ten after six. The time schedule looked like it might be right, but it would have to be rigidly adhered to.

Her heels tapped up the stairs and then she came onto the landing. She had her head bent as she searched her purse for the apartment key. She found it and straightened up and then she saw us standing there outside her door.

"Again, Lieutenant?" she said in a low voice.

"I'd like you to meet Mr. Lee Moss, Mrs. Farnham," I said. "Mr. Moss is from the United Insurance Company."

"Oh?" There was a flicker of something for a moment in the back of her eyes and then it was gone.

"How do you do, Mrs. Farnham," Moss said courteously. "We did meet once before, I remember. A day or so after the unfortunate accident."

"Oh, yes," she smiled at him. "I remember now."

"It's about the claim," he said. "A few details before it's paid."

"I've been beginning to think it never would be paid," she said and put the key in the keyhole of the door.

"These things are bound up with so much red tape," Moss said vaguely. "You know what big companies are like."

The door swung open. "If it's big companies that cause the delays," she laughed harshly, "United Insurance must be about the biggest."

"And you'd be pretty right about that, Mrs. Farnham," Moss said, laughing gently. "May we come in?"

"Of course," she said.

Moss stood to one side to let her walk in first, then followed her in. I came last. I held the handle of the door, then turned back and slammed it. It sounded as if it had been shut, but it wasn't. I let go of the handle gently and the door swung inwards an inch. I didn't think she'd notice. I crossed my fingers that she wouldn't.

She took off her hat and went into the bedroom. She was there a couple of minutes and then she came back. She was wearing a sheer nylon blouse and a grey skirt. The delicate lace edging to the top of her slip rose and fell gently under the nylon.

"Won't you sit down, gentlemen?" she said.

Moss pushed chairs around, fussing. He fussed fine. When we sat down, Mrs. Farnham sat at an angle to the door so that it wasn't in her direct line of vision, but she would be in the direct line of anyone entering the room—or watching outside.

"I've answered so many questions, Mr. Moss," she said. "I hope these won't take long." She looked at me with hatred in her eyes. "Lieutenant Wheeler is the world's prize question-asker. In five minutes he has you believing you said things you haven't. In ten minutes he's got you denying that you said the things you never said."

Moss laughed appreciatively. "I don't think you'll find these questions too hard, Mrs. Farnham. After all, Lieutenant Wheeler is a policeman, isn't he? It's his job to ask questions."

"Yes," she said curtly.

Moss took a cigar out of his top pocket. "Do you mind if I smoke, Mrs.

Farnham?"

"No," she said impatiently. "Look, Mr. Moss, I don't want to be rude, but I have a lot of things to do tonight. Would you please start asking your questions?"

Moss made a production of lighting his cigar and looked at me quickly. I glanced at my watch and nodded.

"All right, Mrs. Farnham," he said. "I'll come to the point. I'm a claims investigator for United. That means that when anyone makes a claim that is suspect in the least degree, I investigate it. Particularly in a case such as yours when a large sum of money is involved."

"Go on," she said indifferently.

The politeness and good humour had gone out of his voice. "I am asking you to sign a waiver to your claim, Mrs. Farnham—in your own interest."

"What?"

"Exactly," Moss said harshly. "Relinquish all claim on your husband's insurance."

"Are you crazy?" she said in a high-pitched voice.

"No," he said. "I'm offering you an alternative, Mrs. Farnham. Take the money and face a double-murder indictment, or waive the claim and we won't produce our witnesses."

"Witnesses?"

He leaned forward in his chair. "I don't know how familiar you are with the processes of the law, Mrs. Farnham. But under common law, everyone has the right to protect their own property. In our case, we have the right to protect our money which would be paid out on a false claim. Lieutenant Wheeler asked me to come here. He cannot force me to reveal the names of my witnesses, if I withhold them to protect our property. You understand?"

I crossed all my fingers. Moss was putting over a line of sheer hokum, but he was doing it very well. He would have been an asset to Annabelle's dramatic club.

"Witnesses?" she said. "What witnesses?"

"For your protection," he said, "I'll call them Mr. X and Miss Y. Mr. X is the man who planned with you the murder of your husband by running him down in a stolen car. He's the man who called here in the afternoons sometimes before your husband was murdered."

"You're crazy," she said.

He shook his head. "What do you want most, Mrs. Farnham? Money— or life? You've got to make a choice. Mr. X is the man whom Cole knew was your co-partner in the murder of your husband. Mr. X is the man who was blackmailed by Cole as you were, for half the insurance money as the price of his silence. Mr. X is the man who hid in that room there," he flung out his arm dramatically and pointed to the bedroom. "Who hid there on the night of Cole's death. The man who, after you had hit Mrs. Cole with that umbrella and knocked her unconscious, put a gun to the back of Cole's head and fired the two shots that killed him."

The lace surged under the nylon. Her eyes narrowed to pinpoints and her nostrils flared slightly. "You're lying," she said. "You're inventing this story. You made it up the way he made it up." She pointed in my direction. "You just don't want to pay the money. All right, we'll see about that. We'll see what the newspapers have to say about United Insurance—the company that won't pay their debts."

He smiled at her. "Where do you think I get this information from, Mrs. Farnham? Miss Y is the witness to the times you and Mr. X were together. Miss Y is the witness who saw him leave this apartment just on midnight the night Cole was murdered."

Her lower lip quivered. "You're still lying," she said in a small voice.

"Look," he said patiently. "How do you think I know exactly how everything was planned for both murders? How do I know that Cole was blackmailing the two of you? Miss Y couldn't tell me—she could only identify Mr. X as the man she saw you with and saw leaving your apartment on certain occasions."

"I know everybody around here," she said shrilly. "There isn't any Miss Y."

"Perhaps I should say Mrs. X?" Moss said sharply. "His wife he deserted eighteen months ago in San Diego. She came here to find him. She wants to divorce him—to be rid of him. She was spying on him, watching his movements. But she didn't tie him in with a murder plot until she realized yesterday that she had seen him leave your apartment at the time when Laurence Cole was murdered there—or a couple of minutes after.

"Fortunately for United," he went on casually, "I had been investigating Mr. X's background. I discovered he had a wife. I traced her to San Diego and then back here. I found her while she was making up her mind whether to tell the police or not. I persuaded her that United would be her better friend."

She thrust a closed fist into her mouth and bit down hard on the knuckles. "I won't believe it," she said.

"Don't be a fool," Moss said curtly. "As I said, she couldn't know the details of the murders—how Cole was blackmailing both of you. There was only one person who could tell me that—and that's Mr. X himself."

"I don't believe it!" The white bloodless circle where her teeth bit into her knuckles was widening. "You're trying to trick me."

"I wouldn't advise you to be loyal," Moss said cynically. "He's talked loud and long to try and save his skin. He told me how you enticed him into planning to murder your husband. How, when Cole started blackmailing the two of you, it was you who suggested a way of getting rid of him and letting his wife be convicted of murdering him. He told me how you used your beauty to drug his senses and ..."

She stood bolt upright, the chair crashing back onto the floor behind her. "I won't believe it," she whimpered. "I'm not going to believe it."

I heard the footsteps outside, mounting the stairs. "Here they come," I said.

"Who?" She turned to face me like an animal at bay.

"Mr. X and Miss Y, of course," Moss said calmly. "Who would you think it would be? Two of my men held them downstairs for twenty minutes. I thought if I couldn't convince you in twenty minutes, I never would. And I haven't, have I? It only remains for them to make a formal identification of you, Mrs. Farnham, and the rest is up to Lieutenant Wheeler."

"Identification." She stared at him. "What for?"

"Murder, Mrs. Farnham," Moss said gently. "On two separate counts."

The footsteps sounded louder and she turned to face the door. I thought that didn't matter now. I crossed all my fingers again and pushed my chair back so I wouldn't be seen immediately when the door swung open.

Eve Farnham stood like a woman transfixed, watching the door as the footsteps came up to it. Her bosom heaved and her eyes had a glazed look. I could almost feel sorry for her.

Then the door swung open and Annabelle stood there. She half-turned her head, obviously talking to someone behind her.

"Darling," she said. "I'll wait, Mr. Moss promises that the worst you'll get will be five years as an accessory to the murders. I don't mind waiting five years—now we're together again. It won't be forever."

She turned her head almost negligently. Her eyebrows rose slightly as she saw Mrs. Farnham standing there. "That's the woman, all right," she said. "No doubt about it. Come in, darling. We might as well get this over as quickly as possible."

There was an animal snarl from behind her and Annabelle lurched forward suddenly into the room, losing her balance and falling flat on her beautiful face on the floor.

Joe Williams stepped into the room, a gun in his hand. "What the ..." he started to say.

He didn't get a chance to go any further.

"You dirty, lying, two-timing mongrel!" Eve Farnham almost screamed at him. "It was you who started it! You and your dirty job of locating people. You called and I was fool enough to ask you in and when you heard my husband was out, you attacked me like an animal! And afterwards when I told you about him, it was you who got the idea of killing him and collecting the money."

"Shut up," Williams snarled.

"You can't stop me talking!" she screamed. "I won't stop! When Cole said he followed you and knew you'd been seeing me and he saw you steal the car—it was you who came up with the idea of murdering him so we wouldn't have to share the money with him. It was you who made me make love to him, so you could be sure he'd be here when you rang his wife and told her where to find him. It was you who hid behind the bed and waited with a gun. It was you who shot him through the back of the head."

She started towards him, her fingers hooked like talons to tear and scratch his face.

"Get back, Eve," he said. "You're crazy."

"Crazy, am I?" One arm flashed up and her nails raked down the side of his face.

The gun in his hand exploded twice and she staggered back, a look of horror on her face. She pressed both hands just above the suede belt that separated her blouse from her skirt. She whimpered with pain like a kitten, then slowly she bent forward, her knees sagging so that she rolled onto the floor rather than fell.

Wheeler was too slow. I admit it. I tried to make up for it. I grabbed the thirty-two out of its holster and it was halfway out of my jacket when Williams swung towards me.

"Drop it, Lieutenant," he said tensely.

I thought if I dropped it, it wouldn't make any difference—he would still shoot me, anyway. He fired once and the room seemed to explode in front of my eyes for a split second.

I pressed the trigger of my own gun in an automatic reflex and pressed it twice more. My vision cleared except for a smear over my right eye.

I saw Williams was leaning against the wall, his gun on the floor. I lifted my gun again and then I saw the expression on his face and I knew it wasn't necessary. He was dying, and dying quite fast.

I touched the top of my head and felt blood. I explored with my fingers cautiously and found that the slug from his gun had ploughed a minute furrow across the top of my scalp. An inch lower and I would have been a verse on a chunk of granite.

I looked at Williams. "Why did you do it?" I asked. "Why did you start it in the first place?"

He coughed and took a shuddering, uncertain breath.

"Thirty thousand bucks," he said. "My chance of a break. With that sort of dough, I could spit on Cole's hundred a week and his sarcasm and his snide way of operating. And I would have had the dame, too."

He looked down wonderingly at her body on the floor.

"It was mostly the dame," he said. "I never did meet a dame in all my life before." His lips set in a thin line and he straightened himself up a couple of inches. "Or should I say, Lieutenant," he whispered. "In all my death before."

He slumped forward, away from the wall and I caught him in my arms and lowered him gently onto the floor. When I got him there I realised I needn't have bothered to lower him gently. He was past all pain.

Moss was trembling like a floating cigar in search of a pair of teeth. I went to help Annabelle onto her feet and she was out in a cold faint. I lifted her gently into my arms.

"This is my girl," I explained to Moss. "I'm going to take her to my place."

He opened his mouth to say something, but his teeth chattered so much he had to close it. He nodded feebly.

"Somebody has to explain to Lavers about all this," I said. "Somebody should tell him. You."

Moss shook his head violently.

"You," I repeated firmly. "You're his friend. He might believe you—I don't say he will, but he might. For sure, he won't believe me."

Moss unhappily nodded his head in agreement with the last part. He made a great effort and managed to get some words out. "I still don't see how you picked Williams?"

"I didn't, really," I admitted, being honest for one minute of my life. "The process of elimination worked down the line and only Williams was left. If Farnham was murdered, his wife didn't do it so someone else was implicated. And the only reason for murdering Farnham was to get the insurance money, so his wife who would actually collect it, had to be part of the murder plot."

"I'm with you so-so-so far," Moss said, then bit down hard to stop his teeth chattering and left his tongue between them. While he squealed with anguish, I went on.

"Who was there? This finance company and their locaters. I felt sure it was Edna Bright and Vince Schaeffer at first—then I found they were in another racket altogether. Then Cole was murdered and that meant Farnham was murdered. I thought it must have been Cole who was Eve's partner and she bumped him off to save splitting the money with him, and also because she couldn't stand the thought of having him around for the rest of her life. But I found that Cole was in his office at the time Farnham was run over.

"So that only left Williams. And then I started thinking about Williams, I started remembering things. Edna Bright had told me he missed the easiest locate of all time in Farnham. Had he? Then things he told me himself. That Cole was the all-time louse to work for. That Cole would even trail his employees through the city to see if they were working or not. That Cole was always after the fast buck. And I remembered Cole's terrific interest in what progress I was making with my investigation. The evening of Cole's death I was in the Camille bar and I met Williams there. He was half-drunk. When I left him, he told me he had a date that night and roared with laughter.

"Depending on your sense of humour," I said cautiously. "You could laugh with him. He had a date to crouch behind a bed, waiting to murder the man who was making love to his girl."

"I don't have that sense of humour," Moss said.

"You need a criminal mind like mine," I told him.

He looked out of the corner of his eyes at me and I could tell right then that Lee Moss would never recommend me as a good insurance risk to United.

"I had tried scaring the hell out of Eve with the theory that Cole did it," I said. "And it didn't work—because it was wrong. When I realised that Cole must have followed Williams the day he murdered Farnham, and had decided to blackmail him rather than turn him over to the police, there was horribly obvious reason for Cole ending up dead.

"But it needed somebody new to scare the hell out of Eve. I'd tried it too often. And you were the boy to do it—and if I may say so, you did it magnificently."

Moss looked pleased and automatically reached into his top pocket to hand me a cigar.

"So with you to hound Eve and Annabelle as bait to bring in Williams at the psychological moment," I said. "We were set."

"What exactly did Annabelle do?"

"I told her to call into his office and say she was a close friend of Eve's. Say she lived in the apartment on the floor above, and Eve had rung her to ask her to contact Williams and tell him it was urgent that he come to see her at six-thirty tonight. And be there exactly at that time. Williams would be worried that something had gone wrong. She was to tell him that she didn't know any more than that, but Eve had sounded terribly worried on the phone.

"Then she was to use her celebrated charm on him and suggest as it was early, why didn't they have a drink until it was time for him to see Eve. And of course she'd come with him to the apartment house and walk up the stairs with him—so far as he knew, she lived on the floor above. That was where the timing was vital. Then Annabelle suddenly stepped into Eve's apartment and made her pitch. You had to have built Eve up to a breaking point so that Annabelle would be one shock too many. And she was."

The body twisted suddenly in my arms and Annabelle smiled at me. "I was magnificent, too—wasn't I, honey-chile?"

"You most certainly were," I said. "And it's time we got going before a lot of horrid policemen arrive and trample over everything."

Moss looked at me anxiously. "You want me to say anything to Lavers for you?"

"Tell him on behalf of Lieutenant Wheeler that he has gone in search of Sebastian Macaron—the terrorist," Annabelle said gravely.

"Huh?" Moss jumped as if somebody had just paid a claim without him knowing.

"You knew," I said.

She giggled. "Of course I knew, Al, I could see your shadow against the glass partition—and anyway, you don't sound a bit like the Commissioner."

I kissed her fondly. "Just love that girl from the South."

Moss tugged at my sleeve anxiously. "What about Lavers?"

"Tell him … no, tell Jerry Schultz to look after Natalie Cole when she's released," I said. "And tell him it will be worth it."

Annabelle jabbed a thumb into my solar plexus. "That's quite enough of that," she said sternly.

"What about the Commissioner?" Moss pleaded. "Please."

"Oh, sure," I said. "Tell him that Al Wheeler bears him no grudge. Tell him that ostracism by one's fellow officers of the law is part of the cross a man has to bear for being unorthodox. Tell him—oh hell, tell him I'm going home with his secretary to listen to hi-fi and drink Scotch and, well, tell him if he as much as rings my phone tonight, I'll take a poker to him."

I picked up Annabelle in my arms and headed towards the door.

"There's just one thing more …" Moss said.

"I quite agree," I said. "But it's strictly none of your business!"

"I didn't mean …" His face started to redden.

"I should hope not," I said coldly. "You're old enough to be her father."

"Now, wait a minute."

"No time to waste," I said. "Not even a second!"

Annabelle giggled suddenly. "You're awful!"

"You have no proof of that."

"I don't need any proof," she said. "A girl's intuition can be relied on in these things."

"I would say your intuition will be proved right very shortly," I said.

"Well," she said impatiently. "Don't let's waste time here just talking about it—call a cab!"

The End

Alan Geoffrey Yates Bibliography
(1923-1985)

As Carter Brown/
Peter Carter Brown

Series:

Al Wheeler (no U.S. edition unless
otherwise stated through to
Chorine Makes a Killing)

The Wench is Wicked (1955)
Blonde Verdict (1956; revised for
  the U.S. as The Brazen, 1960)
Delilah Was Deadly (1956)
No Harp for My Angel (1956)
Booty for a Babe (1956)
Eve, It's Extortion (1957; revised
  as Walk Softly Witch!, 1959,
  and further revised for the U.S.
  as The Victim, 1959)
No Law Against Angels (1957;
  revised for the U.S. as The Body,
  1958; 1st U.S. Wheeler)
Doll for the Big House (1957;
  revised for the U.S. as The
  Bombshell, 1960)
Chorine Makes a Killing (1957)
The Unorthodox Corpse (1957;
  revised for the U.S., 1961)
Death on a Downbeat (1958;
  revised for the U.S. as The
  Corpse, 1958)
The Blonde (1958; reprinted in
  the U.S., 1958)
The Lover (1958)
The Mistress (1959)
The Passionate (1959)
The Wanton (1959)
The Dame (1959)
The Desired (1959)

The Temptress (1960)
Lament for a Lousy Lover (1960)
  [includes Mavis Seidlitz]
The Stripper (1961)
The Tigress (1961; reprinted in
  the UK as Wildcat, 1962)
The Exotic (1961)
Angel! (1962)
The Hellcat (1962)
The Lady Is Transparent (1962)
The Dumdum Murder (1962)
Girl in a Shroud (1963)
The Sinners (1963; reprinted in
  U.S. as The Girl Who Was
  Possessed, 1963)
The Lady Is Not Available (1963;
  reprinted in U.S. as The Lady Is
  Available, 1963)
The Dance of Death (1964)
The Vixen (1964; reprinted in the
  U.S. as The Velvet Vixen, 1964)
A Corpse for Christmas (1965)
The Hammer of Thor (1965)
Target for Their Dark Desire
  (1966)
The Plush-Lined Coffin (1967)
Until Temptation Do Us Part
  (1967)
The Deep Cold Green (1968)
The Up-Tight Blonde (1969)
Burden of Guilt (1970)
The Creative Murders (1971)
W.H.O.R.E. (1971)
The Clown (1972)
The Aseptic Murders (1972)
The Born Loser (1973)
Night Wheeler (1974)
Wheeler Fortune (1974)
Wheeler, Dealer! (1975)

The Dream Merchant (1976)
Busted Wheeler (1979)
The Spanking Girls (1979)
Model for Murder (1980)
The Wicked Widow (1981)
Stab in the Dark (1984; Australia
  only)

Larry Baker

Charlie Sent Me (1965; revised
  from Swan Song for a Siren,
  1955)
No Blonde Is an Island (1965)
So What Killed the Vampire?
  (1966)
Had I But Groaned (1968;
  reprinted in the UK as The
  Witches, 1969)
True Son of the Beast (1970)
The Iron Maiden (1975)

Barney Blain (no U.S. editions)

Madam, You're Mayhem (1957)
Ice Cold in Ermine (1958)

Danny Boyd

Tempt a Tigress (1958; no U.S.)
So Deadly, Sinner! (1959;
  reprinted in the U.S. as Walk
  Softly, Witch, 1959, 1st U.S.
  Boyd; different version of the
  Wheeler title)
Suddenly by Violence (1959)
Terror Comes Creeping (1959)
The Wayward Wahine (1960;
  published in Australia as The
  Wayward, 1962)
The Dream Is Deadly (1960)
Graves, I Dig (1960; revised from

Cutie Wins a Corpse (1957)
The Myopic Mermaid (1961,
  revised from A Siren Sounds
  Off, 1958)
The Ever-Loving Blues (1961;
  revised from Death of a Doll,
  1956)
The Seductress (1961; published
  in the U.S. as The Sad-Eyed
  Seductress, 1961)
The Savage Salome (1961; revised
  from Murder is My Mistress,
  1954)
The Ice-Cold Nude (1962)
Lover Don't Come Back (1962)
Nymph to the Slaughter (1963)
Passionate Pagan (1963)
Silken Nightmare (1963)
Catch Me a Phoenix! (1965)
The Sometime Wife (1965)
The Black Lace Hangover (1966)
House of Sorcery (1967)
The Mini-Murders (1968)
Murder Is the Message (1969)
Only the Very Rich (1969)
The Coffin Bird (1970)
The Sex Clinic (1971)
Angry Amazons (1972) [includes
  Randy Roberts]
Manhattan Cowboy (1973)
So Move the Body (1973)
The Early Boyd (1975)
The Savage Sisters (1976)
The Pipes Are Calling (1976)
The Rip Off (1979)
The Strawberry-Blonde Jungle
  (1979)
Death to a Downbeat (1980)
Kiss Michelle Goodbye (1981)
The Real Boyd (1984; Australia
  only)

Paul Donavan

Donavan (1974)
Donovan's Day (1975)
Chinese Donavan (1976)
Donavan's Delight (1979)

Max Dumas (no U.S. editions)

Goddess Gone Bad (1958)
Luck Was No Lady (1958)
Deadly Miss (1958)

Mike Farrel

The Million Dollar Babe (1961;
  revised from Cutie Cashed His
  Chips, 1955)
The Scarlet Flush (1963; revised
  from Ten Grand Tallulah and
  Temptation, 1957)

Rick Holman

Zelda (1961; 1st U.S. Holman)
Murder in the Harem Club,
  1962; reprinted in the U.S. as
  Murder in the Key Club, 1962)
The Murderer Among Us (1962)
Blonde on the Rocks (1963)
The Jade-Eyed Jinx (1963;
  reprinted in the U.S. as The
  Jade-Eyed Jungle, 1964)
The Ballad of Loving Jenny
  (1963; reprinted in the U.S. as
  The White Bikini, 1963)
The Wind-Up Doll (1963)
The Never-Was Girl (1964)
Murder Is a Package Deal (1964)
Who Killed Doctor Sex? (1964)
Nude—with a View (1965)
The Girl from Outer Space (1965)

Blonde on a Broomstick (1966)
Play Now… Kill Later (1966)
No Tears from the Widow (1966)
The Deadly Kitten (1967)
Long Time No Leola (1967)
Die Anytime, After Tuesday!
  (1969)
The Flagellator (1969)
The Streaked-Blond Slave (1969)
A Good Year for Dwarfs? (1970)
The Hang-up Kid (1970)
Where Did Charity Go? (1970)
The Coven (1971)
The Invisible Flamini (1971)
The Pornbroker (1972)
The Master (1973)
Phreak-Out! (1973)
Negative in Blue (1974)
The Star-Crossed Lover (1974)
Ride the Roller Coaster (1975)
Remember Maybelle? (1976)
See It Again, Sam (1979)
The Phantom Lady (1980)
The Swingers (1980)

Andy Kane

The Hong Kong Caper (1962;
  revised from Blonde, Bad and
  Beautiful, 1957)
The Guilt-edged Cage (1963;
  revised from That's Piracy, My
  Pet, 1957; published in
  Australia as Bird in a Guilt-
  Edged Cage)

Ivor MacCallum
(no U.S. editions)

Sweetheart You Slay Me (1952)
Blackmail Beauty (1953)

Randy Roberts

Murder in the Family Way (1971)
The Seven Sirens (1972)
Murder on High (1973)
Sex Trap (1975)

Mavis Seidlitz

Honey, Here's Your Hearse
    (1955; no U.S.)
The Killer is Kissable (1955; no
    U.S.)
A Bullet For My Baby (1955; no
    U.S.)
Good Morning, Mavis! (1957; no
    U.S.)
Murder Wears a Mantilla (1957;
    revised for U.S. as same title,
    1962)
The Loving and the Dead (1959;
    1st U.S. Seidlitz)
None But the Lethal Heart (1959;
    reprinted as The Fabulous,
    1961)
Tomorrow Is Murder (1960)
Lament for a Lousy Lover (1960)
    [includes Al Wheeler]
The Bump and Grind Murders
    (1964)
Seidlitz and the Super Spy (1967;
    published in the UK as The
    Super-Spy, 1968)
Murder Is So Nostalgic (1972)
And the Undead Sing (1974)

Unrelated Novels/Novelettes (all
non-U.S. unless otherwise noted)

Death Date for Dolores (1951)
Designed to Deceive (1951)

Duchess Double X (1951)
Forever Forbidden (1951)
The Lady Is Murder (1951;
    reprinted as Lady is a Killer
    with Murder by Miss Take,
    1958)
Three Men, One Love (1951)
Uncertain Heart (1951)
Your Alibi Is Showing (1951)
Alias a Lady (1952)
Blackmail for a Brunette (1952)
Blondes Prefer Bullets (1952)
Hands Off the Lady (1952)
Kiss Life Goodbye (1952)
Larceny Was Lovely (1952)
Meet Miss Mayhem (1952)
Murder Sweet Murder (1952)
She Wore No Shroud (1952)
Sssh! She's a Killer (1952)
Chill on Chili/Butterfly Nett
    (1953)
Cyanide Sweetheart (1953)
Dead Dolls Don't Cry (1953)
Dimples Died De-Luxe (1953)
Judgement of a Jane (1953)
Kidnapper Wears Curves (1953)
The Lady Wore Nylon (1953)
The Lady's Alive (1953)
Lethal in Love (1953; reprinted as
    The Minx is Murder, 1956)
Madame You're Morgue-Bound
    (1953)
Meet a Body (1953)
The Mermaid Murmurs Murder
    (1953)
Model for Murder (1953;
    different from 1980 Al Wheeler
    title)
Moonshine Momma (1953)
Murder is a Broad (1953)

Penthouse Pass-Out (1953; reprinted as Hot Seat for a Honey, 1956)

Rope for a Redhead (1953; revised as Model of No Virtue, 1956)

Slightly Dead (1953)

Stripper You're Stuck (1953)

Widow is Willing (1953)

The Black Widow Weeps (1954)

Felon Angel (1954)

Floozies Out of Focus (1954)

The Frame is Beautiful (1954)

Fraulein is Feline (1954; reprinted with Moonshine Momma & Slaughter in Satin, 1955)

Good-Knife Sweetheart (1954)

Honky Tonk Homicide (1954; reprinted with Chill on Chili & Butterfly Nett, 1955)

Homicide Harem (1954; reprinted with Good-Knife Sweetheart & Poison Ivy, 1955; with Felon Angel, 1965)

The Lady is Chased (1954; reprinted as Trouble is a Dame, 1957)

A Morgue Amour (1954)

Murder—Paris Fashion (1954)

Murder! She Says (1954)

Nemesis Wore Nylons (1954)

Pagan Perilous (1954)

Perfumed Poison (1954)

Poison Ivy (1954)

Shady Lady (1954)

Sinsation Sadie (1954)

Slaughter in Satin (1954)

Strip Without Tease (1954; reprinted as Stripper, You've Sinned, 1959)

Trouble is a Dame (1954)

Wreath for Rebecca (1954)

Venus Unarmed (1954)

Yogi Shrouds Yolande (1954; reprinted with Poison Ivy, 1965)

Curtains for a Chorine (1955)

Curves for a Coroner (1955)

Cutie Cashed His Chips (1955; revised for U.S. as The Million Dollar Babe, 1961, as Farrel series)

Homicide Hoyden (1955)

Kiss and Kill (1955; reprinted with Cyanide Sweetie, 1958)

Kiss Me Deadly (1955; reprinted as Lipstick Larceny, 1958)

Lead Astray (1955)

Lipstick Larceny (1955)

Maid for Murder (1955)

Miss Called Murder (1955)

Shamus, Your Slip Is Showing (1955; reprinted with A Morgue Amour, 1957)

Shroud for My Sugar (1955)

Sob-Sister Cries Murder (1955)

The Two Timing Blonde (1955)

Baby, You're Guilt-Edged (1956; reprinted with Pagan Perilous, 1959)

Bid the Babe Bye-Bye (1956)

Blonde, Beautiful, and – Blam! (1956)

The Bribe Was Beautiful (1956)

Caress Before Killing (1956)

Darling You're Doomed (1956)

Donna Died Laughing (1956)

The Eve of His Dying (1956)

Hi-Jack for Jill (1956)

The Hoodlum Was a Honey (1956)

The Lady Has No Convictions (1956; reprinted with Slightly Dead, 1959)

Meet Murder, My Angel (1956)

Murder By Miss-Demeanour
(1956)
My Darling Is Deadpan (1956)
No Halo For Hedy (1956)
Strictly for Felony (1956)
Sweetheart, This is Homicide
(1956)
Bella Donna Was Poison (1957)
Cutie Wins a Corpse (1957;
revised for U.S. as Graves, I
Dig!, 1960, as Boyd series)
Last Note for a Lovely (1957)
Lethal in Love (1957; different
than 1953 title)
Sinner, You Slay Me (1957)
Ten Grand Tallulah and
Temptation (1957; revised as
The Scarlet Flush, 1963, Farrel
series)
That's Piracy, My Pet (1957;
revised as Bird in a Guilt-Edged
Cage, 1963, as Kane series)
Wreath for a Redhead (1957)
The Charmer Chased (1958)
Cutie Takes the Count (1958)
Deadly Miss (1958)
Hi-Fi Fadeout (1958)
High Fashion in Homicide (1958)
No Body She Knows (1958; with
Slaughter in Satin, 1960)
No Future Fair Lady (1958)
Sinfully Yours (1958)
A Siren Signs Off (1958; with
Moonshine Momma; revised for
U.S. as The Myopic Mermaid,
1961, as Boyd series)
So Lovely She Lies (1958)
Widow Bewitched (1958)
The Blonde Avalanche (1984)

As Tod Conway (western stories)

As Caroline Farr

The Intruder (1962)
House of Tombs (1966)
Mansion of Evil (1966)
Villa of Shadows (1966)
Web of Horror (1966; reprinted
in the U.S. as A Castle in Spain,
1978)
Granite Folly (1967)
The Secret of the Chateau (1967)
Witch's Hammer (1967)
So Near and Yet... (1968)
House of Destiny (1969)
The Castle on the Lake (1970)
The Secret of Castle Ferrara
(1970)
Terror on Duncan Island (1971)
The Towers of Fear (1972)
A Castle in Canada (1972)
House of Dark Illusions (1973)
House of Secrets (1973)
Dark Mansion (1974)
Mansion Malevolent (1974)
The House on the Cliffs (1974)
Dark Citadel (1975)
Mansion of Peril (1975)
Castle of Terror (1975)
The Scream in the Storm (1975)
Chateau of Wolves (1976)
Mansion of Menace (1976)
Brecon Castle (1976)
The House of Landsdown (1977)
House of Treachery (1977)
Ravensnest (1977)
The House at Lansdowne (1977)
Sinister House (1978)
House of Valhalla (1978)
Heiress Of Fear (1978)
Room Of Secrets (1979)
Island of Evil (1979)
A Castle on the Rhine (1979)

The Castle on the Loch (1979)
The Secret at Ravenswood (1980)

As Raymond Glenning (stories)

Ghosts Don't Kill (1951)
Seven for Murder (1951)

As Sinclair Mackellar

Prompt for Murder (1981)

As Dennis Sinclair

Temple Dogs Guard My Fate
  (1968)
Third Force (1976)
The Friends of Lucifer (1977)
Blood Brothers (1977)

As Paul Valdez
(stories & novelettes)

Hypnotic Death (1949)
The Fatal Focus (1950)
Outcasts of Planet J (1950)
Jetbees from Planet J (1951)
Escape to Paradise (1951)
Fugitives from the Flame World
  (1951)
Kidnapped in Chaos (1951)
Killer by Night (1951)
Suicide Satellite (1951)
The Time Thief (1951)
Flight Into Horror (1951)
Murder Gives Notice (1951)
The Corpse Sat Up (1951)
The Maniac Murders (1951)
Satan's Sabbath (1951)
You Can't Keep Murder Out
  (1951)
Kill Him Gently (1951)

Feline Frame-Up (1951)
Celluloid Suicide? (1951)
The Murder I Don't Remember
  (1952)
Kidnapped in Space (1952)
There's No Future in Murder
  (1952)
The Crook Who Wasn't There
  (1952)
Maniac Murders (1952)
The Mad Meteor (1952)
Operation Satellite (1952)

As A. G. Yates

The Cold Dark Hours (1958)

As Alan Yates

Novel:

Coriolanus, the Chariot (1978)

Stories & Novelettes:

Client for Murder (Leisure
  Detective #7, 195?)
The Corpse on the Carpet
  (Leisure Detective #8, 195?)
Farewell, My Lady of Shalott!
  (Action Detective Magazine #6,
  1952)
Hush-a-Buy Homicide (Leisure
  Detective #9, 195?)
Margie (Action Detective
  Magazine #5, 1952)
Merger with Death (Leisure
  Detective #12, 195?)
Murder in the Family (Leisure
  Detective #11, 195?)
Murder Needs Education (Action
  Detective Magazine #2, 1952)

Murder! She Says
  (Detective Monthly #2, 195?)
My Love Lies Murdered (Action
  Detective Magazine #7, 1952)
Nemesis for a Nude! (Leisure
  Detective #10, 195?)

Genie from Jupiter (Thrills
  Incorporated #14, 1951)
Goddess of Space (Thrills
  Incorporated #20, 1952)
No Pixies on Pluto (Thrills
  Incorporated #22, 1952)

Planet of the Lost (Thrills
  Incorporated #17, 1951)
A Space Ship Is Missing
  (Thrills Incorporated #16, 1951)
Spacemen Spoofed (Thrills
  Incorporated #23, 1952)

Autobiography

Ready when you are, C.B.!: The
  autobiography of Alan Yates
  alias Carter Brown (1983)

www.ingramcontent.com/pod-product-compliance
Lightning Source LLC
Chambersburg PA
CBHW071732190726

48292CB00003B/719